THE PREY

OAKMOUNT ELITE
BOOK THREE

J.L. BECK

BECK ROMANCE BOOKS

Copyright © 2024 by J.L. Beck

Cover Design by: Cover Couture

Editing by: Editing4Indies

All rights reserved.

No part of this book may be reproduced in any form or by any electronic or mechanical means, including information storage and retrieval systems, without written permission from the author, except for the use of brief quotations in a book review.

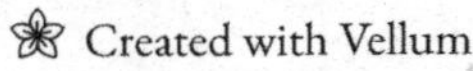

THE PREY

We're all broken in some way but that doesn't mean we're beyond repair. -Unknown

Author Note

Please be advised The Prey is a dark romance, with enemies to lovers, and bully themes throughout. Sebastian isn't morally gray, he's morally black. He does things that you will not like, that might piss you off, and maybe even make you want to stop reading. BUT if you look between the lines and dive deep into his story you'll see why he makes the decisions he does. Try your best to stick through it. I promise it will be worth it in the end. Below is a complete list of triggers. Some may contain spoilers.

Triggers include: knife play, stalking, violence, sexual assault, molestation, rape (not by MC), pregnancy, death, blood play, kidnapping, voyeurism, dub-con, bullying, substance abuse, trauma, child abuse, murder, hallucinations, amnesia, forced oral, primal play, cognitive impairment, manipulation, human trafficking, chasing, masked men, humiliation, gun violence, use of drugs, animal cruelty/death/abuse, and gaslighting.

PROLOGUE

This may be hard to believe, but I don't just go around killing people. Many perceive me to be this ruthless, coldhearted murderer, but much to their dismay, I don't make a habit of homicide. Death is messy and the easy way out if you're asking my opinion. I prefer to give my enemies the hardest path possible if they want to escape me.

As I stand here in my grandfather's study, I realize there's no blood on my hands—not physically, at least—and no indication that anything terrible has happened except for the echo of the gunshot ringing in my ears.

A glass of whiskey sits abandoned on the desk alongside a cigar, the tip still smoking faintly in its marble ashtray. A fire roars in the grate, the wood crackling and popping like it's trying to escape.

I stand frozen in the center of the room, suspended in time, my entire body trembling. The rich scent of leather from the books and furniture mingles with the pungent odor of gunpowder, like metal and wood, filling my lungs with each shallow breath I take.

I blink, slowly returning to awareness, my gaze skittering around me. Papers litter the burgundy rug on the floor, and I sink to my knees, my free hand landing palm down on one of them.

At the top of it, in what might as well be flashing neon lights, is a single word: ***CONTRACT.***

It's unmistakable. Typed out in big, bold letters.

Fuck. Why would he do this? Take a girl—no, a woman—as payment for a debt? Even for him, it's a new low.

Acid climbs up my throat. This is what started the fight. Me proclaiming that you can't own another person, not in the way he proposed to, not with bars and cages and contracts. I was all about control, but not even I could stomach this.

My grandfather had laughed in my face, the sound almost bitter with the depths of his disappointment in me. The thing is —I'm not stupid. I know you can own someone, with fear...with love. Even with heartbreak and hope, but not with locks and windows with bars over them.

I own the fact that I am unwell—maybe insane, even—but I don't come close to this level of depravity.

And I don't want to.

Standing, I peruse the crumpled paper in my hand. I am fine with tormenting people. Fucking with those who deserve it, and hell, some who don't. I am even fine with letting my dark side come out to play. I consider myself among the cruelest of the cruel, but I could not silently stand by and allow him to do this.

Even I have lines I don't cross.

He never seemed to understand that about me. The harder he tried to mold me into something I wasn't, the harder I would fight. That doesn't matter now, though. Fighting was pointless. I've trapped myself in the cage and thrown away the key.

How had I let this happen?

Giving my head a slight shake, I snap myself back to reality and snatch my phone out of my pocket, letting the gun and the contract slip from my other hand as I do so. The paper flutters while the gun clatters to the floor loudly. I don't care. I'll dispose of it later. I scroll to my messages, my fingers hovering over the group text that I have with my friends, my most trusted allies.

They would be here without a second thought to help me if I called them.

I know this, but...

Do I really want to involve them?

To drag them into this twisted, dark mess I've created for myself? *No.* The answer is no, but I still hesitate. They're my people, the closest thing to family I have.

Fuck. I'm selfish, but I can't risk bringing them down with me in the event this goes sideways. I navigate back to my contacts and pace. Two steps to the right. Two steps back. I don't have a lot of options available. I thought I could handle it myself, but I can't, and now, I have to fix the problem.

How could I be so stupid?

Gritting my teeth, I tug at my hair above my temples. My gaze strays, drawn by blood and pale skin, and I pull my focus forcibly back to my phone. There's only one other person I can call, but once I do this, there will be no going back. Saving her will intertwine our lives. The alternative is worse, though—another guilt stacked on the pile of others that will forever stain and tarnish my soul.

I could let her die, but then this will all have been for nothing...

Fucking hell. *There's no other option.* Unsurprisingly, my subconscious chooses then to remind me of that. Swallowing my own frustration, I hit a number I've never needed to call before. It's a mistake that I even have his number to begin with.

The sound of ringing fills the space as I put the phone on speaker. If he's smart, he'll answer the damn phone, or maybe he won't, and both our fates will be sealed. Maybe it would be better if that happened. At least it would be out of my hands.

The ringing stops, and the line fills with static, but there's no greeting. I clear my throat. "Dr. Brooks?"

A sleep-gruff voice answers, "What do you want?"

"I need you at the Arturo estate as soon as possible."

There's a pause. "You know the rules?"

I don't have the energy to posture right now. "No."

He releases a groan."I won't kill anyone. And my fee will be billed; payment is due in cash."

I nod, then remember I'm on the phone, eyes squeezed shut. "That's fine. They're already dead, I think. I just need to have you confirm it. To do...whatever it is you do."

He hangs up without another word, and I stumble back to sit on the couch under the window. Pressure builds in my chest, and all I want to do is cut the pain, my heart, my lungs—rip all of it out. Rip it all away until nothing is left. No reminder of the beast beating inside me. I can't believe I did this. I can't believe what he forced me to do. I stare at the papers covering the ground, blood seeping up over the edges.

What he's going to force me to do.

I'm not sure how many minutes pass as I sit, my thoughts attacking me. *Nothing more than a fucking disgrace.* I catch sight of movement out of the corner of my eye, and it drags me back to the present.

A man kneels on the floor over my grandfather's body. I blink a few times, trying to determine whether I'm seeing things. When he doesn't disappear, I convince myself that he's real. "You're right, he's dead."

I swallow hard and let my features fall into the arrogant asshole mask I've perfected over the years. "Of course."

He tips his head to the side and looks at the entryway, where the office door is cracked to reveal a slice of light. "I can't do anything for him, but there is still hope for her."

I blink. "Really?" *Shit.* I thought they were both dead.

I stare down at my hands, expecting them to be coated in blood, every sin visible for the world to see.

"Sebastian, right?"

I blink again, looking up from my hands to stare into the storm-gray eyes of the doctor. He shines his penlight across my face a couple of times. "Nod if you can hear me, Sebastian."

"Of course I can hear you." I jerk away and shift back onto the couch, putting ample space between us. If I snap again, all hell will break loose.

Fuck, man, get ahold of yourself.

"What's the plan, Doc?"

He tilts his head to study me, and I force myself to return his scrutiny with a calm I don't feel. I don't have a clue what he's thinking right now, but I need him to take care of...them. Not me. Finally, his eyes narrow, and he rises, seeming to arrive at a decision.

"Nothing. Sit here."

He crosses the room to the bar and grabs a bottle of expensive whiskey, then walks it back over to me and shoves it into my hands. With a brief nod at the bottle, he turns and strides away, walking back to the foyer.

I swallow thickly around the knot in my throat. I can see her from here, her dark hair fanned out against the white marble like a raven in the snow.

And creeping beneath that, the blood.

Fuck. My stomach churns, and I wonder if I'm going to vomit. *Pussy.* This isn't my first time seeing death and destruction, but seeing her blood spilled across the floor in my family's name... I can't bear it.

The doctor opens the door wider and kneels beside her unmoving body. The world around me spins, and I need something to hold me in place. Using my teeth, I uncork the whiskey bottle and toss the stopper to the side, then raise the bottle to my lips with a shaking grasp. I tip the bottle back, letting the liquid fill my mouth. It burns across my tongue and slides smoothly down my throat.

I ignore the burn and the nearly dead girl in the next room and chug that shit like it's water until I have to take a breath; then I cradle the bottle against my thigh and slump farther into the couch, wishing it would swallow me whole.

Soft murmuring and a whimper carry in from the other room. The sound cuts through me like a knife, eliciting something close to an ache in my chest. My fist tightens around the bottle.

No. I can't do this. I'm part of this world now, and a woman's soft cry isn't supposed to affect me this way. I need to be stronger, to close it all down, to shove it deep inside until all there is, all I am, is what's best for me and my family name.

A tiny tendril of doubt snakes into my mind, working its way through my thoughts. If the doctor takes the girl away, then I can erase it all. I can disappear. Start a new life somewhere else and be free from the chains of this one.

You'll never be free. As quickly as it surfaces, the hope burns out. There's no going back. I'm man enough to admit I won't survive without money, without my contacts and resources. All those things come with my name and my house. If I walk away, I'd lose everything, and who would get it all?

Fucking Tanya.

I'd rather die in agony, a painful, terrible death, than give that bitch one cent of my money or my inheritance.

I have only one choice, and it's not even an actual fucking choice. I take another long draw from the bottle and stand. In the foyer, the doctor whispers softly. I exit the study, closing the door behind me. I'll deal with all of that after I deal with her.

The doctor's attention swings to me as he turns and surveys my features. "You better now?"

I let out a mirthless grunt. "Not even close."

He slides his hands under the girl's all-but-lifeless body, and I drag my gaze over her. Her white sundress is stained red, along with her fingers. I'm not sure how I manage it, but I force myself to look at her face. It's battered and bruised like someone used her as their own personal punching bag. *Did my grandfather do that to her?*

The doctor eyes my hands, then my face again, his expression carefully neutral. "Did you do this to her?"

I shake my head, tilting my clean, unhurt fingers to the light. "No, I didn't."

Seeing these marks on her makes me want to fucking destroy someone on her behalf, and I don't even know her. Inspecting her features a little closer, and even through the bruises and marks, I recognize her as someone I've seen on campus at Oakmount a time or two. *Fuck me.* Of course she attends Oakmount. Because nothing in my life can be complication-free.

"Help me lift her," the doctor orders. He's staring at me expectantly like he's had to repeat himself while I wandered off mentally.

I nod once, crouch, and help him lift her slight weight. He probably could have lifted her by himself. She's a tiny thing, fine-boned and fragile feeling in my arms. "We can take her to the staff wing. There's no one back there right now, and she'll have the space to herself."

He nods, and I lead the way, both of us carrying her. We walk through the kitchen to the back of the house before turning down a long corridor. Once we reach the narrower hall, I shift the girl away from the doctor and more fully against my chest.

"I've got her. Just...keep going. Right through there."

The doctor continues in front of me. The lighting is minimal, illuminating several doors farther down. I choose the first door we arrive at and adjust my hold while the doctor opens the door. Thankfully, fresh sheets are on the twin bed, tucked tight into the basic wooden frame. I gently place the girl on the gray wool blanket and take a wobbly step back.

Red. Blood.

It coats my fingers now, and I'm transported back in time.

My uncle's drenched in blood, lying in the middle of the floor. The same floor covered in blood all over again. I blink, trying to make the memories fade, but that only intensifies them.

Tanya's hands run over my shoulders and up my neck.

There's so much blood.

"It'll be okay, Sebastian."

"Sebastian," someone calls in the distance.

"Sebastian, are you with me? I need your help." I snap back to reality with a shudder. Sweat beads on my brow, and a shiver courses through my body. I know the doctor needs me, but I can't help him. I can't even help myself at this point.

With fear and panic clinging to my bones, I leave the room to rush down the hall and up the stairs, stopping only once I find the haven of my own room. On the nightstand is a bottle of whiskey, the one constant in my life. It's never let me down, never hurt me. I rush across the room, grab it, and clutch it to my chest, knowing it's the only thing capable of keeping me afloat in these dark waters.

Releasing a sigh, I bring the bottle to my lips and chug down the brown liquid inside. It doesn't even burn. It's like I'm drinking water.

Am I numb to the pain, or am I just too far gone to care?

The answer is irrelevant. Soon enough, the alcohol will kick in, stopping the runaway train of memories threatening to take me back to that night when I was sixteen. Fuck me, that was only five years ago now. Back then, I thought I was happy. That I would one day run a legitimate company with my uncle, who had raised me as his son.

She ripped it all away, though, leaving me with a fist-sized hole in my chest and memories I'll never be able to scrub from my mind.

In an instant, I became a Mafia prince. Heir to the Arturo family's considerable wealth and privilege, but also their secrets and their corruption. Locked inside the family legacy with death as the only way out.

I guess my grandfather was right when he said you can own a person. Even though he's gone now, his name owns me. His family—the Arturo family—owns me, and I'll never be free of them.

A flash of dark hair soaked in blood appears in my mind. The girl—Elyse, according to the papers scattered on my grandfather's floor—is right there with me. I almost pity her. If I was kinder I would've let her die, but I didn't, and now she's just as trapped in this darkness as I am.

A crazed laugh bubbles out of me.

At least I'm not alone.

I snicker to myself and continue drinking. I don't stop until the bottle is empty, and all I'm left with is the warmth of the alcohol chasing away the memories and pain.

It's funny how things can go from bad to worse in an instant. The next night, I get a phone call from the hospital. At first, I'm confused, but then I meet my real mother, and as if God hasn't hurt me enough, He arranges things so I arrive just in time to witness her passing. Something inside me died that day, whether it was whatever remaining pieces of my heart existed or whatever juvenile thoughts about the life I might get to have now that I was free from my grandfather still lingered.

It all becomes grains of sand in an hourglass when I learn the truth about my sister, Maybel Jacobs. She needs me, needs my support and strength. It may appear that I've lost it all, but I've gained something in return, and I'll be damned if I'm going to let anything happen to her. My fate might be sealed, but if I have to choose between freedom and protecting the only remaining family I have left, I will always choose her.

I

ELYSE

There is no one I hate more than Sebastian Arturo. I thought my father was the most loathsome person on the planet, but I learned fairly fast that it's that smug asshole with his icy personality...that beautiful man who I swear is broken inside and out who is the epitome of hate.

Who cares if he's my boss? If he saved my life? If he provides me a place to live?

None of that matters or negates the fact that I absolutely loathe him. Considering the life I've had and how I've spent the last ten months since I was brutally beaten and shot by my own father, that's really saying something.

The sound of the door slamming in the foyer still rings in my ears. He always fucking slams the door, as if its presence and the fact that he had to open it at all is offensive to him. I guess I should be used to his crazy antics by now, but unfortunately, I'm not.

I inhale deeply through my nose and try to let it out slowly to release the anger that kindles the moment he comes near me, talks to me, or even looks at me.

Not that he's going to grace me with his presence today.

The second the thought flits through my mind, the door to the staff wing flies open and slams against the wall again, making me flinch. *Shit.* Apparently, we're doing this again. I swear the guy is always one second away from losing his damn mind. I wonder what his vendetta against doors is and why he slams them to announce himself.

Having played this song and dance a time or two, I know I have only seconds before he comes stomping into the room. I'm tempted to cower in the corner, but I've learned cowering doesn't stop the inevitable from happening. If someone wants to hurt you, they'll do it no matter what.

Quickly, I move toward the dresser, gripping the edge of it to steady myself. My knees tremble, and a sheen of sweat forms against my brow, both telltale signs of fear. It's been difficult to handle the anxiety that comes with living with someone like Sebastian. Fear has been the one thing that helped me survive this life, and I'm so used to living with it and letting it guide my every choice that even though part of me knows I have nothing to worry about when it comes to Sebastian, I can't shake the lingering panic.

Yes, he's dangerous. I know anyone standing within ten feet of the man would assume he's a menace, but instinctively, I feel safe with him. Which is strange, considering I want to stab him in the eye almost daily.

As I predicted, he comes powering through the door like an F5 tornado, hell-bent on destroying anything in his way. He barely manages to stop in time, but not before partially barreling into me, the toes of his expensive leather loafers scuffing against my worn Chuck Taylors. I fall back against the dresser with a breathless *oomph* as he straightens himself, too close for comfort.

Glancing down at my feet so I don't have to meet his gaze, I'm reminded that we do not come from the same worlds.

The typical fear and anxiety that trickles into my veins any time he comes near me makes it hard for me to swallow, to think, to do anything but stand there looking like an idiot. I hate this feeling of helplessness. There's no reason he should have this effect on me. He may be painfully good-looking, powerful, and filthy rich, but he's just a man.

That's all any of them are.

Swallowing my fear, I lick my lips and force myself to look up from my feet and into his dark green eyes.

Sebastian thinks he hides his scars well, but I know better. I know that beneath that soulless, annoyed expression he gives everyone lies a man who's both damaged and hurt. A man haunted by his past and future. And it's sad because maybe if he wasn't such an asshole, I'd be willing to help him. Or I don't know, at least try not to hate him. But not now, not ever.

He wears his usual irritated expression.

Is it really necessary to slam every door in the house?

The question sits on the tip of my tongue, but the thought hardens into concrete on my lips when his annoyance morphs into anger right before my eyes. Even knowing that I'm not truly afraid of him, I can't make my body react differently. All I can do is stand here trembling.

Dammit.

I'm so disappointed in myself. I don't know why I thought this time would be different, that I'd be able to stand up to him. I'm not really surprised; angry men have a habit of making me fear for my life. It doesn't help that my employer is perpetually angry at the world either.

His gaze rakes over my skin as he assesses my navy blue polo, khaki pants, and sneakers. He's silently judging me...*again*.

I straighten my shoulders and tug the hem of my uniform shirt down. I'd really just love to have one day when I don't feel self-conscious in my own skin.

"Wh-what do you want?" The words don't come out half as strong as I want them to.

His full lips twist into a scowl as he drags his gaze back up my body, stopping once he reaches my face. "Did you really just ask me that?" He shakes his head like I asked him to buy me a new car or something. "*What do I want?* How about, how can I help you, Mr. Arturo, or can I get you something, Mr. Arturo? Now if you're done wasting my time, you can start packing your bag."

Huh? Packing my bag. What on earth is he talking about? I stare at him, hoping to convey my confusion without using words, but it doesn't seem to work. He doesn't explain, so I blurt out my question after a moment.

"What do you mean, pack my bags? I don't understand."

"For fuck's sake," he growls, then turns his attention to my dresser. The same one I'm gripping the edge of. Without care, he rips open the top drawer. Shock morphs into embarrassment when he starts rifling around inside.

What the fuck?

"What are you doing? Stop that!" I place my hand flat on the drawer and attempt to push it back in so I don't have to see his long, graceful fingers clutching the lace and cotton of my underwear, but it's useless.

He doesn't miss a beat, doesn't even spare me a glance as he brushes my hand away and continues his assault on my underwear. After tossing a handful onto the top of the dresser, he moves to the next drawer down, where my shirts are neatly folded.

"Why are these all uniform shirts?"

If I had more balls, I'd probably say what's on my mind at this very moment and ask him if he's stupid or just oblivious. He has to know I do nothing but attend classes and work for him. I have no time for a social life. I refrain, though. There's no point in instigating the beast.

Instead, I say mildly, "Because you paid for them, and all my wages go to attending school."

I watch his forehead wrinkle, and he shoves his sandy-blond hair out of his face to crouch down, continuing to dig through my sparse pants drawer.

"What the fuck, Ely?"

I flinch at the stupid nickname, the one he adopted and keeps using simply because he knows how much I hate it. It's the same name my father used to call me while he beat me. I don't bother telling him the real reason I hate being called it; he'd only use it against me, and he doesn't need more ammunition.

"Please stop calling me that!"

His features sharpen, and he freezes at my protest, and I swallow it hastily. "Never mind. I-I don't know what you expect." His lips settle into a thin line. I know that look. When you've spent a good portion of your life making sure you don't piss others off so you don't have to deal with another beating, you learn to read other people's facial expressions. And that expression tells me he's on the cusp of full-blown rage.

"All you have is the employee-issued uniform; is that what you're telling me?"

I swallow hard, my own anger and fear clogging my throat in a tight knot. I can barely squeeze out the words. "Clothes aren't important. Not as important as other things."

He stands in one smooth motion, his frame towering above me. "You mean not as important as school and, say, the menagerie of pets you've been housing and feeding gourmet food to in the old groundskeeper's cottage?"

Shit. Heat blooms in my cheeks. I was certain no one saw me sneaking in there. "It's not a menagerie. Just, like, one cat and a dog. Plus, they were sick." I wave a hand, trying to distract him. "It doesn't matter. I'm not going to argue with you about it."

He takes a calculated step toward me, eating up the tiny amount of space separating us, and I keep my feet rooted into the ground. Even after months of being around him, there are still instances when he surprises me. You can never be too sure with him.

"The animals don't matter. What matters is the clothing you don't have, the clothing that I need you to have."

"Why?" I try to strip the anger out of my voice, but by the way his eyes narrow, I know I've failed.

"Why must you always ask a million questions?" He snarls. "Because I have places to be, and you're coming with me." His annoyance makes a mockery of me, as if it's so inconvenient for him to be here rummaging through my meager possessions.

My chin lifts as my own annoyance flares to life, and I forget for a single blessed moment to be afraid.

"Well, this is what I have. If you don't like it, I suggest you provide me with something else. Maybe Bel has something I can borrow?"

He cocks his head to the side and purses his lips, his full bottom lip poking out invitingly. Nope. Not even going to let my thoughts go there. *I bet he's a terrible kisser.* No one in their right mind would take that invitation and saddle themselves with his emotional trauma or the repercussions of crawling into bed with him.

I've been around long enough to hear what happens in his bedroom. Thinking about it sends an involuntary shudder down my spine. I've had to listen to the screams and the moans; I've had to wash blood from his sheets. Sebastian isn't the gentleman the world thinks he is, I'll tell you that much.

I hold my head high while the urge to look down at my shoes and crumple at his feet tempts me. With nothing more than a nod, and in a deceptively calm tone, he says, "Let's go see what she has in her closet. There should be something suitable, and considering I bought most of it, she won't mind sharing."

He gives me no time to react as he snags me by the bicep. I fight against his grip, but all I end up doing is tripping over my own feet as he hauls me behind him. I have to put in twice the effort to keep up with him since his legs are so long.

"I can walk by myself, you know."

"I know that, but ask me if I care?"

He doesn't even turn to look at me as he speaks, pulling me along behind him as he stalks down the long hall of the staff wing and up the stairs to the kitchen. I barely catch a flash of stainless steel and granite before we're in the foyer.

My head spins, and I stumble, a wave of dizziness slamming into me. *Stay on your feet, E.* The last thing I need is to fall to my knees in front of this man. By sheer willpower, I remain upright until, thankfully, Bel's bedroom door is only a few feet away. He stops directly in front of it, and even with his back to me, I know he wears an expression of annoyance. The closed door is nothing more than another hurdle.

I don't want him ambushing her on my behalf; then again, it's really his problem that he wants me to wear something I don't own.

Releasing a sigh that might be frustration, he raises his fist and knocks. The sound of his fist on the wood vibrates through me, and a shudder ripples down my spine. A moment passes, and when there is no response on the other side, he grabs the doorknob and twists it, shoving it open.

Without blinking, he steps into the room, dragging me behind him as he makes a beeline for the closet. *Jesus.* I nearly sigh when he finally releases me, apparently needing both hands so he can open the closet and turn on the light.

I blink a few times to adjust to the light, and then I notice the clothes. Rows of sumptuous wools, creamy cottons, and gorgeous leather, all perfectly pressed and lined up on hangers. I should know...I'm the main person who does the laundry around here.

I skim my fingers over some of the soft taupe fabrics. She doesn't wear much of this, preferring her old hoodies and sweaters to most of the luxury outerwear and slacks. What I wouldn't give for a closet like this. Everything is so pretty and well-tended. Nothing like my threadbare wardrobe with pieces I've had to mend too many times.

My father never had money for new clothes. And when I got dumped on Sebastian, I'd only had the one old sundress I'd been wearing. That's long since been discarded for the blood spatter, and you know, the prominent bullet hole.

Thinking about it makes my arm ache, and I shake it out while focusing on Sebastian. "I could help if I knew what I was looking for."

He doesn't even spare me a glance, sifting through the hangers like a competent secretary flicks through files. The hangers make soft shushing noises on the metal rod above our heads, almost lulling with their constant motion as he searches for some great unknown. After a few minutes, he stops, clearly finding something he likes. With a flick of the wrist, he grabs it from the hanger and holds it out to me.

I take it so it doesn't fall to the floor since he releases it almost immediately, holding the green satin dress against my body. I don't have Bel's full curves or voluptuous chest. I've always felt more shaped like a box than anything else. This dress will look awful on my somewhat flat chest and shapeless body.

I clear my throat, thinking to warn him of this, but he shoves another couple of outfits at me, then turns to look at the shoes. "What size do you wear?"

I squeak out an answer. "Um...seven." Bel and I happen to be the same size. I know because I might have tried on a few pairs of the beautiful heels she absolutely refuses to wear unless Drew asks her to.

A slight shift in the air and a soft noise alerts me to the presence of someone else. I glance back to find Bel braced in the doorway taking in the scene, a smile on her lips. "So...uh...what's going on here?"

2
ELYSE

I freeze. Shit. Bel isn't privy to why I'm here although we've gone out for coffee, studied together, and even gone to the movies a couple of times. She always talks to me and tries to include me in things, but I'm pretty sure she still considers me to be *the maid*. The maid her doting brother hired out of the goodness of his heart. Which is basically a load of shit. I doubt Sebastian has said a damn thing to her about *that* night.

Thankfully, Sebastian saves me from having to explain. "Ms. Silver has agreed to do me a favor. You know I hate going to those business events alone, and since you and Drew are properly attached now, I find the attention I get at these things tiresome."

Bel chuckles. "You want to take Elyse to a business event to save you from being hunted by other women?"

He clears his throat, and all I can do is stare, still frozen. I notice the pink of embarrassment creep up his cheeks instantly. It reminds me how guarded and different he is with Bel and with his friends.. The person he is with his sister is warm, kind, and gentle —possibly the real him. A man few others get to see.

His gaze ping-pongs between us before he settles it back onto

Bel. "When you put it like that, it makes me sound like a pussy. But yes, I need someone there to keep them away from me. I can't be bothered with distractions. I need to conduct actual business."

She leans against the doorframe now, smiling at her brother. "And where are you going?"

He shakes his head and shoves past me and then Bel as he moves into the bedroom. Bel follows, and I emerge a moment later, my arms still laden with the stack of clothing. The fabric is so soft and lovely.

She gives me a smile. "If you find anything you like in that closet, Elyse, feel free to keep it. I've barely worn any of the clothes hanging in there. It's probably nothing that I care for if it's still hanging in there since most of my belongings and clothes are at Drew's place now."

Sebastian grumbles, "Don't remind me. I don't like the thought of you living there most of the time. But at least it's not The Mill."

Bel scoffs. "Well, for your information, we are currently alternating between The Mill and Drew's house. So we can give his mom some privacy and have our own from time to time."

"I'll continue this conversation with you later. We're already running late." There's an edge of annoyance to his tone, and I know it's only because of me. Sebastian could never be annoyed with Bel. Not even when she's disobeying every one of his rules.

"Of course. I don't want to keep you." Bel smiles, and Sebastian turns to head for the door. I take a step forward, intending to follow but am stopped when Bel places a hand against my shoulder. I look down at her hand and then back up to her face. She's smiling softly, but her eyes look...concerned...worried maybe?

"I know he's my brother, but that doesn't mean anything. Don't let him push you around, E. Us women gotta stick together. Stand your ground, and if he hurts you, come to me. I've got your back."

Bel is what I consider to be my one and only friend in this whirlwind of a life, and while I appreciate her so much and accept her desire to care for me, I won't ever pit her and Sebastian against each other by dragging her into the mess I've gotten myself into with him.

"I know you do," I whisper and give her a smile in return.

"Sebastian has a lot of bark but no bite. At least, not to those he cares about. Don't let him scare you into submission." She gives me a wink and then releases me, her hand falling back to her side.

I'm not sure what that means, but I don't have the time to read into it. Not when Sebastian starts yelling my name.

"Coming!" I reply and scurry from the room like there is a fire behind me. I find him standing in the hall, wearing the same look of impatience from earlier.

"The time to socialize isn't now. What part of we're already running late did you not understand?" he asks, then starts walking again, forcing me to follow. I'm hot on his heels up until the moment he turns into his bedroom. It's there I find myself pausing just outside the door. *Why does this feel so personal and intimate?* I'm sure I'm overthinking it, but I've never been inside his bedroom, at least not with him inside, and even then, it was only to clean the space. He's not asking me to clean right now, and while I understand the interpretation, I'm not sure I like being invited into his room to do anything other than that.

Turning on his heels, he spots me stalled in the doorway. A look of pure impatience etches into his features. "For fuck's sake, Ely. Get in the room. We don't have time for your uncertainty."

Uncertainty? Am I so easily read? Actually, never mind. While it doesn't feel right, and I can't pinpoint in what way, he takes my hesitation and doubt and shoves them back at me, reminding me once more that he holds all the power.

"I highly suggest you get your ass into this room, or there will be consequences, and I can promise, you don't want to see how creative I can be."

The hard edge of his voice makes me shiver, and I don't dare ignore the warning coating his words. Even though my body urges me to turn and run away, I force myself to do as he says and walk into the room. His usual woodsy sea-salt scent tickles my nostrils as it lingers in the air. Someone so bitter and hate-filled should not smell so delectable, never mind look as handsome as he does. It's like false advertising.

Walking up to his king-sized bed, I drop the stack of clothes. *What does he expect me to do now*? I look down at the clothes and try to figure out where the hell he's taking me based on the clothing. He can barely stand to be in the same room as me most days, so what's brought on the sudden desire to take me somewhere? My instincts scream at me, telling me to think this through properly before agreeing. Unfortunately, my instincts don't understand that I have no choice in the matter. There is no "agreement."

The feel of his eyes on me drags my attention back to him.

"What?" I blurt out before I can think better of it.

"Do you plan to stand there all day staring at the clothes, or are you going to try them on? I need to see what you look like in them and determine if this is even worth the effort."

Wow. World-class asshole right here, folks.

I shouldn't be bothered by his crass response. It's not the first time he's spoken to me that way, and it won't be the last. He's all about cutting me down, reminding me that I'm a bug beneath his shoe and that if he wants to, he can and will step on me.

"You know, if you were a little nicer..." I grit my teeth, only then realizing that he means right here and now. Yeah, he's lost his mind if he thinks I'm going to strip down to my bra and panties in front of him.

"Nice gets you stepped on. I'm not nice. We both know that, so let's skip the pleasantries. Now try on the damn dresses."

All I can do is shake my head and roll my eyes. This man is beyond bossy. I quickly grab the green dress off the stack and turn toward the bathroom. If he wants to see me in the dresses, then fine. Hopefully, I look terrible, and he will change his mind about taking me with him. *A girl can dream, right?* I've taken only a step when he speaks again, "No, Ely, I need to see it all. Put the dress on in front of me."

See it all? Everything in me freezes. "Why can't I just do it in the bathroom?"

"Are you going to be able to get the zipper up on your own?" I open my mouth to respond, but he's talking over me before I can get a word out. "Never mind, your response isn't needed. Besides, I want to ensure that if clothing comes off, you'll at least be adequate enough to be in my company."

If clothing comes off? Where the hell does he think he's taking me? I grit my teeth and ignore his words. He's just trying to break me down, trying to see if he can make me cry. It's like his favorite thing to do. See how much he can hurt me before I snap. I'm not really sure why he hates me so much, and I try not to think about it. No point in worrying over something I'll never get an answer to.

Fear furrows low in my belly. I want to tell him no, that I won't change in front of him, but I can't make the words come out. A startled yelp escapes my lips when he snaps, his voice booming around me. "Stop acting like you have something to hide. You aren't the first woman I've seen naked, and you won't be the last."

Jesus, does he have to be so blunt?

"I don't understand..." I start, but he cuts me off with a singular icy glare.

"Do I look like I give a fuck if you understand something or not? I'm certain I warned you once already about repeating myself. If you intend to piss me off, you've succeeded. I don't want to hurt you, Ely, but I will if you make me."

Hurt me? I don't think he knows what being hurt looks like. Anger boils to the surface, and I clench my hands into tight fists. I really want to punch him in the face for being so condescending, but I'm kinda forced to work with him until my asshole father's debt is paid off. So while I don't punch him in the face, I don't stand there letting him toss stones at me either.

"Fine," I growl and grip the hem of my polo, ripping it over my head with a jerk. My chest heaves with every breath I take, and I know I need to get a grasp on my anger before I unleash it all on him, but honestly, he deserves whatever comes out of my mouth.

I can feel his eyes on me, and I look up in time to notice his smoldering gaze as it flicks over the threadbare lace of my bra. I'm barely a B-cup, and while I'm slim, I'm also short. Never mind that I'm missing the sensual curves most women my age have. That doesn't seem to matter to Sebastian, not when I notice the ember of desire glowing deep in the depths of his emerald gaze. A look that wasn't there just moments ago.

Over the course of the months I've been here, I've learned things about Sebastian. Although he doesn't vocalize every emotion, he feels things deeply. And so I know that look, because I've put it there more than once or twice before, and as much as I loathe his existence, I find it hard to breathe when he looks at me like that. Hard to exist.

The moment is ruined when a voice carries from the hallway to the room through the still-open door. "Well, well, what do we have here?"

Ugh, no. As if this situation couldn't get worse. I let my eyes flutter closed and hug the cotton shirt to my chest, trying to shield myself from her gaze. Of course *she* would stumble upon us when I'm half naked in Sebastian's room. *Innocently*, half naked.

"Mrs. Arturo, what can I do for you?"

When I open my eyes again, my gaze automatically shifts to Sebastian. I'm pretty sure it's obvious to everyone but her how much he dislikes her—either that or she doesn't really care. Sebastian does his best to hide his irritation and annoyance of her, but sometimes his mask slips, and other times his feelings are so profound they slip through the cracks. I've never bothered to ask what the problem is and why he dislikes her so much, kind of like I've never bothered to ask why he hates me. It's better not to know the truth sometimes. Though I've never done anything to earn me so much hatred from him. Who knows, maybe Tanya hasn't, either?

Maybe he just hates people for the hell of it?

It's impossible to miss the tightening of his jaw and the slight clench of his teeth. He turns to stone instantly, his body becoming rigid, his eyes narrowing, the typical emotionless mask he wears around everyone except me falling over his face.

No, he saves all his anger and hate for me. And enjoys making me see it.

Tanya creeps deeper into the room, sucking all the air out of the space. Just like always, she's beautifully polished and put together from head to toe. Her ruby-red lips pull up into a predatory smile as soon as her gaze lands on me. I wish the floor would swallow me up and spit me out back in my bedroom, but I don't get that lucky.

"Am I interrupting something?"

3
SEBASTIAN

Am I interrupting something? The list of things that are starting to piss me off seems to be getting longer and longer. Maybe if Elyse hadn't wasted so much time and had fucking suitable clothing—anything other than a damn work uniform—in her dresser, I wouldn't be in this room with her and Tanya right now.

Who am I kidding? Rationally, I know none of this is Elyse's fault, but that doesn't mean I won't make it seem that way.

Something about her begs me to give her a hard time.

Tanya, technically my aunt, although she calls herself my stepmother, has been living in the house for ten months now, and when I say *living*, I use the term loosely since I haven't seen much of her in that time. *Thank fuck.* She tells me—like I actually give a shit—that she's been balancing her time between here and the house she has in Miami. I don't really give a fuck what she's doing as long as she stays away from me. For some unknown reason she's been hanging around a little more lately, though, and I don't like it. Just looking at her makes me sick. It makes me want to crawl inside a bottle of bourbon and never come out. I will deal with her for now, until I can figure out how to convince her to let me buy out her part of the house's deed.

"Yes, you're interrupting something, but we don't have time for it now, anyway, so no apology is necessary." I give Tanya a hard glance and peer back down at Ely, noticing how she clutches her shirt tight in her hands, hands that are visibly shaking.

Good.

I need her fear like I need oxygen because it means I'm in control. I feast on it, and she gives it to me so easily, it's almost pathetic. And keeping her afraid shouldn't be a problem after she finds out where we're going. I've gone easy on her the last couple of months, but I know it's only a matter of time before she remembers things. Dr. Brooks warned me that once her memories trickle in they may come and go like waves. He also said she might not ever regain her memories from that night, so it's crucial that I maintain control over her so I know what she's remembering and not remembering. My own life and future hangs in the balance of her recall.

"Elyse, go pack up whatever else you're going to need, and hurry back. We're leaving soon. As in, in an hour soon. You don't show up, I hunt you down and drag you out the door. Is that clear?"

She blinks up at me, her big doe eyes wide and shining with fright and maybe a hint of something else. Something I'm not even fucking touching right now. Maybe she doesn't think I've noticed her lingering stares or the heat in her eyes, which she tries to hide beneath a hateful glare every time I say something shitty. She might be good at hiding from the rest of the world, but she can't hide from me. I notice everything when it comes to her. In fact, sometimes I have to remind myself that she's my employee, and this can only end one way. Developing an obsession for the quiet, fearful brunette is not necessary to my end goal.

If I wanted to, I could have her. I could fuck her any way I want, however I want, even if she said no and begged me not to. She belongs to me, after all. I pride myself on control, though, being in control and maintaining it. Giving in to those impulsive desires would be the same as letting her win, and I refuse to let her break me down to that level of baser instinct. Plus, nothing good comes from making choices with your dick. My aunt/stepmother, Tanya, is proof of that on my uncle's part.

When she doesn't immediately start moving, I clap my hands, and she jumps, startled by the sound. "Move it!" I taunt. She springs into action, scurrying from the room.

I return my focus to Tanya, un-beloved auntie, adopted mommy, stepmother. *Mother* is a generous term for a woman who didn't do anything to actually raise me; nor did she give birth to me. It was my uncle, Mitchell Arturo, whom I consider my adopted father, who raised me. Not my grandfather, who took credit for turning me into a brutal, sadistic asshole, and definitely not this bitch who thinks she can have what's mine.

My family is beyond fucked up. Just the thought of it makes my head hurt, but Tanya's presence is a constant reminder of all that I try to forget. My mother, who I reconnected with before her untimely death mere months earlier, had an affair after giving birth to me that resulted in the birth of my sister, Bel. Since my biological father was psychotic and abusive, among other amazing attributes, my mother wanted to leave him. She struck a deal with my grandfather, her own father, where she signed over her rights to me, giving him guardianship and allowing him to raise me, and he allowed her to leave, free to live her life as she saw fit. I guess that's what she wanted, since that's what she did, without a single penny to her name.

I'm past the point of hating her for it. In fact, part of me respects her for it. I can understand her desire to escape this place and these people and live a different sort of existence—even if it meant leaving me behind.

I can understand, because I'm living the nightmare she managed to escape right now.

Which brings me back to the present situation.

"What do you want, Tanya?"

Her smile widens, her lips shining in the afternoon light that beams through the windows on the far side of the room. I usually keep the curtains drawn, as it's far more fitting for my mood, but *someone* must have left them open after cleaning.

"No *'hello,'* or *'how are you?'*" She bats her long lashes at me. "I'm actually a little hurt that you don't want to know how I'm doing. Meanwhile, you're seducing one of the employees in your bedroom. Really, Sebastian. What on earth were you thinking? Can you imagine the scandal? Please, tell me, why did she have her shirt off?" There's a hint of suspicion in her question and tone.

"It's none of your fucking business; now get out," I snap but immediately regret it.

Her eyes flash with murderous rage, and she closes the distance between us in remarkable time, given her four-inch stiletto heels. Honestly, I should anticipate her attack. I'm not sure why I don't. Her fingers ghost against the flesh of my cheek, and I flinch.

It's a small movement, inconspicuous unless you're looking for it, but it's all the victory she needs. Sinking her fingers into my skin a little deeper, she gently drags her nails down the side of my face. To the casual observer, it would look like a caress. A motherly one. Only we know otherwise.

"Watch your tone when you speak to me, Sebastian. You might be the big bad overseer of the family, but everyone has a weakness if you dig deep enough. Don't make me expose yours."

"I don't have any weaknesses," I growl.

"Oh really?" She cocks her head to the side. "Bel isn't a weakness? What about the little maid?"

"Elyse is nothing to you, and neither is Bel. I won't warn you again, Tanya. If you fuck with me, I will fuck you back, and it won't end how you want it to."

"Are you flirting with me?" There's a hint of humor in her voice.

Of course she thinks this is a fucking game. Everything is a game to her.

No matter what, she'll never win against me again. With Bel in the picture, I have something to live for, something to fight for, and I won't let Tanya's bitterness bleed off into her. Bel's an innocent, and I refuse to let the dirty dealings of this family touch her.

"Only you would think this is a game."

"Isn't it?" She leans into my face, her lips curling in a smile. "It's been so long since we played, Sebby. Why don't you bend me over the desk and teach me a lesson?"

My gut churns, the contents of my stomach threatening to climb up my throat. I'm transported back to a time when I was too stupid and weak to say no. Too naive and dumb to fight back. I can feel that weak little boy, the one who always feared her, the one who still fears her in so many ways, threatening to crumble.

You're stronger than this.

You're stronger than her.

You're stronger now.

I repeat the mantra over and over again in my head, waiting until I believe the words.

"Come on, Sebby. Don't you want to play?" She taunts me, her breath caressing my ear. Beads of sweat collect against the collar of my shirt. I can feel the ghost of her lips against my cheek as she moves her head.

"Oh fuck. Who knew you could fuck better than your father?" She pants in my ear while shoving her fake tits in my face.

Even as I fight against the pleasure building low in my belly, I know I won't be able to escape it. The orgasm is inevitable.

"Yes! Your cock feels so good inside me. So good, Sebby. I want

you to fill me with your cum." Her voice rains down on me, drops of acid falling from the sky.

"Sebby....where did you go?"

"Nowhere. Now leave. I don't want shit from you," I snap.

I know I could push her hand away, and I want to so I don't have to spend the next hour scrubbing my skin raw, but I don't. I won't give her the satisfaction of knowing she affects me. My mind wanders again, and I slip into a dark space where no one can reach me, all while pasting on the bored expression that gets me through dealing with her and all the others like her. It might not be today or even tomorrow, but eventually, she will learn her place. Even if I have to beat it into her head, she'll come to understand she no longer owns me.

Her lips form a pout. "That makes me very sad."

I'm sure it does. I barely stop myself from rolling my eyes.

"I'd prefer if you stop with the riddles and tell me what you really want. Why are you here?" My flat tone is devoid of the emotion she loves to draw out of me.

"Fine. I'm sorry. I just wanted to know what was going on at home. That's all."

Her toxic scent of raspberry and Chanel No. 5 fills my senses, and I nearly gag on air as I suck a ragged breath into my lungs. Memories continue to assault me, threatening to drag me back down into the abyss.

No. Not right now. I suppress them as best I can, hoping to bury the memory of her hands, her punishments, her skin against mine but they still linger right near the surface.

I need something else to think about. Something to distract me. I don't mention the fact that she's been gone off and on for months and never cared to know what was going on before today, mainly because I don't have the tolerance to deal with any more of her bullshit.

"If it's that big of a concern to you, then I'll tell you. I'm attending a business meeting and taking Ms. Silver with me to assist."

Her eyes narrow, and she cocks her head to the side. "Assist with what...and why on earth would she need to remove her clothing to help you?"

"Not that I require your permission or need to share what I do or do not do with my staff, but I'm taking her to Pound of Flesh. And before you rudely interrupted me, I was having her try on a few dresses I had picked out."

As badly as I'd love to tell her that I was getting ready to fuck Elyse, I don't. I have no doubt in my mind that she would murder Elyse just to spite me if she thought for even a moment that the girl was competition.

Tanya smiles, all sadistic curiosity. "You're taking that innocent little thing to Pound of Flesh? Have you lost your mind?"

I shrug. *I have to wonder about that myself.*

Tanya's gaze sharpens, and her grin widens, white teeth flashing, sharp like a shark's. "Oh...no...are you going to sell her? In that case, things might be different. She'll fetch a pretty penny. Especially with how innocent-looking and doll-like she is. The men will eat her up and spit out the bones."

I want to deny it. To shove her away from me and make my escape, but I don't dare. It will only encourage her to sink her nails in a little deeper. "What I do with her is my business. If I want to sell her, I will. If I want to use her to draw someone else's attention, I will do so. She's my property."

Her eyes narrow, and I realize I've given too much away. Like always. I hate these fucking games. I repeat myself so, maybe, even if Ely fights against it, Tanya will know. "She is my property and, therefore, out of your reach."

4

SEBASTIAN

With a shrug of her shoulders, she steps closer, surrounding me and choking me with her perfume. That, mixed with the proximity of her body, makes it difficult for me to breathe or focus on anything but keeping myself from vomiting. "Maybe for now she is, but think of this. Wouldn't it be more fun to sell her off and get yourself someone with a little more experience? Someone who can handle a good, hard fucking? Remember, I know exactly what you like and how you like it, and that girl isn't going to deliver. You'll break her in two by the time you finish with her."

I swallow hard and meet her cold eyes. "I'm good. Haven't you heard? I've made an art out of taking a girl's virginity. They wear my cuts on their skin, showing them off, seeking me out to parade them around. So no, I don't need anyone with more experience. Virgin or not, I fuck them how I want, and they beg me so pretty to do it." I put enough bite in my tone that I expect her to retaliate in some way, but all she does is smile, blinking at me lazily, like a cat coiling to pounce.

"Darling..." She cups my chin in her warm hand and forces my head back. We are almost the same height with her heels on, but while I'm looking down my nose at her, this is anything but a submissive stance.

With her thumb under my chin and finger anchored behind my ear, she's firmly in control. "Why did you have to be so damn beautiful?"

I speak slowly since she's still holding my chin, and it takes effort to get the words out. "You mean, why didn't your father sell you to marry me instead of Mitchell? Isn't that what you always wanted?"

She hums. "Maybe...you weren't much to look at as a child, but after witnessing the man you've grown into, I can't disagree. Your father was old even when I was young. It was a business arrangement and nothing more. There were no feelings between us. He had his dalliances, and so did I."

I flinch, and she smiles, knowing she's struck a nerve. "I'll let you get packed. Make sure you bring your weapons; you're going to have a hell of a time protecting that little thing once they find out she's a virgin."

She flicks her fingers from my face, dismissing me like I'm a crumb beneath her nail, and turns to head for the door, her heels clicking loudly against the hardwood.

"No one is going to find out. They won't get the opportunity to."

She shrugs but doesn't look back. "Maybe I'll call some old friends, let them know what's coming their way."

Of course she would do that. Anything to spite me.

In the hall, she pauses and turns back, throwing me a smirk. "Good luck with that one. Nosy little thing, isn't she?"

I race to the door and glance down the hall to the stairs, but find it's empty. *Was Elyse really out here listening to us, or is Tanya fucking with me?* It's a fifty-fifty shot at this point.

Heaving a disgusted breath, I face the stack of clothing on the bed. "It'll suffice. We'll only be gone a few days."

Something in the back of my mind warns me to leave Ely here, that taking her will only cause more trouble. I can't leave her to Tanya's mercy, though. She'd just end up being used by her to betray me.

No. She is mine, and she'll stay with me. There is no other solution.

I square my shoulders and shove thoughts of Tanya out of my head. Time to pack my own bag. The housekeeper offered, but I don't want her to accidentally find the weapons cabinet built into the bottom of my closet. For as long as I've been living back in the house, my closet has been off-limits except to put away clothing, which is mostly Elyse's job, anyway.

Fuck it. It is Elyse's job; I'll make her do it.

I turn to march out of the room and crash directly into her small body. I grip her by the arm in an attempt to steady her and notice the old, ratty backpack she's brought with her. All I can do is roll my eyes and shake my head.

"Do you own anything that isn't fucking thrift store chic?"

She flinches, and it feels good. I need this. I need to take back the power it feels like Tanya has stripped from my bones. I haul Ely up by her bicep, and she stumbles forward. The clean scent of soft skin and soap bubbles wafts from her. No thick cloying perfumes, nothing choking me. I let myself breathe her in, erasing the memories of Tanya from my mind. When I realize I've been holding onto her far longer than necessary, I release her with a small shove. She stumbles backward, and I revel in the anger that flashes in her eyes while I take the armchair by the bed.

"Perfect timing. I need my clothes packed."

She blinks. "But I thought you were going to pack your own bag."

"Well, I changed my mind." I eye her body and the stack of

clothes. "That is, unless you would rather resume what we were doing before we were interrupted?" I toy with her, knowing her response will be a shuddering *no*, and on the off chance she tries to surprise me with a challenge, I ensure the door is closed this time.

"No, of course, not." Her voice wavers, and she walks over to the closet. The light cuts across the dark hardwood, and I sit in my chair, watching her. What type of person does it make me if I admit that terrorizing Elyse has become my favorite pastime? I mean, since she belongs to me, why the hell not, right? Our verbal sparring matches are what gets me through the day sometimes, but I would never confess that to a soul.

As much as it annoys me most days, I've come to respect Elyse's sunshiny personality and drive. Even with the odds stacked against her daily, she still finds a way to be happy. Like just breathing is enough for her, and I guess I'm a little jealous of that. Or how, no matter what is thrown at her, she can somehow still find the smallest speck of good in the bad.

I can't seem to take my eyes off her, and it's definitely hate simmering in my blood right now. My balls ache, and my fists tighten as I stare at her perfect, heart-shaped ass. Months of confinement in this damn house with her are going to my head.

Hate. Not lust.

Remember who she is and what she represents. That reminder transforms desire into disgust.

Yes, let the disgust and anger lead you. Not the desire. Never the desire.

She pulls one of the designer suitcases from the top shelf and opens it, placing it just outside the closet, giving herself ample room to move around. "How many days should I pack for?"

There's something intimate about this moment...me watching her as she moves around in such proximity to my personal possessions, her fingers touching them... alarm bells blare in my head. "Five days should be sufficient."

"Five days?" she murmurs. "I didn't pack for five days."

I shrug. "It doesn't matter. Where we're going, clothes are optional." I keep my expression blank, even as adrenaline zips through my veins when I see fear filter into her blue eyes. Those same blue eyes beg me to meet her gaze, as if I'll confirm she'll be safe with me.

Yes, give your fear to me, Elyse. Give me all of it and let me drown in it because the alternative is so much more frightening.

She has no fucking clue what I would do if another man saw even an inch of her flesh without permission. I'd have to gouge his eyes out and remove his brain so I could take the memory from his mind. In every definition of the word, she is mine.

I'd never let anything happen between us, but she doesn't have to know that, nor will she ever. Not even when my use for her has ended.

She returns to the closet and, a second later, brings a handful of suits back out. "Evening wear? I presume a tuxedo?" Her eyes dart to the clothing on the bed, and before I can respond with some asshole remark, she mumbles to herself, "Duh, a tuxedo is needed."

I remain quiet and let her continue packing my belongings. She's just a maid. An infuriating, stubborn maid. A warm feeling takes root in my chest when she brings out a stack of my socks and underwear. *It's just socks and underwear. Get a grip.* But it's more than that. I know it, and I'm certain she knows it, too. Unlike all the others, I trust her, and it shows when I allow her to touch the most intimate items I own.

Thus bringing us way too close to the surface of something I don't want to fucking touch. I need a distraction, even if I don't have time for one. I whip out my phone and hit one of my most recent calls. "Hi."

I can feel Elyse's eyes on me, but she doesn't pause.

"You free right now?"

A sleepy mumble filters through the phone as Lee wakes up enough to answer. "Mm...yeah, I guess. What did you have in mind?"

I put on a wicked smile, making sure Elyse sees it. Not that she would miss it. Her eyes always have a habit of finding me. I think she's as attuned to me as I am to her. "Oh, I don't know. You, me, a bottle of whiskey. Maybe we'll take a dip in the hot tub?"

I have no plans at all to go anywhere with Lee but I sure as hell don't want Elyse to think I'll be sitting around here waiting for her. I could call one of the twenty girls I have in my contact list, but I'm not in the mood to deal with the extra shit that comes with making those calls.

Lee is good enough to make Ely think I'm going off to be with someone else.

More alert than before, Lee responds, "Sebastian. I'll definitely agree if you finally succumb to my wiles, but something tells me this isn't that."

I chuckle, low and deep. "No, it's not that. I'm looking to blow off a little steam before I head out of town on a business trip."

Out of the corner of my eye, I catch Elyse's mouth crimped tight in a thin line. Her hands pause as she stops packing. I stand and saunter over to her, still holding the phone to my ear. If making her life miserable was a sport, I'd be the champion.

I glare down at the suitcase and shake my head. "If you do it that way the suits will be wrinkled, and I won't have anything to wear when we arrive." With the toe of my leather shoe, I tip the suitcase up and over, spilling the contents onto the floor.

It's assholery at its finest, but someone has to do it.

Her pert mouth pops open, and her big blue doe eyes glisten with tears. “W-Why did you do that?”

“If you did it right the first time, I wouldn’t have to correct you. Now, do it again.” I lean in close, dragging one long, deep breath of her clean soap scent into my lungs. *Fresh. Clean. Perfect.* “And this time, do it right. I’ll be back in an hour, maybe two, depending upon my mood. Be ready to leave as soon as I arrive.”

She flinches and stares down at the mess on the floor, but to my surprise she doesn’t cry. Oh no. I can’t have that. Not if I want to keep this wall up between us. For good measure, I kick the suitcase, sending it sliding through the clothes, scattering everything everywhere. The shirts become wrinkled as they slide across the floor. “Make sure those are pressed again, too. If they’re wrinkled, even the slightest bit, I’ll have you re-press and re-pack the entire bag all over again.”

She turns those baby blues to me in an icy glare. The tears I previously spotted fade away to a liquid heat mixed with a good amount of hate, making it difficult for me to distinguish between the two. It doesn’t matter. She’ll never say what she really wants, anyway. I can hear her screaming in her mind, railing at me, cursing me. Yet all she does is glare until she looks back down at the mess.

Whatever remains of a heart I have left splinters away against every confrontation we’ve ever had. All the good inside me died the day I saved her life. She’ll never know that, never understand the significance, but I’ll make certain if she ever remembers the details she knows just who it is she’s standing against.

I walk out of the room, feeling accomplished. Feeling closer to the new me than previously. Tanya has a way of stealing all my strength, but through Elyse, I found a way to gain control again. It’s fucked up in every way, but I need the strength, the willpower and I can get that by taking it from her.

When it comes to Elyse, I already know there is no way I will fall into those pretty doe eyes, or succumb to that soft voice. Nope. Never again. I'll never let anyone control me again. Not Tanya, not Elyse. No one.

The only person who will ever own me, is me.

5
ELYSE

Is this a punishment? If it isn't, it certainly feels like one.

Maybe I haven't been kicked enough by life itself lately? I'm not surprised fate is out to get me, but did it have to leave me stuck with him? The crown prince of fucking cruelty. He makes a professional sport out of being mean. Well, he's not mean just to me, but for some unknown reason he appears to enjoy tormenting me the most. Just once, I wish I had the balls to talk back, to put him in his place.

I kick the suitcase hard and then huff, kneel, and rub out the rubber scuff mark that's left on the fabric.

Dammit. I hate him. I hate him. I hate him. I hope he stubs his toe on a table and forever has a piece of food stuck in his teeth...

As I think of silly things like that, my anger recedes, and I let out a long exhale and inhale slowly through my nose.

Maybe if I keep telling myself I hate him then I'll actually believe it. It's unlikely but possible, someday. The reality is, it's hard to hate the person who took you in at your darkest moment, even if he's under some insane delusion that he owns you.

He doesn't own me. No one owns me.

I know he doesn't deserve my kindness, but it's hard not to give him some when it's all I have to offer. So even though I want to run his clothes through a shredder instead of picking them up and repacking them, I do what I'm asked. I stack the clothes again, carefully folding each piece and organizing them inside of the suitcase with origami precision.

But if he complains again I'm walking out and making him pack his own shit.

Well, I'll seriously think about walking out and making him pack himself.

Once everything is organized, I stare at the bathroom door, which is shut mostly, minus a sliver of light cast across the floor. *Does he want me to pack his toiletries too?* I mean...how should I know which of his overpriced colognes or body soaps he wants packed?

No. Better to let him do that himself. It's one less thing I can make a mistake on. Instead, I stare down at the suitcase and its contents. It looks good, great even, but I can hear his voice in my head, and I'd much rather be ignored by him than berated. With my anxiety heightened and the fear of making a mistake rattling in my ear, I drop to the floor and sit cross-legged in front of the suitcase.

Then I straighten the already straight lines of clothing, again and again. I become immersed in making sure everything is perfect, so much so that by the time I snap out of it I find myself wondering when he's going to return, like his approval is life itself. The reality of that thought breaks me, and I remember how bitter and cruel he is.

Heat climbs up my neck, until my ears are burning and my nails cut into the palms of my hand as I clench them. Why am I sitting here, like a dutiful wife doing as she's told?

I'm tempted to tip the case over and tell him to fuck himself.

I'd regret it instantly; I know it, but this fucking dick thinks he can order me around like a dog, then bully me into doing what he wants. *And stupidly, I do it.* Yes, he's my employer, technically, but damn him, he orders me around like I'm more of a pet than a paid worker.

I shove off the floor and re-enter the closet, staring at the long row of his perfectly pressed clothes, some still wrapped in their dry cleaning bags. Under the hanging suits and slacks, low shelves are lined with shiny leather shoes, athletic clothing, and other accessories.

It's all perfectly organized, thanks to me. Not that it wasn't before I started working here and doing most of the laundry—it's just that no one else ever touches his things. According to the kitchen staff, I'm one of the few workers who gets to enter his room and closet.

I skim my fingers across the fabrics, watching the sheen of the overhead recessed lighting reflect off their surfaces. A box on the far side of the closet holds a line of watches, cuff links, and perfectly wound belts.

My gaze catches on something shiny next to the box. I shouldn't...but I do—what's that saying, curiosity killed the cat?

Consider me dead.

I move closer as if I'm tethered to the object, and the glint of a knife edge gleams back at me. I nearly gasp as I take in the sight of it. It's eight inches long, has a black handle, and a long, shiny, silver point. I've never seen a knife like this before; then again, who the hell needs a knife like that?

Don't do it. Do not touch it.

Against my better judgment, my hand moves on its own, and I gently pick up the knife. Grasping the handle tightly, I lift it toward my face to get a better look at it. The blade is shiny, without a speck of dirt, blood, or any imperfection.

What does Sebastian use a knife like this for?

I think back to some of the rumors I've heard about him from those who attend Oakmount, and even some of the staff. It's been said that he has a thing for blood and pain in the bedroom, among other darker things I refuse to think about. A shiver ripples down my spine at the thought. Okay, I need to stop thinking about this. Even as the memory of scrubbing blood out of Egyptian cotton rises up.

I swallow thickly, my attention gravitating back to the shimmering blade. *They're just rumors, Elyse.* That's what I tell myself, even if I know better.

What if it were me he was using this knife on? No, that's a foolish thought. He might look at me with heat flickering in his eyes every now and then, but that means nothing, not when he's almost always cursing my name or shoving me around to do his bidding.

I'd rather climb in bed with a panther than sleep with him. Hell, I'd probably climb out with fewer injuries.

I tighten my grip on the handle and stare over the edge of the blade, my gaze darting to the fancy line of clothes hanging just inches away. I don't know a damn thing about this knife, but I know the blade will cut through wool and cotton like butter. I can feel it. Sense it.

A smile tugs at my lips. And wouldn't that be the best payback for how he treated me? How he made me watch while he tore up my hard work. Ahhh, yes. Let's see how he likes having his hard work destroyed.

Before I can think better of it or stop myself, I lunge forward and stab the knife into the breast of the expensive designer suit, piercing through the plastic of the dry cleaning bag and into the material. It takes nothing but a flick of the wrist to drag the blade down, shredding the wool all the way to the edge of the jacket and snagging the pants as I pull it free.

It feels good. Too good.

I pause, the knife suddenly feeling heavier in my hand as I reflect on what I've done.

This suit probably costs thousands, yet all I can think is that it's just another dollar added to the growing debt I'll never be able to repay. It's wrong. I know it. My mind orders me to stop, that the repercussions aren't worth the deranged man's wrath, but I don't care.

I'm on a high, and making certain Sebastian knows where I stand is all that matters to me. Turning my attention to the next suit, I do the same thing, stabbing the knife deep and hard until the hilt meets the fabric—no plastic on this one. Watching the blade slice through the rich material is almost mesmerizing. It's petty revenge, but revenge at its best. I attack the next two suits, slicing cleanly through them. Each suit is a semblance of ribbons now, and that fills my chest with pride.

My hand shakes as I remove the knife from the last one, a shiny gray material that catches in the light. I've seen him wearing this exact one, and I squeeze my eyes closed against the memory of how it spread across his broad, football-honed shoulders. He looked so charming and gorgeous in it.

Not anymore. Charming and gorgeous on the outside.

I take a step back, admiring the damage I've caused.

But venom and tar on the inside.

It dawns on me then that he's probably going to kill me in retaliation. Then skin me and wear my skin as payback for destroying his expensive clothes. It's inevitable at this point. There would be no way to hide the evidence of what I've done. Better to own up to it.

I look at the other side of the closet. Those clothes are still pristine, without a single wrinkle. Would it be too much to think that he might not notice? At least until we get back.

I can always hope, right? I turn on my heels and lean forward to place the knife back by the box of cuff links, but as I do, I lose my grip, and my thumb slips off the handle, pressing against the sharp blade. I pull my finger away instantly, but it's too late. The blade has already cut through my skin, and a stinging sensation followed by pain zings along my finger.

"Dammit!" I gasp and shove my thumb into my mouth, sucking on the wound so I don't drip blood all over the floor. It's not deep, thankfully, but I know the blade itself is sharp enough that it could've very well cut my finger off.

Because of my anxiety and years of dealing with my father's alcoholism, I'm attuned to every little sound. It's why when I hear a scuffle just outside the door, I freeze, my thumb still in my mouth. Fear latches onto me, but instinct keeps me in place.

I'm dead. He's going to kill me.

Slowly, I return to my senses and place the knife back in its hiding spot. Then I do the only thing I know how to do. I run. I race out of the closet and shut the door, but it bounces off the frame instead of closing all the way, leaving it cracked open. One glance inside, and I'll be ruined. *Dammit, Elyse. Why did you have to be so dumb?*

I throw myself down in front of the suitcase and pull my thumb from my mouth, tucking it into the side of my jeans to keep from getting blood on his clothes. Lord only knows what he would make me do if I stained his precious clothing. The irony of what waits in the closet makes me tremble harder.

My gaze moves to the door. There's a scrape of shoes over a rug, then the sharp crack of the sole of a foot slapping against the hardwood floor. Anticipation builds low in my belly. I know he's coming, and I can't stop what's going to happen, but that doesn't prepare me.

The door swings open in a rush, and he steps inside. *Fuck.* I should look away and hide my eyes because they're a portal to my guilty conscience. The heavy thump of my heartbeat fills my ears, and I'm right on the fringes of panic as I stare up at him, wide-eyed and afraid.

Very afraid. I've never done something so stupid, so reckless, something that is so not Elyse.

"Why are you staring at me like that?" It's merely a question, but I'm still stuck on the way his voice sounds, how low it is, carrying with it a different level of darkness.

Shit.

I shake my head and stare down at my trembling hands. "I'm not." My voice squeaks out, sounding high and stupidly suspicious. "I mean, no reason." I couldn't be any more obvious if I tried.

Stalking closer, he cocks his head to the side, his eyes narrowing. "What did you do, Ely?"

I flinch at the nickname but don't answer; nor do I call him out on using it like I usually do. I'm far too worried about what might happen to me next than to squabble over something so stupid. No response is a good response, right?

Wrong.

He clicks his tongue at me."Oh, Little Prey, what have you done?"

I'm not sure that nickname is any better, but at least he—*my father*—never called me by that one, so the sound of it on someone's lips doesn't make me want to curl up and die.

Somehow I manage to swallow around the knot in my throat and keep myself from vomiting. "N-nothing. Just packed your clothes like you asked. Now that I think about it, we should probably get going. You wanted to leave immediately, right?"

He steps closer when I shift to my knees to stand, halting my movements with a hand planted on my shoulder. The weight of it is heavy, pressing down on me, and that dark, pensive gaze of his roams over the suitcase, the bed, and the floor around me. Like a damn bloodhound, he's sniffing for the scent, seeking out my crimes.

"Mmm, not so fast. You're acting way too guilty to have just packed my clothes."

Fuck. He knows. Like a predator, he peers around the room, stopping only when his gaze reaches the closet. *Please, lord*. If you spare me, I promise not to do anything else so insanely stupid... maybe, like for a whole day.

The ground beneath me crumbles when he lifts his hand, the pressure on my shoulder disappearing. *I need to get out of this room. If I can escape, then I might be okay*. I rush to stand right as he takes three massive steps in the direction of the closet. Out of the corner of my eye, I see his hand press against the door. He shoves it open, and I know there's no way he isn't seeing the destruction I've caused.

Move, dammit, I order my body, but I'm too consumed by the raw fear that my body has frozen itself.

"What the fuck?" His booming voice trails off, and the sound of plastic shifting, as if he's moving it out of the way, filters into my ears.

I try to ignore the sounds and stare intently at my feet, wondering how I can make myself smaller. What's done is done, but what can I do to make the punishment less? Because he *will* punish me. He hasn't before, but I've also never made such a stupid choice either.

"Elyse..." My ears burn, my name punctuated sharply, just like the skin I cut with his blade. Even knowing he expects me to say something or react, at least, I don't move, and I don't respond.

When he steps out of the closet, I'm left confused. His face is perfectly blank; there's no expression whatsoever, except for the tight clenching of his jaw, accentuating his jaw, making him appear more like the cruel beast he is. His body language is another story, though. There's no missing the anger that rolls off him in waves, threatening to sweep me under and drag me into its dark depths. My eyes dart down to his clenched fist, which is strangling a scrap of gray material. He holds it up for me to see as if I don't know what it is he's shoving against my nose. As if I don't know I've dug my own grave in one irrational act of vengeance.

6
ELYSE

"What the fuck is this?" The words are spoken through clenched teeth.

I can tell he's restraining himself, but barely. I've seen him angry many times, over various things, and while he's been mean and downright terrifying to others, he seems to hold back a little with me. That doesn't lessen my fear of him right now, though.

My lungs burn with a need for oxygen, and I force a ragged breath into them. His face shows nothing; it's like he's a robot, incapable of showing any emotion, but I know better. I can hear his rage, feel it in every word he speaks, and see it in the tight clench of his fingers. See it in the veins bulging in his neck and flames of revenge burning in his eyes.

Run, you idiot. Get out of here.

"Maybe you can't hear me?" His devious lips tug up at the ends, and he looks completely villainous. *Demented. Cruel. Broken.* "Let me speak a little slower in case your tiny brain cannot compute what I'm trying to say."

He takes a step closer, leaving little to no space between us. I tremble, my entire body quivering to the point that my knees threaten to give out beneath me.

"What. The. Fuck. Did. You. Do?" Each word is a growl of rage.

I need to say something, to respond, but I can't, and that's terrifying all on its own. I'm not sure how long he stands there staring at me, anger rushing off him and slamming into me like a truck. When he lifts his hand, I flinch, thinking maybe this time he will hit me, that he'll punish me like my father and my father's friends used to do, but instead, he pinches the bridge of his nose.

I don't dare hope. Hope is a seed that you learn very early on not to plant.

Exhaling, I suck a wobbly breath into my lungs and then force the first words that appear in my mind out of my mouth.

"I-I'm sorry. I..."

He drops his hand and shakes his head, and I stop speaking.

I watch cautiously as he crosses the room, taking a seat in the armchair in the corner. "Sorry does not fix the clothing you've destroyed, Elyse. I'm not sure what you thought shredding my suits would do or how it would make me feel, but I can assure you it's nothing compared to what I'm going to do to you."

"P...please..." My voice trembles, and I hate it because I promised myself months ago I would never beg someone to stop hurting me again, but lo and behold, here I am.

"Shhh. I think it would be smart of you to keep your mouth shut right now because I'm barely restraining myself as it is. But if you want to see what happens when I snap, go for it. I can sincerely promise that you won't enjoy what I do to you, nor likely will I."

With shaky fingers, I swipe at my cheeks and feel the wetness there. I didn't realize I was crying, not until this very moment. It only makes me look and feel weaker than he already sees me as. I should've learned that crying doesn't fix anything a long time ago, but my body doesn't seem to understand that. Every time my fight-or-flight instincts kick in, I end up a blubbering mess.

"Twenty thousand dollars, give or take." His voice cuts through the air like a whip, and I jump, startled by the sudden sound. "That's how much those suits you decided to cut up cost, and now how much more you owe me, on top of your father's debt."

I nearly sigh with relief. Maybe that's my punishment in all of this. I can handle that. Not like I'll ever pay it off, anyway. With force, he shoves out of the chair and stands, buttoning his black suit jacket. He tugs the edges down hard, stretching it across his broad shoulders and chest.

"Luckily for you, I don't have a lot of time, so your punishment will have to wait until we return, or at least until we arrive where we're going. We're already pressed for time. If we don't leave in the next five minutes, I'm not sure there will be any point in going."

He extends his hand to me, and I blink, confused, until I notice the pill he's holding between his thumb and forefinger.

"Take this."

I shake my head. "What is it?"

"Doesn't matter what it is. I'm telling you to do something, and it would be in your best interest to do it. You've pissed me off enough this evening."

"I don't like pills." I'll do a lot of things that he tells me to, but I draw the line at allowing him to drug me.

Before I have the opportunity to react, he pounces. With one hand, he grasps my jaw, his fingers digging into my cheeks hard enough to leave bruises. I open my mouth, a scream on my lips, and he presses the pill onto my tongue.

"Swallow."

The cold edge of his voice chills me to the bone, and I shake my head, my teary gaze unwavering from his.

His nostrils flare, and his gaze hardens to steel. "Fucking swallow it, Ely."

I scowl at the name but don't move. The bitter pill melts on my tongue. If I don't want to take it, I need to spit it out now, but even I'm not naive enough to think he doesn't have a backup plan. If I spit out the pill, he'll just find an alternative.

My thoughts shift when one of his legs slides between mine, his body radiating heat that wraps around me like a dark cloak.

With him so close, I have to tip my head back to peer up into his emerald eyes. It's darker around his pupil, like the evergreens at night, fading to lighter around the edges with a few flecks of gold. He's so stupidly handsome that my breath hitches in my throat with one look.

He's so close I can see the very faint stubble blooming across his perfect jawbone. The gold in his sandy blond hair as it curls across his forehead. *Damn.* No man should be so beautiful. Too bad his beauty hides such anger and fury. Every breath, every word he utters, is lined with that heat. He hides it well, but I was raised looking for it, hunting for it in my father to keep myself safe, and I see it in him every single day.

"Little Prey, you're trying my fucking patience." His voice is soft, but his hot temper still underlines each word. "Swallow, or I will stick my fingers into that sweet mouth of yours and shove this pill down your throat."

He...wouldn't? Who am I kidding? Of course he would.

Especially after what I just did. I'm sure it would be nothing but a pleasure to him. The time to make a choice is dwindling away, and if I don't swallow the pill, things will just get worse. But the thought of simply rolling over and taking it makes me volatile. While I'm willing to make the best of a bad situation, I know that if I'm ever going to make it out of all of this alive, I can't just keep saying yes. I can't keep doing as I'm told simply because I'm told to do it.

I have to draw lines.

I spit the pill back at him, watching his face transform from a mask of boredom to downright fury. Perhaps the robot has emotions after all?

"I'm tired of taking orders from you and being treated like a possession instead of a human. You might be my boss, but that doesn't mean I should be treated as less than." The words come out weaker than I intend, but they come out, and that's all that matters.

"You're nothing but a toy to me, and it's your own fault for thinking otherwise." He snarls and plucks the pill off his shirt where it landed, pinching it between two fingers. "Since you want to do this the hard way..."

"Stop. I won't let you drug me." Panic zips through me, and I whirl around, but the bed is right there, and the only other way out is through him. I'm tiny and fast, but Sebastian has no problem hitting below the belt to get what he wants.

"Keep acting like you have a choice in the matter. It's more fun that way." A sinister chuckle escapes him, and then he attacks.

I'm trapped in his dark web without any escape. In no more than a step he's got me cornered against the bed. I fall back against the mattress in my haste to get away from him.

His reaction time is much faster than mine, and he has me pinned to the bed beneath his body before I can blink. I swear I can feel the hard length of his cock against my thigh, but I don't even consider mentioning it.

His thick fingers sink into my cheeks once more, and I fight through the pain, struggling against him, doing whatever I can to stop him from drugging me because who knows what he will do next.

"If you do this, I will never forgive you. I will never trust you..." I barely get the words out between heaving breaths.

A wicked glint of satisfaction appears in his eyes. "Oh, Ely.

Your first mistake was thinking you could ever trust me; your second was pissing me off. Now you'll pay the price."

His fingers sink deeper into my cheeks, and the pain becomes unbearable.

"Don't make me have to hurt you more than necessary," he speaks softly.

My lips part as a whimper escapes them. It's at that instant that he takes the remainder of the pill and shoves it past my lips and into my mouth. The bitter tang of it is all I can taste, and I open my mouth to spit it back at him, but he's prepared this time.

With two fingers, he pinches my nose closed and leans forward, his hot, formidable lips hovering over mine. *He's not going to kiss me, is he? No, you idiot, he's trying to kill you.*

His hand slaps over my mouth, and real fear kicks in. I start to thrash against his grasp, but he's got me trapped, and just like a python, the more I struggle, the more his grip tightens. It doesn't take long for my limbs to grow heavy, especially when my lungs are starved for air.

"Swallow," he whispers cruelly.

The fear of the unknown, of him truly hurting me finally becomes a reality. The fight drains out of me, and every second without precious air brings me closer to the dark.

My hands slip from his arms and eventually fall to the mattress beside my body. My lungs burn; my brain screams at me to move, to do something, but I'm helpless. Black spots fill my vision as I try to hold on a little longer.

"You should see yourself right now, Ely. Your eyes are like frigid pools of water shimmering in the sun, and they look even prettier filled with fear. Fear put there by me." I want to respond, to tell him to fuck off, to fly a kite to Mars, but I'm barely hanging on, afraid of what he might do to me once I'm unconscious.

The harder I try to hold on, the further I slip away. My eyelids flutter closed, and then open, and I can barely make out the shape of him in front of me, but I swear, before the entire world goes dark, he leans in and ghosts his lips against mine.

"It's time to let go...nighty-night, Prey," he taunts. "Enjoy your reprieve because when you wake up, you'll discover I'm so much more of a monster than you ever imagined I could be. I'm ready to play...are you?"

7
SEBASTIAN

What the fuck am I doing?

Exactly what I fucking shouldn't be doing, that's what. Ely is nothing to me—less than nothing. Her existence in my life is a reminder of how trapped I am.

If that's true, why do you always have to remind yourself that you hate her?

My subconscious is playing Russian roulette today, and I'm considering killing the fucker. Elyse's only real fault in all of this is that she happened to be at the wrong place at the wrong time, and that's only because her father manipulated her presence there in the first place. It's not like she wandered in of her own accord. I have no other reason to hate her outside of that, but it's because of her and those circumstances that I'm now trapped in the family business.

A victim of the very same shit I always said I'd never succumb to.

For one fleeting moment, I consider leaving her at the mansion to take care of herself while I take care of my business. Or I could ship her off somewhere so that I don't have to look at her face anymore. As soon as the thoughts pop in my head, I dismiss them.

Both are very appealing ideas, but I could never go through with either. As much as I despise what she represents, I need to make sure she doesn't spill my secrets to the world, and I can't keep her in line if she's on another continent. Combine that with my desire to own her, and well, it's not looking good.

Her body goes completely slack beneath my grasp, her eyes fluttering closed. I exhale and slowly lift myself off her, removing my hands from her soft skin. If I don't stop touching her, I might do something I'll regret.

Still, even as I tell myself to walk away, my feet refuse to move. I remain there, planted like a fucking creep, hovering over her and watching her breasts swell with every slight rise and fall of her chest. Fuck, the things I could do to her right now. And the knowledge that there isn't a damn thing she could do to stop me —it's intoxicating.

I lift my thumb, wiping at the moisture forming at the corner of my mouth. I could fuck her, take her however I want, and she would never even fucking know. It wouldn't matter, even if she did know. She's mine to do with as I please.

The temptation is so fierce, I reach for her without further thought, my fingers flicking at the top buttons on her shirt to reveal a small peek at what's beneath.

Smooth, porcelain skin reflects back at me in the lamplight, and I stroke a single finger down the center line of her chest, starting at the pulse that beats frantically in the hollow of her throat, ending at the last button, just beneath her breasts. Her skin is silky smooth, against the rough pad of my finger.

I want to trace it with my tongue. Discover its flavor.

For some reason I hesitate. All I would have to do to see more is twitch my finger a bit to the right or the left, pulling back the fabric, and all of one little tit would be revealed. I bet I could swallow it whole. *Shit.* My throbbing cock presses against the zipper of my pants, reminding me that even if she pisses me the fuck off she still has the power to awaken me with need.

Now would be the perfect opportunity to relieve myself. While she's lying so perfectly still, so vulnerable and helpless. The perfect prey.

It wouldn't take long for me to come. I could rub it into her skin, coat her with my seed. *Mark her. Make her even more mine than she already is.* Would she be confused when she woke up and found the dried residue of my cum? Disgusted?

Or turned on? My fingers brush against the button of my slacks like they've already made their choice.

Don't let her win. Don't let her gain control of you.

A tiny voice rings in my mind, an annoying reminder that snaps me out of the hazy fog of lust and back to reality. Disgust coats my insides. She's the enemy, the very thing I need to stay away from. Touching her, even if she would never know, would only complicate things. I'd know what I did, and that would fuck me up enough in itself.

Fighting against every impulse in my body, I force myself to take a step back. I curl my fingers into my palms to alleviate the temptation to touch her.

But goddamn, she's beautiful. Her features are delicate, tiny, and breakable.

I look away from her still body and back to the ravaged closet. Anger simmers in my blood, demanding an outlet. One that I do not have at the moment. It's easier to allow myself to feel anger than lust for my little prey. If I lean into the anger, maybe I can forget how much I desire her in other ways.

My gaze catches on the suitcase that's sitting on the floor, and I move to inspect the contents. At least she packed adequately. I let out a sigh and grab the pile of clothes I set aside for her earlier off the bed.

I cast her still body one last lingering glance and trudge into the closest to grab another suitcase. I toss the clothes inside, along with a few toiletries I stole from her room while I was gone, and because you can never be too prepared, I add a gun, a couple of knives, and some spare clips. I don't anticipate trouble, but that doesn't mean it won't find me on its own.

Once I've gathered everything I need, I call for the driver to come grab the bags while I remain standing at the edge of the bed staring down at Elyse's unconscious form. She'll wake up in about twelve hours with a hangover from hell. Not that it matters. It's worth it knowing I don't have to spend eight hours in a steel box thirty-five-thousand feet in the air listening to her whine about her animals, trivial life, and how I've ruined it all. In reality, she hasn't said much about it to me or how much I've destroyed her future, but I'm waiting for the day she blames me for the choices her father made.

Crouching by the bed, I prepare myself for what I need to do. Touching her both disgusts me and intrigues me. I grab her by the arms and lift her, tossing her over my shoulder so I can carry her out to the car. She's as light as a feather, too light for my liking honestly, but her eating habits haven't been my priority.

I might have to change that.

The driver averts his gaze as I bend and load her inside the back seat before sliding in behind her. I straighten in my seat and stare down at her sleeping body, slumped against the door.

"Fucking hell," I mutter under my breath and then lean forward, yanking the seat belt around her. It gets caught on her pants, and I jerk at the fabric in frustration, jarring her small frame to the side. Thankfully, it gives way, tearing her pants a little in the process.

Not like it matters. She doesn't pay for the uniform.

I click the buckle back into place and ease back in the seat, glancing her way only once more. She looks uncomfortable as hell, and if we got into an accident, there's no saying she wouldn't break her neck anyway, but at least I won't have to listen to the fucking annoying ding of the car. It's the only reason I buckled her in.

That's what I tell myself, anyway

It only takes a few minutes to get to the airport. In a college town chock-full of rich criminals, there's always quick access to a safe exit.

The jet is prepared and waiting for our arrival. My agent took care of the paperwork for both of us, and it should only take about forty minutes to reach the hotel once we arrive in London, giving us just enough time to get ready for the event.

I calculate the timeframe again and again in the car as we drive to the airport. She stirs a few times, and I wonder if I should double down on the pill with a shot, but I decide against it. I know her medical history from Dr. Brooks, but I don't want her to be drugged up and drowsy during the event tonight. I don't trust her enough to leave her in the hotel by herself, and I might need to use her to get the attention of the man I seek.

The driver opens my door, and I walk around the car to grab Ely out of her side. The lone flight attendant helps with the bags and completely ignores both Ely and me until we are sitting and buckled in.

These are the kinds of advantages to being wealthy. I'll accept —the ability to get away with murder, figuratively speaking.

Literally speaking, too.

The flight attendant brings me a whiskey and takes her own seat near the cockpit door. I eye her down the aisle. Long brown hair bound up in a braid at her crown and a carefully pressed uniform I want to shred just for the sake of it.

What would Ely do if she woke to me fucking the pretty flight attendant with my knife to the woman's throat? *Would she be scared?* I give the idea some thought. It would benefit me to scare her, scare her enough that she runs away for good and leaves me the hell alone. But then it would make my job ten times harder because I'd have to chase her around, stalk her, and ensure she doesn't tell anyone anything.

I sip the whiskey and stare out the window while we taxi down the tarmac. Money ensures we get out of here fast, and I amend my time calculations as we take off. Still on schedule at least, even with Ely trying her best to fuck everything up.

I drag my attention back to her across the small polished table between our chairs. She's slumped in the seat, the belt cutting hard across her thin hip bones. She's still in the house uniform, but that's fine. No one important will see her until I'm ready for them to.

Once the pilot turns off the discreet seat belt sign by the entry door I lean my chair back as far as it will go and settle in for the eight-hour flight. A little fuck with the flight attendant might help my mood, but I don't want to have to hire a new one before the trip home, so I leave it for now and just stare out the window until I drift off to sleep.

When I wake, the sky is dark outside the iced-over window. The lights are dim. My gaze catches on Ely, who is still slumped and sleeping in the opposite seat. Something eases in my chest like she might have managed to escape at thirty thousand feet, but she's still out, as I expected when I calculated how much of the medication to give her.

The flight attendant saunters down the aisle toward me with an exaggerated swish in her hips.

"Mr. Arturo." Her voice is low and soft as she crouches next to my chair, her skirt riding high up on her thighs. "We'll be landing shortly. Your agent has confirmed the customs details are already handled." I watch as she trails her manicured hand up my thigh. "Is there anything else I can do for you before we arrive?"

I shake my head, still a bit groggy. "No, thank you."

She has no idea what kind of monster she's inviting to her bed right now. If I had more time, I'd show her, just to teach her the lesson. Fortunately for her, I don't.

"Just make sure everything is quickly deplaned once we arrive. We are in a bit of a hurry."

She nods once and gives me a last, lingering look. "As you wish, sir."

It only takes about a half hour to deplane and carry Ely to the already waiting sedan. The traffic from the airport eats the time, though, and we arrive according to the original calculations I made.

It's fine because we are still on schedule. I throw Ely over my shoulder again and carry her through the posh London hotel lobby. This is a frequently used hotel for Pound of Flesh members, so no one bats an eye at my fireman carry as we move onto the elevator. I punch the button for the floor and stare straight ahead. The ride up is smooth, and when I step off the elevator, our room is right around the corner.

The door key card is in my luggage, courtesy of the travel agent. I grab it from the front pocket and get us into the room, our bags following us. Once situated, I wave the bellman off and shut the door, leaving him with a hefty tip in his hand.

The room is perfect, with sleek modern lines and glass from one end of the bedroom into the en suite bathroom. Even the small sitting room is glassed-in on one side, the better for seeing the London skyline in the distance. It's dark now, but lights dance along the buildings, shining off the River Thames.

I breathe a sigh of relief now that we are here. So much is riding on this event—getting to Mondrake and convincing him to take over the Arturo holdings, all while hopefully leaving Bel out of it, of course, so I can cut ties and finally escape.

He's the only one with the power, the influence, and the interest to take over my family's holdings, and he can't say no.

Even more so if I dangle Ely in front of his face. Rumor has it he has a thing for pretty, petite brunettes. It's why he attends the Pound of Flesh gathering every year. He likes them young and unattached to anything, or so I hear.

Ely, beholden to me and with her bastard family out of the picture, is the perfect bait.

8
SEBASTIAN

I stand near the bed and strip out of my suit jacket while I stare down at her. Her beauty—that fragile, elfin sort of prettiness—is exactly what Mondrake likes. Big doe eyes that draw a man in, a cute button nose.

I draw in a deep breath. I understand the appeal.

She looks utterly breakable. Porcelain in a sea of crockery.

Once I toss my jacket over a small leather armchair, I undo the top couple of buttons of my dress shirt. It would probably be best if I change while Ely is getting ready. I blink back the haze of exhaustion lingering from yesterday, from the trip, from my fucking life. It's time to get this shit show on the road. Gently, I shake her khaki-clad thigh.

She jolts but doesn't open her eyes. I lean and tap her cheek gently with the side of my hand. The last thing I need is her flailing awake and hitting me in her confusion, but after a moment, it appears there isn't another option since she's not waking up as easily as I had hoped.

With another deflated sigh, I tap her cheek a bit harder, but not enough to put any sting into it. That must do the trick because she wakes with a startled gasp. She blinks her eyes open as she rolls over in the bed, a groan escaping her mouth as her gaze fastens on me.

"What the hell did you give me?"

I step away, putting distance between us. "That doesn't matter. It's time to get up. You might have a bit of a headache, but the upside is you probably won't suffer any jet lag."

She squeezes her eyes closed again and rolls her top half onto her belly, then pushes up to sit. "Jet lag? How long was I out?"

I check the vintage Rolex on my wrist as I finish unbuttoning my shirt. "Ten or so hours."

"Hours?" She repeats my word back to herself, her brow furrowing with confusion.

"While I know you love to chitchat, we don't have time for that. I need you to get ready now, because we have an hour before the event starts, and arriving late isn't an option."

She blinks out of her confusion, her gaze going wide-eyed as she drinks in my completely bare chest. "What the hell are you doing?"

I turn away from her to find my luggage. It would have been better to hire someone to unpack for us, too, but I don't want anyone touching my weapons or going through my things.

"Getting ready, which is what I told you to do."

Turning my head to the side, I gaze at her over my shoulder. Another blink, another long stare. *Are you kidding me? I don't have time for her bullshit.* Whatever patience I had built up for her is gone now. I stalk back to the bed, my shirt flapping open along my ribs.

"Wake the hell up and get moving. Bathroom is over there." I point at a door leading off the bedroom. "I'll grab you something to wear."

Fear trickles into her eyes, and I can see the hesitation building. "Wh-where are we?"

I take her chin in my hand and squeeze it gently. "Ely, darling, if you don't get moving, I'm going to drag you to this event naked."

There's a dark layer of menace in my voice now that she doesn't seem to be grasping.

She blinks again, and as the words sink in, she jerks her face from my hold and glances around the room. Once she spots the windows, she glances back at me, then scoots backward across to the other side of the bed, walking over to the windows. It's a gorgeous view, and I don't begrudge the little gasp that escapes her lips as she cups her mouth.

"Are we...is...is this London?"

"Sure is. Now get dressed."

Of course she doesn't listen to anything I'm saying, and I have to stalk back to her side, grip her by the bicep, and drag her to the bathroom door. "Go, or I'll be going in with you to make sure you actually listen to me."

She cranes her neck back and looks up at me, and I see the usual haze that comes from the use of that medication. It still lingers in her system, which would be fine if I didn't need her to be a little more alert. Her legs wobble as she steps into the bathroom, and thank the fucking lord she does. I slam the door closed behind her and release a sigh of frustration.

If she were anyone else, I would've ruined her by now, but every time I think of crushing her in my fist, I see that broken and bruised image of her from that night in my mind, and I can't bring myself to hurt her.

On the far side of the room is a small coffee maker that sits on the bar. I stalk over to it and hit the button for an espresso, placing a small glass *demitasse* beneath it.

Coffee should wake her the fuck up, and if it doesn't, then I guess she'll have to deal with my assholery keeping her in line.

A few minutes later, she exits the bathroom and scans the

bedroom hesitantly, her gaze finding me. The espresso machine spits out the final drops of coffee, and I take the tiny cup over to her.

She takes it from me, staring at the brown liquid suspiciously. "Did you drug it?"

My annoyance climbs once more. "No, the drugs were to keep me sane on the long flight, and keep you alive by stopping me from tossing you out the damn exit hatch. This is to wake you up."

"How can I trust that you're telling the truth?"

I might murder her. I just fucking might.

"I told you the biggest mistake you could ever make is to trust me, so trust is a non-issue here, Prey. I'm not a good guy. I will hurt you if it gets me what I want. Don't make me do that; just do what I fucking say and stop questioning me because, in the end, I don't care if you trust me or not. What I care about is you waking the fuck up and making yourself presentable. That's what I care about. So don't trust me...trust me. It's all the same."

Her eyes narrow, the blue catching the light, but she doesn't respond, thankfully. Instead, she sips the espresso like we have all the time in the world. That only pisses me off more. I can feel my blood pressure rising. I roll my eyes in place of taking the cup and pouring the contents directly down her throat. "Just fucking drink it, already!"

Maybe she can sense how close to the edge I am, or maybe she's finally decided to get moving; either way, I can't complain when she places the cup on the end table and starts doing as she's told. In an effort to move things along, I grab a dress out of the suitcase for her. "Here, put this on."

She pauses and then starts examining the shimmery green fabric. "This...I don't remember this being in Bel's closet."

"Okay? And your point is? I didn't ask if you wanted to wear it. I told you to wear it."

Her blue eyes blink rapidly, and I look away before I fall into their depths. "I can't. It's way too short; never mind the fact that I'll look like a can of busted biscuits in it."

All I hear are complaints when what I need is for her to do what she's fucking told. I'm irritable and snappy and just need her to do what I say, when I say it.

"Enough," I shout but then slam my mouth shut, my teeth clashing against one another, and I realize a moment too late that she's enraged me to the point that I'm yelling.

I strive for control, and somehow, this tiny scrap of a woman has found a way to shatter that. When it comes to her, I go from zero to a hundred in an ,instant.

I need to calm down before I do something really fucking stupid. I force a ragged breath into my lungs, hoping the fresh oxygen will stop me from strangling her. *Nope, not helping.* I let my eyes fall closed and sink into that feeling of relief. Okay...let's try this again. I blink my eyes open, and this time I glance from the floor, then back up to her face.

Like a random rainstorm, the anger, annoyance, and frustration return, threatening to pour out of me. I drag a hand through the mess of my blond hair and tug at the strands to the point of pain. It's only ever Ely. Only this one infuriating female who can—

Fuck.

This stops now. All of it. I refuse to let her crawl under my skin and undo me from the inside out. No more threatening her. No more excuses. It's time that I play my part. It's time that I show her who I really am.

"I'm not trying to be difficult..." Her voice wobbles, a slow tremble rippling through her slim body. She's afraid, but the drugs that linger in her system make her braver, more flexible.

I snarl my upper lip and leer toward her. "That's the problem. You tell me you aren't *trying* to be difficult, but you still are. So let me make this easier for you..." I reach for the knife I carry on me at all times. It's a small switchblade, but it will do the job.

I tug it free from my slacks and open it in one swift motion. The knife cuts through the air with a swish. Elyse reacts with a gasp, her blue eyes shining with fear. She takes a step back, and being the prey that she is, instinct alone is ordering her to run. Part of me wants to tell her to do that.

Do it. Run, Little Prey. It'll make hunting you down and taking what I want all the more fun.

The other part of me, the saner side, knows her running will not end well, for me, yes, but her, not so much, Which is why I choose to go a different route entirely.

Regarding the blade of the knife, I point the tip at her. "What am I removing first?"

"W-what?"

"You heard me, Ely! Is it really that difficult? Put the goddamn dress on, or I'll take you to the event naked, and trust me, Little Prey, this isn't the sort of place you want to go stark-ass naked. It might lead someone to believe you're for sale or, worse, that you want to play in one of their games. The choice is yours: belong to me or belong to a stranger. But stop dicking around, or I'll make the choice for you."

I take another step, bringing myself even closer. The tip of the knife catches in the dim light that illuminates the space from the bathroom. It gleams, and for a moment, I wonder what it might look like with her blood on it, but before I let that image bloom in my mind, it disappears.

Staring her down, I gently press the blade against the spot where her heartbeat beats a frantic tattoo at the hollow of her throat.

"What's your choice, Prey?"

9
ELYSE

The cold edge of steel grazes my skin, and I squeeze my eyes shut, anticipating his next move. Maybe if I don't look at the sharp blade, it won't hurt as badly when he cuts me with it. Memories pour in, another blade, another time, and I grit my teeth, pushing them away. I can't deal with those right now.

This is it. This is what I get for ruining all his clothes, for the smart-ass remarks, for the way he grinds his teeth every time he looks at me, like my very presence is a burden to him. It's time to pay for my sins, and his form of currency is blood.

The sharp, slick sound of my shirt slicing apart punctuates my panting breaths. Cold air brushes my skin as he rips the remnants of my shirt off. It catches on my arms, twisting and stinging as the material tightens around my flesh, even more so near the scar from the bullet wound on my shoulder.

"Fuck," I curse and twist so I can pull the ripped-up sleeves off myself. "Dammit, Sebastian, I can do it." I barely recognize the antagonism in my own voice.

The fear and the drugs create the perfect storm of self-indulgence that I forget, for one heartbeat, who I'm yelling at.

He raises one imperious brow at me and flips the knife expertly in his palm so the sharp edge points down along his wrist, then jerks the waist of my pants away from my skin and slices downward. The flat edge of the steel brushes along my hipbone as the serrated metal slices away more fabric, the thin khaki giving way far too easily.

It almost peels away instead of cutting or ripping.

I'm greeted with the kiss of more cold air on my bare flesh, and I shiver, both at the chill and the feral look that shines in his eyes and reflects back at me.

The ribbons of my pants hang on my thin hips, and he moves to slice the other side of them. I need to put an end to this before it goes too far, and he really does cut me. I hold my hands up and plead with him.

"Please, let me do it. This isn't necessary." I try to inject a level of calm into my voice, hoping it projects onto him in some way, but I know I failed when my words come out breathless and shaky.

"Then fucking do it, Ely, or I'll continue to do it for you. I told you I wasn't fucking around. I don't have time for your bullshit today, nor do I give a fuck about your modesty."

All in all, as far as modesty goes, I think I'm holding things together rather well. I'm mostly naked here, and now that I think about it...fuck I'm standing in front of my savage animal boss in nothing more than scraps of cotton. I swallow hard and quickly jerk off the remains of my pants. Then I use my hands to cover all the bare areas I can.

The green dress fills my vision, then my face, the sequins scratching softly against my cheek before slipping down into my hands. I catch it on reflex and shift it so I can look at it again. *Shit.* It didn't somehow gain more coverage since I saw it the first time.

"Get dressed while I change; then we are leaving." His voice is calmer now, but it's the sort of calm I don't trust. Not while he still has a manic glint in his eyes and the sharp knife in his grip.

I drag my attention back to the dress, studying the slinky fabric. There's no way in hell I can wear this. Everyone will see my scars, the ones my father gave me. Not to mention the still red and tender bullet wound in my shoulder, and...other ones I can't think about right now.

Never mind that I haven't been able to shave my legs in forever, as it would seem that messing up the tendons in your shoulder limits some fine motor functions. I risk glancing back at Sebastian. Something tells me if I try to explain all that to him he's going to blow up like an atomic bomb.

I don't realize how long I've stood there, frozen, the dress clenched tight in my fist as I try to rack my brain for a solution until Sebastian's gruff, angry voice pulls me out of the darkness.

"Ely, I'm not fucking around," he warns, his voice menacing now, all hints of his barely restrained calm gone.

When I don't move, he stalks closer, kicking the remains of my pants away from his feet. His gaze sweeps the length of my body, and he gives my soft white cotton underwear a disdainful look. At least he doesn't say anything. Instead, he rips off the rest of my shirt. When he makes a swipe at my bra with the knife, I shake my head and take a small step back. I cradle my breasts against my arm, the dress squished between.

"Please..." I try to rationalize with him.

"Don't beg, Ely. You should know by now that it doesn't have the effect you want it to have on me."

Cold fear douses my insides, and while I know he's serious, I need him to understand. To see that it's not that I want to disobey him, but more that I'm uncomfortable. "Please, Sebastian. It's not that I don't want to get dressed. I just... I can't wear this."

"You can, and you will wear the dress," Sebastian orders, taking a step closer.

I try to shield more of my nudity and let whatever shame I'm feeling go. "I haven't been able to shave my legs in a long time, not with the bullet wound, and my fingers don't work as well as they used to. Shaving hurts, and it's messy. I just can't, and while I don't expect you to understand, I won't wear such a pretty, short dress with hairy-ass legs."

Something dark enters his eyes, and he drops his gaze down to all the bare skin I can't cover with my hands. The tight lines of his shoulders drop fractionally.

"Have you tried shaving with something bigger than just a razor? Those things are tiny and finicky."

I blink at him. *What the hell else would I shave with?* He rolls his eyes and turns his knife in a blindingly fast swish so the hilt faces me. "Try this."

"Did you not hear me? I just told you I don't have the fine motor skills needed to control the razor. If I try to shave with that thing, I'll end up bleeding to death. Also, are you really sure you want to give me something sharp right now? I could sink it into your gut and then just go home."

He shrugs one shoulder, and somehow, on him it looks graceful. "Don't threaten me with a good time, Little Prey."

A good time? I barely have time to process what he said when the rough touch of his hands circle my waist. In a flash, he lifts me like I weigh nothing and carries me into the brightly lit bathroom. I give the room a quick scan, noting how big and luxurious it looks with gold accents and marble everywhere. A small leather toiletry bag sits on the sink, a white shopping bag beside it and a hand towel next to that.

I let out a squeak when he places me down on the counter, the cold stone pressing against my bare thighs.

What is happening right now?

Heat radiates off him, and I shiver involuntarily. He shouldn't be this close, and he especially shouldn't have his hands on me.

His long fingers drag down my sides until he reaches my thighs, where he clutches them right above my knees. I'm lost in a daydream for half of a second, and then it becomes a nightmare when he tries to pry them apart.

Out of pure instinct, I move to snap them tight shut again but then catch his narrowing gaze and clenched jaw out of the corner of my eye.

"Do you really want to fight me on this? I'm stronger, faster, and more than capable of forcing you to do what I want."

It's okay, Elyse. It's okay.

I force myself to breathe through the panic bubbling up in my mind. I can't do anything to stop him, but at the very least, I know he won't hurt me. Or at least he hasn't yet, so I have no reason to believe otherwise.

I shake my head because my brain is past the point of forming coherent words.

"Good. Then be a good girl and do as you're told."

Good girl? What is it about those two words that calms me? I try not to delve too deeply into it, but it's hard since the person saying those words generally has the opposite effect on me. *Please don't tell me I'm developing a praise kink.* I gulp and tighten my hold on the counter, then slowly allow him to readjust my legs.

I can feel his hot gaze on my bare skin, and he skims his hand up the front of my shin to graze over my knee. "Mmm. You're so fucking tiny, Ely. Tiny and breakable. Like a little porcelain doll."

I lift my chin and let him see what's left of me there. "Looks can be very deceiving. I'm tougher than you might think."

He looks from my legs and up to my face like he's looking for something, but then he looks away, the connection severed when he turns on the faucet, pulls the tab for the stopper, and waits for the sink to fill. The entire time he keeps his eyes on the water, and I sigh, grateful I don't have to meet his gaze while he does this.

There's a vast difference between staring at his face and staring at his hands, and I find a strange combination of comfort and pleasure coiling in my stomach as I watch his graceful hands while he soaks a white washcloth in the water before he gently scrubs it down my right leg.

He does the same with a rich lather of soap he works in his hand from the provided toiletries by the sink. I realize very suddenly how intimate this is, and I can't help my need to say something.

"This really isn't necessary," I quip, trying to focus on anything but the way his calloused palms feel on my wet, slick skin.

"If it wasn't necessary then you wouldn't have brought it up," he responds while keeping precise focus as he dips the knife in the water. I hold my breath when he turns the blade and runs it up the length of my soapy shin and over my knee, stopping right before he reaches the curve.

I'm mesmerized by the action. It's in the flick of his wrist, the deliberate control he maintains, as if he's painting a picture and not gliding a sharp-as-hell knife over my skin. Rinsing, he repeats the action carefully, methodically, until my skin is slick and shining in the bright overhead lights. He's surprisingly gentle around my knees and even shaves up the inside curve of my thigh. I flinch as that sharp blade reaches closer and closer to the junction of my thigh and pussy.

My heartbeat skyrockets as he climbs higher, and I tighten my grip on the counter.

Say something. Tell him to stop.

One wrong move and your lady bits are gone forever.

I swear he adds pressure to the blade just for the hell of it because it feels as if it's gliding harder against my quivering muscles. When he reaches the edge of my pussy, he pauses, and I stare down at him, frozen with fear. He looks up at me, and I can see the predator lingering just beneath the surface.

"Never forget who's in control." The words are a whisper, but he might as well have yelled them with how loudly they echo in my mind.

It's a warning, a reminder that no matter what, I'm at his mercy. He switches to the other leg without hesitation while I can hardly draw a full breath into my lungs.

He repeats the same process, only this time he drops down to his knees to carefully carve off the hair around my ankles.

Fuck, why does he have to be so pretty? Why does he look so good on his knees for me when I know he's only there to get into the best position to strike. The most advantageous position to cause the most pain and suffering. That's what he lives for—to hurt people, to hurt me. Even if his touch is gentle, there's always the promise of pain and suffering lingering in the background like a wisp of latent tobacco smoke.

He finishes the second leg, then cleans the sink, re-wets the washcloth, and mops up the remnants of soap still left on my skin.

Now that the job is done, all I can think about is asking him why he did it and what he expects in return from me? But I can't seem to bring myself to break the spell. To crack the silence and see what fresh hell comes out of his mouth.

"Do you need me to do your underarms, too?"

Somehow, my face and ears burn hotter at the question. He's stared directly into my underwear-covered pussy, he's shaved the hair on my legs, and now I'm blushing at the thought of him running that knife over my armpits.

Come on, Elyse.

"No," I tell him. "I'm good. It's a smaller area, so I can usually shave that just fine."

He nods once and focuses his attention on washing his hands. After drying them, he plucks the dress he'd tossed on the other side of the counter up and holds it out to me. I lean forward to grab it but he shakes his hand, and instead opens the top to slide it over my head.

"I'm not a toddler. I can dress myself."

He narrows his eyes. "If you could, then you would already be dressed by now, wouldn't you?"

I grit my teeth and let him settle the dress down over my hips. He stares at my bra straps, like he wants to cut them off too, but instead he reaches around and unfastens it, like he's an expert. "You can go without a bra; the dress has enough coverage."

I question him with a lifted brow. "Says the man who isn't running around with his tits out."

The corner of his mouth twitches, barely. "Fair enough, but you'll still go without."

I say nothing since we both know he's right, and there's no point in arguing. Not right now, with the shine of the knife on the counter next to my hip and the way his eyes keep roving over my skin like somehow, by grooming me, he owns even more of my body than he did before.

It's like this small act changed something between us. I can't pinpoint what yet, but I'm even more terrified now. Not of him, precisely. But of this feeling, of the unknown.

I'm shaking as he steps away, and there's no hiding it. I know he sees it, too.

"Hurry up, or I'll do what I promised to do to begin with and drag you along beside me, clothes or no clothes." He says the last almost half-heartedly, like he's already somewhere else, thinking about something else.

I nod once, not wanting to draw the monster out of him anymore than I already have. I've pushed him enough already, and knowing myself like I do, it won't take much more to irritate him further, and I have an entire evening to spend with him.

IO
SEBASTIAN

She doesn't notice that I exit the bathroom with the wet cloth still clutched tight in my hand and the knife in my other since I wasn't about to leave that in her possession. I saw what she did to my clothes, and while I'm far more agile and capable of protecting myself, I'd prefer it if I didn't have to break her hand when I force her to drop the knife.

I close the bathroom door behind me and pray she takes the hint and stays inside. If she interrupts me now, there's no way I'll be able to stop myself. Not with the feel of her slick, soapy skin under my palms still so fresh in my mind.

There aren't many places for privacy in a shared suite so I have to be creative. I wait until I hear the sink turn on before I duck into the closet and close myself inside. It's a small walk-in, and the perfect space for a moment of peace. I brace my back against the door to face the row of plush white robes hanging on the rack.

Why am I so weak for her? How could I become so consumed by her that I let her bring me this close to the edge, where I either live in or risk losing complete control.

It takes two seconds to unzip my pants and pull my aching

cock out. I almost whimper from the sheer relief of the friction on my skin when I fist it, dragging my hand up and down in a long, lingering stroke. *It's not enough, though.* The low-burning ember of desire sticks in my gut, but I'm missing that bang, the igniter.

I rotate the knife in my palm one-handed and press my thumb to the base of the crossguard. It slides along my skin as easily as it did Ely's, and my entire body hums with approval as I watch the blood well in thick droplets. I use it to slick up my own skin and then release a sigh.

This is what I need. No, that's not true. What I *need* is Ely on her knees, my cock down her throat while she cries big fat tears for me, but that's not going to happen.

It can't. It won't.

I settle for my own hand instead, and while I stroke myself, I try not to think of her smooth skin or the way her soft, small tits would fit so perfectly in my hands.

In my mouth. I could suck the whole of those little handfuls between my teeth until she mewls for me. Fuck. I wonder what she tastes like and if she'd scream as she falls apart or whimper, begging me to stop. The image sends me straight over the edge, as does the sharp bite of pain in my palm, and sticky spurts of cum splash against the washcloth.

So much for not thinking about her.

I mop up the blood as well and toss the mess on the floor, clean the knife, and bend down to slip it into the minimal sheath around my ankle. I need to consider getting laid more, especially if I'm going to force myself to be in her presence.

When I open the closet door, I find her hovering just outside the bathroom, her face a flurry of apprehension. However, as I drink in the sight of her, I wonder if I made a mistake. The dress hugs her body tightly, giving her slight, muscular form more curves. I've noticed her running on the property early in the morning or late in the evening...that must be where she gets her spare, defined shape that's nonetheless feminine as fuck. My mouth goes dry at the shadowy hint of cleavage bared by the dip of the dress.

Shit. I want people to notice her, but I don't want to have to fight anyone off either.

She raises her eyes slowly to mine, and if she knows what I'd been doing in the closet she doesn't indicate it.

I pull a tie off the bed, loop it up, and then shrug on my jacket. Once I fix my cuffs, I point at the shoes on the bench at the end of the bed. "Put those on."

She rushes to the bench and quickly slips on the tall, strappy heels. "I don't think I'm going to be able to walk well in these."

I pretend to ignore how sexy her legs look and then shake away the thoughts of her bare skin again. "Don't worry about it. If all goes well, you'll be sitting or kneeling most of the night."

A line creases the center of her forehead, and she gulps loud enough for me to hear but thankfully, she might be learning after all, because she doesn't argue or question me.

It only takes a few minutes to get down to the car, which is waiting for us since I already had the time set for pickup. I help Elyse into the car and then take the seat next to her. She's quiet, almost too quiet, on the drive, but thankfully traffic is light. Even so, I keep checking my watch. I wanted to be there over a half an hour ago to find the perfect spot to approach Mr. Mondrake Sidorov. Everything needs to be perfect. This might be the only chance I get to fix this, to rewind things enough so I can still break away from this life, from this world.

If the past few months have taught me anything, it's that I have the mind for it—the temperament, I guess—but I don't want it. Tanya ruined my desire to take my rightful position within the company. I don't care about the power or the money, the driving forces of most of this world. I don't give a shit about anything or anyone except Bel and my freedom.

Nothing else...I glance over at Elyse, who stares out the window into the city, her red-painted mouth slack as she takes in London for the first time. I can't imagine what's going through her head right now. I suppose if I was halfway human, I'd feel guilty for dragging her all the way here for a flesh market instead of actual sightseeing. Good thing I'm not.

But we packed enough for a week, just in case. Maybe I can take her to a few touristy places. The Tower of London. Buckingham Palace. Big Ben. One of those red phone booth things.

We pull up to an old warehouse, derelict and seedy-looking, but the streets outside boast millions of dollars in vehicles, all being parked and seen to by the sprinting valet drivers who linger near the huge industrial double doors. The car rolls to a stop, and I exhale slowly, preparing to slip into that dark place in my mind.

The door to the vehicle opens, and we're greeted by a smiling valet. I step out of the car and offer my hand to Ely, who takes it automatically. Once she's on her feet, I interlock our arms; it's more of a cover than concern, as I don't want her to topple off her heels before we even get in the door.

Men like the ones who frequent Pound of Flesh don't like their property damaged.

At the door, a willowy, blond young man extends a tablet, and I pull out my phone and hold up the QR code I was sent as an invitation. He scans the code, the doors open automatically, and I lead Elyse inside.

"What is this place?" she asks curiously, leaning close so I can hear her over the sudden barrage of thumping house music.

The internals of the warehouse are set up in tiers, progressively sinking down like the levels of hell. We walk up to a steel railing and stare down into the pit. Stairs lead down to each level, with couches, tables, and bars lining each level. Everything is black and gold with red accents. Gaudy as fuck, but I guess these assholes want to feel fancy with the decor that will be used for exactly two nights a year.

It takes me a minute to find the spot my informant had identified—the tier and couch area where the man I'm hunting for will be. I find us a seat on a nearby sofa and unbutton my suit jacket. Ely perches on the edge of the red velvet couch next to me.

"Hey. You didn't answer me. What is this place?"

I scan the crowd that lingers nearby, and I can feel Ely's gaze slip off me. There's a mixture of couples, groups of people, and some single individuals dancing. Everyone seems to be having fun. A woman crosses in front of us, a leash in her hand, the collar attached to another blond woman who is on her hands and knees crawling beside her.

I wave at the room and down to the roiling dance floor below. "This, Little Prey, is where those with the most depraved fantasies come to play, and one special day a year, they hold the world's biggest flesh auction."

"A flesh auction? What is that?" She blinks at me, her sooty black lashes brushing her cheeks as she digests what I've just said.

I shake my head and nod toward the bar, where someone is handing off a brick of cash. "It's exactly what it sounds like, Ely."

It takes a second for my words to sink in, but when they do, her shock morphs into pure horror. "Oh God. Please, tell me you didn't bring me here because you want to sell me?"

I can barely hear her above the music, and a sigh shudders out of me. I resist the urge to tell her to stop being so dramatic and instead roll my eyes, "If I wanted to sell you, I could have done that from the comfort of my home. I didn't come all this way to sell you, but keep in mind if push comes to shove, then I'll easily put you up on the block."

I watch her little throat work and notice the fresh tears swimming in her eyes.

"Please, Sebastian. I-I'll do better. I'll work more hours and pay you back faster. You don't have to do this. I'll stop being so annoying and asking so many questions. Whatever you want me to do. I'll do it."

I shake my head. "It's not your decision. Just don't tempt me, and you'll be okay."

A couple walks over to us and takes a seat on the couch beside Ely. She flinches and scoots closer to me, her thigh pressing tight against mine. I grit my teeth and ignore the heat of her body, the proximity of her bare flesh to me. Having her this close, the temptation to do dark, despicable things to her nearly undoes me.

I swallow my desire and scan the crowd, looking for Sidorov. When I don't see him, I flick my chin at the bar a few yards away. "Why don't you go and get us a couple of drinks? Perhaps some alcohol will loosen you up."

She blinks, opens her mouth, but then reconsiders whatever it was she wanted to say. *Smart.* Standing stiffly, she tugs at the hem of her dress, trying to make more fabric appear. When she realizes there isn't any point she starts toward the bar, her legs wobbling like a newborn fawn's taking their first steps.

Staring at her backside, I notice the way her shoulders are hunched in, like she's trying to make herself seem smaller, unnoticed. Unfortunately there's no point. There's not a single hot-blooded man on this tier who could ignore her silky dark hair and the way it brushes her lower back, or those huge doe eyes of hers filled with tears and fear. She's the perfect combination—afraid of her own shadow, but submissive enough to do anything to please you.

I continue watching her until a commotion near the stairs draws my attention. A big man with wide shoulders, nearly the identical size of my friend Aries, cuts through the crowd. No, that's wrong. More like they throw themselves out of his way. I watch from my seat as he sinks into a leather chair. A server rushes over to him to take his order.

Great. Everything is finally coming together. Now I just need Ely. I turn my attention back to the bar, and that's when everything goes to shit. I spot a man approaching her from the other side of the bar. I clench my hands into tight fists to stop myself from going to her right away. *Let her swim with the sharks for a bit.* I grit my teeth and watch as he stops right in front of her. Without speaking a word he reaches for her, his fingers splaying over the bare skin on her exposed back shown off by the cutout in the dress.

Blinding rage pulses in my veins, and the only reason I don't react immediately is because of the way she reacts to his touch, as if it's poison, and she's trying to escape.

Tilting my head, I hesitate, watching.

This is a new development. An unexpected one.

This shark acts as though he might know my Ely. As though he has some claim to her.

Ely's mine, though. My eyes narrow as I watch the shark circle, and everything in me clamors to gut him. I wait, though. He'll find out soon enough.

11

SEBASTIAN

I wait because despite the instinct tugging at me to protect Ely, another instinct is telling me there's something here worth paying attention to, something that will give me greater insight into who she is and where she came from. That is until I notice the way her body stiffens, then turns to stone, like a statue, the freshly made drinks in her hands slip from her grasp. They smash onto the concrete floor, sending fragments of glass and liquor everywhere.

Fuck. It's time to jump in.

I shove from my seat, rushing to her aide while at the same time forcing a smile onto my lips, burying the anger and trying to appear calm and collected. I close the distance between Elyse and myself quickly and stop only once I'm pressed firmly against her back, trapping his hand between our bodies.

My anger spikes when the man doesn't bother to glance my way or acknowledge my presence. *Who the fuck does he think he is?*

Leaning into her ear, he's speaking low and soft in a language I don't know but recognize as Russian. After a moment, he moves his hand, but only the placement of it, not off her skin, but simply sliding it around to her belly.

I should break each finger and feed them to him.

Instead, I clear my throat. "Take your hands off my property. Now."

Finally, the fucker looks at me. A smile draws onto his lips, recognitioning blooming in his eyes. "Oh, it's the little pup." He lets out a chuckle. "It's so nice to see you. I'm sorry about my poor manners. I couldn't take my eyes off Ely."

"Or your hands?" I sneer. Inwardly, my mind races, all neurons firing as I attempt to figure out the puzzle before me. He speaks as if he knows her.

"Are you sure she is *really* your property? I don't think so. She's only yours via inheritance, correct? If you'll be so inclined, I'd like to buy her from you. Then she will be mine, as she was always meant to be."

Ely trembles, and it's enough to make me sick to my stomach. I can feel her fear, smell it, acidic and pungent and for the first time it doesn't turn me on. It pisses me off. I didn't put it there. I don't control it.

"I'm not so inclined. She's not for sale."

"No? Are you sure you can't be swayed? Everyone has a price, pup. What's yours?"

"The only one who will be paying a price is you, if you don't remove your hand."

His gaze hardens, and he scans the space behind me, then my body, like he expects me to pull out a gun, but instead, I reach down and snag my knife from its hiding spot. I've got it in hand before he can even resume eye contact.

Let's see how many fingers you're willing to lose, fucker.

Keeping my voice calm, I barely resist snarling. "Tell me, how many fingers are you willing to lose?"

As if he realizes how serious I am, he lowers his hand back

down to his side. "I'm not scared of you, pup. You don't know shit about me, or my and Ely's past. This is a family matter. It was a mistake for her to be given to you. Respectfully, I've already offered to buy her from you. I don't know what more you want."

I keep my eyes on him, but I direct my question at Ely. "Is this man your family?"

She shakes her head again, wisps of dark brown hair fly, as she presses back into me. "No. No. He's not."

I know what she's doing, seeking my protection, assuming I will save her but unfortunately she has no idea that I'm just as bad as this man, In some ways, I may be even worse.

The man curls his lip, his icy gaze on her. "That's not true. Ely was promised to me by her father many years ago, to be delivered once she turned of age. Regretfully, he sold her out from underneath me to your grandfather. The deal was settled many years before he made the mistake of going back on his word."

Ely. Awareness zings through me. All the times *my* Ely flinched at my casual use of the nickname. *Please stop calling me that.* It had something to do with him. He has no right to let it cross his lips. Whatever he did to make it ugly in her ears, I'll have to undo. It's *my* name for her now.

Needing to make this tool disappear and prove she belongs to me and only me, I clasp her around the waist with my free hand, splaying my fingers across her smooth flat belly.

"The past is the past. As of today, she is mine and will belong to me until her father's debt is paid in full." Her body jolts against me, but she doesn't say anything.

"What seems to be the problem?" A booming voice questions from behind the little leech who thinks he can take what's mine.

Sidorov.

My quarry approaches and stops behind the smaller man. "Yanov. What is happening?" Sidorov's eyes bounce lazily from me and then to Ely, where they pause and darken. "Oh, you found a little toy."

Yanov, or whatever his fucking name is, stiffens. "No, she is not a toy. She is mine. I don't share."

Mr. Sidorov grins while holding his hands up. "Oh, wvell," —his accent is thick— "then all is good. No problem."

I take a step back, bringing Ely with me. *Damnit.* I'm trying to conjure up a response, a way to salvage this shit show. I need Sidorov so that I can get out of this mess, and with the way he's looking at Elyse right now, I could use her to my advantage. But can I bring myself to go through with it? That I don't know.

Looking down, my eyes catch on Elyse, her bare shoulder that's littered in scars. She doesn't notice me staring. Her entire body is a bundle of nerves, and her own gaze is cast down to the floor submissively.

What...?

I squint, trying to read the letters that look as though they've been etched into her skin.

YANOV.

Each letter is carved into the back of her shoulder in jagged slashes.

This fucker. This piece of shit.

My stomach roils, the contents threatening to climb out of my throat. I'm supposed to wear a mask of boredom, but how can I when I see something like that? The irony doesn't escape me—his mark is similar in aspect to what I do with my Oakmount conquests. It's a type of branding. The only difference is that the girls I slice beg me for the blade. They want my mark—it's part of the whole Sebastian Arturo experience and they wear it proudly, showing it off like a damn gold metal.

This though... This is different, and I know without asking that Ely didn't ask to be branded by this man.

I grit my teeth through the nausea and breath through my nose, tightening my grip on her.

"Elyse, who is this man..."

She trembles against me, and leans her weight backward so much that I have to widen my stance for better balance. "He's... he's a friend of my father's."

I stare the man down, ready to explode. Who the fuck does he think he is? I feel even more compelled to protect her against this twisted fucker now. He's either got a death wish, or he's dumber than a box of rocks. I don't really care what the excuse is, but he's soon going to find out what happens when you fuck with the wrong person.

His name might be carved into her skin, but that don't mean a fucking thing.

Elyse is mine.

MY FUCKING ELY.

The asswipe takes a predatory step closer, and Mr. Sidorov slams a hand down on his shoulder, stopping his progress, as if he knows where this is going.

"Yanov..."

Unfortunately, his friend isn't listening, and it's even more unfortunate that my patience is threadbare. I didn't come here to draw attention to myself, but I'm very close to saying fuck it and slitting the fucker's throat just to prove a point.

"Ely, don't lie," he spits out the words, and she flinches at their impact. "Tell this man the truth. Tell him you belong to me."

Elyse's trembling becomes full-on shaking now. *Shit.* She's probably on the verge of a panic attack.

"It doesn't matter what she says. Legally, she belongs to me."

Yanov snarls at me, spittle flying from his lips. "Paper is useless. Prove it, here. Now. If she belongs to you, show me."

"Show you?" I growl. "She's not a fucking dog; she doesn't do tricks."

Yanov looks into my eyes, and if I thought I was a soulless asshole, this guy is ten times worse. I see an endless pit of darkness, and I can understand why Elyse fears him so much. He's a slimeball who needs his face used as a fucking mop.

"Perhaps you don't know her as well as you claim. Ely does all kinds of tricks, don't you?" He snickers like he knows something I don't. Fucker is going to end up gutted like a fish if he continues with the stupidity.

"Don't talk to her." I hiss through my teeth.

I shouldn't have brought Ely here. I could have figured out some other way to approach Sidorov—

"Territorial, are you?" He laughs. "I can understand the obsession. There's something special about her, isn't there? Something intriguing." His reptilian gaze measures me, finds me wanting. "It makes you hard, doesn't it, pup? You think about sinking your cock into that sweet pussy—"

Sidorov clears his throat, halting Yanov's vile commentary, and I couldn't be more grateful for an interruption because tucked tight against me like she's trying to make herself disappear is Ely, her entire body shaking like a leaf.

"Why don't you show us then? Everyone knows a man who takes a woman as his property must train her well in all areas." Yanov's gaze slides over Ely, oily and full of hidden intent. There's no doubt in my mind he's speaking from his own twisted agenda, that he's always meant to "train" Ely in whatever fucked up ways he deems suitable. "He knows she will do as she is told, no matter what. No matter where. No matter with whom. So prove it."

I'm Sebastian Arturo. Powerful. Successful. A king among peasants. I have nothing to prove to this fuckhead, or anyone else in the room, but that doesn't matter.

Not when he challenges me the way he is right now. Sure, I

could turn him down, but it would be viewed as a sign of weakness. *One fuckup.* That's all it takes for someone to think they can take you on. I may hate my position as the head of the family and want to do nothing more than abandon it, but looking weak is not an option as long as I'm in control. After all, image is everything, and weakness is blood in the water. It'll get you stepped on. It'll get you killed.

I look down at Elyse, and I know she's not going to be happy with my next words. I remind myself that it doesn't matter; not if I can get us both out of here without making a scene.

"As you wish." I growl in resentment.

I give Ely's hip a squeeze, drawing her attention to me. She peers up at me through thick lashes, and I see both fear and hope brewing in her icy blue depths. I don't have the heart to tell her there is no saving us. If she wants to survive she'll have to fight for it.

"Get on your knees, Ely. Show them who you belong to."

12
ELYSE

Did he just tell me to get on my knees?

I'm fairly certain I'm hearing things, so I hesitate a second longer than necessary but then he releases me and pulls away, leaving me without the protection of his body.

"Ely, I will not ask you again." His commanding tone is dark and tempts me to disobey just to see what he might do if I don't listen, but with Yanov lingering so close I don't have the luxury of teasing. Or of getting out of this.

And then there's his friend...Sid-something? His gaze makes me feel like ants are crawling over my skin, and something unpleasant lingers on the edge of my mind. An instinct that tells me never to be caught alone with him.

My legs wobble like towers of jelly while I try to navigate to my knees without toppling over. Using my hands, I lower myself to the ground, pressing my palms to the sticky, cold concrete to help balance myself. By the time my legs touch the bare concrete, I'm dizzy and afraid I might vomit all over the floor.

It's this or Yanov; choose the lesser of the two. Getting away from Yanov was the only good thing about my father selling me off to pay his debts to the Arturo family. I had hoped I would never see the man again, but like all things in life, I never get what I want. My entire body shakes, and goose bumps crawl up my arms.

The cold concrete beneath me isn't helping matters.

What is Sebastian going to do to me?

I don't see him forcing me to have sex. Yes, he lacks morals, but I know he doesn't want me, not like that. He may give me a lingering look or two but nothing has ever happened between us.

Well, not until today.

He can barely stand to be in my presence. *So what's the plan, then?* Uncertainty coats my insides, but I remind myself that it doesn't matter. I'll do whatever he asks of me so long as he doesn't let *him* touch me or take me.

I cast my gaze to the floor, not daring to look at Yanov for fear that he might take it as an invitation, and if he touches me again, I will absolutely lose it. Sebastian takes a step toward me.

I know this because the tips of his expensive leather shoes appear in my line of vision. His unique sea-salt scent fills my nostrils, and I nearly gasp when his warm fingertips graze my chin. With minimal effort, he tilts my chin up, forcing me to meet his gaze. His pretty green eyes twinkle in the light, and I sink into their depths, becoming almost mesmerized. How can someone so cruel and heartless be so beautiful and tempting at the same time?

"Are you my property, El...Little Prey?"

I inhale sharply as awareness arcs between us. For the first time, he understands the ugliness of that name; he realizes that's what Yanov and my father always called me. Gratitude spears through me that he's calling me something else. I'm not sure he'll continue with the nickname after tonight, but right now I appreciate the tiny gesture.

My tongue feels heavy in my mouth, but I force the word out. "Yes."

Cocking his head to the side, he eyes me curiously, and there's something soft in his eyes, even as his shoulders are set tight and rigid. "Are you sure? Because this asshole doesn't seem to believe me. I think he needs a visual since his ears aren't working all that well."

I swear I hear someone snort, maybe in laughter, maybe in derision—I don't know. I'm trapped in this dark trance that Sebastian put me in, and strangely I don't want to leave.

"What do you want me to do?" I ask.

When he speaks, his voice is soft, coaxing. "Be a good girl and crawl over to the red chair. I'll be following you."

The connection between us flickers out when his fingers slip from my chin. For one moment, I hesitate, wondering if there is another way out of all of this, but as soon as I consider the idea, I shove it away. I don't know what I'm doing. I need to let Sebastian lead to get us the fuck out of this situation and to save myself.

Ugh. I hate myself a little bit more right now for how much I need him.

I do as he instructs and crawl across the floor, trying not to look as awkward as I feel.

I've almost reached the chair when I hear a loud, booming voice behind me.

"If you're going to put on a show, at least make it good..." It's the other guy, the one with the S-name, chiming in. I grit my teeth and try to forget that he's still here, that Yanov is here. That I've put us in this horrible situation by simply existing.

The chair is now in front of me, so I sit back on my knees but keep my gaze on the floor. I can feel the heat of embarrassment blooming in my cheeks. It's a matter of survival. I understand that, but I can't explain how much shame I feel being watched as I crawl across the floor.

Sebastian slips into the seat in front of me, and I look up from the floor dragging my gaze over his legs, until I finally reach his face. Our gazes collide, and I swear my entire body lights up. Every cell becomes electrified. *What is wrong with me?* I should not be reacting like this to him. I should be terrified. Shaking like a leaf in a thunderstorm, but no, I want to lean into his darkness, to let him corrupt and taint me.

I notice two shot glasses cradled in his hands. He takes one and tips it back into his mouth, swallowing the clear liquid like it's water. I try not to notice the way his lips shape to the rim of the glass or how sexy he is when he isn't being a complete asshole.

"Get on with it," Yanov interrupts.

I flinch at the sound of his voice and breathe deeper, trying to keep myself calm. Just having him near me makes my skin crawl.

"Shut the fuck up," Sebastian snarls and slams the shot glass onto the wooden end table beside him.

"You're dragging this out because you know she doesn't belong to you, pup. If she were mine, she'd have already put my cock in her mouth. Just admit it and stop wasting my time."

No. No. I don't belong to him. I stare into Sebastian's eyes, hoping those words resonate, that he can see them.

"I'm not dragging it out. It's not my fault you have no patience. I think you're jealous that she is mine, and if that's the case, then maybe you shouldn't stick around for what happens next." Sebastian's hard gaze moves from Yanov, who I'm certain is standing behind me somewhere, to me. I try my best to forget Yanov's here but that's pretty difficult when he starts talking.

"Keep your eyes on me," Sebastian commands, and I nod, staring only at him, trying to forget where I am and who else is here. It's terrifying how my body reacts to him, like there is this imaginary rope tethering us to one another. My core clenches in anticipation, desire swirling low in my belly."Open your mouth, Little Prey."

I don't question him. I simply open my mouth and stare up at him, waiting for his next instruction. I have no other option but to put my trust in him. He's my dark angel, swooping in to save the day. I swear I see the side of his lip lift in the ghost of a smile, but when I blink, it's gone.

"Wider. Open your mouth nice and big for me." I'm not sure what he plans to do, but I tip my head back a little and open my mouth wider, hoping that's enough.

He nods, as if approving, and then clasps the other shot glass with two fingers, and brings it to his lips. Instead of downing it and swallowing, he simply holds the liquid in his mouth. I blink, watching, confused, as he leans forward and pinches my chin between two fingers.

Shock gives way to something sinister and sickening when he spits the contents in my mouth. I'm both appalled and strangely turned on by the act. The vodka burns against my tongue, and I swallow it down quickly to ease the burn. My eyes water from the alcohol, and Sebastian looks down at me like I'm a star pupil, releasing my chin and patting my cheek gently.

Pulling back, he settles into the cushion. I lick my lips, the vodka in my belly warming me from the inside out. *Okay, I can do this.* From the position I'm in, I've gathered where this is going to go. I've watched enough porn. It shouldn't be that hard, right? I just need to unbuckle his pants, pull his penis out, and put it in my mouth.

It's no big deal. Women do it all the time, E.

The fact that *I* myself have never done it doesn't matter, right? Never mind the attention we're gathering. I can feel eyes on me, and it makes my already hot skin, hotter.

As if Sebastian can smell the anxiety rolling off me, he reaches forward and gently caresses my cheek. "Undo my pants and take my cock out." Each sharp word is clipped.

The opposite of his gentle touch.

My heart skips a beat at the demand. I stare down at his lap, then up at his face, and back down again. I force myself to move and reach for his belt buckle. My fingers tremble as I thread the leather through the loops until the ends hang loose across his lap. I'll use every ounce of courage I have left to get through this very moment.

With a deftness I don't feel, I unfasten the top button, then slide his zipper down. It's a little awkward since his zipper is backward. In typical Sebastian fashion, he leaves me to struggle. When I finally get the zipper down, I give in to the growing desire to see his face.

I look from his lap and into his eyes. I'm not really sure what I anticipate finding there. *Anger? Desire? Hate?* I'm greeted with none of those emotions. Instead, I find his gaze narrowed and the corner of his mouth tucked tight in his teeth like he's trying to focus his attention on something else entirely.

I'm not sure what that look means, but it only intensifies my anxiety. I don't want to mess this up—if it's even possible to mess up a blow job.

Swallowing around the ball of fear threatening to clog my throat, I focus my attention back on him.

"It's obvious you don't own her and have not trained her properly. Look at her trembling hands." Yanov interjects, and I find myself retreating into my mind.

I can't do this. I can't.

"She's nervous, asshole. I've never made her do this in front of an audience, so sit down and shut up before I make you suck my cock." Seb growls. Yanov stares at him balefully before sitting. Beside him, Sidorov hides a smile. "Now if you're done interrupting, my Little Prey will continue. "

He stares down at me, hypnotizing me with that intent green gaze, and I find myself nodding.

I'm ready.

13

ELYSE

I blow out a breath and reach for his length. I've barely grazed the fabric of his pants when his hand comes out of nowhere, his fingers circling my wrist and halting any further movement. I whimper from the pain that radiates up my arm and try to pull back, but his grip only tightens.

I glance up at him, needing to understand what I've done wrong. He merely shakes his head when I open my mouth to speak. "No hands, Little Prey. We're doing this my way and my way only. Do you understand?"

All I can do is nod.

"Good girl. I'm going to free my cock and then feed it into your mouth. You'll take every single inch, won't you?"

I nod again, but this time, that's not enough.

"Tell me, tell them," he urges.

"Yes," I whisper.

His hold on me relaxes a smidge, and with a knowing smirk, he uses his free hand to pull out his cock. It's thick and long, and I have to wonder how the hell he does anything with it. It stands straight up, then bounces back to rest against his stomach.

Oh God. I can't do this. He's going to choke me to death with it. I'm panicking, and I know it, but I also know I have no other option. I have to do this.

Taking his cock into his hand, he gives it one rough stroke as he says, "I'm going to fuck your throat, Little Prey. I won't be gentle, and I won't stop until I've painted the back of your throat with my release, do you understand?"

It's not a question or demand. It's a promise, and I can't seem to shut down the small excitement and arousal I get from his words. I risk looking into his eyes once more, and what I see there makes it difficult for me to breathe. Dark, deep-rooted desire reflects back at me.

"Yes." I nod.

He smiles. "You want me to come in your throat, don't you? To treat you like my personal slut. Fill you with my cum, and use your body for my pleasure."

It's wrong. So fucking wrong, but his words, they spur me on. They give me the encouragement I need to play my part.

"Yes, please." I bat my eyes at him.

I want, *no*, I *need* to prove myself to him, to please him. Braced on my knees with my thighs pressed into the couch, I lean forward, tentatively licking the thick, swollen head. He tastes like salt and smells both musky and clean. Not bad at all. I take the tip of him between my lips, and his thighs clench tight around my torso in response.

I suck the head of his cock back into my mouth and take as much of him inside as I can. Of course, he's thick and long, so I don't get very far, or at least, it feels like I don't. My eyes water as I gag around his length, but I try to ignore that fact and hollow my cheeks out, sucking harder while gliding my tongue over the head before pulling back.

His thighs tremble against me, and I freeze. *Does that mean he likes it?* The thought makes my core clench and burn hot. How did I manage to make a man as callous and powerful as him tremble? Yes, I might be the one on her knees, but I've never felt more powerful in my entire life. Something about this moment is so exhilarating.

I want more. Need more.

The thought of pulling such a reaction out of him consumes me. And I repeat it all over again, this time sucking on him a little harder. This elicits a deep mewl from low in his throat, a sound that vibrates through my entire being.

"Look at me, Prey." It's an order, and I follow it eagerly.

With my eyes locked on his, he releases my wrist slowly. Then he leans down and retrieves the knife he'd pulled out earlier. Shit, I didn't even notice that he put it away. It rests in his hand along the outside of his leg. Panic flutters through me briefly as I wonder whether he plans to carve me as Yanov did.

He merely tucks his thumb against the blade, though, initiating a shallow cut.

"Keep your eyes on me. Only I get to see how pretty you look while choking on my cock," he growls.

I blink and look back at him, keeping my gaze locked with his as I drag my mouth up and down his length, taking as much of him as I can. When he flexes his hips up, forcing the head of his cock to the back of my throat, I start to struggle. I try to meet each thrust of his hips, but even I know I can't take all of him.

"Relax, Little Prey. Unclench your jaw and relax your shoulders. I want to see how much cock that tiny throat of yours can take."

Even though I'm afraid to do as he says, the desire to please him is more prevalent than any other emotion right now. So I drop my shoulders and let my jaw go slack.

Drool pools in my cheeks and dribbles out the sides of my mouth as he slips out and then threads himself back between my lips. I brace my hands on his thighs to give myself a little leverage, and he takes the opportunity to piston his hips forward.

A river of tears leaks from my eyes as he slides deeper, past my gag reflex and into my throat smoothly. I do my best to swallow against the pressure telling me I can't take another inch. *Yes. This feels right.* I breathe through my nose and dig my nails into his thighs.

A small hiss of pleasure escapes his lips. And at that moment, it feels like I've won something, earned something.

"Yes, just like that," he praises. "You're doing such a good job taking my cock into your pretty mouth like a good girl. Letting me fuck your throat."

His words flutter through me like butterflies, and I can't help but work that much harder, if only to have him praise me again in his deep baritone voice. Anything to hear something good, something nice. I don't get praised often...or ever, really.

I up the suction while taking him deeper into my mouth at the same time. His green eyes bore into mine, and I notice the tight clench of his jaw. It's almost like he's angry, but that can't be. *Maybe more unhinged?*

I can't be sure. Whatever semblance of control he has left slips away with every harsh press into my mouth. It only takes seconds for him to completely snap, and when he does, his fingers spear through the hair at the nape of my neck. Panic grips me with a vengeance while he presses my head down, forcing my nose against the base of his cock.

I dig my nails into his thighs and try to pull away, but his hold is steel, and the lack of oxygen makes me dizzy. Sensing this, he whispers harshly into my ear, reminding me once again of what I need to do.

"Breathe through your nose, Prey."

More tears leak from my eyes and trail down the apples of my cheeks. Even though I know what to expect, I'm still unable to stop myself from panicking when he does it a second time, especially when it seems like he's trying to choke me to death.

He lifts his hips and drives my head down into his lap, making my chin bounce on his balls. I whimper around his length, unable to suppress the response. I'm not sure if it comes from a place of fear or arousal...maybe both? It doesn't really matter because when the sound reaches his ears, I swear I hear him respond with a growl of approval.

"Fuck, your mouth feels like heaven. How will I live without it now that I know how good it feels?" His whisper is feral, sharp like the knife blade pressed against his thumb.

I blink through teary eyes and try not to think about what that means while he fucks my face harder. *Does he get off on pain?* The ache in my jaw intensifies, and I squeeze my eyes shut to focus on finishing the job. Sebastian isn't having that, though.

"Hell, no. Fucking look at me, Elyse. Now," he snaps. "I want to see your face when I come down your throat."

I immediately snap my gaze back up, even though I can barely see his face swimming behind a layer of tears, but that one quick look is all it takes to see how close to the edge he is. His entire body is strung tight like a bow; his jaw clenching tight, his nostrils flaring with every sharp inhale.

It occurs to me, then, that I want this. I want to make him come, to see him vulnerable and at my mercy. To see him unravel at my touch. The desire encourages me, so I match his brutal pace, gagging around his length while I struggle to take more and more of him. Strangely, the more I struggle, the more excited he becomes.

"Yes, fuck yes. Take me deep into your throat. Choke on me." He tightens his grip on the back of my head and forces my head down, choking me with it.

I dig my nails into his thighs, trying to fight off the panic and spots that fill my vision. Meanwhile, I can feel my own arousal dripping down my thighs, my hard nipples grinding against the fabric of my dress.

I want this. I want him.

Without warning and with a guttural groan, he explodes, his grip tightening to the point of pain. I stop moving as thick, salty ropes of cum fill my mouth.

I gag at the intrusion, forcing myself to swallow. My cheeks burn, my mouth aches, and I can only imagine how my makeup looks.

A soft clap sounds from behind me, and that only amplifies my shame and embarrassment.

I just let him fuck my face in front of a crowd of people.

"That was well done," the big man says, congratulating me.

Sebastian gently eases himself out of my mouth, and a trail of cum crosses my tongue to drip out of my mouth and back onto him.

"Clean it up," he snaps.

I lean forward and tentatively lick his skin.

"You can do better than that."

I swallow nervously and try again, sucking the head of his cock between my lips and cleaning up the errant drops. Once he's satisfied, he tucks himself back into his pants. My thighs are wet, my jaw aches, and my throat is raw, but I'm hopeful that's enough proof for Yanov.

It better be.

After a moment, Sebastian extends his hand to me and helps me to my feet. I move to stand beside the chair but make it all of one step before he's tugging me down onto his lap. I perch on his thigh and lift my head slowly, just enough to see if anyone is staring at me.

The big man laughs heartily from the couch opposite us.

"You are your mother's son, after all." My quick peek shows him looking at me with a heavy-lidded gaze. His tongue darts out to lick his bottom lip and then disappears again, the gesture making me shrink back against Sebastian reflexively. "I believe Yanov got the message; he left in a huff. Me, though..."

Something about his statement makes Sebastian tense, but I can't bring myself to ask him if he's okay. Not when I realize that Yanov is gone. I'm almost disappointed that I don't get to see his face after what I just did.

Sebastian's hold on me tightens, and I won't lie— I like the possessive way he forces me to remain seated on his lap like I'm a trophy to display.

"I'm no longer interested. We're leaving. There will be no negotiations today," Sebastian announces abruptly, and for some reason, that terrifies me—probably because I know nothing will ever be the same between us after tonight.

14
SEBASTIAN

My entire plan is a wash. I had Elyse dangling like forbidden fruit right in front of Sidorov, and I couldn't bring myself to offer her up to him. Fuck.

What the hell is wrong with me?

Why bother asking myself that question? I already know the answer.

Elyse. She's the fucking problem. The whole problem.

I fight with myself for the next twenty-four hours, trying my best to stay in control, balancing on the edge between right and wrong. The alcohol helps to dissolve some of the desire. It keeps me tipsy enough to numb most of my feelings, but it never brings me to the point that I'm sloppy. Even if it's tempting.

I let my eyes fall closed for half a second, and I'm reminded all over again why I haven't slept a wink. It doesn't help that we're stuck in this tin can together at thirty thousand feet, her clean scent surrounding me, her sunshine personality making me want to slit my throat. Escape is impossible at this point, but that doesn't mean I need to continue torturing myself.

And still, my brain refuses to think of anything else. I can still see the way she looked up at me with so much trust in her eyes. I remind myself that she only felt that way because I was the lesser of the two evils in the scenario; still, it doesn't change the fact that she had my cock in her mouth.

I spear my fingers through my hair in frustration. The memory of her warm mouth on my skin and her little nails digging into my thighs will be my undoing. *Dammit. I need another drink.* I can feel her eyes on me, even if she thinks I can't since she looks away as soon as I look at her. I'm not dumb. I know she has things she wants to say and maybe even questions she wants to ask, but I don't have the mental fortitude to deal with all of that right now, nor do I ever want to deal with it.

I'm barely keeping myself in check as it is. God forbid we talk about what happened. It might spark me to do something irrational, like take her back into the bedroom, bend her over, and fuck her until she screams my name. Thinking about sinking inside her wet heat is the only other thing I can seem to think about after the blow job. My brain keeps reminding me that I could have all of her, every single inch. I could let Sidorov have her too, but I'm too much of a pussy to do it.

Jesus fucking Christ. I should just jump out of this plane right now. Fucking pussy.

"We haven't talked about what happened, and I don't really want to return home with this strange awkwardness." She gestures to the open space between us.

"There's nothing awkward, at least not on my end." I shrug, dismissing her feelings entirely. I don't even bother looking at her as I speak. I don't want to encourage this conversation to continue. I just want the plane to land so I can put more than five feet of space between us.

"Okay, sure." She huffs out a breath. "Well, there is for me."

"And what is it that you want me to do about it? Apologize?" I snap.

I know I'm being an asshole, but it's either be this way or put her on her back and fill her with my cock until my balls touch her ass. I think being an asshole is a better choice.

"No, but I didn't expect you to give me the silent treatment either. You're acting even stranger than normal, which says a lot." I notice the way she anxiously wrings her hands together in my peripheral vision. I'm honestly shocked she held back this long. I was positive she would word-vomit all over me last night but she shocked the hell out of me when she didn't make a peep. Most likely internalizing everything that happened.

That doesn't matter—hell, her feelings don't really matter, not when it comes to keeping myself in check. In the long run, she should consider this a favor. Stopping myself from claiming her offers her a chance at freedom—if she ever pays off her father's debt, that is.

I cling to the frustration hovering just beneath the surface, because the alternative is not something we're thinking about right now. "Jesus Christ, Ely, it was a blow job. I didn't take your virginity. It doesn't have to be a big deal. Don't make it something that it isn't."

She drops her gaze, and I pin her with a glare.

"What?"

"Nothing."

"It is something." I eye her speculatively, playing back what I said until it hits me. "Fucking hell." In essence, I did take one of her virginities because I'd bet money that was her first fucking blow job. Mixed with an unexpected and weird sense of shame is a feeling of victory. Mine was the first cock that took her throat.

Play your cards right; it could be the last. Could be the only.

I shove that thought away and concentrate. Ely's talking, her soft, earnest voice doing something to my insides.

"That's just it. I'm not trying to make it anything, but you're acting weird, making it difficult for me to let it go."

"I don't know what you want me to say or do. All I'm doing is sitting here. Would you have preferred I let him have you?" It's a shitty response, but I need her to shut up, and the easiest way to make someone do that is to hit them where it counts.

"No. That's not what I would've preferred. I'm sorry. I wasn't trying to make a big deal out of it. I just wanted to reassure you that nothing has to change between us. If it were up to me, I'd forget it even happened."

"Sounds like it." I arch a brow in question at her. "You're the only one talking about it, and somehow you want me to think you want to forget it happened?"

Her mouth opens and then closes like a fish out of water. After a few seconds, she finally mumbles, "I do."

"Then shut up about it. What's done is done."

"Okay," she whispers, tucking her bottom lip under her top. I look away, my desire for her growing tenfold, burning hotter than the sun. *Fuck her.* Fuck this need she's planted deep inside my chest with her pretty eyes and her soft lips and her and delicate features. She's making me crave things I have no right to take. I want to hurt her for making me feel this way. Mark her skin. But touching her would only set me off at this point, so my only other option is to cut her with my words.

"You really don't need to worry about anything changing between us. I can promise nothing has changed. You're still the maid who owes me a debt that you'll never be able to repay, at least not in this lifetime. Sucking my cock doesn't change that... although maybe I'll let you do it again, just for the fun of it."

It happens in a flash, so quick that I don't even have time to react. One minute, she's sitting, and the next, she is out of her seat, her palm colliding with my cheek. The sting of her slap ripples across my face and twists my head to the side from the impact.

"You're despicable. I hate you."

Lord, please explain to me why my cock is harder than it's ever been in my entire life? Her violence makes me harder than steel, and I find it even more difficult to focus. I'd love nothing more than to show her what happens when you fuck with a man like me, but I can't cross that line. *I won't cross that line.* Swallowing down my arousal, I focus on her anger. I cling to it, because if she hates me then she'll stay away from me, right?

"Weird, you weren't saying that yesterday. In fact, you said you'd do anything I wanted you to as long as I didn't sell you. Maybe I made a mistake when I didn't let Yanov take you home? Or maybe Sidorov? He wanted to fuck you, too."

Red spots bloom on her cheeks, confirming her embarrassment, but beneath it is fear. It shines like a beacon of light in her eyes. I know I'm an asshole, but someone has to be. I need her to hate me, need it like my next breath. She takes a trembling step back, her lip quivering, and I can physically see her slipping somewhere else in her mind.

"Did I? Did I make a mistake, Elyse?"

"Please...I'm sorry. Please don't let him hurt me again."

"*Again?*" I growl, my emotions spiraling. I'm caught off guard by her words. She's so fragile, broken. As bad as I want to hurt her, I want to protect her, too.

How the fuck is that possible?

"Wait, you need to go back to the beginning and explain this to me because, after everything I did to save your ass, I deserve an explanation." I don't deserve shit, but I'm not telling her that. "Like, why are his initials carved into your shoulder? Why did your father agree to sell you to him?" I shouldn't care. Shouldn't even be asking these stupid questions, but I need to know. "I know he did something to you. I could tell by the way you shrank back from him and how he acted, like you belonged to him. Now tell me what happened, and don't lie to me. Otherwise, I might go to your father and ask him myself."

Her big blue eyes fill with worry, and she shakes her head. "No, please. I'll explain."

"Then do it," I snap.

She sags back down into her seat, tugging her legs up to her chest so she can wrap her arms around them. Without looking at me, she speaks. "From the moment I turned fifteen, he's had an interest in me. He begged my father to give me to him, even going out of his way to endear himself."

"Give you to him? What, did your father owe him money, too?"

She lifts one shoulder in a shrug. "That, or a favor. I don't know, really."

"So how did that end with his name carved into your shoulder?"

Her gaze goes hazy, and I wonder if she's going back in time.

"I don't know, exactly. When I was sixteen, my father threw me a birthday party, but it wasn't really a party for me. It was a party for his friends. He wanted to show his newly grown-up daughter off to his friends. Yanov didn't like this at all. Sometime during the party, he cornered me and dragged me into a back hallway. One second, I was okay, and the next, I was so sleepy I could barely stand. All I remember is falling asleep, and the following morning, when I woke up, I was in my bedroom, my shoulder aching and crusted with blood. Ever since that day, he's considered me his property."

Why didn't I kill him when I had the chance? Stick my knife in his stomach and gut him like a fish?

"I don't care what hold he had on you before. You're mine," I snap. "My property," I add at the last moment.

The words send her diving headfirst back into reality. The hazy look in her eyes disappears, and instead, the Elyse I've slowly watched her transform into reappears.

"I'm no one's property. I belong to myself. And even if I

didn't, I'd never willingly belong to that asshole. I'd rather die than return to him or my father."

Apparently, I haven't made myself clear enough. "I don't care about Yanov or whatever disgusting obsession he has with you. Until your debt is paid, the one from your father and the one you accrued all on your own in my closet, you're mine. Every breath, whisper, tear. It's mine. You belong to me entirely, and I'll do whatever I want with you."

She nods, even though the look on her face tells me she wants to fight me. "Whatever. I get it. I'm forever in your debt."

"Exactly. We're not equals. And don't ever think that we are because I won't hesitate to remind you of the truth."

"Thanks." She shakes her head and turns away from me. "You only care about me enough to ensure my father's debt to you is paid. Not because I'm a human who deserves to be cared for, right?"

Wrong. I want to tell her so badly it hurts, but this can only end one of two ways, and I'm not going to lead her along. I can't have her, not beyond the capacity of her debt being repaid.

"Right, Little Prey. My only care for you is to ensure you stay alive long enough to repay your father's debt."

"I hate you," she whispers, and I almost tell her that I hate myself, too. Instead, I take a drink of the whiskey and let it burn away the guilt that's threatening to choke me.

"Get in line, sweetheart. There's a lot of fuckers who hate me, and you are merely a number at this point."

15
SEBASTIAN

Several silent hours later, I find myself staring out the window on the opposite side of the plane as we land in Oakmount. I've had far too much time to think about what happened between Elyse and me and what I said to her when she finally broke the silence and asked her questions.

Now I feel like an asshole, and there's nothing I can do to fix it. I mean, I'm supposed to be an asshole, but I can't help the pang of guilt that stabs my chest every time I cut her down. The guilt is getting harder and harder to cover up.

Everything that could possibly go wrong is going wrong. I suppose there is hope, a silver lining in all of this being that we're finally home, and I won't be confined to this damn tin can with her a moment longer.

I've got enough shit on my plate without having to worry about Elyse having a psycho stalker, and even if it isn't my problem, I've made it mine. After witnessing the way he talked about her, and touched her, I won't rest until I find a way to make him disappear.

Adding Tanya into the mix just gives me a headache. I couldn't have predicted how far she would go to secure her position in the Arturo family, but one thing is clear: Yanov was at Pound of Flesh because Tanya tipped him off.

Maybe I'll call some old friends, let them know what's coming their way

Tanya's wily as fuck. She's bound to have realized why I was so intent on going to the flesh market and parading Ely in front of Sidorov...none of which would have been advantageous for her. If I were to sell out to Sidorov, she'd stand to lose everything she'd become accustomed to. I knew she'd try to block me at some point; I just didn't anticipate this particular move this soon.

How does she even know Sidorov? There was no reason for her to have ever attended Pound of Flesh; therefore, there was no reason for her to be in contact with him. I can't wrap my head around all the things going on. There are too many moving pieces, and I'm starting to underestimate those closest to me. I need to get back on track.

And the first thing I need to do to ensure that happens is to keep Elyse as far away from me as possible.

The plane finally comes to a stop, and the flight attendant opens the door. Ely stands and slides past me, out the door, and down the small staircase in a flash. I follow her but keep my gaze alert. I don't think we've seen the last of Yanov, not by a long shot. His obsession with her runs bone deep, and I'll need to stay vigilant if I'm going to try to get rid of him.

Nevertheless, regardless of what I manipulate Elyse into believing he will never get his hands on her again. I make a mental note to get in touch with my PI. I need all the information available on him. It's clear that fucker, Yanov, doesn't know how powerful my family is, because if he did he wouldn't be challenging me like he is.

It doesn't matter, though. He might think I'm young, maybe

even naive, but he has no idea who he's fucking with. I'm not soft, nor am I empathetic. If you fuck with me, I will fuck you back, and I won't use lube.

Ely is in the car, waiting and ready. I slip into the seat beside her, but she ignores me. *Who's giving who the silent treatment now?* I guess I should be happy she's not yapping my ear off, but for some reason, her silence infuriates me more now. The entire drive to the estate is filled with silence, and the pressure inside the car becomes suffocating.

Funny how silence isn't silence at all. In fact, it's just a space where unsaid words hover between two people. I can't explain the relief I feel when we pull up the long driveway to the house. It's so nice to be home, even if Tanya is here.

The car has barely come to a stop, and Ely is opening her door and hopping out. I follow more slowly. Not like she can get very far on the estate. I'll give her a few minutes of alone time before I make my next demand. After all, the things that happened at Pound of Flesh changed nothing. She's still the maid. I'm still her boss.

I clear the foyer and head directly to the kitchen for a proper drink. There's a bar in my room, but I need an ice bucket and a lot of whiskey to recover from the past twenty-four hours.

Of course God couldn't spare me a single second of peace. I've barely stepped into the kitchen when I spot Tanya braced against the countertop, her long hair hanging in shiny waves over one shoulder. I give her a brief glance, noticing she's wearing a red dress that hugs her slender curves today. As I approach, she extends a perfectly manicured hand my way, and I look down to find a crystal glass filled with amber liquid.

Usually, I would ignore her and go to the bar to get my own drink. But right now, between Ely, Tanya, and the entire bottle of whiskey I killed on the plane, I'm not thinking straight.

I throw back the glass, set it on the counter, and head to the bar to get another one. "What do you want, Tanya, and let me preface this entire conversation with the fact that I'm not in the mood for your shit. Especially with the knowledge that you fucked up the deal I went all the way to London to make."

She frowns. "So you didn't sell your little friend then? Pity. I guess the maid I interviewed won't be needed after all."

I don't answer because she's not talking to me; she's posturing. "Again, what do you fucking want?"

Standing up straight, she shifts the empty glass on the counter with a *clink*. "You will not speak to me that way. "

I meet her eyes over my fresh lowball glass. "Is that an order from the aunt, my adopted mother, or the woman who took my virginity?"

She snarls her lips at me. "Shut up. I'm telling you as the woman who will make your life hell if you don't treat her with the respect she deserves."

Exhaustion washes over me in a wave, and I can barely remain standing upright. It has to be jet lag. Definitely not the lack of sleep. Or the alcohol diluting my blood. "Hate to spoil it for you, but my life is already hell, and there's nothing you can do to make it worse at this point."

"Don't be pitiful, Sebastian. It's not very attractive, and I know you can do better. Let me know when you want to speak to me civilly."

She sashays out of the kitchen leaving me with nothing but the click of her high heels on the floor. *What-the-fuck-ever.* I fill my glass to the rim with bourbon and take a massive gulp, letting it fill my belly with warmth. Once I've drunk close to half of it, I finally get up the strength to meander up to my room.

I'm so beyond done with this day. I want a hot shower and to fall face-first into my bed. I've just walked into my bedroom when my phone vibrates. I swear to fucking God, if it's any one of my dickhead friends, I'm going to murder them.

Lucky for them, they'll live to see another day since it's only my head security guy, Rambo. He doesn't text me often, so I take it seriously when he does.

Rambo: Someone is lingering outside the gate entrance.

With a sigh, I turn on my heels and head back downstairs.

It's never a good thing when someone lingers outside your gate. People don't do that...well, except for Drew. And that's just because he doesn't know when enough is enough. I jog down the stairs, counting the steps to distract myself, and then head out the front to go down the drive. As I get closer to the gate, my steps slow, and I slip on the invisible mask I've perfected from attending boring party after boring party.

The mask I wear as the older wives grope my ass, the mask I wear when I do anything I don't want to do. I approach with my hands deep in my pocket, even if I want to have my knife clutched there. Better not escalate this unnecessarily...*not yet.*

I'm partially baffled and partially pissed to find Yanov standing on the other side of the gate, peering toward the house with a maniacal grin on his face. His smile widens as soon as he spots me. "Oh, good, you do live here, Pup. Glad to know my information was correct."

I signal to the security guards, who are inching closer to the gate. They stop immediately, watching while I finish walking down to the gate, stopping only with a few feet between me and the metal.

"Didn't like how things ended the first time so you decided to show up here for a personal viewing?"

"Just because you got her to give you a blow job doesn't mean you own her. I've got her to do lots of things, things she doesn't even know she's done."

My stomach twists into a tight knot, and I really, want to fucking reach through the gate and strangle the life out of him.

"Doesn't really matter when she's mine, now does it?"

He shrugs. "You mean, for now."

I scan him quickly, looking for any weapons he might have. I catch a glimpse of silver metal. He definitely has a gun tucked into his pants, hiding under his trench coat.

"No, I mean until I choose to release her, and when and *if* that time comes, I can promise you I won't be releasing her to you," I tell him, then gesture to the security guards. "This man is not allowed on the property. I don't care what he tells you. He doesn't get past the gate. If he does, whoever allowed it will pay in blood."

The guards nod, eyeing me, no doubt picking up on the growing tension between Yanov and me.

"I hope you don't think a few security guards and some metal gate will stop me from getting what I want." He taps the gate with his hand. "I'll find a way around it. Now that I know she's here I won't have far to go when I'm ready to take her."

"If you step foot on my property you will regret it immensely."

"Are you threatening me, Pup?"

"It's not a threat." I grit out. "If you don't believe me, do it and see what happens."

He only grins, his smile slightly unhinged. He has to be at least twenty years older than Elyse. All the things she told me about this fucker come rushing back to my mind, giving me even more fuel to end his pathetic life.

I might hurt Elyse with my words, but everything I do is to protect her. This fucker doesn't want to protect her. He wants to hurt her, and I will end his life before I let that happen again.

Leaning down, I tug the knife from my ankle sheath. Expertly, I roll it over my palm and flip it so the blade points toward Yanov. "Are you sure you don't want to fuck around and find out? It would save me some time."

He shakes his head. “Sorry, I can’t play your little kid games right now. I'm under orders at the moment, but don’t worry. The day will come soon enough when I’ll return to take her from you. Maybe I’ll let you stay alive long enough to watch it happen.”

“The day will never come fuckface. I might look naive, but I’m a lot harder to kill than you think. If you want Elyse, it will come at a cost, and I don’t know that you’re willing to die for her.”

That only earns me another shrug, then he peels back one side of his coat to flash the gun I knew he was already hiding there, but it's not the gun I latch onto. No, it’s the shiny surface of a badge glinting on his belt.

Well, that complicates things. “You don’t know a damn thing about me, but you will, soon. In the meantime, make sure you take good care of my girl, and let her know I’ll be coming for her soon.”

It's a shocking development, yes, but it also fills me with a different kind of anger. Ely told me what happened, but she didn't give me this one very important detail.

That he’s a fucking cop.

“I warned you what will happen if you step on my property, so when you show up here again, don’t be shocked, because police badge or not, I’ll end your life and deal with the consequences later.”

“I guess we'll see what happens, won’t we?” He slowly backs away from the gate, and I track his movements.

“We certainly fucking will.” I try to play it off like I don’t give a fuck what he says, but keeping the mask of indifference in place is difficult as fuck when I want to murder him with a glare alone. I stand there watching him disappear down the driveway. I want to make sure he’s gone before I go back inside the house.

Dealing with this fucker is my top priority.

My phone vibrates with an incoming text, and this time, when I pull it out and open the message, it's the group chat I share with my best friends. I haven't been active in the group for weeks now, and I know it's my own fault for pulling away from them. Guilt flares deep in my chest. I haven't shared anything with them about my grandfather, Elyse. What my future plans are. I know I could go to them, but they each have their own shit going on, and I don't want to burden them, nor do I want Bel to find out how bad everything has gotten.

Still, I read through the messages, smirking, wondering when things became so fucking hard. *Life. School. Work.* To be a kid again. Mmm, then again, my childhood wasn't any better really. I'm dragging my feet by the time I march back up the driveway, my vision hazy. Fuck, I guess I didn't realize how exhausted I was. Now that the adrenaline is wearing off, the mix of alcohol and lack of sleep are in full effect.

I blink, but the world moves in and out of focus. I make it through the door, the ground beneath my feet shifting. It takes substantial effort to keep my eyes open, but somehow, I manage to fight off the exhaustion just long enough to get inside.

I stumble through the first door I find, the world spinning around me. I recognize the room as my grandfather's office, and I slump down onto the long leather couch. I'm hit with a wave of nostalgia. A reminder of the numerous nights I fell asleep on this very couch while my grandfather and or my uncle worked. Even with the memory of what happened in this room, it still feels like home. I let my eyes drift closed, and I'm assaulted by her. Even in my dreams, I can't escape her sassy mouth and piercing blue eyes.

Ely. My perfectly innocent fucking Ely.

Nails sink into my skin, raking down the side of my cheek. The smell of soap, clean skin. Her scent fills my nostrils. Hot breath fans against my throat, and I grip her by the hips with both hands and press her warm cunt against my throbbing cock.

Yes. This is what I want, but I've been too stuck in my own head, too afraid to do anything about it.

"Elyse..." I whisper her name.

She's perfect. Just like I always knew she'd be.

16
ELYSE

After the London trip, the days blend. I bounce between nonstop cleaning and schoolwork with an occasional catnap in between. It takes me a good portion of the week to catch up on all the housework I missed when I was away for just a couple of days, but I guess the silver lining in being busy is that I don't see much of Sebastian.

I shut down the part of myself that misses him.

Instead, I try to remind myself a million times over that regardless of the reason for it, what we did was wrong, and I have no right to be fantasizing about sleeping with my boss—yet I can't pretend I didn't enjoy what we did. Even if the entire reason it happened was because of Yanov.

Yanov. Even thinking of him makes me nauseated. I had assumed that when I disappeared, shipped away by my father once again, he would conclude that something happened to me and move on. My father had stupidly promised me to him as his bride, but that was years ago, and several thousand dollars in debt later, he had to use me to pay for his debts. I wasn't complaining about the circumstances, though. For the most part, I was content living here, happy even. I didn't live in fear anymore, and even if Sebastian was a bully at times, he never treated me like my father did.

Was it too much to hope he thought I had died? Fate apparently had other plans because now he knew I was alive and well here. That discovery only ignited the embers of an obsession that had never burned out. Yanov isn't just a stalker. He's worse, so much worse, and I hope I never have to tell Sebastian about the things he's done to me.

Speaking of, I can only imagine what he thinks of me now.

Weak, probably? An idiot, for sure. I don't know. He saw me in my most vulnerable state, and while he had the chance to break me down further, he didn't. I'm not dumb enough to think it's because he has a heart, though. No, he's most likely storing whatever he can away to use it against me later.

That's just the way he is.

I amble back down the staff corridor to my room. I'm exhausted, practically dragging my feet as I walk, and all I want right now is to fall into bed and sleep forever. Before last week, I'd never been out of the country, but I now understand what people mean when they talk about having jet lag, which makes them sleep for days. It's no joke.

When I reach the door to my room I let out a sigh of relief. *Home at last.* I unlock the door and shove it open with my shoulder. I can't wait to fall into bed. Except sleep is the last thing that enters my mind when I catch a glimpse of my bedroom. I blink against the faint rays of evening sunlight that slice through the window.

What the fuck?

The place is trashed...torn to shreds. There isn't an item left in its original spot. All I can do is stand there, staring in horror. The bedding hangs over the edge of the bed, slashed to ribbons, the stuffing from my pillows strung out across the floor. The dresser's been ransacked, the clothing ripped out of it, or rather, hanging out of it.

What the hell? I try to keep it together, but the more I look around at the one place I could call my own, the only place I've been able to view as a kind of sanctuary, the closer to the edge I get. But it's the sight of a couple of my academic books, the pages ripped and tossed half under the bed, that makes me completely lose it.

A whimper slips past my lips, and I clench my fists together as my knees buckle. I can't afford to replace them, but I also can't study without them.

What am I going to do?

The memory of Sebastian tearing into my dresser and throwing my clothing out onto the floor in a similar manner appears in my mind. *Sebastian.* He did this. It had to be him. No one else in this house would put this much effort into hurting me. No one hates me like he does. This is probably his way of getting back at me for having to *"save"* me at the club and messing his plans up.

I wouldn't have needed to be saved if I hadn't been there in the first place.

Forcing air into my lungs, I latch onto reason even though what I really want to do is march up the stairs and confront the asshole. If he thinks this makes us even, he's in for a rude awakening. I blink back the sting of tears, reminding myself that I'm stronger than this. That I've been through worse.

I'm burning with rage, but I know confronting him will only end in a fight, which I also don't have the energy to deal with, so I choose to take the remainder of my energy and funnel it into cleaning up the room. I shove the clothes back into the drawers, telling myself I can fold them and put them back nicely when I've had more sleep.

I can't do much about the pillows or blanket. Those items are trash, but thankfully, the extra linens are just down the hall. About twenty minutes later, the room looks a little more put together. Once I have the bed fixed, I start picking up the floor. I pluck the two books I need for class up off the floor and pray they're salvageable. As soon as I open the first, pieces of torn paper fall out and drift across the floor.

"What the hell!" I growl angrily and bend down to pick them up so I can shove them back into the book. The tips of my fingers barely touch the first piece when I see bright red writing on the page. It's a single word, written in all caps.

YOU

Fear and confusion become one. I can't stop my hands from trembling, and my stomach knots to the point of pain. I look at the other pieces of paper that litter the floor. They have the same bright red ink staining their pages, each with one word scribbled on them. I practically fall to my knees, the impact not registering in my mind as I scramble to put the pieces together. As the words come together, the blood in my veins turns to ice.

YOU. MIGHT. BE. HIS. FOR. NOW.

BUT. YOU. WILL. ALWAYS. BE. MINE.

I'm suspended in a moment of time. The pounding in my head intensifies, and I press my palms to my temples to try to alleviate the pain.

No! No! No!

It's not Sebastian at all. It's Yanov.

This can't be happening. But it is. He's here. He's coming for me.

Dread swamps me. *What do I do?* I have to leave, to go somewhere, to get away from him...but there's nowhere to go. No one to protect me.

There's Sebastian.

No. I shake my head, sending the thought away. Confiding in him will only make all this worse. It's not his job to save me or protect me. I owe him enough already, and I'm not about to hand him another reason to hate me. My pride can't take anymore hits.

My only option is to deal with it myself, but that seems impossible. I can't even be in the same room with him without being paralyzed by fear. *How will I ever fight back against him?* How will I ever be free? Tears sting my eyes, and when I blink I feel the cold trail they leave behind. It's so hard to be strong when you're tired, and not just the physical kind of tired. It's like fate wants to see how much more shit it can stack on my shoulders before I topple over. Now I have to think about where I'm going to sleep since my room isn't a safe space anymore. I'll have to go back to being hypervigilant and sleeping wherever I can. Whenever I can.

I'll have to find a closet. Or a bathroom. Somewhere small without windows. The thoughts swirling in my head leave me reeling. I wonder if he's out there now? Outside the window, watching me, laughing in the face of my fear.

I look around the room at the destruction he's caused, and I can't bear to stay in here another moment. I grab my bag and a few other belongings I'll need for the night. I hate the idea of sleeping somewhere else, but the risk of him finding me here alone outweighs that uncomfortable feeling.

Next time, there won't be a warning or the piddling destruction of my things.

Yanov's one and only motive is me. I knew this would happen. Why did I think I'd get lucky, and he would forget about me? If anything, seeing me at that club reignited his sick obsession with me.

With my things in hand, I leave the bedroom and climb the stairs to the first floor. My immediate response is to hide, at least until I can figure out a plan that doesn't involve bringing Sebastian into it.

Because that worked so well the first time.

I guess there's one thing I have now that I never did before: protection. Sebastian technically owns me and will continue to protect me as long as I remain under his ownership. I'm reminded of his hold on me at the club and how he came to my rescue when he spotted Yanov touching me. Even if he denies giving a shit about me, denies how attracted he is to me, there's one thing he can't deny, and that's that I'm his. So even if the only reason he protects me is to keep me, to own me, I'd rather be owned by him than abused and used by Yanov any day.

17

ELYSE

In the two weeks that pass, I slip back into the shell of the girl I used to be.

I'm exhausted and so jumpy I scare myself sometimes. I haven't slept in my room since that night. Instead, I've made a makeshift bed out of blankets and pillows in the closet of a spare room on the second floor. Even without windows or a way for anyone to sneak up on me, I haven't been able to get restful sleep. The worry and fear of Yanov getting close enough that he could easily kidnap me terrifies me.

I'm in a permanent state of exhaustion with no end in sight, which is probably why I nearly trip over my own two feet and slam face-first into Sebastian's chest. My body bounces off him and sends me backward along with all my cleaning supplies.

Bottles of chemicals and towels cascade to the floor, and I catch myself against the wall. I blink back tears when I catch sight of the mess on the floor. *Deep breath.* Clean it up and move on. You'll be fine.

I suppose that would be easy enough if I hadn't run into *him.* I've been doing everything I could to stay out of his way so that I don't fuck up and give him a reason to send me away. Not only that, but my reaction to his presence makes me forget that we can never, ever be a thing. That no matter the attraction between us, he will always be my boss, and I'll always be indebted to him. That, and I need his protection from Yanov more than I need anything.

"What the hell, Ely?" He jumps back. "Pay attention to where you're walking."

"I'm sorry. I didn't mean to..." I trail off, hoping to minimize the damage. At least I didn't ruin another one of his suits. *Right?*

I look up from the floor to be sure I didn't spill anything on him and find his shirt free of any mess. *Thank God.*

"I'll just clean this up," I say, my voice shaky.

Taking a step forward, I reach for one of the many towels I dropped so I can soak up the glass cleaner, and that's when things go from bad to worse. My foot slips through the puddle, and before I realize it, I'm flat on my back, my head bouncing off the floor. Pain ripples across my scalp, and black spots appear in my eyes.

I lie there for a moment, trying to gather my wits, my thoughts swimming, the glass cleaner seeping into my clothes. I peer up at Sebastian. His huge body looms over me, and those green eyes of his fill with confusion. His lips move, but I can't hear what he's saying.

A sudden rush of dread encompasses me, and when I blink, darkness overtakes me.

A man looms over me, but it's not glass in his hands. There's a blur; the man morphs before my eyes, and where Sebastian previously stood, now Yanov stands.

"No, please..." I croak and lift my hands to shield my face. My eyes catch on the blood that stains his tattooed and bruised knuckles. There's so much of it. So much. The air in my lungs wheezes out of me.

I'm a shell of pain, waiting for the moment when my heart stops beating so I don't have to endure another second of this. I can only hope death will save me now.

"You'll never escape, never be free. You'll always be mine," he growls and then grips me by the hair, dragging me across the floor.

With a gasp, I escape the memory and lift my hand to press it against my cheek. Beneath my fingertips is warm skin. *There's no blood. No pain*. It's okay. *You're safe,* I repeat to myself. *But am I really safe?* Was that a real memory, suppressed due to the trauma in it, or was that simply something my imagination conjured up, given the current events?

I can't be sure unless I talk to Sebastian or the doctor about it, and I don't want to do that right now.

My heart thunders against my rib cage, and I breathe deeply, trying to calm myself. Fear still has its claws dug into me, and I scramble into a sitting position, scurrying backward and sending bottles of cleaner flying. I stop once my back collides with the wall.

"Elyse!" Someone calling my name way off in the distance yanks me back to the present.

Shit. I scramble to my feet and move, focusing on cleaning up the spill. Don't think about the memory or what happened. A dull ache forms at the back of my head. I'm still trembling when Tanya waves a hand in front of my face.

"Hello...Elyse?"

Oh crap. "I'm so sorry. I didn't hear you."

Looking up, I scan the hallway, finding Sebastian first, staring down at me. Tanya stands beside him, a bit closer to me with a confused look. "Are you all right?"

I glance side to side, anywhere but at Sebastian, and then realize she's still talking to me. "Oh, yeah, fine. I'm fine. Just not sleeping well."

She doesn't respond, but then again, she doesn't need to. The expression of disgust etched into her features is all the response I need.

I swallow the bile rising in my throat. "Did you need something?"

She waves at the floor. "Well, yes. I need someone to clean this up. How about you go get one of the kitchen staff to help you. I'm not sure what your problem has been recently, but you need to start paying better attention to what you're doing. Otherwise, you might not have a job in this house anymore."

The threat is clear, and I know while Tanya isn't really my boss, she could easily convince Sebastian to fire me and send me back to my father. The mere thought repulses me. Yanov would certainly get me once I was back in my father's care. I'd discover very fast then what's a memory and what's my imagination.

"Please... I'm sorry. I'm just... I'll do better," I squeak the words out.

Sebastian shifts, lingering in the doorway of his room. I still don't risk more than a glance in his direction. He stares down at me just as Tanya does, and even if his eyes aren't as cold as hers, they're still inspecting, watching for any little imperfection.

"Stop. You don't have to apologize to Tanya; she's not your boss," Sebastian orders, shoving his hands into his pockets. He seems to do that a lot, especially when I'm in the same room as him. Is it so he doesn't strangle me? *Probably.*

"I understand that, but she is right. I have been very clumsy lately and forgetful, but I promise to work harder and pay better attention." I look away from Sebastian and back at Tanya, whose eyes have only grown colder.

I hate how desperate I appear, but with the threat from Yanov hanging over my head and Tanya's warning, I know it'll only be a matter of time before the other shoe drops. Without Sebastian's protection, I'm as good as dead. I know it, and surely he does, too.

Looking away, I quickly gather up the rest of my supplies.

"This is your only warning, darling. Next time, you'll be out the door," Tanya states matter-of-factly, and I can feel the tension rolling off Sebastian.

"Tanya," he scolds. "Elyse isn't any of your concern. I told you that once before."

I duck my chin to my chest. Doing my best to ignore their presence, I work hastily to dry up the spilled chemicals.

"Anything that affects me, my home, and those I care about is my concern," Tanya snaps at him.

"It's barely your home, only in a legal sense, and nothing Elyse does or doesn't do has any effect on your quality of life, so again—not your concern."

"What do you mean?" Tanya growls, clearly insulted by Sebastian's words. "It's obvious something is wrong with her. I shouldn't have to explain how I want my things every time she cleans my bedroom. Being a maid is not that difficult of a job," she huffs. "Now she's spilling things and making bigger messes. I'm telling you, if *it* doesn't get fixed, I'll hire someone else."

Sebastian makes a rude noise. "Maybe have that bodyguard of yours do it. I don't know how he can be *'guarding'* you while you aren't even in his presence. Then again, he probably won't like that he can't meddle in my business if he's busy cleaning toilets."

"I think you're jealous, Sebby." Her voice drops to a seductive tone. "Am I not giving you enough attention?"

My skin crawls, and I can feel bile climbing up my throat. It's been clear since I started living here that something terrible happened between Sebastian and his aunt/stepmom, and every day that I'm around her, I draw closer to the conclusion that she's the predator in all of this.

"There, all clean," I announce and shove off the floor with the supplies in my hands.

I need to get out of here and away from these two before I vomit on the floor and make a bigger fool of myself. I'll have to remember to try harder and complete my tasks without so many errors so I don't risk Tanya trying to change Sebastian's mind.

"Oh goodness, I forgot you were still there." Tanya smirks at me, her eyes dropping to the floor to assess my work.

Yup, time to disappear.

Whirling around on the heels of my shoes, I start back the way I came, but I make it all of one step before a hand lands on my shoulder, stopping me.

The touch catches me off guard, and I twist back around, my heart racing in my chest.

Sebastian. Shit.

"Wait, we need to talk," Sebastian says and drops his hand from my shoulder. I nod but say nothing. I doubt he wants to talk about anything good. I should probably start packing up the minuscule box of things I own and prepare for what's to come.

My throat tightens as bubbles of panic rise slowly to the surface.

He abruptly turns his attention back to Tanya. "It's been nice chatting with you, Tanya, but I need to discuss some things with Elyse, so carry on with whatever it was you were doing before."

"Excuse me, but you cannot just dismiss me like that," Tanya huffs.

"I'm not dismissing you. The conversation is over; now move along."

Shaking her head, she sneers at me, her gaze sending pinpricks of awareness across my skin. After a second, she looks back at Sebastian, and only then can I breathe again.

"Each day, I have to wonder how you turned into the cold, callous man you are today. I know I raised you to be more respectful than this."

"Tanya," he growls impatiently.

"Whatever, but we're not done with this conversation," she

warns and stalks away, but not before she slams her shoulder into mine.

It's a miracle I keep all the items locked tight in my grip. Can't say the same about my body since I sway like a leaf being carried away by a gust of wind.

Sebastian notices and steadies me with both hands pressing down on my shoulders.

I look up at him, trying to read his features. *There's nothing there. Not even a hint.* It's hard to tell what he's thinking when he's wearing that stupid mask to hide his emotions.

"Uh, what did you want to talk to me about?" I ask nonchalantly, trying to act like I'm not close to my third nervous breakdown of the day.

"Did you not realize you hit your head when you fell?"

I shrug. "I did, but I was more concerned about cleaning up the mess. I don't want to upset Tanya any more than I already do."

He shakes his head. "Fuck her. I don't give a fuck about the mess. You could've left it there; someone else would've cleaned it up." The bitterness in his voice drains out into his words. I don't tell him that I care about the mess, especially since I'm the one who made it.

"It's okay. It's my job to clean stuff up, and it's done now, so it doesn't matter."

We haven't talked, but maybe a few words here and there recently, more so him telling me what he needs done or what I should be cleaning, so it's weird to have a full conversation with him right now.

"Sure." He sighs. "How does your head feel?"

I'm confused. Why does he care? He's bound to have some kind of ulterior motive...right?

But no...he's not the one who left me for dead after beating me and shooting me. "Fine," I say finally. "It feels like a head should feel."

He nods, but he doesn't look like he's okay with that response. Every inch of his body is rigid and drawn tight like a bow. *Shit, is he going to fire me now?* Maybe he was just bringing up my head so he had something to lead the conversation with.

"Dr. Brooks wants to do a checkup soon. He asked me to ask if you remembered anything from that night or if you've had any flashbacks?"

I tighten my grip on the supplies. This conversation makes me feel incredibly vulnerable, but outside of Sebastian being a total prick most days, he's never used that night against me, so I've never felt uncomfortable talking to him about anything pertaining to it. Not until now, that is.

I have this sudden urge to lie to him, and I don't understand why. Fighting against it, I force the words out. "I mean, there have been some things, but it's nothing major. I've been a little spacey lately."

The flicker from earlier resurfaces in my mind.

Yanov beating me and dragging my body across the ground.

I could feel the bruises, feel the impact of his knuckles as they landed on my skin, jarring my bones, dousing my entire body in pain. It felt like a memory, as if I had experienced the events in real time.

"There's no reason to lie to me, Elyse. If you remember something, you can tell me."

I look up at him and stare deep into his penetrating gaze. Yes, I want to know if it was my imagination or a suppressed memory from that night, but I also wonder if that will make things worse. Because what if it was a memory, and what if what I've thought or come to know all along hasn't been the truth at all?

"I'm not lying to you."

His nostrils flare, and his mood sours instantly. "Could've fooled me. You act like you're hiding something."

I press my lips firmly together to stop myself from saying anything else. I already told myself I wouldn't drag him into the Yanov mess, and I don't want to discuss the memories right now. Not with how skittish I've been lately. He might ask other questions, and knowing myself, I'll end up spilling everything by accident.

Lifting my chin, I give him one final, narrow-eyed look before I turn decisively and walk away. "I said I'm fine, and I mean it. Now, if you'll excuse me, I have work to do."

18
SEBASTIAN

Days later, the hallway incident, as I've come to think of it, still bugs me. I step into my bedroom and close the door behind me, running a hand through my hair with a frustrated sigh. Striding over to my minibar, I pour myself a drink and tip it back, letting the whiskey burn a path down my throat as I grapple with shit I have no easy solutions for.

I've been doing my best to ignore her, but Ely always seems to be right in my path. I've considered her words, played them over in my mind a thousand times, and I still feel, in my gut, that she's lying. She remembers something from that night, something that she could use against me, and she doesn't want to tell me because she's afraid. It's the only thing I can think of that fits with her sudden behavior change.

The fear, the forgetfulness, how easily distracted she's become...like she's lost in her head somewhere far away...it's not like her. Even if it isn't her memory returning, something is going on, and I need to figure it out.

When I clench my fists around the lowball glass in my hand, a few drops of cold condensation wash over my fingers, breaking the spell. I throw myself down into the chair near my bed so I don't send the glass flying.

I'm better than this.

Get ahold of yourself, dickface.

Why is every day an even more difficult test of my control? Control of my anger and of other things...my mind immediately shifts to the memory of her kneeling on the floor with my cock in her mouth. I clench my jaw at the sheer need that ripples beneath my skin.

So what? I want her. That's not news. It also doesn't mean I have to act on that desire. In the end, it'll be easier if we continue to avoid one another. It's worked this long; there's no reason it won't continue to. Yeah...if I can stop myself from looking at her, watching her every move, even when she doesn't think I'm watching her.

If I wasn't watching her, I wouldn't have noticed the change in her demeanor. On top of that, I swear she's lost a couple of pounds, and that, coupled with the heavy bags that always seem to be under her eyes, tells me she's not getting enough sleep. Maybe I need to monitor that, as well.

Just in the interest of making sure my employees remain healthy.

I throw back another swallow of whiskey and consider what else I might do to ensure she doesn't go off the rails. Finding a new maid isn't an option. Especially with Tanya sneaking around. No doubt she'd hire someone she can trust, someone I'd never be able to rely on...even for just cleaning. So for now, I need to keep Ely safe and as healthy as I can.

After all, if she's not cleaning or doing what I need her to do, then she's not really working to pay off her father's debt, which is only half the reason she's here. The other half she has yet to discover, and hopefully, she never does because that would change things between us. In a bad way. I finish off my drink and slide the glass onto the bedside table. I need to stop drinking to get a grasp on everything, but without the whiskey to dull my senses and desires, I run the risk of losing control, and control is all that's standing between myself and my little prey.

With that in mind, I stand, button my suit jacket, and head out into the hall.

The house is quiet, but that's okay; I prefer it this way. I'm not particularly interested in seeing Tanya or her pet bodyguard. I doubt he's her fucking bodyguard, anyway.

Well, maybe the fucking part. Heh, heh, heh.

I head downstairs to the back room that houses the security cameras and guards. It's an open space without a door. It leads right into a room with a bank of monitors, with a small armory against the wall and a set of lockers for the guards. A room next door houses some bunks and a small kitchen for them. It's the best I can offer, and at the very least, it stops them from traipsing through the length of the house, making a mess and drawing attention.

I hear one of the guards chuckling softly and stop just outside the entrance.

The first guard nudges guard two and points at the cameras. Quietly, I creep closer to get a better look. They are pointing at an upper hallway, where on the screen the video plays, and I spot Ely in the frame. She tiptoes into the spare room with a bundle of blankets in her arms.

What the hell? I lean against the wall and listen as the first guard laughs again. "She's been doing this for a while now, and the other day, I got curious and went upstairs to check what was going on. I thought she was sleeping in the room, but nothing was out of place when I walked in. The closet door was cracked, so I opened it, and that's when I saw all the blankets piled up. It looked like a damn bird was roosting in there with how she had it all arranged."

The other makes a humming noise and laughs, too. "What a fucking weirdo. Why stay there if she has her own room down here? Wouldn't having an exit make her feel safer?"

I consider what they are saying. Ely is sleeping upstairs in the guest rooms? How did I not know about this? And in the fucking closet, no less. I'm both pissed off and concerned. I'm angry with myself for not noticing. For not knowing about it. Yes, I saw the change in behavior, but I didn't realize other things were going on.

I've been so wrapped up in my own shit and in trying to keep away from her that I missed the biggest sign that something is going on.

"She's weird, sure, but I'd definitely fuck her. Did you see how tight that ass is?"

I lift my gaze and lean my head back against the wall. I concentrate on their words, listening a little bit more intently. I'll let them finish before I fucking destroy them with my presence. Let's see how deep they dig their own graves first.

There's some typing, and I slowly peek around the corner, watching as the first guard points at something on the camera. "But yeah, you're right. They say the craziest ones are the hottest in bed. Any of the women in this house..."

I snap, like a string pulled too tight, and step into the room before they sign their death warrants in earnest. "If I hear either of you utter another word, I'll cut out your tongues." The weight of my knife rests in my hands, and I blink, trying to recall when I pulled it out.

It doesn't matter.

Both men spin in their chairs to face me, bracing their backs against the computer console table. "Sir, you...we didn't..."

"Well, obviously, you fucking didn't know I was here, or you wouldn't have been so damn stupid to talk out of your asses."

The guard on the left gulps, his worried gaze ping-ponging

between my face and the blade. I step closer and lean in a little bit. I want to make certain that both of these fuckers know that Elyse is off-limits to them and everyone else in this house.

"Keep Elyse's name out of your mouths, or I'll ensure you don't speak again. And if you so much as glance at my sister, no one will ever find your bodies. Are we clear?"

Both men nod frantically.

It's starting to feel like I can't trust anyone in this house.

I release a sigh of frustration and fight against the desire to sink my knife into their guts. I need to think rationally and not with murder hazing my mind. I take a step back and weigh my options. Attacking them won't fix the issue, nor will it give me the information I need when it comes to figuring out what the fuck is going on with Elyse.

"I'll deal with Elyse. Your jobs are to find actual threats and make sure no one that isn't supposed to be here gets in or out. Elyse isn't a fucking threat, so forget about her. Put your efforts into other shit."

I'm past the point of annoyance now, and I can't tell if it's because of these fuckers and what they said about Elyse or if it's because she's been sleeping on the floor in the guest room closet. If I'm being honest, neither of those things should evoke such a strong emotion out of me, but when it comes to her, I don't know what's up or down.

Elyse has a chokehold on my emotions and my heart in her tiny little fist.

"I'm sorry, sir. It won't happen again."

"Damn right it won't happen again because if it does, you'll be helping each other put your intestines back in your bodies."

My phone buzzes in my pocket, interrupting my thoughts, and I fish it out. I check the message, noting it's from Bel.

BEL: *Are you coming to dinner, or am I just eating alone?*

I squeeze my eyes shut for all of a second and shake my head at myself. *Fucking shit.* I forgot we were supposed to meet for an early dinner. How the fuck did I forget? I spin the blade around in my hand to point the sharp edge down my forearm and type out a quick response.

ME: *Be there in ten.*

When I turn my attention back to the guards, I stare them down. I really want to fuck with them a little, scare 'em, teach them a lesson, but right now, I need to get to my dinner date with Bel. I hate that I forgot and that she's been waiting. That's not like me at all.

"Get your asses back to work. I'll be checking in with both of you later," I announce, checking my watch before I step out of the room.

All I can do is shake my head in disappointment, mainly toward myself. My fixation with her has backfired on me. While I accomplished avoiding her for the most part, I've failed in other areas. I've missed big things going on right under my own nose and in my own fucking house. Now I'm late for a dinner that I set up. I barely recognize myself right now.

I jog down the hall and toward the exit leading to the garage.

It only takes a minute to hop in the car and speed down the drive to the gate. Once on the road, I slam my foot on the gas. There's little-to-no traffic since everyone is finishing classes. I make it to the restaurant in minutes and leave the car with a valet. We come here often, even Ely, since they have a great to-go coffee counter next to the bar. It's also close to campus, so it's not a surprise to see a good number of students sipping coffee and sharing a meal.

The hostess opens her mouth to greet me, but I shake my head. "The person I'm with already has a table." I find Bel in my line of sight as I peer over the woman's shoulder.

Bel looks up from the table and right at me, her face lighting up instantly. When I reach the table, she shoves herself up and out of her chair and wraps her arms around me, engulfing me in a tight hug. I hug her back, allowing myself to enjoy her touch. Ever since I found out Bel was my sister, small parts of my heart that I was certain would never beat again did just that. Supporting her and caring for her throughout our mother's death brought us closer.

It was because of Bel that I felt I had a purpose. She needed me, and I needed her so fucking much. She just didn't know it.

When she pulls away, I apologize, "Sorry I'm late. I've been distracted." My watch tells me she's been waiting fifteen more minutes since she texted me.

"It's okay. No big deal. It just surprised me since you're hardly ever late." She waves me off and twirls the glass in her hand, sending the coffee and cream mixture swirling with the ice and straw. "I ordered you a whiskey, but I think maybe you should drink some water instead. How much have you had to drink today? You smell like a distillery."

I ignore the way she wrinkles her nose at me, fighting against the prevailing anger building in my gut at her judgment. "You're not my babysitter, Bel. I don't need you to dictate when and what I can drink or eat."

I don't need to look at the menu, so I just wait for the server to return. She glances between us, at me in my Armani suit and Bel in ripped-up jeans and a hoodie with the Oakmount logo printed on the front. I can already see the questions in her mind, but she doesn't ask anything, thankfully. She takes our orders quickly before heading back to the kitchen.

The restaurant is pretty busy, and there's a short line at the coffee stand a few feet away. "How many cups of coffee have you had?"

It's her turn to narrow her eyes. "You're not my babysitter, Sebastian," she mocks, using the same tone I used on her.

"Fine. I get that you're worried about me, but you have

nothing to worry about. I didn't come to dinner so that I could argue with you. I just wanted to share a meal and spend some time together. Can we do that?"

She blinks at me slowly as if asking, *can we*? "Sure. We can do whatever you want."

Her tone still holds a smidge of attitude, but I decide to ignore it and move on.

"Okay, so you said you wanted to talk about something?"

She ducks her chin to her chest like she's insecure, and I watch her carefully. "Yes. I've been thinking about it for a while, and I want to see if I can find my dad. My real dad, that is. Find out who he is...and if he wants to meet me."

My knee-jerk response is to tell her *no* because if he wanted to see her, he would've tried to find her already, but then I remember who I'm talking to. *Bel. My sister.* The light to my darkness. I can't berate her for wanting to know more about her father. And Bel's so stubborn that if I tell her no, she'll do it anyway, and in a way that leaves me out of it. The thought of anything happening to her makes me feral.

"What if he's not a good person? What if you regret meeting him?"

I think back to my own father, the fucking asshole who beat my best friend for most of his life. Who made our lives miserable. Yeah, not a great guy. I was shocked for all of five minutes when I found out the truth, but it didn't stop me from ending his pathetic life. He deserved what he got.

She shrugs and adjusts her glasses. "But what if he's a good guy who has been searching for me?"

I sigh and sip my drink, letting the alcohol burn through some of my anger. We have to change the subject. I'm unstable as it is, and now I have to try to wrap my head around Bel wanting to meet her father. Our mother claimed he was a good man, but he could very well be a terrible person by now. Yeah, doesn't sound like a good idea.

"Let me think about it and see if I have any information that might help. Before we do anything, we need to find out the type of person he is."

She nods and then leans in a little closer, a smile tugging at her lips. "Sooooo...how is Elyse? How did it go in London? Did she love it there?"

A sharp pang of guilt knifes me in the gut. "It was a very short trip, for business only. She didn't get to see much." She actually hadn't gotten to see anything, a fact that makes me wince a bit when I allow myself to think about it. I had been knocked so off-balance by Ely's mouth on my cock and the grimness of the situation surrounding Yanov and Sidorov that I wasted no time getting us back on the plane and home.

"Then why did you take her?"

"I needed help, remember?" It's not a lie, but it's also not the whole truth.

If Bel found out the real intent or discovered how Elyse truly came to be a part of things, she'd lose it. I don't like withholding information from her, but she has no idea about the decisions that must be made on behalf of our family, nor would I ever share that information with her. I decided as soon as I found out she was my sister that I wouldn't let the darkness of our namesake taint her. I haven't done so since that day.

Her green eyes narrow with suspicion. "I remember, but I also think you could have taken Lee, or Aries, or any other one of your ridiculous friends. They can fend off the cougars just as well."

I scoff. "My ridiculous friends are your ridiculous friends, remember?"

"Don't remind me. Things have been crazy busy, and I haven't seen her lately. Is she doing okay?"

It's my turn to shrug. "I guess. No one told me she's dead."

"Seriously?" Some of the light leaves her eyes. "I can't... What is wrong with you?"

"Okay, maybe that was harsh." I swallow thickly. "To be honest, it's not like I sit around waiting to see what she's doing. We don't talk regularly. She cleans and goes to class. Why would I know about how she's doing?"

"Oh well... I guess I just thought..." There's a certain reluctance to her voice.

"What," I snap, losing my patience. "You thought what?"

She frowns, shaking her head, and I hate to see her withdraw from me right before my eyes.

I grimace. This is Elyse's fault. I haven't been the same since that trip to London. She's under my skin, in my lungs, and in my head. I take a calming breath and gentle my tone.

"What did you think, Bel?"

She stares down at her coffee, not even looking up at me when she speaks. "It's nothing. She's just different—super sweet and kind. The two of you seemed to be spending a little time together. I thought that meant you liked her, and that maybe you'd stop sleeping around with all The Mill bunnies."

Trying my best to stifle the frustration I'm feeling on the subject, I pinch the bridge of my nose and breathe through the anger. I remind myself that Bel doesn't know anything about Elyse and me. She doesn't know a lick of how I came to be the head of the family.

"First, I haven't slept with anyone who hangs around *The Mill* in months. Second, Elyse isn't anything to me. We haven't been spending time together. She works for me, remember? I'm her boss, and ethics and morals aside, to sleep with her would be breaking every rule there is. Never mind the fact that she's the fucking maid. I told you she went with me to London because I needed help. She did her part. It wasn't a date. It wasn't anything."

Bel's gaze shifts away from me, and her lips part like she wants to say something, but I don't want to hear it right now. I need her to understand, to fully grasp the concept that there is no *us.* Elyse and I do not exist, nor will we ever. "No. Let me finish, please. I need you to understand so you stop pushing the matter. Elyse means nothing to me. She's my employee, and that's it." Bel looks back at me, her eyes hard, and I get the feeling she doesn't believe me.

Fuck. "She's the fucking maid, for God's sake. You don't think I might aim a little higher?"

That hits the nail on the head. Bel's mouth snaps shut, her eyes glaring. "And I think I've had enough of your asshole attitude for the day."

I grit my teeth, pressing my lips together. *Why do I keep fucking things up?* Bel shoves out of her chair and gestures to something, or maybe even someone over my shoulder.

Shifting in my chair, I notice Elyse standing there, her delicate features pinched tight like someone slapped her. There's no guessing whether she heard what I said. All I can do is shake my head in disappointment, at myself, at this entire fucking situation.

I open my mouth to speak. To say what, I don't know. Not that it matters since Elyse whirls around on her worn sneakers and disappears in the flurry of bodies. As soon as she's out of sight, the guilt trickles in. My stomach twists into a knot of despair that I can't untangle. I look back at the table, wondering how I can fix this.

Bel throws some cash down even though she knows I always pay, and when I spot the disappointment shining in her eyes, I find it hard to breathe. "When you're done being a dick, come find me so we can actually talk. But not until after you apologize to Elyse."

I sit in silence, watching as she walks out of the restaurant.

Fuck. I don't feel like myself anymore. I'm even more careless than usual, and now it's fucking up my relationship with Bel. The only person I really give two shits about. I have to fix this, even if it's only to make Bel happy.

It doesn't matter if what I said was or wasn't true. The further I can push Elyse away, the easier this will all be. If anything, I made things easier for myself. But easier for me doesn't change the fact that by saying those things, I've hurt Bel because Elyse is her friend.

I don't want to do it, but I know I have no other option if I expect Bel to talk to me ever again. As much as I need Elyse to hate me so that I don't lose control and claim her like I've wanted to every night since London, I can't lose my sister.

So even if it pains me, I know she's right. I have to apologize to Elyse. I just hope she doesn't look too deeply into things because I don't know if I can continue to fight against my impulse to claim her. I want her so badly that some days it physically hurts me.

All of this would be easier if I could play my part as the evil monster in her story, but I can't. Not when I want to be the predator who hunts down all those who have hurt her, forcing her to be at my side and trapping her in a cage of gold that she'll never escape.

19

ELYSE

She's the fucking maid. Just the fucking maid.

I shake my head as I cross the street, walking back toward campus. There's a shorter route, but I could use the walking time to clear my head right now.

I can't let what Sebastian said bother me. Even if it really fucking does.

Not when I know deep down what I felt couldn't possibly have been fake. Yeah, he might see me as "*just the maid,*" but he definitely feels something for me. He's just too stubborn to admit it. A shiver skates down my spine, courtesy of my constant paranoia, and I turn to look over my shoulder, reminding myself to stay vigilant. Yanov is still out there, and I don't intend to fall into his hands again.

I sip my iced coffee, but I've lost my appetite after Sebastian's words. It's not the part about calling me a maid or even the part where he said I meant nothing that really hurt. It's the coldness in his tone when he spoke about me. Completely devoid of warmth, of the heat he had in his voice that night at the club as I stared up at him.

I shake the memory away and take another sip of the coffee.

A hand lands on my shoulder, and I spin, slapping the hold away.

Bel bounces back, hands up in surrender. "Whoa, ninja, sorry. I didn't mean to scare you."

My heart is still clogging my throat, leaving me unable to speak once I realize it's her. When I shake the fear off, I brace my free hand against my belly and breathe. *Crap.* She wouldn't have scared me so much if I hadn't been thinking about Yanov literally two seconds ago.

Once I catch my breath and my heart rate returns to a normal rhythm, I give her a small smile. "No, it's okay. Sorry I'm so jumpy. I don't know what's gotten into me," I lie.

She smiles, dropping her hands. "Don't apologize, girl. You have no reason to be sorry. If anything, it's me who should be sorry. For my brother's shitty attitude and poor manners."

I frown. "I didn't mean to ruin your dinner."

She waves me off. "You didn't ruin anything. He did. Plus, he was super late and irritated before you even appeared."

I let out a long sigh, finally feeling calmer. "Yeah. Okay."

"Do you want to talk about it?"

Do I want to talk about the fact that my super-hot boss, who I want to climb like a tree, is disgusted by my presence? *No. Not really.*

"I don't see the point in talking about it. It seems pretty straightforward to me. No need to beat a dead horse."

She tilts her head to study me. "Are you sure? I thought something was developing between you two."

"We aren't even friends, Bel. He's been kind most of the time, but that's it. And that's probably only because you and I are friends."

I'm not sure if she buys it. A glint of suspicion lingers in her eyes. "Okay, well, would you want to go"—she waves at my still mostly full coffee—"get some food with that coffee?"

This is to keep me awake, in the hopes I can try to sleep in my own room tonight. Sleeping on the floor in the closet is killing me. Not that I'm about to tell her that. "I would love to, but I had a late lunch."

We stand together on the sidewalk. I can feel her gaze roving over me, but I can't look at her. "Did you need something else?"

She shakes her head, and then a shadow cuts between us. I nearly startle but calm myself when I see it's just Drew, her obsessed boyfriend, walking up behind her. He snakes an arm around her waist and tugs her back into his chest. She smiles, and I can see the love shining in her eyes. His nose skims the side of her throat, and his lips move against her ear, but I don't know what he says.

Whatever it is makes Bel's cheeks pinken.

Pulling back with a smirk, he finds my eyes immediately, pinning me to the spot. "Elyse, right?"

I nod once, swallowing nervously. It's not an easy thing being the focus of Drew's attention. I'm not sure how Bel can stand it.

"What's going on?" he questions, sensing my dismay.

Bel chimes in first. "Sebastian. He's being an asshole again, so I'm being a good friend and making sure I don't have to get a shovel and start digging him an early grave." She winks at me.

Drew's gaze roves over me again, but not in a sexual way. It's more like he's assessing me. "Unfortunately, asshole is his default setting. All I can say is don't take it personally. It's definitely a Sebastian problem and no one else's."

I shrug. "Yeah, I don't. If I did, then I'd be in a mental hospital with the shit he puts me through, but anyway... you two get back to doing whatever it is you were doing."

Bel reaches out and snags my free hand. "Wait. Please. Are you sure you're okay? Is there anything we can do to help?"

Drew glances at her over her head like he did not sign up for helping the maid, but Bel plows on, oblivious to him. "I mean it. We're friends, and I'm here for you."

I nod once, trying to give her the smile that I know will ease some of her worries. "I'm okay, Bel. I've dealt with worse people in my life than your brother. He can't say or do anything that hasn't already happened to me or that I haven't heard at least once before." Even as I say the words, the echo of him calling me *nothing* plays on repeat in my head.

It's going to be a while until I come to terms with it. It doesn't matter. I've done my best to avoid him lately, and I'll continue to do so until my debt is paid or I find another way to clear it and get out of this whole terrible town.

Bel sighs, and Drew tugs her hand away from mine. "I know you want to save everyone, but you can't. Leave the girl alone, Wallflower."

The slight edge to his tone scares me, but Bel doesn't seem to notice or care, for that matter, because her eyes remain on me.

"Stay out of it," Bel mumbles to him. Then she continues to me, "If you need anything, and I mean anything at all, you know where to find me. I'm always here for you."

"I know, and I appreciate your friendship, but I'm okay. I promise."

She hugs me wearily and then releases me, and I turn and start walking again. After a few minutes, I turn around, half expecting her to chase me, but she and Drew are gone now. I can finally relax. I love Bel and her kind little heart, but she tries too hard sometimes. Some people you just can't fix; they have to fix themselves, and while I might be in need of fixing myself, I like all my broken pieces just fine. Sometimes it's not the whole pieces that make you who you are, but the broken, chipped, and mismatched pieces you force together that make you...*you*.

I won't deny that I thought maybe Sebastian and I might fit our broken pieces together in a way that might make a whole, but that ship has sailed now. I refuse to pine after a man who clearly doesn't want me. I pick up my pace, trying to get back home.

No. Not home. It's just the place where I'm keeping a few destroyed things for now. Sebastian's house is no longer my home, and I'll never be safe inside those four walls again. Not with the knowledge that Yanov got inside, even if it was only long enough to destroy my room. It leaves me wondering how safe I am in other parts of the house.

Yanov isn't afraid of anything, and I know he'll do it again. Hurting and scaring me are all he lives for. I just hope, even if I'm *nothing* to Sebastian, that he won't let Yanov take me. Even if it's only out of a sense of challenge...to his property, no doubt—even if that's all it is, I'll take it.

After a few minutes, I find myself back on the estate grounds. I jog up the driveway, and when I reach the front door, I slip inside. I head straight through the kitchen, down the back hall, and into the hallway leading to my room. It's chilly down here since I haven't turned the heat on.

With trembling fingers, I unlock the door to my room, shove it open, and survey the scene.

I check the toothpick I placed at the top hinge. It's not broken, so...no one was here.

The relief I feel makes me lightheaded. Inside the room, I stare at the neatly made bed and then back at the stack of ripped-up books. I'll have to use them for now since I can't afford to get different ones.

Gingerly, I take a seat on the edge of the bed and place my plastic coffee cup on the bedside table before I fall back against the mattress. I stare up at the ceiling, wondering what the hell I'm doing. This room has lost its appeal, its safe aura. But it's the first place that was all mine, where I felt okay for a period. Now it's been tainted, and I don't know how to fix it. Or if I even can.

The only way I'll feel secure again is if Yanov disappears, if he forgets my existence.

Did he come at my father's order?

I haven't seen him since the night he beat me into unconsciousness and shot me. *Thankfully.* But just because he hasn't reached out or initiated a conversation doesn't mean he's not out there, looking for a way to make my life worse hell than it already is.

You're going to be okay. Everything is going to be okay.

That's been my mantra for months, and it's worked well until that night at the club. I wrap my arms around myself, trying to shake away the feeling of being watched. Ants march down my spine, making me shiver. The longer I think about it, the worse my thoughts become. Fear begins to claw open my chest, and I heave myself off the bed, crashing into the opposite wall.

I tried to do it. I tried, but I can't. I can't stay in this room.

What if he finds me while I'm sleeping? The fear spikes, reaching its height, and I rush into the hall, up the stairs, and into the kitchen. It's a relief that it's still empty. The last thing I need is to run into Sebastian or Tanya right now.

Not wanting to chance a run-in with either of them, I grab some leftovers I know neither will touch and slip out the side door onto the patio that leads out to the lawn. There's one other place I can go to hide away from the rest of the world that makes me calm and brings me joy. A place that I doubt Yanov would ever think to look for me.

The abandoned groundskeeper's cottage. It's where I house all my *"pets,"* as Sebastian calls them. The mere reminder of his name sends me into a tizzy. He's so patronizing and dismissive. Why does he care if rescuing little animals and nursing them back to health makes me feel better?

It's not my fault he doesn't have the ability to show compassion, at least outside his own needs. I'm glad no one told him about the dog I've been caring for.

I found him wandering the property a couple of nights ago. He was limping, so I assume he has a sprained paw or something. I've been trying to get out to the cottage to check on him more than once a day, but that's proven to be difficult.

I'll just have to try harder.

I rush down the slope of the lawn toward the old groundskeeper's cottage. I'm focused on the task of getting there inside, so much so that I miss the man dressed in all black popping up out of nowhere.

He cuts into my path, forcing me to stop or run directly into him. I dig my feet into the ground, stopping at the last second. I'm a bubble of fear that's ready to pop. I only manage to pull myself together when I realize it's just one of the security guards and not some masked stalker who's coming to kidnap me. One glance at the guard's face and recognition blooms.

He's the usual guard on patrol when I sneak out here. His blue eyes fill with concern as they roam my face. *Robin*...I think is his name.

"You okay?" He greets me.

I straighten my shoulders and stand a little taller, trying to look less exhausted and afraid. "Yeah, I'm fine. Just checking on Cobalt."

"I heard him barking earlier, but I didn't know if you had told the boss about him yet, so I led the other guard away just in case. Hopefully, he's feeling better soon."

I beam up at him. "Thank you. It looks like it's just a sprain. I'm hoping he'll be all healed up in a couple of days. I'm sure it helps that he doesn't have to go scavenge for food."

He tucks his hands into his protective vest and nods. "Of course. Just try to keep him from barking."

I nod once and head to the cottage.

It's a rustic place but serviceable. There are two rooms, one a big open space where I spot Cobalt sitting on a worn rug. A sleeping bag is rolled up on the hearth, and I tug on it and lay it out flat.

"Come here, boy. Lie down. You need to rest."

Cobalt lets out a loud yipping bark, and I clamp my hand over his muzzle.

"Shhhh, Buddy. Be quiet. If Mr. Grumpypants finds out I've rescued another animal, he's going to lose his mind." I check his brace, which looks good. "There. Good boy. I'll lie down with you for a while. I could use the company."

I run my hand up his long muzzle to the top of his head and then to his left ear and give him some scratches. He leans into my touch, and that makes me smile as well as eases some of the tension in my muscles. Why are animals so much easier to deal with than humans? At least with animals, I know what they want from me. *Food. Care. Attention.* Easy enough.

People are the hard ones.

I use both hands to scratch his ears, and then I place a kiss on the top of his muzzle. It's a little dusty, so I bet he was sniffing around this place while I was gone.

Once I take a seat on the bag, he turns, scruffs his feet into the fabric to bunch it up, turns again, and then lies down right over my ankles.

All I can do is laugh. "You dork. Those are my feet. They will fall asleep if you lie on them."

He regards me with steady brown eyes, and I imagine him telling me he doesn't give a shit. I snuggle into the sleeping bag, exhaustion pressing down on me.

If I lie here for a bit, I'll feel better.

I can always go back into the house in a couple of hours. It's not like I can sneak into the closet to sleep until everyone else is in bed, anyway, or at least retreating to their rooms for the night.

I tug Cobalt closer so I can nuzzle him. He obliges, curling his body against mine, and I stroke his back gently. With each stroke, my eyes grow heavier. It doesn't take long for my exhaustion to overpower the caffeine roaring in my veins.

Okay, maybe I lied. I'll just take a tiny nap.

20
SEBASTIAN

Apologizing sucks dick, and not just any dick, but dick that's been wrapped in razor wire. To apologize is to take accountability for your actions and admit you were wrong. If you ask me, I have no issue doing either, mainly because I'm usually never wrong.

Except in this instance.

I've fought against myself, agonizing over how I would approach Elyse and wondering exactly what she heard. If I apologize, it will mean that what I said was a lie, which might make things worse, but if I don't apologize, then Bel may never talk to me again.

Okay, that's a lie; she'll probably talk to me at some point, but knowing she's disappointed in me eats away at my resolve.

It makes me feel slimy and bad.

But being an asshole to Elyse isn't the only place I went wrong. I missed the entire thing with Yanov. When she moved into the house, a house I still can't really think of as mine, I checked her out.

Both on paper and in person, she's everything that she portrays herself to be.

Kind. Studious. Never been in any type of trouble.

Everything lines up. The only issue I now have is where Yanov fits into the puzzle.

There's nothing about him in her paperwork; nor did her father mention him. It's like he appeared out of thin air, which makes me uneasy and feel like I'm missing something.

So while apologies might be outside my capacity, at least for now, maybe I can feel better if I find another way to fix things. To keep her safe and out of that sick fuck's hands. I snag my phone off the bed and switch the drink into my other hand to scroll through my contacts. Information is king in the world that I live in. If you know things about someone, you can use it against them. When I reach Grady's number, my PI, I hit the call button. It's late, but for how much I pay him, he should be available to take my calls at any time, day or night.

The phone rings for a while, and when he doesn't answer, I call again.

"What? For fuck's sake, what?" the deep Irish voice barks through the line.

"You talk to all your clients that way, Grady?"

There's a pause. "I didn't check the name, but considering the time, I'm not fecking apologizin'."

I don't give a shit, so I press on. "I need all the information you can get me about a man named Yanov. Works for Sidorov, the flesh merchant."

Another long pause. "You got anything else? Something to go off that isn't a couple of names that sound like damn characters from *Game of Thrones*?"

I roll my eyes. He's always such an asshole when I wake him up. "Yanov is a cop here in town, and he's friends with...likely working under an officer named Silver...at the police department."

"That's better. I can work with that. How fast do you need the information?"

"As soon as you can get it. I've got this guy eyeing something that belongs to me, and I'm not about to let him blindside me when he tries to take it."

There's some shuffling on his end, and I wait.

"I'll call you when I get something that will help him see things your way."

"Do. The usual rate, of course."

He curses softly, too soft for me to make out the words. "Fine. Usual rate."

He cuts the call without a goodbye, and I toss my phone back on the rumpled covers. I tell myself this is so I stay prepared, but really, I know it's all for her. I miscalculated. I didn't anticipate her worming her way under my skin, and I didn't expect to be attracted to her goodness like a bee to a bloom.

Now I'm the one left guilt-ridden, feeling like an asshole for doing everything I can to keep distance between us. For shutting down other people's thoughts on *"us"* when there is no *"us,"* and not because there couldn't be, but because there can't be. I know my words hurt her. I fucking know that, and I know I need to apologize, but I can't help but think how apologizing will have the opposite effect on things.

On top of that, I've been meaning to have a conversation with her about what I overheard the guards discussing. I know now that she's no longer sleeping in her room, but instead in a closet inside one of the spare rooms.

No matter how much I try to convince myself that it's none of my concern, the less I believe it, and the more annoyed I become at the prospect of her sleeping on the floor in a closet when she has a perfectly good bed downstairs. *Does it have something to do with Yanov?* I haven't forgotten his threat, and in the midst of everything else happening this week, I've been waiting for the other shoe to drop. It's the other reason I'm strung so tight.

Irritation zips across my skin. It's easier during the day to keep my mind busy, to focus on other things and forget that she exists. Once night comes and the restraint holding my patience and tolerance for bullshit is thread-thin...it snaps.

Fragments of her goodness, of that sunshine personality, seep through the cracks in my mind and do their best to poison everything—if goodness can be a toxin, that is.

I check my watch. It's late, and the house is quiet. *Too quiet.* I take a sip of whiskey and allow another minute to pass. I keep my gaze trained on the liquor in the glass, if only to give myself something to focus on, something to keep my ass in the armchair and away from Elyse. I'll lose my fucking mind if I find her in that closet down the hall, so the best thing to do is keep my ass in the chair and do nothing.

After the events at Pound of Flesh and the aftermath, including the new closet development, she continues to keep her distance. I know I should be grateful since it's for the best, but in the evenings, when I'm at my weakest, she has a habit of entering my mind. I look forward to our sparring matches and seeing the fear and desire pool in her baby-blue eyes. Fuck, it makes my cock hard just thinking about it.

I switch gears and force myself to think of something else. The plan with Sidorov didn't go well, but I know one person who wants this life and the power I hold. I just don't know if I have the stomach to turn it over to her. Not after what she's done.

Memories assault me, and I squeeze my eyes closed, forcing the thoughts into the past where they belong so they don't take over in my drunken state. Bare flesh sliding on bare flesh flashes in my mind nonetheless, and I flinch. *No.* I can't go back there. I can't be reminded of how weak and powerless I was.

She no longer controls me. No longer owns me.

I force measured breaths into my lungs. Some will say I need to see a therapist; others will question how I can stand to be within ten feet of her after all she's done to me, but none of them will understand the basic desire to simply forget. To want simplicity. I don't need to heal from my trauma. I don't even require justice, really. I just want to forget it ever happened. A humorless laugh escapes me. That's where Elyse got lucky by losing her memories from that night.

The memories twist and contour in my mind, but it's not Tanya lingering at the fringes who makes my stomach curl—it's Elyse. Memories of her slam into me—the way her pouty lips looked wrapped around my cock and how she clenched her thighs together like she wanted to be there on her knees just as much as I wanted her there.

It's an illusion.

I blink away the memory, then stand and cross the room to the bar. I refill my drink, the liquid settling perilously close to the top.

Why can't I stop thinking about her? About that night?

It was nothing but a blow job, one of many I've had in my life, but somehow it was the best fucking one I've ever had. Maybe I need to get laid? Yeah, that's probably what it is. I've forgotten what decent sex is like.

My phone chimes from on top of the rumpled bedding. I'm a little groggy as I cross the room and check the notification that's popped up on the screen.

Shit. It's security. The need for sleep is driven away with the spike of adrenaline that's been injected into my veins. I gently slide my glass onto the bedside table, then snatch the device off the sheets, open it, and check the text. It's from my head of security, Rambo.

Rambo: *We've got movement out at the old groundskeeper's cottage.*

I clench the phone tight in my hand. My first thought is Yanov. *Is it possible he's been hiding out there?* I didn't have it searched since I know Elyse likes to sneak her little charity projects out there. That and the thought of being notified every single time she's out there would drive me insane, but now I'm worried I've made another mistake. That there's been a security breach, or worse, that I missed something important.

I type out a quick response and hit send.

Me: *On my way.*

I tuck my phone into my gray sweatpants and adjust my black T-shirt. Before I leave the room, I throw on a hoodie and slip my feet into a pair of sneakers. It's easier to go down and check it out myself. I doubt it's anything serious and definitely not worth sending the entire team out to investigate, but on the off chance that it is something serious...

...it's better to be safe than sorry.

I pause in the doorway and look back at the bedside table where I keep a handgun loaded and ready for whenever I might need it. I think about grabbing it, but instead, I walk back to the bed and snake my hand under the pillow.

My fingers clutch onto the knife hidden there in its leather sheath. It takes me a second to buckle it around my ankle, but there's no describing the sudden rush of relief I feel at bringing it with me. I doubt I'll need it, but if I do, at least it's there. My security men carry guns on them, but I prefer a more hands-on approach. Hence the knife being my weapon of choice. It's ironic when you think about it. Head of a multibillion-dollar arms-dealing franchise, and I choose to carry around a knife.

It doesn't take me long to find myself at the patio doors that lead off the ballroom. I slip outside and move down the slightly sloped lawn toward the cabin. The air holds a chill, reminding me fall will be here soon. In the distance, I spot the cottage. It's run-down and hasn't been maintained in many years, as the mansion hasn't had a groundskeeper who stays on-site in over a decade. Not that it matters. The inside still holds furniture, and I know Ely keeps it as clean as she can for her little animals.

Not that they give a shit.

At the bottom of the hill, I spot two of my men. They stand about ten feet away from the cottage, their flashlights pointed at the ground.

I stop when I reach them. "What's going on?"

The one guard, fuck I can't remember his name, or maybe I never knew it, though he looks vaguely familiar, answers. "We were doing our roving patrol, as Rambo asked us to do. That's when we spotted a light on through the window. We haven't been inside yet."

I nod and scan the cabin. It's small, two rooms if I remember correctly. Nothing much more than a bedroom and open living area with a kitchenette. The building is livable, but the roof leaks, and it smells like wood and dirt. Or at least it did when I was a kid.

"I'll check it out. You guys stay behind me."

They share an apprehensive look. "Sir..."

I wave them off. "Don't bother. Just stay behind me unless I say something."

They step into place behind me as I stride toward the cottage door. I check the knob, giving it a little twist, and surprisingly, it's locked. Whoever's hiding inside was smart enough to lock the door. It only takes a minute for me to grab the spare key I keep hidden under the frog figurine on the porch. Plucking the key from its hiding spot, I unlock the door and then twist the knob, pushing the door open gently.

Faint candlelight glows from the far side of the room by the empty fireplace. I freeze when I see a familiar face, her angelic features reflecting back at me in the dim light, her tiny body sprawled out on a sleeping bag.

What the hell is she doing out here?

The tension in my body eases, and I let out a sigh. Twisting around, I wave security on, letting them know there is no threat.

"Continue your patrol. It's not a threat. Just one of my other employees."

They don't argue with me, taking my word for what it is, and turn to walk back toward the mansion, while I slip back inside the cottage. The place still smells of dirt and nature. I can't help but wrinkle my nose.

Why would she subject herself to this? Is her room not good enough? The thought turns the blood in my veins to lava. If I find out she's sleeping out here with these animals, I will punish her even if it shatters my self-control.

My attention catches on a small cat that sits on the mantel of the fireplace across the room, its orange fur barely visible in the low candlelight.

I can't stand animals. They're messy and demanding of attention, two things I have no patience for. I catch the low rumble of a growl as I inch closer to Elyse, and then I spot the culprit, a black dog poking its face out of a small blanket near her knee.

"Watch it, Mutt," I whisper as I crouch beside her. "Bite me, and it'll be the last thing you do."

My gaze moves from the dog to Elyse, and for one fleeting second, I do nothing but stare. She is beautiful but in the simplest of ways, without any fillers or makeup. I allow myself to memorize each inch of her delicate face, her pouty lips, and button nose. A whimper escapes her lips, and worry lines crease her forehead.

Dammit. I try to remind myself that she's none of my concern, but I'm sure we both can see how well that's going. My thoughts shift, and I'm back to thinking of my original question.

Why the hell is she out here?

Maybe she fell asleep while taking care of the animals, although that's pretty unlikely. She's been out here numerous times and never fallen asleep. *Is there something else going on?* I consider the alternative. Is she hiding out here to avoid me? With Yanov sniffing around, this is the last place she should be. I can't protect her if I have no idea where she is. No one would even be able to hear her scream for help if he decided to show up and take her.

The mere thought sets fire to my blood.

Mine. She is mine. My property.

I nudge her shoulder. "Wake up, Elyse."

Nothing.

I shove a little harder this time, and that does the trick. She wakes with a squeak, then scrambles backward into a sitting position, rubbing at her eyes. "Sebastian?"

"Expecting someone else?"

"What?" She blinks slowly, then scans the room, relaxing when her surroundings come into focus. "What are you doing out here?"

I shove at the bag with my hand. "I don't think you're in any position to be asking the questions. Now why don't you tell me what the hell *you're* doing sleeping out here?"

My protective instinct when it comes to this girl is mental. She's not my fucking problem, but for some reason, I can't sit back and let her be.

Sleep still clings to her eyes, and her dark hair is matted and sticking up on the side where she was lying on it. "I wasn't *sleeping* out here. I fell asleep while taking care of Bow."

The little black mutt lifts his head and blinks his big brown eyes at her when she says his name. Even the homeless, emaciated dog is smitten with her.

I shake my head and remind myself why I came out here in the first place.

"For some reason, I don't believe you."

"I'm not asking you to believe me."

My patience for her bullshit is stretched thin as it is. I didn't expect her to come to me and tell me why she's been sleeping in the closet, but finding her hiding out here asleep leaves me even more on edge. She claims it's because of the mutt, but I know better. She's going to tell me what's going on before we leave this cottage.

I suck a slow, steady breath in through my nose and try to calm myself. "Anyone ever tell you that you're a shit liar?"

She looks confused, but I know it's a front. "No. But I don't really care what other people say about me."

I'm reminded of the words I spoke to Bel. The words that she overheard. Do I apologize now? I'm so caught up in my own mind. Fuck me. Elyse has a terrible habit of winding me all up and making me lose my fucking mind.

"What's been going on with you lately?"

"What are you talking about?"

"Don't play stupid with me. You know exactly what I'm talking about." I pin her with a glare.

She sits up a little straighter, flecks of doubt and suspicion appearing in her eyes. "I don't."

I smirk and reach for her, the need to touch her in some capacity overcoming me. It's a terrible idea because I know the moment I touch her, the more I'll crave her, but I can't be denied. Gripping her chin between my fingers, I force her to look at me. Really look at me. "I'll give you one opportunity to tell me the truth, Ely. One chance. That's all you're getting, and remember it's one more chance than I typically give to others."

21
SEBASTIAN

One chance.

Her little throat bobs, and I know I've caught her. Trapped her. I can practically see the panic bubbling to the surface, and she tries to look away, but I pinch her chin a little harder, stopping her.

"Now, tell me, Prey. What has caused you to start sleeping in the closet versus the bedroom I provided you in the staff quarters?"

"I...." Her lips tremble, and I'm tempted to bite them just to see if she tastes as pure and sweet as she looks at this very moment. When I look back into her eyes, I see ice-filled lakes of fear, and that makes me pause. My stomach churns, the whiskey I drank threatening to climb up my throat. My thoughts go to the worst.

Something happened. Something bad. Something she doesn't trust me enough to tell me. And of course not, why should she trust me?

As much as I love seeing her vulnerable, all her hard layers peeled back to expose her softness, I'm the only one allowed to break her down. I'm the only one allowed to taste her fear.

"Tell me. Now," I grit out, trying my best to keep my voice soft.

She looks at me defiantly. "It's not your problem. I'm just the maid. Remember?"

That stings, but I deserve it. I'm an asshole.

The longer we stare at one another, the more I see how much my words hurt her. How could she ever believe she is merely the maid?

Oh, I don't know, idiot. You treat her like it.

I could kick myself in the ass right now as I search my mind for the right words to say. I didn't think I'd be put on the spot to apologize, but I find it admirable that she expects me to and holds me accountable.

She remains staring, exuding beauty and patience.

I exhale. "Okay, I'm not good at this, but well... I'm sorry. I didn't mean it badly. You know, what you heard me say to Bel. I don't think you're just the maid."

"I would believe you, but I don't think you even believe yourself," she challenges me.

What the fuck? Are we even still talking about the apology, or is this something else?

"You don't get to tell me what I do or don't believe. I'm apologizing to you, and instead of accepting my apology, you're critiquing it."

She shrugs one shoulder. "Don't apologize unless you mean what you're saying. I don't accept half-hearted apologies."

"Then don't accept it. I don't really give a shit."

"Sure, whatever." She frowns, then schools her expression. "Apology done; you can leave, conscience free of any wrongdoing."

"What the hell is wrong with you?" I growl, surprised by her change in attitude and response. I won't lie. I kind of expected her to accept the apology and move on. Instead, she's throwing it in my face, and I don't like it.

"Nothing is wrong with me. I'm just done letting you believe that I don't see things for what they are. I'm tired of pretending since we both know you didn't come out here to apologize or make sure I'm okay. Since we know *'maid'* status doesn't get that kind of treatment, I figure what's the point."

"Look, I said I was sorry. You misinterpreted what you heard."

"And I told you I don't accept your apology, so let's move on."

I shake my head because my only other option is to grab her by the throat and kiss the fuck out of her, and that's not going to help either of us right now.

"Outside of apologizing, I came out here because security sent me an alert that someone was in the cottage. I figured it was you, so I told them I'd come and check it out myself."

"Great, well, you checked, and all is well. As you can see." She gestures at herself.

"Yeah, I don't really believe that, and if you're trying to evade the question I asked earlier, I'm not leaving until you tell me what the hell is going on."

There's no witty comeback or immediate response, and my heart sinks into my stomach as the seconds drag. Her gaze darts from mine, and I see raw shame filling her blue eyes. She can hide from everyone else, but she can't hide from me.

"Elyse," I warn. "I'm trying really fucking hard to let you tell me what happened and not force it out of you, but my patience only goes so far."

"I know." Her voice wobbles.

"Then tell me what happened so I can try to help."

She releases a harsh breath, her body sagging. "Fine, but I'm only telling you because you're making me and not because I want you to do anything."

I nod in agreement, and she speaks again. "When we returned from the trip, a couple of days after or something like that, I came home from classes and found my room trashed. I thought maybe it was you trying to get even with me."

"What? Why would I?" I pause, and then it dawns on me. *The suits.* She thought I would be getting revenge on her. "Sorry, continue..."

She exhales slowly. "I was going to find you and give you a piece of my mind, but I decided instead to clean up the room first. Cool off a little. Then I found a note."

Her entire body quivers at the confession, her gaze far away.

"A note from who?" I have a sneaking suspicion, but I need her to say it just to be sure. To make it real.

She looks away. "Yanov."

Fuck. I release her with a snarl and shove to my feet. *How did he get in the house?* I thrust a hand through my hair and start pacing the small room so I don't return to my bedroom, grab my gun, and hunt the fucker down myself.

My thoughts are going a million miles an hour. How did this happen? Why didn't my security tell me?

I should've anticipated this, should've been prepared.

"And this is why I didn't want to say anything to begin with. I'm not looking for sympathy or help. I have it figured out already; in fact, I'm going to handle it myself," Elyse tells me almost proudly. *Or fucking stubbornly.*

I let out a dark, humorless chuckle. "You're going to handle it? By doing what? Waiting in the trap he set for you? By offering to suck my cock again? By begging him pretty please to let you go?"

Stupid, stupid girl.

She wrinkles her nose at me. "There's no need to be mean. I said I'm going to deal with it, and I will. I'm not some princess in need of rescuing."

I snort. "Good, because this isn't a Disney movie, Elyse. This is real life. Real fucking life. Life-and-death."

"You say that like I don't know what it's like to be on the fringes of death. News flash, Sebastian, but I've been dealing with Yanov for the better portion of my life. I'll take care of it."

The more she tries to push me away and dismiss her own safety, the more pissed off I become. No, she doesn't need to be rescued, but that doesn't mean I'll stand by and let her get hurt either.

I shake my head. "I don't care what happened in the past. I don't give a fuck if you dealt with him by yourself or with an army of people. You aren't alone now. You're protected." I let out a sigh of frustration. "Why didn't you think to tell me?"

She stares at me like I'm stupid. "What good would telling you have done?"

"A lot of things."

"What? Like what you're doing now? No, thank you, and I don't really want a replay of what happened in London." Color climbs into her cheeks. "Sorry, but I don't need to be reminded that I'm only here to satisfy my father's debt either. You've told me many times over. I'd much rather just deal with it on my own. And it doesn't really matter anyway; nothing else has happened."

"*Yet*," I hiss. "Nothing's happened yet."

She corrects me. "Nothing would've happened anyway. I've been careful. Secretive. Did you forget I survived all this time without your protection? I'd rather have no protection than have you offer me safety out of pity."

Pity? I wish I could show her that the last thing I see when I look at her is pity. I don't pity her. I envy her because she's so much stronger than me. Stronger than a lot of people.

"It's my job to protect you, Ely, and I can't protect you if I don't know what's going on."

The possessive need to protect and claim her in every way

possible eats away at my crumbling resolve. *Mine. She is fucking mine.* Yet only mine because of a debt her piece-of-shit father owes. Not because she actually belongs to me in any real sense of the word.

"It's not your job to protect me. It's your job to make sure I'm capable of repaying my father's debt to you."

The anger in my veins boils over. Elyse might not be mine in the true sense of the word, but she's not his, either, and I'll be damned if I stand by and let her *protect* herself. That's my job, as her owner, as her boss. As a fucking human. And I'll start by making sure I can keep an eye on her at all times.

Crossing the space separating us, I reach down and wrap my arms around her middle. Her expression turns wary, and she tries to squirm out of my grasp.

"What are you doing?" She squeaks as I secure my grip and pluck her off the floor, tossing her over my shoulder. Shoving at my back with her hands, she tries to get me to release her and starts cursing at me.

"Keep cursing at me, and I'll fill that mouth with something you won't be able to talk around." I swat her hard on the ass, and she releases a whimper. "Your own safety might mean jack shit to you, but it means something to me, so shut up and let me do what I'm going to do."

"Safety?" her voice is lower now but still full of indignation. "As nice as it is for you to show even a morsel of concern about me, I think it's clear that your security standards and capacity for keeping me safe need revisiting. Then again, what do I know? It's not like he already got into the house, destroyed my bedroom, and ruined my belongings."

Touché. It stings, but I let it slide because she's not wrong.

"I don't really care about your opinion right now. You're still safer inside my house than you ever would be in the cottage where no one could hear your helpless screams if he got to you. Do I really need to explain in detail what he could do to you if he got his hands on you? How no one would be able to stop him because no one would even know he's here. Out here, you're as good as dead, Little Prey."

She sucks in a ragged breath I can hear over the quiet sounds of the night. "Out here, I don't have to pretend I'm okay. Out here, I don't have to avoid anyone. I haven't had a full night of sleep in days, and I'm hanging on by sheer willpower at this point."

It's impossible to miss the anguish clogging her throat. I recognize the terrible emotion that's developing in my mind. *Guilt.* I loathe it. Despise it. Yet it's all I feel as I play her response back in my mind.

I haven't had a full night of sleep in days...

Even if I'm not fully responsible for what happened, I'm partially to blame, and like a damn rash, the guilt spreads across my skin, reminding me of my mistakes. I slip out of the cottage and jog up the small hill, trekking across the grass toward the patio door. My toes grow wet from the dew on the grass through my sneakers, but I don't give a shit. I can't be bothered by such trivial things when I know I failed her. In my effort to avoid her, I nearly delivered her right into the hands of that sick bastard.

It won't happen again. Elyse is mine, and I protect what is mine. She lets out a frustrated growl as I jog up the porch, not even trying to be careful of her bouncing body.

The ballroom is dark, but I know my way around this mausoleum like the back of my hand. I climb the stairs quickly, her small body bouncing with each step. When I reach the first spare bedroom, I realize it's right across the hall from my own.

Fuck me. This is such a fucking bad idea, but I was already on my way here before I considered my actions. I want to keep her close, but not next-door-close. Not where I can so easily access her.

Shit. What do I do?

I'm already grappling for control, and now I'm making the choice to keep her across the hall, within easy reach. *I'm losing my fucking mind.* Might as well toss my control out the fucking window along with it. Is there any other option? *No.* I have to keep her close if I want to keep her safe.

Knowing I'm going to hell anyway, I shove the door open, cross the room, and toss the bundle of her and the sleeping bag onto the bed. She scrambles to sit up and kick the bag off her feet. I wait, watching like the predator I am.

If she even thinks about running, her ass will wear my handprints.

The length of her bare legs catches my attention, and I drag my gaze down and then back up to the snow-white patch of lace that's merely a tease, then up and over the very worn gray T-shirt she's wearing. A T-shirt covered in both dust and dirt.

Have I been so oblivious to her needs? Or have I just been suppressing my desires so deeply that I'm just now noticing all these little details? It doesn't matter.

I squeeze my hands into fists and twist on my heels, stalking back to my room. I can't leave her to sleep in that shirt. Not when she has a clean bed and a safe room. I find the nearest clean shirt and return to her with it in hand. Then I shove the material at her face, but instead of taking it, she bats it away like an annoying fly.

"Stop. I don't want your clothes."

"You stop. You're the one who's being stubborn."

She recoils like she's stunned I would make such an accusation. "Stubborn? Because I don't want to wear your clothes?"

"That's what I said, didn't I?"

"I've always thought something was wrong with you, but now I'm certain of it."

She has a habit of making me smile, and that shit needs to

stop, but how can I not smile when verbally sparring with her is the highlight of my day?

"You act like that's new. There's a lot wrong with me, Prey. Maybe you should put more effort into doing what I tell you to do instead of trying to figure me out."

"Maybe you should stop being so bossy, and I will."

I suppress a smile. "We aren't negotiating, Ely."

"I didn't say we were." She pauses, looking down at the shirt I gave her. "Why do you keep trying to dress me?"

I ignore her question and reach for the neck of her T-shirt, deciding that if she won't change her clothes then I'll do it for her. My intention is to jerk it off her so she can see the dirt and dust, but I miscalculate how threadbare it is, and it rips under my grip.

"I could ask you the same ridiculous questions. Like why do you keep fighting me on every single little thing? If I ask you to breathe, will you fight me on that, too?"

She lets out a small gasp and clutches the ripped shirt to her chest while glaring at me. "Yes, in fact, I will." A tiny growl escapes her, and the sound is sexy as fuck. "Sometimes I wonder if a kind bone exists in your body."

"Kindness isn't going to make you listen any better. You live to piss me off. It doesn't matter what I say to you; you're predisposed to defy me."

She stares, refusing to back down. "And you live to make my life hell, so we're even."

The knot of tension between us tightens. I should've known the night I saved her life that she would be my undoing. "We aren't anywhere close to being even, Little Prey."

"Oh yes, how could I ever forget my debt to you?" She rolls her eyes, then unfolds the T-shirt. "Could I have some privacy, please?"

I cross my arms over my chest and sink onto the side of the bed. "Could you? *Certainly.* Will I give it to you? Not today."

She huffs and tugs the ripped shirt off her head, revealing a lacy white bra. It suits her. *White. Innocent. Pure.* But while she's mostly an angel, I know a part of her clings to darkness. Light cannot exist without darkness, or darkness without light. We all carry fragments of the darkness that threaten to snuff out our light. She drags my football shirt over her head, her slim body disappearing beneath the material.

I feel a sudden surge of relief now that she's wearing something clean, something that's *mine.* Giving her one more quick glance, I check to make sure there isn't any more dirt on her shirt, but honestly, I just want an excuse to look at her.

The longer I stare, the more I see a sleepy, pissed-off, porcelain doll. My shirt is far too big for her and drowns her small frame, but I can't ignore the profound warmth that fills my chest at seeing her wear my number. *Lucky number seven.* I didn't intentionally give her one of my jerseys, but now that she's wearing it, I'm not sure I want it on anyone else.

Ever.

Dammit. That's such a stupid thought.

I cannot fuck her. I cannot cross that line.

With that reminder fresh in my head, I shove off the bed, needing to put some distance between us. I risk glancing over at her and notice her watching me.

Can she feel it? The tension? The desire?

Of course, she can. I try to moderate my tone when I open my mouth again, then realize I don't even know what I was about to say.

I'm not ready to leave her presence yet, but I don't have anything else to talk to her about right now. I filter through my thoughts and circle back to her little charity cases. I can't tell you how many of them she's nursed back to health since she arrived here.

"Why do you do it? Why do you care for those fleabags?"

She adjusts the shirt, frowning at it as she shoves it around her thighs to make sure she's covered. "What do you mean?"

"Your pets. They aren't your responsibility, but you've made them your responsibility. You care for them, using what little money you have to buy them food and pay their vet bills."

Her blue eyes find mine in the dim light from the hallway. "It doesn't take much effort to be a good person. They didn't ask to be born into the situation they're born into, no more than you or I did. In my mind, they're innocent, a casualty to someone else's wrongdoing, and if I can ease a little bit of their discomfort, then I will."

As shitty as the situation is with Elyse, somehow she manages to be a good fucking person. The kind of person who deserves way more from life than what she's been given.

"And what do you get in return? The satisfaction of doing something good?"

She nods. "I could ask you the same thing. Why care about me? Make me your responsibility? You don't owe me anything." She narrows her eyes. "Or maybe you do? What happened that night, Sebastian?"

"What are you talking about?" The abrupt change of subject catches me off guard.

"The night my father brought me here," she replies without blinking, awareness flickering in her gaze. "You say I owe you, but lately, the way you've been acting has been anything but an indication of that. It's almost like you care what happens to me. Almost like *you* owe *me*. So you tell me. What happened that night?"

I sputter, then stop and blink, wide-eyed, at her. I can't hide my shock. Like a knife to the chest, she's killed me with her words, watching as I bleed out. She's too close, too deep. All I can think to do is lash out.

I let a lazy smile spread across my face. The mask I learned to perfect in my grandfather's presence as a teenager slips into place.

"Careful, Ely. I wouldn't call fucking your face caring for you. Caring for myself, yes."

She's not the least bit fazed by my response. "Maybe the act itself wasn't proof that you care, but you didn't have to offer to prove that I was yours. You didn't have to be gentle with me or help me through it. You had a choice in all of this, and no matter how you try to paint yourself to me, I know there are good parts to who you are."

The bitter taste of denial sits on my tongue. She's not wrong, and she knows I know it too. That makes her far more dangerous than even she realizes.

"Don't mistake my kindness for weakness. Just because I show you compassion doesn't mean I won't choke you with my cock and leave you begging for your next breath the next time you offer yourself to me. You're my property, and that means the only person who gets to hurt you, scare you, or make you cry is me."

This time she's the one sputtering, and I leave her that way, pissed off and mad as I head for the door. My fingers twist the lock into place on the handle. I'll use any means necessary to ensure I don't cross the fucking line.

"Go to sleep, and keep this door locked at night." I pause with my hand on the doorknob. "Yanov isn't the only monster hunting you."

22
SEBASTIAN

It's only been a few days since I moved Elyse into the room across the hall, but I'm still suffering the consequences of that choice. *Sleep?* What is that? I find it harder to sleep now than I did before, and I was barely sleeping before. Every little sound makes me climb out of bed and check the hall, my eyes gravitating to the door across the hall. I haven't checked to see if she's locking her door at night like I instructed her.

It's disturbing how much I care about her, her safety, and my lack of self-control.

I'm rudely pulled from my thoughts when something hits me in the back of the head. I glance down to see an orange land on the floor beside me with a thwack. *What the hell?*

I swivel around on the stool where I'm eating at the kitchen counter and spot Lee and Aries standing on the other side near the patio doors. I already don't like where this is headed, and neither of them has opened their mouths yet.

"I guess we don't use the front door anymore?"

"Why use the front door when there's a perfectly good entrance right here?" Aries asks.

"Honestly, I prefer to enter through the back door, but I'm not going to lie, it's not usually this easy to get into. Most of the time, there's a lot more prep work..."

"Are we talking about the same thing?" Aries interrupts Lee before he can finish what he was going to say. Sometimes I wonder how I became friends with these fuckers.

I rub at the back of my head. "Can't you two be annoying elsewhere? Some of us have adult stuff to do."

Lee raises one imperious eyebrow. "And have you miss out on the fun? Nope."

"Oh yes, because it's so fun being annoyed by you." I roll my eyes.

"Why are you so grumpy?" Lee questions.

"I'm not."

Lee exchanges a look with Aries. "He is, though, is he not?"

Aries nods. "He is."

I wasn't grumpy before, not really, but now that they've accused me I might as well be.

"You both can fuck all the way off. I know you have other shit you could be doing right now. Shit that doesn't involve annoying me."

"Of course we have other things we could be doing...people, as well." Lee winks and continues, "Speaking of people...where is that little maid of yours?"

I blink slowly, trying my best to regulate my breathing and not react. I've known Lee for years, and his favorite pastime is annoying the shit out of everyone. If he can piss you off or get a reaction out of you, then you've already lost the game. Good thing I already know his antics and can spot them a mile away, which is why I don't fall into that trap.

"The maid is busy cleaning and not making my blood boil like you two."

"When are you going to admit you like that little brunette?"

Lee ignores what I've said and carries on like he didn't hear me at all.

"Never, because I don't like her." *Do I like her?* I wouldn't call it *like*. It feels closer to obsession, with a dash of need to protect what's *mine.*

"Could've fooled me. I swear my cock gets hard when you start your foreplay banter."

I shake my head and sigh. "Please, stop. I don't want to hear about your hard cock."

Aries shrugs. "Everyone wants to hear about my cock."

Lee snorts. "Sure. Everyone but you know who..."

"Shut up!" Aries shoves him, and Lee bursts into a fit of laughter.

I can't help but feel a little nostalgic over having them in the kitchen berating one another. It reminds me of a time not too long ago when we were all on the same page, without so many secrets separating us.

"Anyway, even if it's funner than fuck to bust Ari's balls, we didn't come here for that. We're here on official Mill business."

"Okay...and why couldn't you do this on the phone?"

Lee tugs out his cell phone, and his fingers fly over the screen with agility.

What the hell is he doing? I hear the faint ringing of my own phone from inside my pocket. This asshole thinks he's funny, doesn't he? I tug it out and set it on the counter, hitting the red decline button. *Fuck off.*

"Holy shit. It's a miracle. It really works."

My lip twitches up at the side, but I don't smile. "Why the hell wouldn't it work?"

"Oh, I don't know, maybe because you never fucking answer it when we call or text you."

"Yes, I do."

"Lies. You haven't been active in the group chat for almost a month," Lee postures.

"It's time to face the music, Seb. You're being a shitty friend." Aries crosses his arms over his chest, staring me down like I'm a child who disobeyed their parents.

"I'm not being a shitty friend." *Lies.* I'm being a terrible friend.

"Liar, liar, pants on fire," Aries taunts, echoing my thoughts.

"Sure, keep on telling yourself that. Like we don't see you avoiding us. Drew's busy, too, but even he still makes time to hang out," Lee mutters.

A sliver of guilt cuts across my chest. Okay, so I haven't been a great friend, but I've got a lot of shit going on, and I can't fathom burdening them with any of it. They couldn't help me even if I was willing to accept their help. I'm not dumb; sometimes you have to fight the battle on your own.

"Did you come here to berate me, as well, or are you going to tell me what this official business is?"

Lee smirks and cuts across the kitchen, acting like I invited him in. He pulls out a stool across from me and plops down on it.

"Sure, of course. Come in, have a seat."

"Shut up." Lee snorts. "We've been planning all the senior activities for The Mill, including this year's annual hunt. It feels wrong that you aren't actively a part of things. Every time we need your help or opinion on something, you're nowhere to be found."

I look down at the bowl of food for a moment, and when I feel I've got my emotions in check, I look back up. "Not sure if you noticed, but I have shit going on. You're lucky I've been making it to practice. Where's Drew?"

"Inside your sister." Aries smirks, knowing full well his comment will make me lose my shit. I clench my hand into a fist, ready to punch the smugness off his face.

Lee snickers, and I shift my glare to him. "He can stop

fucking for five minutes and plan something." Filled with irrational anger, I scoop up another bite of blueberry oatmeal and shove it into my mouth.

Lee huffs. "No worries, we have your help now."

"What do you need my help for? You act like this is your first year putting the event on. It's the same thing but with a slight difference. Send the invites out, buy the alcohol, come up with new rules, and show the fuck up when it's time to start."

This earns me an affronted look from Lee. "You say all of this like you didn't spend months planning who to send out invites to last year."

I don't have the time or patience for this. With a long sigh, I shake my head. "If it's of such importance, then send them out to the same people as last year and move on. I don't have the time to do this right now."

Aries hops up on the counter next to Lee and snags a banana out of a nearby bowl of fruit.

Lee glares between us. "It's not that easy."

Aries peels the banana while speaking. "It's the biggest event we hold, and it's our senior year. The last one before they send us out into the great unknown. We need to end the year with a bang. The whole night needs to be unique, an unforgettable experience, per se."

"We aren't Disneyland. Isn't it enough they get to live out their sexual fantasies for a night?"

Lee shakes his head at me, his gaze pressing like he's trying to look deep inside me. "Tell me what's wrong."

"Nothing is wrong," I grind out.

"Why are you lying? I thought we were friends?"

"Yeah, you've never been a good liar." Aries frowns. "How can we help you if we don't know what's going on?"

"If I needed help, I'd ask, but since I didn't, I think that means I don't need help."

"Yes, you do. You're here, but not. No one can get you to show up for anything. I mean, I guess you did show up for your date with Bel, but you were late, which isn't like you." Lee rubs his chin as if he's pondering something, "Oh, actually, no. Sorry. You were in attendance at Pound of Flesh. Weird how you can travel overseas to attend some obscure flesh market, but you can't make it to The Mill meetings or answer the fucking phone when your best friends call you."

I really don't want to have this conversation right now, or ever, for that matter. My friends sort of know what's been going on in my life since my grandfather died, but they don't know the gritty details. They don't know how much I'm struggling or what I'm willing to sacrifice to be free of this noose tied around my neck.

I'm not ignoring them by choice, and I'm not attending events for fun. I need to get Sidorov to take over so I can slip into oblivion without question. How the fuck can I explain to them that the only reason I went to Pound of Flesh was so that I could meet with Sidorov? In what way could they help me escape this shit show?

I swallow down the words before they can spill out. The need to confess to someone, anyone, eats at me from the inside out.

There's a sound at the door, and Elyse stumbles into the room. She freezes in the doorway when she sees us gathered around the counter. "Um...I'll just..."

Aries smiles at her and then hops off the counter. "Ahhh, there she is. We were just talking about you, little pet. So cute and tiny."

I ignore him and her. Reacting to anything he says or does gives him ammunition that he can use against me later. But my lack of response pisses Aries off, and he stalks closer to Ely. If he touches her, I just might fucking lose it.

Lee's eyes ping-pong between Elyse and me, suspicion

building in their depths. “Is *she* the reason you haven't been pulling your weight?” I grind my teeth together so hard I’m shocked they don’t crack. “Fuck. Don’t tell me you’re pussy whipped, too?”

“If you haven’t claimed her yet, I might be interested.” Aries grins and leans in closer, his nostrils flaring as he inhales her scent. *My scent.*

His single saving grace is the fact that Elyse flinches away from him like she despises the idea as well.

“I… I think I should go,” Elyse stutters awkwardly.

“But you just got here, sweetheart…” Aries raises his eyebrows.

I grit my teeth. If I show even the slightest response, these fuckers will know what’s up, but I won’t stand by and let them touch her either.

“Leave her alone, Aries. She’s my employee. I’m not fucking her, and neither are you.”

The resounding sound of high heels clicking on the tile greets my ears, and I let out a sigh of defeat. *Could this day get any fucking worse?*

23
SEBASTIAN

Tanya saunters into the kitchen and stops just behind Elyse. "I don't pay you to stand here looking like a statue," she snipes at Elyse, who jolts forward. In a flurry, she rushes past Aries and straight to the cleaning closet on the other side of the room.

Tanya stares after her for a whole second and then crosses to the counter, her skintight dress riding up as she walks. Aries watches her closely, but not in a sexual way, more like how you'd watch a rattlesnake that's about to strike. I always thought he was smarter than he looks, especially concerning human nature. He's a true Casanova and a playboy, but he's also manipulative and cruel when he needs to be.

It's probably how he manages to see Tanya for the snake that she is.

"Oh my, what a pleasant surprise. It's been far too long since I've seen you all." Tanya eyes Aries curiously, while I have to stop myself from vomiting on the floor. "You sure have filled out."

"What do you want?"

"Do I need to want something to walk into my own kitchen?"

I release the spoon in my hand and let it fall into the bowl. I can't fucking stand her, but I can't make her disappear either. Closing my hand into a fist, I press it against my thigh beneath the island and sink my nails deep in my palm. Pain lances across my flesh, awakening my senses and grounding me.

"It's not your kitchen. It belongs to me, according to the Arturo estate."

After my grandfather's death, it became clear to me that I couldn't simply write Tanya off. I wanted to so fucking badly, but there were certain stipulations, certain things that she owned a stake in by virtue of her marriage, and I needed to play it smart if I wanted to ensure that when I left, it would be with my entire slice of the pie. So while I despise her presence, she's nothing more than a necessary hurdle to me getting what I want.

And knowing just how much her touch and mere presence pisses me off, she leans into my side and slices her fingers through my hair. It takes serious self-control to force myself to stay still because any out-of-place reaction will only entice her further. Even with me in control of the Arturo empire, I still can't make her disappear. She's got connections and knowledge. Plus...there's truth in that old saying that it's safer to keep your enemies close.

"Your grandfather was not in his right mind when he finalized the will."

Here we go again. I'm not about to get into another argument with her about what belongs to her or doesn't belong to her. According to the will, I'm to ensure she lives comfortably. It says nothing about whether that's in a shallow grave or a foreign country.

"So you've told me half a dozen times. Now did you need something?" I ask more politely this time, trying to modulate my tone enough that she will get on with it and leave us the hell alone.

She shrugs. "Not really. I only came down for a drink, but I see we have guests, so...I'll stay a moment and chat."

I open my mouth to tell her to leave, but Lee cuts in. "It's good to see you, Mrs. Arturo. It has been a while now that you mention it. I was surprised I didn't see you at the elder Mr. Arturo's funeral."

Her fake-ass megawatt smile slips a little. "Well, I was in Europe when he passed. By the time the funeral was arranged, I was only being notified of his death. Not that those things matter now." She wraps a protective arm around me, hugging me tight around the shoulders. The scent of her perfume is cloying, and I breathe through my mouth to escape it. "All that matters now is that I'm here to take care of my boy and help in whatever way he needs me."

Help? More likely to cause problems.

Her gaze returns to Aries, and there's no missing the way she checks him out, up and down. "I'm here for you boys, too, if you need anything. Anything at all."

Fate clearly isn't on my side today because Elyse chooses that moment to come out of the cleaning closet. Like always, my gaze automatically goes to her. There's no escaping the hold she has on me. I can't look away.

I fucking hate it. Hate that I'm attracted to her. Hate that her existence makes my heart beat a little heavier. Hate that she's the one true weakness I have, and that when all the pieces missing from her puzzle come back together, I'll be the person she sees as the enemy.

Tanya's hand closes around the back of my neck in a vise. "That girl needs to know when and where it's appropriate for her to show up. Real staff are never seen."

I turn my attention to Lee, who is staring straight ahead, but it's too late. Tanya turns to press her chest against my arm, her hand still on my neck, and focuses all her attention on the weakest prey in the room. *Elyse.*

"Ely, dear, could you grab me a drink, please. These young men have me so distracted I forgot why I came in here in the first place."

Ely drops the bucket and items in her hands to the floor. "Oh, of course, Mrs. Arturo. What would you like?"

Tanya winces at the falling objects but recovers with a small smile. "Water." She doesn't say thank you, or please, nothing.

It shouldn't bother me because I don't say those things to Ely either, but it does. Especially because the look in Tanya's eyes says I can and I will squish you like a bug.

Like always, Elyse plays aloof to Tanya's bullshit and grabs a bottle of sparkling water from the refrigerator. She brings it over, placing it on the countertop, the glass bottle clicking against the granite.

Tanya smiles, and I swear if she gets any closer, she'll be in my lap. "Oh dear, could you grab a glass, as well? And ice."

To her credit, Ely does nothing more than spin on her heel and grabs a glass with ice, placing it right in front of Tanya as she asked. I survey Lee's and Aries's faces, but their expressions give nothing away. Whatever they're thinking, they're keeping under lock and key.

Ely turns to leave, and Tanya gasps. "Oh dear..."

I huff, grab the sparkling water, crack it open, and pour it over the ice. "Enough already. You have your drink."

Tanya glares at me and steps away. Small mercies.

I don't look at Elyse as I speak, but she knows my words are for her. "Get what you need, and return to your duties."

At my word, she scrambles to gather up the cleaning supplies and flees from the kitchen like her ass is on fire.

"Why do you coddle her, Sebastian?" Tanya whines, taking a

delicate sip of water, leaving a red lipstick print on the edge of the glass.

"I don't coddle her. Her job is to clean the house, not get you something to drink."

Tanya shrugs. "If I'm paying her, she'll do whatever I want her to do."

"Then I guess it's good you aren't paying her. I am," I snap.

This time, I know I've pushed her too far when her eyes narrow to slits. "Watch your tone, Sebastian. I'd hate for your friends to think you make it a habit of disrespecting your mother."

It's on the tip of my tongue to tell her she's not my mother, that she never will be nor has she ever been, but I bite the retort back. Her husband—my uncle—may have been like a father to me, but despite being my aunt, she was never a motherly figure. I don't think she has a motherly bone in her body if I'm being honest.

Lee pats the back of her hand gently. "Will you excuse us, Mrs. Arturo; we have some very important planning that we need to finish up."

Tanya huffs and scans Lee's face, assessing him. I pinpoint the moment she decides she doesn't have a use for him. It's nauseating. I watch Lee's face, and I know he sees it too. The moment she disregards him, underestimates him.

Not that I'd enjoy her taking an interest in any of my friends. The fewer of my friends she interacts with, the better. I'm just grateful Drew isn't here; he'd have shoved her out the door by now, most likely in tears.

Her attention shifts back to Aries, and I can't stop the smile that curves my lips. Aries would love nothing more than to break her, and if she tried to take him to her bed, she'd learn that, but only after it was too late.

She nods and gives my neck one last squeeze. "I'll let you boys be boys. Don't get into too much trouble without me."

What the hell is she trying to accomplish here?

I'm cautious in her presence, watching as she grabs her glass of water and exits the kitchen. Once she's finally gone, the weight on my chest is lifted, and I can breathe again.

"What a raging witch," Aries states with disgust.

They know about her flirting; they've seen it, but they don't know the worst of it.

The molestation, the abuse. It goes far deeper than any of them could fathom. I can handle it, though. I have for years, and I will continue to.

"I don't want to talk about her. Just tell me what you need, Lee. I'm tired as fuck and running thin on both time and patience."

He frowns. "I think I can handle it. I just...I feel like you and Drew have abandoned us. Planning The Hunt was your favorite activity. Now I've taken over because it needs to be done... and it just... it doesn't feel the same anymore." I can hear how upset he is, but I don't know how to fix it or if I even can. "I mean, are you even going to show up?"

I nod. "I'll have to show my face, right? People would think it's weird if I wasn't there. Is Drew running?"

Aries chimes in. "He is, and he's bringing Bel."

Fantastic. Just what I need, to see my best friend and my sister fucking in the woods. What a perfect highlight to an already stellar few months.

"Wonderful. I'll be sure to steer clear of them."

Lee grins. "This might be exactly what you need. Come to The Hunt. You've been off since last year when everything went down with Drew and after finding out Bel was your sister."

I let out a long sigh and sink down, my shoulders falling away from my ears. "Yeah, well, there's nothing like learning the world you live in is a lie. That everything is a lie."

When I found out the truth about Drew's father actually being my father, I didn't know what to think. I still haven't really wrapped my head around it. Not that it mattered. I wanted nothing from that man. DNA didn't make him a parent. It made us related. That was all there was between us.

"Is there something you want to share? Do you need us to take care of someone? Dispose of a body?"

I need to get out of this fucking house, away from that woman, and out of this life. But there is no quick fix for any of that. This goes deeper than fucking with someone or pissing someone off. There's nothing they can do to help me. I've dug the hole, and I'll have to lie in it.

"No, I'm good, but if I do need something, you'll be the first to know."

Aries nods, and Lee shifts on the stool. "Go take a nap, Mr. Grumpy Gills. I'll finish planning without you. But I don't want to hear you complaining on race day if something isn't the way you like it."

Aries grins and looks at me. "Oh, I think he'll like what we've already planned just fine."

Cryptic. I study them both for a second and then stand. "Call me later if you still need help."

"The phone only works if you actually answer it." Lee purses his lips.

"I know, and I'll answer it, asshole. Now get out of my hair."

"Love you, too." He chuckles.

I leave them in the kitchen. They will find their own way out, the same way they found their way in. I feel lighter after the interaction, like maybe not everything is a piece of shit that's been lit on fire. Then I round the corner, and Tanya's voice pierces my ears. I stop mid-step and spot her at the top of the stairs talking to Elyse.

I'm tempted to intervene because I know how Tanya is, and even if Elyse's presence is unbearable to me at times, that doesn't mean she deserves to be on the receiving end of whatever shit Tanya is stirring up.

But tempted as I might be, I don't move. I don't even breathe. I wait, standing there to hear if she has anything else to say.

"I don't know what his infatuation is with you, but if you aren't going to do the job you were hired to do, then I'll have you fired." The venom in her tone is unwavering.

"I'm so sorry. I will do better." Elyse tells her, and I don't miss the slight worry in her tone. *Does she actually think I would let Tanya fire her?*

"I sure hope so," Tanya sneers.

I take a step forward, preparing to step in since Tanya is obviously losing her mind but also to put Elyse at ease. Just as I do, Elyse sprints away, and Tanya continues her path of destruction up the stairs.

Standing there, I get lost in thought. I can't help but worry that all this time I've been too soft on Elyse. Can Tanya see through the deception? The only thing she wants more than me is the throne, and I'm not desperate enough to offer her that—not yet, at least.

If she discovers Elyse means something to me, big or little, good or bad, she'll consider her a weakness, and there won't be anything to stop her from using her against me. All over again, Elyse will become the casualty of another war she has no business being a part of.

24
ELYSE

You would not look good in orange. You would not look good in orange.

I repeat the mantra to myself for the tenth time today. Tanya's bodyguard, Marcus, is breathing down my neck, and I'm about to become a member of the TV show *Snapped*.

One more insult, or little comment, or slight from either of them and I'm going to lose my shit. It's bad enough that I have to take crap from Sebastian everyday, but Tanya has a way of making me feel...bad. Like, as a woman—something I thought I'd gotten over when I came to Oakmount, saw the blond Barbies traipsing around and just accepted that I'm smaller, more athletically built, and all around not a super feminine beauty. Sure, I'm pretty, but I wouldn't call myself sexy.

And I'm okay with that.

Marcus steps closer as I gently ease Tanya's clean clothes into a drawer. He's crowding me, and I don't like it.

"Do you mind?"

He shakes his head. "Not at all." There's an accent there, but I have no idea where it's from, so I don't bother speculating.

"Did I do something wrong? Is that why you are here...monitoring me?"

He shrugs. "Just keeping you on your toes."

"Can you keep me on my toes from another room?" I deadpan, grabbing the next stack of lacy undergarments and tucking them in the drawer with the others. Thousands of dollars in lingerie, and I'm wearing my cotton Hanes Dollar General bra and panty set.

I sigh and finish putting away the rest of the clothes, then turn to check the bed is made tightly. The last thing I need is her hunting me down in the middle of the night for some trivial thing. Other people work here, but she seems to have designated me as her personal slave.

It's nothing I can't handle, just annoying as hell since she's an absolute bitch. But she's one of those bitches who say really bitchy things in the most polite voice possible. For your benefit, of course.

I tighten down the corners of the sheet and smooth the coverlet, then check the trash can in the bedroom before I go in to clean the bathroom.

Marcus follows me, of course, and I'm thankful it's not a tiny bathroom.

"Aren't you a bodyguard?" I question as I clean the shower drain and spray the inside of the tub with cleaner.

He makes some kind of noise in his throat. I can't tell if it's a snort or what."How can you guard someone when the person you are protecting isn't here?"

"I think you should worry about yourself. It's none of your business what I do," he says, keeping his vigil at the door. I feel his hawk eyes on me as I make my way around the bathroom, wiping up toothpaste, disinfecting, imagining flushing Tanya's head down her own toilet.

I peek back at Marcus as I sweep the floor. Tall and muscular, he definitely looks like a bodyguard with his dark suit and shaved head. I'm not stupid, though, and something tells me guarding isn't the only thing he's doing with Tanya's body. Not to mention her bed is always rumpled on both sides, and he doesn't allow me into his room to clean.

It only takes a few minutes to clean up the floor and shake out the small rugs that decorate the space, considering she makes me clean her entire room every single day. Even the ones I'm supposed to be off for. Hell, I wouldn't put it past her to march up to the school and pull me out of class if I so much as forgot to fold the toilet paper edge on the roll.

I re-lay all the rugs and clean up the sink while I consider how to get rid of my shadow. He's making me nervous, and I'm not even doing anything but cleaning.

"Can you leave while I finish up, please? I'm almost done," I ask as I wash out the sink and then wipe down the mirror. There's toothpaste splatter all over it. Considering I clean this everyday, she must spit at the mirror to make this kind of mess.

"No, I won't leave until I can lock the door behind you."

He's never hovered when I cleaned before, nor has he locked the door behind me...what's going on that Tanya suddenly feels the need to hide things?

I roll my eyes and continue cleaning, having to stretch so tall my calves hurt to reach the top of the mirror.

The granite counters inlaid with black and gold gleam in the overhead mirror lights, and I ensure no water spots remain on the gilded fixtures.

I guess I should be grateful my own suite's bathroom isn't as gaudy as this one.

I quickly clean the toilet bowl, which is still sparkling from yesterday, and grab the couple of items from the bottom of the wastebasket to throw into my bigger trash bag.

I freeze when I spot what looks like a pregnancy test wrapper.

What the fuck? The first thing that comes to mind is whether she should even be having kids at her age? I try to calculate her age, but I know she's Sebastian's aunt, not his mother, and his uncle, Sebastian's adoptive father, was older than her. All of which I caught from conversations with other staff members and Tanya herself in passing. It doesn't matter...it's none of my business. I trash the tissue and the wrapper, then notice some dust on the edge of one of the vanity drawers.

I go back into the other room to grab a clean rag and have to squeeze by Marcus's gorilla-sized frame.

"Excuse me," I murmur, but it comes out like *fuck off*.

He leans against the doorjamb to take up more space once I pass.

Dick.

I turn my back to him and swipe the dust on the drawers, opening the top to make sure I get around the edges. I'm both stunned and confused by what I find there, and my lungs tighten from the effort it takes not to breathe. There's a pregnancy test pressed to the edge of the drawer, tucked face in like she's trying to hide it.

One, that's super unsanitary since her makeup is in here, too, but I can't resist. Shock gives way to curiosity, and I flip the test over to see the result.

Positive.

Oh shit. Marcus, the asshole, is going to be a father...poor kid.

I move to flip the test back over where I found it and accidentally send it sliding.

The door banging against the wall behind me scares the ever-loving shit out of me, and I jump, snatch up the test, and shove it into my pocket. If he gives me a minute of privacy, I can replace it where I found it, and no one will know.

The door, however, wasn't Marcus lunging at me, like my brain so helpfully supplied in my imagination, but is instead Bel.

She stands in the doorway, her shoulder nearly pressing into Marcus's chest.

"Hey, girl, I was looking for you." She smiles, her blond messy bun bobbing as she folds her arms across her chest.

I close the drawer behind me and face her fully, smiling back. My heart slowly eases out of my throat and back down to where it belongs. "What's up? You need your toilet cleaned, too?"

It's a joke, but when the words are out, it feels more like I'm complaining.

Her smile slips away, and I know she can tell something is wrong. "You okay? What's up?"

I shake my head. "It's just been a weird day, and I don't like to be surveyed while I work."

She tilts her head back to look up at Marcus who has refused to get out of her way, or move a muscle. "Can you give us a minute?"

He glares daggers at her, and I doubt he would be looking at her like that if Drew was in the room. "No, I'm doing my job."

Bel smirks. "As far as I can tell, your job includes carrying overpriced luggage and fucking your boss...neither of which needs to be done right now."

"You're lucky..." he snarls and walks out of the bathroom and into the bedroom, knocking Bel to the side as he goes.

"Yeah, and so are you. Because if I told my brother you're trying to intimidate his staff, your ass would be canned."

"Ooo, I'm so scared," he taunts.

She rolls her eyes and steps closer to me. "That guy needs his ass beat. Has he been messing with you for a while now? I'm not joking about telling Sebastian. If he's giving you a hard time, I'll talk to him about the ogre."

I sigh. "No, today's the first time he's ever done this. I'm okay. I'm just tired. It feels like all I'm doing is working or going to school."

She reaches for my hand, but I jerk away and then hold my hands up so she can see the latex gloves I'm wearing.

I strip them off, trash them, then wash my hands in the sink. "What did you need?" I ask as I meet her eyes in the mirror.

She shakes her head. "Nothing important. I kind of want to drag you out of here and force you to have some fun. Sebastian is giving you time off, right?"

I shrug. "Yeah, he is. If only Tanya understood I'm not a twenty-four-seven staff member, then I could actually enjoy it. Maybe I need to leave the house on my off days."

As I say it, I know I can't, not with Yanov running around, knowing where I am and who I'm with. I'll never feel safe out there alone.

"Why don't you come out with me tonight?"

"To do what?"

"Socialize. Relax. It's just a little party."

"What party?"

"The party at The Mill. It's to celebrate the start of the recruitment season and all that. It's really a glorified excuse to drink and hang out, like anyone at this school actually needs one though, am I right?"

There's a noise from the bedroom, and Bel shakes her head. "I think someone is getting antsy out there. Come on." She grabs my hand, and I let her, taking my trash bag in the other.

In the bedroom, I grab my supply bucket and broom and head out behind Bel. We go to the cleaning closet, and she helps me put everything away. Then she waits patiently while I dispose of the trash. I double-check that I have my wallet and my keys in my jacket pockets, and as I'm patting I feel an unfamiliar outline in my skirt pocket.

Oh shit. The pregnancy test. How could I have forgotten to put it back? Panic rises in my chest. If Tanya realizes it's gone before I can replace it, I have no doubt that she'll know it was me who took it. And then what? I need to get rid of it.

"Are you leaving right now?" I question.

"Yes, and I'm taking you with me. I won't take no for an answer. You work way too hard, and you need a damn break." She winks and then grabs my hand, dragging me out the door. I try to dig my feet into the ground and conjure up any response I can so that I can turn around and put the test back without suspicion, but there's no use.

Crap. I'll have to make sure I keep it hidden and that I don't lose it.

"Could you slow down? I have tiny legs," I grumble, and Bel lets out a laugh.

"I'm sorry. I'm just so excited."

Her response makes me smile, and I let her lead me out to a sleek silver car that likely cost a fortune. She jumps into the driver's seat, and I slide into the passenger side. Once inside, she tosses a bag in my lap as she starts the car and buckles herself in.

"Here, I have some makeup if you want to use it. No pressure, but I didn't exactly give you time to get ready."

"No, you basically kidnapped me."

"Touché." She grins.

I smile back at her, take my hair out of the messy braid I'd put it in earlier, and finger comb the dark strands. Then I dig through her bag and find some lip balm and a little bronzer. I refuse to use her mascara because...germs...and quickly shape my eyebrows. I look at my reflection in the tiny compact mirror and give a small nod. I look human and less like the pale maid version of myself. Not that anyone will notice.

In the ocean of sharks at this school, I'm the little seahorse simply trying to keep up. If anyone notices me at this party tonight, I'll be shocked. I do have to wonder, though, if Sebastian will notice my absence.

Who am I kidding? He'll definitely be in attendance. At least one person will notice me. Nervous energy encompasses me, and I start to bounce my leg up and down. I'm out of my element here.

My anxiety rises as we pull up the long drive to The Mill house. I've been here a couple of times since I came to Oakmount, but this will be my first official party here. Bel parks the car in the driveway and exits the vehicle, urging me to follow. I exit the car a little more slowly, and she waits by the hood for me.

The second I'm near, she threads her arm through mine and drags me up the stairs to the huge double doors. "You're going to have a great time. I promise."

One of the doors is propped open with a football, and she nudges it to lead me inside. Music thumps from inside, and as soon as we walk in I'm assaulted with numerous sounds, sights, and smells. The space is already crowded even though by school standards, it's still pretty early. I'm tempted to look anywhere but at the people in attendance, but that would be awkward as hell, so I look up and scan the crowd.

A good majority of the partygoers dance on the makeshift dance floor, red plastic cups in hand, while others linger at the edges, a guy or girl glued to their side. Not what I was expecting. Someone slips in behind us, bumping into me, and I skitter out of the way, in turn bumping Bel and causing us both to teeter.

A pair of strong arms circle her waist, dragging her backward into an ironclad chest. Instantly she relaxes into Drew's embrace, and it's like he's an envelope and she's the love letter tucked inside. Nuzzling the side of her neck, he whispers something into the shell of her ear that makes her smile.

Jeez, watching them makes me feel like I'm watching some sappy rom-com. I'm happy for her, though. The best love stories are the most hard-fought.

Turning away from them, I scan the crowd once more. My gaze stops on a man who's sitting on a throne across the room.

Okay, not a throne but a huge, ornate chair. I find it hard to breathe when I notice those familiar green eyes of his, the same eyes that haunt me in my dreams. He's staring at me, legs splayed wide, leaning on the hand he has propped up on the arm of the chair. His hair is disheveled, and he looks bored out of his mind, but it's hard to tell if he really is or not since that's his usual expression.

He looks away, his gaze cutting from mine as a girl crosses in front of his path and then settles into his lap, grinding herself against his groin. My cheeks heat as if I have a reason to be embarrassed. Yep. This is exactly as I've always pictured him. A king sitting on his throne, giving no thought to the rest of us peasants.

No. I can't stand to see him like that. Not when I know what lies beneath the surface, hidden under that cruelty and emotionless smile.

Without giving him another ounce of attention, I turn and head toward the kitchen to find something to drink. If I'm going to survive this party, I'm not doing it sober.

25
SEBASTIAN

The party is already in full swing when I walk through the front doors of The Mill house. Lee is sitting on the counter, shirtless, sipping a beer. Aries is just outside the kitchen with a girl wrapped around his waist.

As soon as Lee spots me across the room, he hops off the counter and cuts through the crowd, making a beeline right for me. "You made it. I was sure I'd have to come back out to your house and harass you again to get you out here, but I'm glad I didn't."

I sigh. "Is there any purpose for this party, or is it just the usual debauchery?"

Lee quirks a brow and nudges me with his shoulder. "Once upon a time, you loved this debauchery." Then waving over at the throne pulled out for these types of events, he continues, "Drew is coming later with Bel. I doubt we'll see much of them, so you get to lord over the underlings tonight. Take your seat and try to relax a little; you don't always have to be so serious."

With a grin, he shoves a bottle of cheap brown liquor into my grasp, and I stroll over to the chair, knowing it's useless to argue with him. Lee is used to getting what he wants, and if I sulk around all night, he'll only make his presence more defined. I step onto the platform and throw myself into the wooden throne. It's hard and uncomfortable, but I've sat on worse.

I twist the tip of the liquor bottle off and bring it to my lips, tipping back the contents into my mouth. I take a couple of gulps, letting it warm my insides. I set the bottle on the arm of the chair and strip the hoodie I'm wearing off over my head.

I barely have the fabric out of my line of sight when a huge pair of tits fills my vision.

"Sebastian. It's so good to see you," a girl coos.

Hmm, fuck. I don't remember her name. It's not really surprising to me. I don't see a name or even a face when I fuck them. They're more of a means to an end, an outlet for my twisted fantasies. I search through my memory, and when recognition fails to take root in my eyes, she releases a huff of frustration.

"Trish, is it?" It's a guess, but apparently the right one as her eyes light up with satisfaction.

"You remembered me!" She smiles and moves to sit on my lap.

I shift away as much as I can because that's better than sending her running for the hills. She ends up with half her ass on my thigh and the other half on the wood chair. "Where have you been? The cheerleading team feels neglected."

I'm not sure why she feels the need to tell me that. Each girl I fuck knows the score. It's a one-time thing, and that's it.

When I don't respond to her questions, she asks me another. "The Hunt's coming up. Are you excited?"

I shrug. "Sure. I'm excited for every event we put on."

Snagging the bottle of liquor, I take another drink, my attention to the conversation fading as I scan the crowd of people for something better to distract me. In the throng of people, I spot Lee and Aries. They're talking in the corner, their heads bowed.

What are you fuckers up to?

My pulse quickens as irritation blooms, and I look over at the girl. "What do you want?"

She simpers, and I barely keep myself from curling my lip in disgust. Elyse never does that. I roll my eyes. *Why the fuck am I thinking about her again?*

The reminder that I never wanted her in my life in the first place rolls through me, and I bring the drink to my lips. She was nothing but a pawn in a game played by our father figures, a symbol of everything I wanted to be away from with every cell in my body. And now...it's like she's burrowed under my skin, and I can't fucking get away from her.

How did all of this get to be such a fucking mess?

"We had fun last time, didn't we?" Trish places a well-manicured hand against her bicep, and my eyes gravitate toward the movement. Her fingers run along the signature scar I leave on all my conquests. I might feel guilty for it if they didn't beg me so badly to do it.

To mark them.

To hurt them.

"Doesn't mean we are doing it again. How many girls have you seen with two scars?"

She pouts and tosses the long strands of her blond hair over her shoulder. "None, but I could be the first." When I don't respond to her comment, her anger bubbles up and over the top. "You don't have to be a dick about it, damn. Just say no."

I clench my teeth and glare at her, leaning into her face so she can't miss it. What part of "doesn't mean we're doing it again" isn't registering? "No."

"Whatever." She sneers and clambers up and off the chair, taking the stink of her perfume with her. Maybe I should indulge in one of them. Or two...maybe it will keep me from doing something stupid like pinning Elyse to the wall and fucking her silly.

My dick takes interest in that idea, and I cross my legs to hide the raging hard-on growing there, letting my ankle rest on my knee. I notice the curious looks of a couple of girls who shift closer to me, one tripping over her own feet and landing directly in my lap, her ass pressing against my erection.

I could fuck them. It wouldn't mean anything except maybe a reprieve from my lingering thoughts of Ely.

"Your cock is so big." The nameless girl whimpers and writhes against me, her hips rolling, her eyes shimmering in the overhead lights. She's cute. I've seen her at a party once or twice.

Her friend, who has jet-black hair and bright blue eyes, stares down at me. "Sebastian. We've missed you," she drawls, sitting on the arm of the chair while her friend still dances.

I try to play my part, to smile even, but it comes out as more of a scowl. It's fine; girls around here are used to me being a moody asshole. "You missed me, huh?"

She nods, beaming under my attention. I hand her the bottle of cheap bourbon and watch as she takes a long sip, then hands it off to her other friend. The girl in my lap stops dry humping me long enough to take a drink and passes it back to me. I tuck the bottle back into my hip for safekeeping.

"Do you want to hang out with us tonight?" the girl on the arm of the chair asks.

Hang out? I don't know why she doesn't just ask if I want to fuck them.

I look over the shoulder of the girl who's planted in my lap, her ass rubbing against my cock. The strangest thing happens then. A ringing fills my ears, and the tiny hairs on my neck raise with awareness. I feel her presence before I see her. *Elyse.* A sick and twisted longing rips through me. It only intensifies when I see her there, standing in the doorway with Bel and Drew beside her.

Her brown hair lies in soft waves around her shoulders, and even from a distance, I see that she put on some makeup. That's different. Something that feels a lot like jealousy burns in my veins. I hope she isn't trying to impress someone because no one with a brain cell in their head is going to leave this party with her in their possession while I'm here. An irrational need to go to her pops into my head. I shake it, the movement subtle but fierce. *No. She means nothing.* The less interest I show in her, the easier this will all be.

Even with that thought, though, I can't look away. I drag my gaze over her from head to toes, noticing that she's wearing a zip-up hoodie over her jean skirt and ankle boots. Fuck, she looks good, even covered more than most of the girls at this party.

An image of her tiny little body writhing beneath me appears in my mind. Her skin between my teeth. Her pretty lips releasing sweet, intoxicating sounds.

The fucking ways I would ruin her.

I shift uncomfortably in the chair, and the girl beside me laughs. Suddenly, even the idea of being with either of them pisses me off.

Ely's blue eyes find me. I can feel the weight of them on my skin, but her expression is different, unreadable, and I swear it looks like she's looking through me, rather than at me.

The moment ends, the elastic band tethering us together snapping, and I clench my fist, needing something to ground me. Without an apparent second thought, she turns and follows Bel into the kitchen, both of them disappearing from my line of sight for a second because of the crowd.

I stand, pretending to stretch, and the girl on my lap tumbles forward.

"Hey, what the..." She pauses when I resettle into the seat, with a better view now, and tug her back onto my lap.

I'm not going to fuck either of them, but I can use them as a buffer between Elyse and myself.

The nameless girl wiggles in my lap, grinding her ass against my still-hard cock. If only she knew my cock was hard for someone else entirely. I wonder if she would still be working this hard?

The other girl leans in and drapes her arm over my shoulders. "We could go," she whispers into my ear.

I shake my head. "Sorry, I have to stay. Mill business."

She gives me what I assume she thinks is her best puppy dog eyes, and when that doesn't work, she lets out a resounding sigh and turns to scan the crowd. After a moment, she looks back at me, realizing I'm not going to change my mind.

"Let's go," she orders her friend, grabbing her by the hand.

"What? I thought..." The girl in my lap stares between us, confusion filling her eyes.

"He doesn't want to fuck us. Let's go," she announces like she's ashamed and then drags her friend back out onto the dance floor.

Well, there goes my buffer. Whatever, I guess. I look away from the dance floor and back to where Elyse is standing. Bel is there with Drew wrapped behind her back as usual.

I notice there are a few other girls standing around, but none of them draws my attention like Elyse. I watch as she strips off her hoodie and ties it around her waist.

Drew says something and then passes her a cup, which Ely takes without question. I unclench my fist, not realizing how tightly I was holding it. *Relax.* She's not your problem. I mean outside of her obligation to pay her father's debt. Still, it's a relief that she isn't taking a drink from some random guy. I can trust Drew.

He doesn't want her, wouldn't even consider giving up Bel for her, not with how obsessed he is, but it's not him that's the issue. It's the other fuckers in attendance. Interest reflects in their heavy stares, the way they look her up and down like she's a big, juicy steak they can't wait to get a taste of.

Just try it, fuckers. See what happens. Touch what is mine. I'll feed you your fingers one by one.

When Ely smiles at something Bel says, my heart lurches out of my chest. How have I never noticed how pretty she is when she smiles? I suppose I've never seen her smile like that, since I'd have to give her a reason to smile in the first place. I grit my teeth in anger. It's irrational to be jealous of everyone else who gets to see that smile, but now that I've seen it, I want to see more of it. All the time.

I'm fucking screwed.

My hands reach for the bottle of liquor absentmindedly, and I need the liquid courage to help get me away from this fucking chair and into that kitchen. It's already packed in there, spilling out to where the small dining table usually sits. Even over onto the dance floor in front of where the throne was placed. I can't stay here; I need to be closer to her.

I can't bear to look away from her. She is laughing outright now between taking tiny sips of her drink. I can't help but be reminded how much she looks like any other college girl having the time of her life at a party. Making friends. Socializing. The thought of ruining that for her makes my chest ache.

What if my presence doesn't ruin it? Ha. Laughable. The second I go in there, she'll stop laughing, and all the tension that's been building between us lately will be evident to everyone.

Why did Bel have to bring her?

If I really wanted to be an asshole, I could order her away...tell her to go home, throw her out. I release a groan of frustration. I'd never live that shit down. Not with Lee watching my every move, and that's not even considering the tongue-lashing I would get from Bel. No, I can't do that.

God, I'm a fuckhead. She deserves to be here just like everyone else, but her presence is doing crazy things to my head.

A group of girls form into a circle a few feet away from Bel and Ely, and they whirl around to join in on the conversation. Even from my spot across the room, I can feel the shift in the air. The fun, easygoing conversation has taken a nosedive in a different direction.

I take in Bel's glare of disgust, aimed at the blond girl closest to her.

"What the fuck?" I mutter to myself, watching as Drew tightens his hold on Bel, tugging her backward like he's afraid she might launch herself at the girl.

If someone is fucking with Bel... I pause for a moment, and my attention turns to Ely, who is staring straight ahead, her eyes glazed over, looking as if someone has slapped her. I shove out of the chair and watch them with confusion as the crowd surrounding them turns their faces toward me.

Fuck, they have to be talking about me. Why else would they look over here?

Bel yells something, but I can't hear it over the beat of the music. Then she lifts her hand and points at the door. I step down onto the makeshift dance floor, intending to stalk over there and figure out what the hell is going on, but then Ely whirls around and cuts back through the kitchen, crossing directly into my path.

She freezes in her tracks when she spots me, and the look of horror in her eyes is unmissable. I've done many things to her, said many things to her, but she's never looked at me like that. Like I'm a monster.

I open my mouth to say something, anything but she spins around and trudges back into the kitchen, fighting her way through the crowd to the back door.

Goddammit. I shouldn't give a fuck what it is that's suddenly made her thoughts on me shift, but I can't make myself not care. Not when it's about her. Or anything that concerns her.

"Elyse, wait," I call after her, but the music is too loud for her to hear me.

Anger replaces whatever I felt before, and I stalk over to where Drew and Bel stand, talking to one another.

"What just happened?"

Bel eyes me out of the corner of her eye. "You happened. Your little harem told her about your ritual, among a couple of other things. I think she just needs a minute to cool off."

I'm so confused. "What the hell are you talking about?"

Bel drags her finger up the side of her bicep. "That thing you do to the girls you've been with."

"Okay?" *What does that have to do with Elyse?*

Bel shakes her head, looking at me with disappointment. "Do you think the rumors about girls fawning over their desire to wear your signature mark never make it back to me? It's disgusting, if you ask me."

"Good thing I didn't fucking ask you, then," I snap, scanning the area for a way to get back to that door. Too many fucking people are in here.

"Watch it," Drew warns with a growl. "I don't care if you're her brother. Talk to her like that again, and we're going to have a problem."

Fucking shit. I need to pull it together. Bel hasn't done anything to deserve my shitty attitude. I release a sigh of defeat and focus my attention back on her.

"I'm sorry, Bel. I shouldn't have said that." I shake my head, trying to reel myself back in. "I'll go make sure Ely is okay."

"I don't know if that's a good idea," Bel warns.

In a perfect world, I'd leave her to her anger, let her go home and sleep it off. Whatever. The mark on her arm was just to release her from that nightmare; it's not like I fucked her. If I'd been inside her, the mark she wears would be much different, deeper, and clear to anyone who looks that she is mine and mine alone.

I swallow the visual, shaking my head, and reach behind them for another bottle of liquor. "I'm not afraid of Ely."

As badly as I don't want to, I need to try to fix this however I can. There's no way in hell I'm leaving her outside, in the dark, alone with Yanov still out there. When I turn in the direction of the back door, my worry of being able to get through the crowd eases when the masses part on their own as I cross the room.

Maybe the look on my face is enough warning, who knows. Or at least it is to everyone except Aries. He doesn't give a fuck if I'm pissed off.

He cuts into my path, blocking me from exiting the back door. "Where've you been, man? I didn't see you get here."

The smell of alcohol and pussy seeps off his pores. "I need to go out that way, asshole. Move."

Grinning, he steps aside with a sweeping bow. "Good luck fixing that clusterfuck."

Everyone thinks Aries is a playboy, stupid and attractive, but they don't have the first clue how fucked up he is, or worse, how dark and malicious he can be. I slip past him and exit through the door, traipsing onto the grass. It's darker than fuck out here.

I scan the dark grounds, but I don't see her anywhere. Nor do I want to call out for her because, depending on how upset she is, I wouldn't put it past her to run away from me. It takes a moment for my eyes to adjust to the darkness, but when they do, I can make out movement near the tree line, and that's when I spot her leaning against the trunk of a tall, fall-stripped oak. The moonlight plays across her fair skin, fading away into the dark of her hair.

My stomach twists into a tight knot as I stalk toward her. I can tell the moment she notices me, her dark gaze resting on me. I pause, waiting to see if she runs.

Do it. Run, Little Prey.

I'm playing with fire here, since I already know I won't be able to control myself if she takes off on me. The thrill of the hunt is too much to resist.

Unfortunately, she doesn't move. She stays right where she is, her back pressed firmly against the tree, looking every bit like the prey I call her, caught in a trap and waiting for the big monster to come and eat her.

I smile. "What are you doing out here alone in the dark, Little Prey?"

26

ELYSE

His commanding voice greets me in the dark. I knew he would follow me as soon as I saw him walking toward Bel and me in the house. I was hoping he would take the hint and give me some time to cool off out here alone, but apparently, even a moment of peace and quiet is too much to spare.

I turn to stare at him, watching as he basks in the moonlight like a god cut from stone. His biceps are accentuated and hugged tight by the dark gray Oakmount T-shirt he's wearing, and there's something about a guy in gray sweatpants that does it for me. There's a feral look in his eyes, his usually perfect hair mussed around his forehead.

Mussed because some bitch had been all over him. I have no right to be angry. He's not mine, and I'm not his. I know that, but I can't stop the jealousy from forming so I grit my teeth and fix my gaze somewhere off in the distance over his shoulder.

"Why do you care what I'm doing?"

"Because I do."

Even though I'm angry, I don't intend to play into his bullshit.

He walks all the way over to me, stopping with only a few inches separating us. With him this close I can feel the heat from his body wafting off him. Looking down, I spot a bottle of liquor in his hand. The guy has a drinking problem, but I know better than to tell him that. It never helped when I told my father, either.

"Don't you have someone else to harass?"

"I do, but no one I get as much joy out of harassing as you."

"Well, stop getting joy from it and go bother someone else." I try not to sound as hate-filled as I feel.

"Nope, not going to happen." He takes a swig from the bottle and wipes the excess alcohol from his lips with the back of his hand. "So are you going to tell me what the fuck you're doing out here alone in the dark with Yanov lurking around? I believe we had a conversation once before regarding your safety."

His words sting, and I scan the dark trees, suddenly feeling exposed and vulnerable. He's right; Yanov is still out there. *Waiting. Watching.* It's only a matter of time. I swallow around the knot of fear that forms in my throat at that reminder.

Sensing the darkness lingering on the fringes of my mind, Sebastian uses his free hand and tips my chin up, forcing me to look at him, bringing me back to the present.

"Relax. He's not out here. I would have noticed."

I'm still angry over seeing him with those girls. I want to hurt him and make him bleed. *Why do I care so much?* "Noticed? You're kidding, right? How can you notice anything with your lap covered in girls while you down a bottle of alcohol?" I shake my head in disgust. I know I shouldn't wear my emotions on my sleeve, but I can't continue to hide how I feel.

His gaze narrows, and his grip on my chin tightens."There are very few things related to you, Little Prey, that I don't notice."

I jerk my chin free from his grasp, and a breath shudders out of my lungs. "What the hell is that supposed to mean?"

We've been on this teeter-totter of emotions, going back and forth. The attitude I'm giving him is nothing like my usual self, but I feel like I've been pushed to the limit. I can't keep living like this. Every time he enters a room, my lungs tighten, and I forget how to breathe, how to exist. I don't know if it's from fear or lust, but the more I try to ignore him, the more I crave him.

Seconds tick on, and I can feel his eyes on me. I can hear those stupid girls in the kitchen talking about their scars and asking how I got mine because God knows he'd never touch someone who looks like me. I let my anger lead me and thrust my arm out toward him.

The scar, still scabbed over from his knife, is visible in the moonlight. "What does this mean? That I'm just another one of your conquests? Did you fuck all those girls?" I don't know why I'm asking him that when I already know the answer. Maybe I just want him to give me another reason to hate him.

"We both know I don't owe you an explanation," he whispers, his eyes on the mark like I've bared more than that skin up to my shoulder. He inches closer, and instinct tells me to retreat, but that's not an option with the massive oak tree at my back.

"No, you're right. You don't owe me an explanation for fucking every girl on campus." My tone is hard as I try to ignore my body's reaction to his proximity.

Before I can make sense of what's going on, he's got me trapped, caged in, his arms resting on either side of my head. The bottle of liquor bumps against the bark, emitting a soft clink. I shouldn't do it. I know I shouldn't but I breathe deeply, letting his cologne fill my lungs. It's then when all my senses seem to go out the window.

Clean. Home. That's what he smells like.

My entire body lights up, from the tips of my toes to the tips of my fingers. My core aches, my arousal soaking the cotton of my panties. How am I already aching for him? I want his hands on me so much it takes immense effort not to tip my hips up into his.

"Careful, Little Prey. If I wasn't so sure you hated my guts, I'd say that sounds a lot like jealousy. Or are you mad that it's not real? That I didn't fuck you before I marked you? Are you upset you didn't get the complete experience?"

Asshole. I can't hold his gaze when he's talking so crudely, and I know all it would take is one look for him to know the truth. "I'm not jealous of them. You're an adult; you can do what you want. Who you fuck has nothing to do with me."

"Yeah, you say that, but it's a bullshit response." He slams his hand against the tree near my face, and I jump, startled by the sudden movement.

"What do you want me to say? That I want you to fuck me? Oh please, Sebastian." I mock softly. "No, I think it's pretty clear we can't cross that bridge. Look what happened after the blow job. You can't look at me or even be in the same room as me for longer than five minutes." I trail off, shaking my head in disappointment because, once again, I've shown him how vulnerable he makes me.

When will I ever learn?

Never. Which is why I keep finding myself in these stupid situations. I lift my chin and prepare to escape the cage he's trapped me in, but when my gaze catches on his, I see something there that I've never seen before. *Guilt. Sadness.* It's only a brief glimpse, but it's there, reflecting back onto me.

"Fuck. Haven't you realized by now that it's not because I can't stand to fucking look at you, Ely?"

Oh God. This is when he destroys me for the last time. When he cuts out my still beating heart and tosses it at my feet. I turn my face away from him because I don't want to see his eyes when he lands that final blow. But nothing is ever simple with this man, and as soon as I turn away from him, he reaches for me, his fingers against my chin, dragging my gaze back to his.

"No, look at me. Fucking look at me." There's so much command in his voice I can't help but do so. I try to wipe my face clean of all emotion, but I can't. I'm not like him. Almost like he knows this, he frowns. "Ely. It's not anything that you're thinking. I can't be in a room with you or fucking look at you because it takes every ounce of self-control I have not to strip away your clothing with my knife and fuck you against the nearest surface until all you know is me. Until all you feel is my cock inside you, my weight above you, my cum dripping out of you."

I don't know what to think. How to react. It's like I'm having an out of body experience. All this time, he's been avoiding me because he's afraid of losing control?

"But... I thought. You've told me so many times that I'm nothing to you, and now you're saying you've wanted me this whole time?" The words fall from my lips with a bite of rage.

"Oh, Ely. I don't think you understand. You're this beautiful fucking parasite, eating away at all the darkness around my heart. I've had to tell myself you're nothing in hopes I could make myself believe it, but I can't. I never have. You're under my skin and in every fucking breath I take. You've destroyed me, and I fear there's no going back to where we were before. "

Wait, what? I part my lips, ready to explode on him, but my brain short-circuits the words, preventing them from coming out because Sebastian's firm, full, warm-as-hell lips press down on mine. I can barely comprehend what is happening right now, but what I do know is that I don't want this moment to end. Weeks of anger and resentment make me crave something I shouldn't, something I know is bound to only end in heartbreak.

Yet even with that warning in my mind, I press closer, not wanting a single inch of space between us. Our tongues tangle, and the taste of bourbon explodes in my mouth, and fuck, it's like coming home after being gone for months.

As usual, Sebastian takes complete control, one hand cradling my cheek, the other dropping the bottle of liquor so he can cup the other side of my face. He angles me in such a way that allows him to deepen the kiss, his thumb coming under my chin to tip my mouth back just right. I clutch onto his arms, my body melting into his, my knees trembling, threatening to give out on me. *Who knew a kiss could have such an impact?* Then again, this isn't just any kiss.

This is hate, want, desire, and lust all packed into one.

Laughter carries from somewhere off in the distance, and I jolt back into my body like a lightning strike. Wait...we can't do this. We shouldn't. I don't want to be another mark on his bedpost. I want to be special. More. Releasing my hold on his arms, I move my hands to his muscular chest and give him a shove to break the connection.

He breaks the kiss, pulling away just enough to stare down at me in the dark, his erratic breathing matching my own.

"Don't tell me you don't feel it?" Desire drips from his voice.

There's more laughter, and I hear someone's lilting voice. "*Sebastian, why don't you come play with us?*"

No. I'm just another tally, another girl he's claimed, minus the actual fucking, which I guess makes me less than them. The reality of that feels like being punched in the throat. I have to get away from him. I can't bear to be seen as nothing more than a stone when I know damn well that I'm a diamond, even if he doesn't see it. Tears prick my eyes, and I blink them away, because I do not want to cry in front of him. Titling my face away from him, I shove at his chest again, harder, but he barely moves, not even an inch.

"What's wrong?" His voice echoes in my mind.

"Everything." I shake my head. "Everything is wrong. This. Us. I'm not a toy. You can't just kiss me and play with me when you want, then toss me aside when you've had your fill. I'm not that type of girl, and I won't be treated like one. Hell, you've barely spoken to me lately, and when you do, it's filled with nothing but anger and hate."

"I don't hate you, Elyse."

I turn my face to look at him. "You do. I know hate when I see it. I was raised by a man who hates me, who can't even look at me without reminding me that I'm the reason for my mother's death. I know what hate looks like, Sebastian."

"I. Don't. Hate. You. Ely." He enunciates each word like that will make me believe him more. Stupidly, I scan his features for any proof that he's lying, but his face doesn't give much away.

"Even if you don't hate me, you've been acting like you do. You went from ignoring my existence to showing concern to acting like you don't care about me. It's a lot of hot and cold, and I can't handle it anymore."

"You're something else," he mutters under his breath.

"Just tell me what you want, Sebastian. Tell me what you want from me so I can stop second-guessing every interaction we have," I ask, needing to hear the answer.

He's given me part of it, but I need more.

When it comes to him, I'm so conflicted. I don't know what to do or believe.

"That's such a loaded question, and I have a million answers for it, but my biggest want, need, and desire is for you to shut that pretty fucking mouth of yours"—he strokes my cheek gently—"and let me kiss you."

All I can do is blink, and when he smirks at me, I swear my heart soars out of my chest. Leaning in, his lips brush against mine sensually, our breaths mingling together, and all there is, is him.

His scent and taste threaten to drown me and consume me from the outside in. "I never lied when I said you were my property. You've belonged to me since the night I found you, and not just because of your father's debt. You're mine because I say you're mine, and in every single way, Ely. Every. Fucking. Way."

27
ELYSE

Before I breathe, think, or form a coherent response to what he's said, we're kissing again. He devours me like he wants to crawl inside me and live there. My hands roam his chest, mapping a trail across flesh I've only ever dreamed about exploring until I reach his back and sink my fingers into his shirt, clinging to him.

The tree behind me digs into my back, even buffered by my hoodie, but I don't care about the pain. I don't even want to stop my hips from tilting up against him.

His rock-hard erection presses against my belly, digging in, and dammit, I wish we were lying down so I could have him put it right where I need it most. I'm greedy for more—an addict and he's my drug. His teeth graze my lip, nipping hard, and I whimper as the pain ignites my senses. He smiles against my skin as his mouth moves down my chin, his teeth grazing the sensitive flesh at my neck.

"Don't stop," I moan into the night.

He continues nipping at my flesh and lapping at the spots with his tongue after biting, making my heart beat wildly. I can't get enough of him. His big hands slide down my neck and circle my waist before slipping to the hem of my skirt.

Do I want this? Yes! A million times, yes.

I spread my legs without thought, giving him room to move between them. Anything he wants, he can have. Anything he wants, he can take. I just don't want him to stop. A whimper escapes me, and he pulls away to look at me, desire and need shining in his eyes.

"There's no backing out now, Little Prey. It's time for you to be as consumed by me as I'm consumed by you."

I swallow thickly at the low, deep menace in his tone like he's about to rip me apart with his bare teeth and make me beg him to do it again.

A glint of metal catches my eye in the dark as he bends. As he lifts the blade, I take in the wicked-looking knife that hovers an inch from my mouth. It's the one I've seen him with several times, the one he marked me with when I'd succumbed to my nightmare. I bite back a gasp, and the air between us crackles, sparks igniting and shooting off like firecrackers.

Fuck, what is he going to do with that?

With my anxiety never too far from my mind, a tiny warning goes off, telling me this could end badly, but I'm too caught up in the sensations to tell him to stop. Not that he would. The feral, unhinged look returns to his eyes, and he presses the flat edge of the knife against my mouth, the point resting against my cupid's bow.

Staring down at me, he orders, "Lick it for me, Ely."

I swallow hard. This knife is fucking sharp, but there's no give in his eyes, no room for negotiation. It's his way or no way. Some of the lingering fear and tension eases out of me, and I relax at the thought. All I have to do right now is feel.

Slowly, I part my lips and let my tongue slip out, caressing the edge of the blade with hesitation. His eyes gloss over, his pupils dilate, and the corner of his lip twitches up. He likes it. He fucking likes it, and more than that, I like seeing him so undone and at my mercy.

"I'm going to corrupt you, Little Prey. Ruin you for all others so you know nothing but me. My scent, my cock stretching your pussy, my name falling from your lips." It's a warning, but I'm past being warned away.

He could push me off a cliff, and I'd go gladly at this point.

He pulls the knife away, and I watch it disappear while he uses his free hand to ruck up my denim skirt, jerking it up over my waist. Goose bumps erupt across my bare skin, and I shiver as the cold air reaches my inner thighs and lower belly. Dropping to his knees, he slides the knife along the edge of my panties and then gives them a tug, the fabric biting into my flesh when he pulls them from my body.

Fucking hell, that shouldn't be so hot.

With the scrap of my panties slipped down to my ankles, he twists them off and tucks the cotton into his pocket. Dropping the knife by my feet so he can use both hands, he sinks his fingers into my thighs and wrenches them apart with bruising force, hiking my body up the tree. I catch myself, digging my nails into the bark.

"Sebastian." I whisper his name, and I'm not sure if it's to tell him to stop or to keep going.

Moving my legs to rest on his shoulders, he looks up at me over my mound, strands of hair curling against his forehead. He's so beautiful.

"Don't, Ely. Don't tell me to stop because I can't. I can't fucking stop. I need you. Need to taste you. Taste what's been mine this entire time."

Hell, how could I even consider stopping him with a confession like that? After a heartbeat, when he knows damn well this is happening, he pounces.

One second he's spreading my legs, his eyes on me, and the next, his teeth are tugging against my clit. Red hot pleasure rips through me, and my body curls toward him on instinct, my hips bowing up to give him better access. I bite my lip between my teeth to suppress a moan. I knew it would be good, but I didn't think it would be this good.

That skilled tongue of his flicks over my clit, teasing it before gliding down my center and to my entrance. My eyes roll to the back of my head. Using his tongue like he might his cock, he dips in and out, fucking me with it. It's perfect, but not enough. I need more. As if he knows this he drags his hands up to my thighs and curls a digit through the slick arousal coating my folds.

I'm burning hotter than the sun, flames of desire licking at the edges of my soul. I don't fear the burn, though, not with Sebastian between my legs. Keeping one hand braced against the tree, I grab his head with the other, sinking my fingers through his damp curls. If I'm going to hell, I might as well get the full experience.

"Mmmm. So fucking good," he murmurs against my folds, the vibrations zinging over my sensitive flesh.

"Please don't stop," I pant into the darkness.

"I couldn't even if I wanted to, Little Prey," he growls, and then I feel him at my entrance, his thick finger slipping inside me and sinking deep. I tighten around his finger, the muscles tensing from lack of use. There's a little discomfort, but it soon fades when he moves his finger in and out, slowly at first.

"All those nights I imagined your pussy around my cock...my imagination has nothing on this moment. So tight, so perfect. I'm going to have to stretch you, get you nice and wet to make sure you can take my cock, because you will be taking my cock."

All I can do is whimper, my mouth unable to speak words. Pleasure builds low in my belly, swirling, burning me from the inside out. Sebastian shows no mercy and burrows his face between my folds, his tongue flicking against my clit, carrying me higher and higher while his finger pumps in and out of me.

Without warning, he adds a second finger, stretching me. An uncomfortable ache follows, but it's so subtle that as soon as I feel it, it's gone, washed away in the undertow of pleasure. I clench tightly around his fingers, and it's almost embarrassing how turned on I am, the evidence of my arousal trickling down my thighs.

I squeeze my legs together, trapping his head, and that's when he fucks me with his fingers. I mean really fuck me, in and out, in and out, the pace relentless, my body moving up and down with the movement while his tongue does wicked things to my clit.

He consumes me, and I don't even care. I'd die happily at his feet so long as he lets me come first. My lungs burn, and I realize I'm not breathing. He's stealing the air right out of my lungs, sucking it right out of me with his lips latched on tight to my clit.

"Sebastian," I beg between gasps, "Please. Please."

I'm so close. My toes curl in my boots, every nerve ending on fire, my muscles tightening to the point of pain. He's right, he's going to destroy me for anyone else, and I don't care.

I whimper when he pulls away just long enough to growl out an order, "Come on my fucking tongue, Prey. Let me drink your arousal; let me have what's only made for me."

His filthy mouth adds gasoline to an already out-of-control fire, and when his lips latch back onto my clit, his fingers finding some magical spot at the top of my pussy, I burst into flames.

"Sebastian!" I scream his name as I dig my nails into his scalp, and he makes a noise, something close to a groan of approval, the sound slicing right through me.

With an undeniable need guiding him, he presses his whole face against my pussy, his mouth, his nose, all of it, almost like he's trying to truly devour me. A memory flashes in my mind of him fucking my face in almost an identical manner, and I let it play back in my head as I float back down from heaven.

I'm still catching my breath when he pulls away, his fingers still inside me, which he uses to fuck me lazily. There's a slight ache from the pressure, but it only adds to the onslaught of sensations.

"You beg so pretty, Ely." He grins and then leans in and bites my clit while he thrusts his fingers deep, lazily in my pussy. "Think you can come again for me?"

"I don't know," I tell him, but whine when he tries to pull his fingers out.

"Mmm, you're going to make a beast out of me," he snarls and assaults me with his tongue, worshipping my clit, while he fucks my pussy slowly. I'm high on pleasure, and I don't want it to stop.

I'm not sure how he does it, but he pulls another orgasm out of me, ripping it from my bones and making me scream his name.

I shudder against him, the aftershocks rippling through my body, making it difficult to breathe or exist. He lets me ride his hand through it, easing away only after my knees have stopped shaking and I've gained my footing.

Pushing to his feet, he towers over me, his six-foot frame drawing my five-foot-two one to my feet. I watch as he brings his hand to my mouth. I can see my juices coating his fingers, dripping down his wrist. "You have no idea how beautiful you are, how fucking perfect your face looks when you come. I can't wait to see it as I slide deep into your cunt. Owning you, forcing you to take every fucking inch."

I don't know what to say or how to react. I'm still reeling from the orgasms, and now he's showering me with praise and filthy fucking words.

Bringing the digits to my lips, he smiles. "Lick them clean, Prey. Taste yourself."

It's nothing less than an order, and I obey before I even consider it. Closing my lips around the digits, the slick, salty taste of my own release fills my mouth. It's not a bad taste. In fact, it turns me on to taste myself on his fingers. I flick my tongue against the digits, sucking intently until I've removed every drop of my release while staring into his eyes.

When he finally pulls away, his fingers leaving my mouth with a resounding pop, the reality of what we've done crashes down on me. I look away, hesitant and vulnerable now that he's peeled back my layers.

What happens now?

I want to ask that question so badly it makes me ache, but I don't want to ruin the moment. Sebastian reaches down and snags his knife off the ground while adjusting his bulging erection.

I sway on my feet, a wave of dizziness sweeping through me as he jerks my hoodie sleeve down, the back falling to pool around my hips and baring my arm to him. I look up at him, hesitant at what I might see in his eyes.

I don't know if I'll be able to handle a look of regret or anger. I already told him I don't want to be another girl to him. What I find is neither of those emotions; instead, he's looking at me with satisfaction and need.

My heart clenches in my chest with all these unfamiliar emotions. When he reaches for my hand, I give it to him without hesitation. I think nothing of it when he shifts the knife into my grasp, forcing me to take hold of it. His own hand blankets mine, wrapping around my grip tightly. Then his eyes are back on me. His own gaze is warm, tender.

He lifts the blade to my arm, and I hesitate, shrinking back.

"Sebastian, what are you doing?" I blink rapidly, trying not to sound as afraid as I feel.

"Making certain you understand you're more than they ever were to me." He moves the blade, aiming it right below the other mark. "Do it, Ely. Make the mark and claim your spot beside me."

I've still not caught my breath, and I blink a couple of times, trying to calm myself. He waits patiently, and once I feel I have a better grip, I carefully tip the sharp edge against my skin. My eyes dart from that one spot on my arm and back up to him.

A hiss of discomfort escapes me as a burning sensation zips across my flesh when he adds the correct pressure, guiding the blade through my skin and making a mark right below the second.

I'm mesmerized by the crimson blood that trails in a small stream down my bicep and over my elbow. The red against my alabaster skin is nothing short of an intoxicating image, one I'll never be able to unsee.

I drag my gaze away from my arm, nevertheless, afraid of the slight tingle of pleasure it gives me in my belly.

Looking from his mark and back up to my face, he reaches for me, wrapping a hand around my throat, using his grasp to bring me closer. His lips ghost against mine when he speaks. "*Mine.* You're mine in every sense of the word. The only one to bear my mark twice on your skin, and the only one I want."

It's not the words that terrify me at that moment, but their meaning. From this moment on, everything between us will be different. I can feel it in every beat of my heart.

"Do you understand?"

"Yes," I whisper hoarsely and sway on my feet when he releases me.

He smiles and then kneels to put the knife away. I look down, watching as he does, and that's when my entire world tilts on its axis, because there on the ground, nestled very visibly in the leaves, is Tanya's pregnancy test.

He goes still as his gaze fastens on it.

I'm consumed by dread. *No! No!* He has to understand. I can make him understand. I can explain. My stomach tightens to the point of pain, and I open my mouth to speak, but no words come out. I need to say something. I have to. But I can't. All I can do is watch in horror as his fingers curl around the test. He picks it up, bringing it closer to his face as if he's inspecting it. *No!* It's not what you think it is.

Pushing off the ground, he stands at his full height, towering above me, and I can feel the betrayal, see it etched into his face.

Fuck. Think, Elyse.

Those emerald eyes of his clash with my own, and the look of despair—of defeat—that I see there steals the air from my lungs. He brings the test closer, shoving it in my eyes as if I can't see it. As if I didn't know it was in my pocket all along.

"What the fuck is this, Elyse?"

Say something. Anything. I want to tell him that it's not my test, but fear has me in a chokehold that I can't escape. I part my lips and try to speak, but nothing comes out.

"Tell me this isn't real, Elyse." Anguish and despair thicken his voice, underlined with a hint of rage. I'm drowning in his pain. "Elyse! Tell me. Tell me that this isn't yours. That you're not having someone else's baby."

It's the rage that keeps me from speaking, from telling him the truth. I can't breathe as that anger morphs into old hurts, old wounds, opening up in my mind. My father screaming in my face so that all I can feel is his spit on my chin.

No. I can't see Sebastian that way. Not like that.

My lips tremble, and I open my mouth to tell him *no*, but again, nothing comes out. Not even a squeak.

"Elyse!? Sebastian!?" The sound of Bel's voice echoes over the lawn, calling from somewhere off in the distance. I can't do this right now. I can't stand here, unable to speak. To defend myself.

I don't think; all I do is react.

Before Sebastian can react or make a move, I lift my hand and shove him backward. Caught off guard, he wobbles back on unsteady legs, and I take off on a dead run back to the house. There's no way Sebastian will risk making a scene in front of Bel. At least not with the pregnancy test.

My lungs burn, and I spot Bel off the patio in the distance. As soon as we're close enough to see each other, the smile on her face slips away, and concern takes its place. She opens her arms to hug me, and I run right into them.

Drew hovers at her back like a shadow that never leaves. I try to swallow down the fear and anxiety coursing through me. I don't want Bel to ask me a million questions about what is going on between Sebastian and me. Especially when I have no idea what is going on, but I also know that I'll have to tell her everything at some point.

"Oh my God. Are you okay?" She tightens her grip on me. *No. I'm not.* I want to tell her, but I don't. My biggest priority is getting out of here and putting as much distance between Sebastian and me as I can. We both could use some space, and then maybe he'll come to his senses about what we did, and after I tell him about Tanya's pregnancy test, we can move on. Even if that means I might be fired, homeless, and sent back to my father.

"Can we...can we please go." I stumble over my words, and she releases me, choosing to wrap an arm around my shoulder and tug me into her side.

"Of course. Is...is everything okay? Did...Sebastian hurt you?" She guides me back up the steps, toward the house. Bel radiates a kindness that few others carry with them, and I'm grateful for her friendship.

"I'm okay...he didn't hurt me. It's not what you think it is," I whisper, still feeling the need to defend him even if I'm terrified of what might happen next.

I'm not scared of what he will do to me. I'm scared of the way he makes me feel, scared of the fact that I want to tell him it's not my test, that he's wrong because I can't fathom what I'll do if he doesn't believe me, but more than that, I'm terrified I'm falling for a man I can never have, and nothing is scarier than heartbreak.

28
SEBASTIAN

Rage simmers low in my gut. I'm not angry with Elyse, not specifically—more like the circumstances that got us here.

I'm tempted to chase her, to wrap my arms around her middle and pull her to the ground so I can claim her before I crack her open and spill all her secrets out.

Pregnant. How can that be?

I let my eyes drift closed because if I don't see her walking away then maybe that will curb some of the desire demanding that I go to her. After a minute, I open them, just in time to watch Bel slide her arm over Ely's shoulders while Drew walks them up the soft slope toward the packed driveway. I can still feel the need, the pressure on my chest urging me to go to her. If it was anyone else ushering her along I can't say I'd be standing here still. But it's Drew, and I trust him more than anyone else to keep her safe.

I look away and back down to the pregnancy test, closing my fist around it. It cracks in my hand as I squeeze the cheap plastic, and suddenly, I'm pissed off all over again. This piece of plastic might appear insignificant, but it's the sole reminder that she gave herself to someone else.

After...everything. All of it. I wouldn't be surprised if I made up all of this in my mind. The stolen looks, the tension and searing heat. The desire rips me apart from the inside out.

Having her so close yet so far away is killing me. Wanting her is wrong, especially because when she finds out the truth... *No. Stop.* I refuse to let my thoughts go there. I did what I had to do. I was protecting her.

I don't step out of the tree line until I spot Drew's headlights spin around the top of the drive and in the direction of the road, leading back toward campus. It's only then that I feel comfortable walking back to the house.

I'm still having a difficult time wrapping my head around the prospect of her being pregnant. Without even thinking the situation over in any great depth, I want to murder the fucker in cold blood who did this and raise the baby as my own, but that seems a bit irrational.

Irrational, yes, but not wrong.

There's a slight chill to the air, but it helps to cool my heated thoughts. I need to give myself a little time before I approach her again and force her to tell me the truth, and I should at least let Lee know I'm leaving before I disappear.

He's going to be pissed, as usual, at my absence, but I don't give a shit. He needs to wake up and realize the world is still going on all around him. Away from the parties, and the fucking, and the drinking. Outside The Mill, Oakmount, and his little kingdom.

When I enter the house, the blast of music smacks me in the face, making me grit my teeth. I skirt through the crowd, moving around some and shoving others out of the way. I spot Lee perched on top of the counter, still shirtless and still drinking from an almost empty bottle of gin.

I shout over the loud music as I step closer. "I'm leaving."

He blinks down at me, leaning to the side until he falls over to put his face near mine.

"What?"

"I'm fucking leaving," I bite out.

"Why? The party's barely started? I don't need to remind you that you have certain obligations. People expect to see you and fucking Drew, who seems to have already left."

I want to tell him the expectations can fuck off, but I get this strange feeling that there is something more important going on here. With a long sigh, I ease him into a sitting position by the shoulder until he's sitting again.

"Okay, spill. What's wrong?"

"Nothing's wrong. It's a fucking party, and you're my friend. We're supposed to be spending time together."

I snatch the bottle out of his hand, causing him to shift sideways again, but this time he catches himself on the edge of the countertop.

"All I'm hearing is lies."

"It's not a lie," Lee sneers.

"Sure it's not. You might be able to fool yourself, but you can't fool me, jackass. I know you drink, but not like this." I raise the bottle, then take a long gulp and chug back the rest. The alcohol burns a path of anger and despair down my throat.

"The only jackass I see is you. And nothing is wrong. Everything is perfectly fine."

"Really?" I blink at him, wondering if he really expects me to believe that.

He shrugs. "Oh, before I forget to tell you, you need to prepare yourself for an engagement party."

Startled by his response, I nearly choke on air. "Engagement party? What the hell?" I sputter.

That playboy smile and give no shits attitude he always wears slips from his face, and his eyes take on a murderous glare.

"You heard right. Good ole Mom and Dad found someone who's willing to marry my ass. So I guess congratulations are in order? I'm officially fucking engaged." He leans back to lie flat on the counter and snags another bottle from the other end.

I'm still trying to make my brain process what he told me. "Wait, you mean your parents arranged a marriage for you? And not only threatened it but have followed through?"

He nods and twists the plastic off the top of the bottle with his teeth.

I snatch it from him before he fucking hurts himself and pull the cork out by the small wood disk on the top. Then, even though I shouldn't, I hand it back to him. He's going through shit, and if he needs one night to drink his sorrows away I'm going to give him that.

He *hmms* as he takes a long pull, and most sloshes onto the counter since he's still mostly lying flat, only lifting his head enough to sip the dark liquor.

"Look, I don't know what I can do to help, but I'm here. Whatever you need."

Lee nods, but there's a faraway look in his eyes that I don't like, telling me he doesn't really hear anything I'm saying.

"Don't worry your little head about me. I've already come up with a resolution for my parents' perfectly-constructed plan. They'll never see it coming either." His smile sends shivers down my spine. It's that of a cross between a psychopath and a child who just won a year's worth of candy. In other words, it's downright terrifying.

"Don't fuck up your entire life for a little revenge, Lee."

God, I'm such a hypocrite.

"Oh, I'm not. Now enough about me. Where did that little maid of yours go?" Lee asks, through small sips.

I grit my teeth and clench my fists, forcing my thoughts back to my friend so I don't think about the test sitting in my pocket and weighing me down. "Bel and Drew took her home."

He smiles, "Don't think I didn't notice that you didn't deny her being yours."

I shake my head, and for once, I let the truth spill out. "Whatever is going on between me and her is complicated at best."

"Complicated is better than denial. You deserve to find happiness. I mean, look at Drew, if someone can love his psychotic ass, any of us have a chance."

"Yeah, sometimes I have to wonder what Bel sees in him," I joke.

Drew's changed. Don't get me wrong; he's still fucked up, and I'm not sure if he has any morals at all, but when it comes to my sister Bel, he cherishes her. Puts her first, loves her unconditionally, and I couldn't ask for someone better for her. Okay, maybe I could. Someone a smidge less annoying.

"I bet it's his cock. Have you seen it?" Lee grins, and I smile back at him.

"Please do not talk about Drew's cock or Bel in the same sentence ever again."

"You mean to tell me you don't think about your sister and best friend banging every day?"

While I'm mature, and can obviously understand that Bel and Drew are going to bang like rabbits, it doesn't mean I want it tossed in my face.

"Behave yourself tonight. I'm going home. I don't want any phone calls from the police, either. I mean it."

Lee moves to sit up but then sags back against the counter, thinking better of it. "You got it, dude!"

All I can do is shake my head as I turn to head toward the door, leaving him there to drown himself in his sorrows. I know I shouldn't go to Elyse, but I need answers. I'm desperate for them.

She might've escaped me earlier but tucked into the bedroom across the hall from me, there will be no escape.

I've barely stepped out the door to make my way out onto the front lawn when my phone chimes with an incoming text. I tug it out of my pocket and see the text is from Bel. Fuck me. I can only imagine what she has to say. Knowing Elyse, though, I doubt she told Bel anything. She's had many chances to share her dislike of me with Bel, but she never has, at least not to a degree that would give Bel concern.

I forgo ordering a ride and navigate to my texts instead to see what she needs.

BEL: *Elyse is staying with Drew and me tonight. I don't know what happened between you two, but she's really upset, and I think it would be best if you both gave each other some space.*

I tighten my grip on the phone. Are you kidding me? She was upset? Like she has a fucking reason? Because her secret was discovered? Before I can think better of it, I start in the direction of Drew's place. It isn't that far of a walk, and with this new development I can feel the anger threatening to pull me under. My fingers tingle, my muscles ache, and my heart beats furiously. Who the fuck does she think she is?

I doubt she told Bel the whole truth—that is, if she told her anything at all. From the fear in her eyes when I picked up the test, I highly doubt she's told anyone her news. With anger clouding my judgment, I find it hard to think clearly. I have no reason to be mad at Elyse, not technically, but I am. I'm so fucking angry. *Mine. She is mine.* Yet she's pregnant with another man's baby.

Even thinking about it makes my vision red.

It doesn't take long to arrive at the estate where Drew grew up. As I get closer, the guy at the security gate eyes me but doesn't say a word. Instead, he pushes a button and the gates open, allowing me entrance.

It's fucking weird to be on the other end of things. I can remember when Drew used to stand outside the gate at my house, threatening me and telling me I needed to let him see Bel or else. Fuck, have the tables turned.

As I suspected, security must've alerted him of my arrival since Drew greets me at the door, shirtless, a pair of checkered pajama pants hanging low on his hips.

"What's going on?" he asks in a friendly voice.

"Don't play coy with me, Drew. Where is she?" I grit out.

His brows pull together and he gives me a confused look before waving me inside. "Bel? She's in the bedroom washing her face. No need to show up. You could've called her, being that it's late and all."

I almost laugh. *This guy*. He gets a girlfriend and suddenly he gives a shit what time it is? I shake my head, and shove my clenched fists into my pockets. There's too much energy inside me, too much anger. *Why are you angry?* I ask myself because it makes no sense. She isn't yours. She doesn't belong to you. She doesn't carry your last name. She is no one to you, yet you're acting like she is the entire fucking universe. Pull it together.

Looking back at Drew, I mumble, "Not Bel, Elyse."

I start to pace, back and forth, back and forth. The mask of confusion slips from his face, and he narrows his gaze, almost like he's suspicious of me. "What the hell is going on with you?"

"Nothing. You wouldn't understand," I murmur, clenching my jaw so tightly it aches. The truth is a hard pill to swallow when you refuse to accept it. Maybe that's my problem; I need to stop fighting against fate.

No. I need to turn around and walk out of here.

Go home, give her space. Let her move on with her life, with her baby and whatever man tried to take her from me.

"Try me. I think I have you beat when it comes to dysfunctional." I watch him out of the corner of my eye as he crosses his arms over his chest.

No. I can't do it. The idea of leaving her and walking away for good is equivalent to carving a hole in my chest and expecting to carry on living.

"Fine. I'm trying to do the right thing, but it's hard. Harder than I thought it would be."

Drew nods. "Well, yeah. Nothing you *really* fucking want is ever easy. Sometimes you have to sit in the moment and let the pieces fall where they may."

I pause and look him dead ass in the eyes. "You get a girlfriend, and suddenly, you're Dr. Phil? Giving advice and being inspirational and shit."

He grins while shaking his head. "And shit."

I hear the slap of bare feet on tile before I catch sight of Bel coming down the stairs. As soon as she sees me, her eyes fill with disappointment. "What are you doing here?"

"Whatever I want."

Bel shakes her head. "I told you to give her space, and somehow that means come over?"

I swing on Bel, and Drew grabs my shoulders holding me back, his fingers pressing into the muscle. "I don't care if she wants space. Space fixes nothing." When she doesn't so much as blink, I continue, "How much space did Drew give you when you asked for it?"

Drew makes a scoffing sound, and Bel's cheeks flash pink. "It's not the same, and you know it. Ely is your employee, and you pushing yourself on her isn't fair."

I bite back a retort, the urge to tell her that Ely sure as fuck didn't think I was pushing myself on her earlier or on the night she had my cock stuffed down her throat. Instead of saying that, I release a long sigh and shrug off Drew's hold.

He lets his hands fall away, but he keeps himself close. He's standing here watching me like he thinks I might attack her. She's my fucking sister. I'd never do such a thing.

"Why are you acting like that?"

"Like what?"

"Like that." I gestured toward him. "Like I'm going to hurt her."

"No offense but you aren't really acting like yourself."

"So what? That doesn't mean I would hurt my sister." All he does is shrug, and I'm more disgusted with the thought of how he could think I'd ever do something like that. "If you're worried I'm going to hurt Ely or something, I wouldn't. I've had plenty of opportunities to do that. Remember, she lives in my house and is employed by me."

Bel darts her gaze around the brightly lit foyer. " I think it's you that needs to remember that. Plus, it doesn't really matter what you came here for. If it has to do with her she's already sleeping. It was only minutes from the time I took her to the guest room, and when I came back to check on her, that she was sleeping."

Fuck it. All I needed to know is where to find her. If they won't help me then I'll help myself. Ignoring both Bel and Drew, I start toward the guest rooms. It takes a second to remember where they are but as soon as I reach the end of the hall and cut across the wing, I turn left and shove open the first door I find.

The room is furnished but dark and empty.

Bel races down the hall behind me. "Sebastian! Stop. Leave her alone; she's sleeping."

I turn to face her, my heart racing, my stomach churning. I scrub a hand down my face. It's been hard enough continuing to distance myself, ignoring the desire, the want, and need, but this is pure torture.

"Please, Bel. I just need to see her. All I want to do is make sure she's safe."

She narrows her eyes, the bow of her lip dipping down as she considers what I've said. "Ugh, fine, but you have to promise me you won't wake her up."

I nod. "I just need to make sure she's safe; then I'll go."

Her face tells me she doesn't think it's a good idea, but she waves to the other side of the hall toward a door diagonal from the one we're standing in front of. Relief courses through me, to the point that I hadn't realized how much I needed this moment. I immediately cross the hall and carefully turn the knob.

The room is dark except for a slice of moonlight that's peeking in through the curtains. I hold my breath for a moment. Bel decides then to poke me hard in the ribs then points at my face, eyes wide.

"Don't wake her up," she mouths.

I nod, then slip through the partially open door and shut it soundlessly behind me. I don't understand the pull she has over me, but the way my lungs open, filling with air like it's the first time I've fully been able to breathe, tells me my body already knows.

Slowly I creep across the room toward the bed, and when I reach the edge of it, I stand there, looming above her. I can't bear to take my eyes off her. She's tucked into the covers, her long, dark hair fanned out across the pillow. She's on her side, her hands tucked under her head, looking so small and vulnerable.

This unbearable urge to claim her, to take her, and ruin her for anyone else claws at my insides, begging to be released. Needing something to keep me grounded, I squeeze the wood frame of the four-poster bed, digging my nails into it. Then I force myself to breathe slowly, in and out, until I no longer hear the thundering beat of my own heart in my ears.

Once I have control of myself again, I skirt the end of the bed and lower myself into the chair near the nightstand. Seeing her right now has sealed it for me. I can't let her go. I fucking can't.

Her delicate features are soft, no longer holding the usual hardness that she wears daily, except for a small furrow that has formed between her brow. Even though I know I shouldn't, I gently reach forward and brush a few lingering strands of hair off her cheek. I hold my breath waiting for her to wake up, but she doesn't stir.

The need to be closer to her forces me onto my knees, and I find myself kneeling beside the bed, staring at her sleeping face. So small, so vulnerable, so very fucking breakable. She needs to be protected—from everyone but especially me.

I grit my teeth and clench my hands together as my darker nature once again tries to assert itself. *Take her. Own her. Make her yours.* A feral growl threatens to rip out of me as I battle against myself. I promised Bel I wouldn't wake her, and I don't break my promises, not to her. So even though it kills me, I don't do anything but sit there and stare at her, watching her sleep. After a few minutes my gaze travels down the length of her body, and catches on her rising and falling chest. It lingers there for a long while and then out of nowhere, it hits me.

As badly as I want her to be mine, to keep her, I can't stand by and watch her be with another man. I have to let her go. Let her get on with her life. Or whatever life she's going to have. It's the right thing to do even if the thought of it makes me want to claw my eyes out.

Then again, the thought of seeing her round and swollen and pregnant with a child sends a pang through my chest. The feeling is so foreign I reach up and rub at the spot.

What the actual fuck? It's weird but the idea of her being big and heavy with a child makes me feel like I've lost something. Like her being with someone else has stolen that possible future from me, and the realization of that makes it hurt more.

So much so that I can't even look at her. I think I'm going to be sick. I stand and cross the room, forcing my feet to move. As soon as I'm out of the room I close the door quietly behind me.

Bel is standing across the hall, her back to the wall, looking like she's been waiting for me the entire time.

"Sebastian, will you tell me what's going on?"

I shake my head, squeezing the test in my pocket again. "Nothing is going on. Elyse made a choice, and even if it pains me to all hell, I'm going to respect it."

She follows on my heels as I start down the hall. "What does that mean?"

"It means nothing, Bel. It means nothing." I whisper the last part, feeling as if for the first time in my life, the one thing I want most is out of reach. I spent so long pushing her away, refusing to accept what was right in front of me that inevitably she ended up in the arms of another man. The only person to blame for the heartache I'm feeling is myself.

I head straight for the door, needing to get out of this place. Elyse is safe here. She doesn't need me. Drew steps out of the shadows just as I reach the door, his face twisted into a concerned look, his gaze bouncing between Bel and myself.

I bite the inside of my cheek, tasting the coppery tang of blood on my tongue. Drew's my best friend. One of many people I could tell, but I know telling him wouldn't change anything. It wouldn't make Elyse mine. So I say nothing.

When I step out into the night, my head is reeling.

How do you make yourself forget losing something that was never really yours to begin with?

29
ELYSE

It feels strange to make a bed just for the sake of making a bed. When you spend months cleaning up after others as a maid, it's hard to do nothing. Usually after I make the bed, I clean the bathroom, dust, and do the floors. I'm almost more anxious doing nothing because I feel like I'm going to be scolded for sitting here. Which is whatever since I know the real reason my anxiety is up has nothing to do with cleaning at all.

Every second of this morning has been like walking on eggshells, waiting for Sebastian to come bursting through the door, throw me over his shoulder, and drag me back to his mansion. I'm like a bug caught in a spider's web, waiting for it to come out and eat me.

I perch on the edge of the freshly made bed and stare out the window across the room. It's a lovely room, and I'd gladly stay here if I had no other option, but there's a certain security I feel with Sebastian, and I need to figure out what I'm going to do about everything.

He scared me. *No. That's not right.* He's scary, sure, but some part of me knows, even with the brutality, the knives, and his sharp words, that he'd never hurt me. Not like others have. I wasn't necessarily scared of him, but more of him finding out I stole the test from Tanya and having to admit it.

What if that's the tipping point in all of this? What if he kicks me out of his house? What if I have nowhere else to go? No one to protect me from Yanov?

It seems stupid since I'm working to pay off a debt, but everyone has a point where whatever they're trying to achieve no longer seems worth it. I don't want Sebastian to think I'm no longer worthy of being kept around.

My thoughts shift from the pregnancy test, as the memory of what we did pops back into my mind. It took a long time for my body to come down from the high he instilled last night. How he touched me in ways I didn't even know I'd enjoy.

How could I when my life had been one step away from rape most of my teenage life. I never wanted to do anything that might draw Yanov's attention. Not even when I was alone for fear he'd catch me and see it as some kind of invitation.

As a result, I barely know anything about sex and what I might enjoy in that area, but it's something I still want to explore. The connection I have with Sebastian is one I've never had with anyone else, and especially not a man. Even while I'm afraid of it, I'm more afraid of losing it, so I need to pull myself together and tell him the truth.

I'm about to gather the toothbrush Bel gave me and the clothes she thrust into my arms and told me to keep and head home when a knock against the heavy wood door jolts me out of my thoughts, sending my heartbeat pounding through my body on a wave of adrenaline.

"Come in," I call, having to clear my throat at the end to hide the squeak.

What the hell do I say if Sebastian walks in? I know I said I needed to get my shit together, but I thought I'd have more than ten minutes to do it. I don't get to think about it for long since, to my relief, Drew walks in.

I notice almost immediately that he's dressed very differently compared to his normal attire, wearing a black hoodie, jeans, and high-top sneakers. Dang, he's pretty, but there is an untamed quality to him that terrifies me and seems so at odds with Bel's pure sunshine personality.

I stand and face him, smoothing the short gray dress over the black tights Bel gave me. "Thank you again for letting me stay here. I was just about to grab my things and head back to Sebastian's. I can't even put into words how much it helped to have some time to think things through."

He studies me, his dark eyes clawing into the depths of my soul. Drew has a habit of looking at people in a way that makes them want to spill all their secrets. Stalking forward, he comes to stand beside me, his frame resting casually against the banister of the bed.

"There's no need to thank me. If you need a bed to sleep in, we have one. Actually we have a lot more than one, but you get the point."

I smile. "Of course. Well, I'm thankful, nonetheless."

He shrugs. "If it would help, you can move in."

I know without a doubt he's not offering because he wants to. This is not his idea.

I shake my head, sending my loose hair around my waist. "No, but thank you, really. I hate inconveniencing people. I need to figure this thing out with Sebastian, and I can't do that while living here. I also don't think he would be very happy if I did that."

I don't bother sharing with him that the only place I truly feel safe is with Sebastian. It's bad enough I've shared tiny bits and pieces with Bel.

He nods, his hands stuffed into his front pockets. "I mean, whatever you need help with, Bel and I are here for you. I hope you know that."

"Your kindness is appreciated, but you don't have to lie to me. I know I'm nothing more than an unnecessary nuisance that you tolerate because you love Bel."

He smirks, and when he smiles his eyes look a little less like he's going to eat me alive. "While that may be partially true, you're also someone my best friend cares about, regardless of what he says, or how stupid he is, so your safety and security are important to me by extension. Which leads me to my next question. What if I told you I could help fix things?"

I look away and down to the tips of my Converse. My gaze jumps to the battered tips of his boots, and then I look back up to his face again. "Help? How? In what way?"

He shrugs one broad shoulder. "It's not a guarantee, and most of the time it takes some work on both parts since afterward things can get a little hairy, but it helped Bel and me. I'm only bringing it up since I feel it might make Sebastian see things in a different light."

"I mean..." I consider what he's saying. It's obvious that Sebastian and I have been playing this yo-yo game, going back and forth. It would be nice to know his intentions and feelings. I weigh my options. It seems rude to decline, especially if he has a way to ease the tension between us. It might help lessen the blow of my confession, as well. "Okay, sure. Whatever you can do to help, I'm all ears. I want things to work out."

The corner of his mouth tips up the tiniest bit, and then he nods. "I'm happy to hear that. Apologies in advance for anything that might happen after this moment. It's not personal, I promise."

My brows pinch together as I stare up at him in confusion. "Apologies? What do you mean? Why're you apologizing?"

Before I can think or react, he's got me by the bicep, spun around, and a piece of rope jerked tight around my wrists. *How the...? What is happening right now?* I open my mouth to speak, and he shoves me down onto the bed. I land hard, my chest pressing uncomfortably under the weight.

"What are you doing?" I squeak out.

He lifts me easily by the hips and tosses me higher up the bed. I'm trying not to think the worst here, but it's impossible when my brain sends mixed signals. There's never been anything between Drew and I. He is cordial at best for Bel's sake. And she's my best friend. I would never touch him or do anything to ruin my friendship with her. I didn't think he would either, not with how in love and obsessed he is, but I guess I was wrong.

The possibility of losing Bel and Sebastian—it breaks my heart. I blink away the tears threatening to fall as memories loom at the edges of my mind. "Please, don't do this. I thought you loved Bel. I promise you don't want me."

He ties my ankles with the same rough rope, and the weight on the back of my legs lifts when he moves back to stand.

"Of course I love Bel. But this has nothing to do with her."

"Please... you don't want me." I gasp into the mattress.

"Relax, I'm not going to rape you or touch you sexually in any way. I would never cheat on Bel. She's my entire fucking world."

I nearly sigh in relief at his confession. "Then... what are you doing?"

"You told me you wanted my help, so I'm giving it to you."

I turn and rest my cheek against the mattress so I can breathe and try to catch sight of him from the corner of my eyes. He's looming behind me like a monster who's going to attack. I squeeze my eyes shut to fight off one of the memories of my past that appear in my mind.

Drew is not Yanov. He's not going to hurt you.

I repeat that to myself ten times over, but making my body

and mind believe that isn't easy. Especially not when he grabs me and tosses me up and onto his shoulder.

My imaginings of Sebastian doing this very thing to me make me feel foolish now. The air is pressed out of my gut as my weight bounces on his shoulder. "I changed my mind. I don't want your help anymore."

He slaps the back of my thigh hard enough to sting, and I jerk. "Stop talking and trust the process."

I gulp and watch the floor as he carries me down the stairs and outside. Not a soul comes out of the woodwork to help, and I know Bel must be gone for some reason.

Fuck. What is going on?

"Please, Drew," I pant out, barely able to draw breath with the position he holds me in." I mean it. I don't need your help if it involves me being kidnapped."

I hear a beep, then a soft emittance of laughter from Drew. "Will you just trust me?" I don't get the chance to answer him because he tosses me into the trunk of his car, slamming it closed and leaving me in the dark.

"Trust you? Are you kidding me?" I growl. "You just tossed me in the trunk of a car!!" I slam my hand against the roof of the trunk in frustration.

My lungs burn, feeling like they can't draw in enough air even though nothing stops me from doing so.

I catch his voice through the metal. "I've never done anything to make you believe that I'd hurt you, so calm down. Now, that might change if you start screaming like a banshee, and I have to pull over. I promise you don't want that to happen, and I don't think you want to piss Bel off, do you? Because she'll be upset if I have to do something because you were stupid."

Pissed at me? I squeeze my eyes closed a few times to let them adjust to the darkness. Dread slithers up my spine. Bel is my only friend. I can't lose her, not over some stupid misunderstanding.

Relax. It's going to be okay.

Opening my eyes, I stare into the darkness that surrounds me and repeat the words out loud, as if the sound of them will make them more convincing.

"It's going to be okay."

30
ELYSE

I settle into the trunk and try my best to ignore the tools, or whatever the hell it is that's back here digging into my hip with every bounce.

We drive around for a bit—not long, I don't think—but it's hard to tell time when you are imagining all the ways a situation could go wrong. Eventually, the car rolls to a stop, the engine turning off. Anticipation roars in my veins, my heartbeat picking up again.

The trunk opens, and I blink up at the light, Drew's hulking frame cutting through it. His face is emotionless, a mask. He reaches in and pulls me up and over his shoulder again. It hurts just as bad as the last time, and I know I'll have a bruise.

"You want to tell me what's happening?"At the very least, it's an attempt to distract him while I wiggle my wrists to loosen the ties. They don't budge. *Of fucking course.*

"Did a little ride in the trunk cool you off?" That's all he says. He doesn't tell me where he's taking me or what's going on.

I slump as he carries me. And I watch the grass under his feet turn to leaves, rocks, branches, and brush. *He's taking me into the woods.* Oh God. This is starting to look like an episode of a true crime documentary.

"You aren't planning to murder me, are you? I don't see how that would help things with Sebastian, but I'm a little worried right now so I thought it would be a good time to ask."

"Not today." That's the only response I get, and I won't lie, I'm pretty fucking annoyed at this point. While fear still lingers at the back of my mind, I have to wonder what the hell he plans to do with me out in the woods if he isn't going to hurt me or assault me.

I don't know how long we walk, but my chest aches from the pressure and gravity of being carried over his shoulder. After a few more minutes, his stride becomes smaller, and he slows his pace. We must be getting close to wherever he intends to take me.

Eventually, he shifts and slings me to the ground, and my body lands in a heap. I groan as circulation comes back to my stomach, ribs, and shoulders. "I'd rather you let me walk. Now I'm going to have a bruise the size of Texas on my stomach," I grumble.

Crouching down in front of me, he grabs the rope at my ankles. I thrust my hands toward him, hoping he's going to release me, but he tightens the knots instead and gives me a wink. I narrow my gaze, wishing I could get daggers to fly out of my eyes.

"Whatever game you're playing, I'm done. I don't want your help anymore."

"Too bad, you already agreed to it." He smirks and then turns, giving me his back.

"I didn't agree to anything," I snarl.

"She's all yours now," Drew announces, and my heart shoots back up into my throat as fear drives through me like a spike.

Did he sell me? Oh God. I can't go through this again.

Some of my fear ebbs when another one of Sebastian and Drew's friends pops up from behind a tree. *Lee.* His shoulder brushes over the bark of the tree as he turns in a circle, his sneakers turning up leaves from the forest floor. Backlit by the setting sun, he looks every inch the golden god the school believes him to be.

"Don't hurt her, and don't do anything stupid. If anything happens to her, Bel and Sebastian will have your head on a spike. Got it?"

Lee salutes him with a knowing grin. "Got it, Dad. You act like I'm a monster."

"Wait...don't. Please don't leave me here."

"Monster? No. Manic and completely unhinged at times? Yes."

While I don't know Drew that well, I've had enough interaction with him to know better. Lee, on the other hand, I know nothing about him. I've only ever seen him in passing and at functions where we both happened to be in attendance.

A whimper escapes me.

Drew shakes his head and turns to start walking away. "Don't be a baby. You'll be fine."

I watch his back until he disappears into the darkness. *Fuck.*

Then I shift my focus back to Lee. Rumor has it he is a party boy with a reputation for danger, but he seems the most...*normal* of the group as far as I've been able to tell. Okay, so I realize I'm trying to rationalize the situation so I don't have a panic attack, but it's not really working. My heart hammers against my ribs, and while I've learned to hide my fear over the years, it's difficult when I'm in the middle of nowhere with a man I don't know that well.

"Lee, can you untie me, please? It's almost dark, and I'm cold and tired."

"Unfortunately, I can't do that." The leaves crunch beneath

his feet as he walks over to me, pulling out some black object from his pocket. "Releasing you would ruin the surprise, so while I know you're uncomfortable, you're going to be okay."

How can he possibly know that?

"Says the one who wasn't kidnapped under the false pretense of being *'helped.'*" I shiver. "Just let me go."

"Not an option." He gives me a boyish smirk, and then my world goes dark as he ties something around my face. I feel pressure at the back of my head, like he's placing a blindfold on me, but then he puts something else on top of my head, similar to a headband.

"Lee, please? I'm begging you. Just let me go."

A humming sound emits from deep in his throat. "Oh, Elyse, don't beg me. I might not be able to resist. Actually, no, I take it back. Beg me to let you go, and maybe I will. I'm a sucker for a girl who begs. I'll almost always give her what she wants."

My throat constricts. There has been a lot of begging in my life.

Begging for my father to stop hitting me.

For Yanov to stop touching me.

For some God or whoever to help me.

It didn't once do me any good, so what's the point now? Exactly; there is none. I won't beg anyone ever again. Pressing my lips into a firm line, I glare at him, knowing he can't see my expression.

"Ah, there's your backbone. I knew you had one," he taunts. "Don't worry, Sebastian will take care of that soon enough, and maybe when it's over, you'll be made of steel this time instead of straw."

What the hell is he talking about?

"Stop talking in riddles," I snap. "If you won't let me go, can you at least tell me what is going on?"

He lifts me by the elbows, and the movement is so fast, I

stumble into his chest, catching a whiff of alcohol on his breath. That only intensifies the worrying in my gut. I've dealt with alcoholics my entire life. Any time my father had a drink, it never ended well for me.

"I don't want to ruin the surprise, silly," he jokes. "We should make sure you're properly dressed, though, right? A bunny can't run unless she's all dressed up."

I'm still processing his words when I feel the fabric of the dress part down the middle. Cold air hits my skin, and I recoil, trying to pull away. "Stop. What are you doing? Why are you cutting my clothes?"

"I'm not going to hurt you, Elyse. And I promise I won't look, Scout's honor." His tone is matter-of-fact. Like he's picking out clothes for a party. He spins me around and then cuts the fabric at my wrists.

I'm wearing basic department store white underwear, and I'm almost embarrassed to have him see me in them. Even more so when I'm bound and blindfolded.

His fingers toy with the strap of my bra. "An upgrade, I think."

He cuts the tights off, ripping them off at the ankle. Next is my underwear, and I shiver at the cold edge of the knife on my skin. It's not the same way Sebastian's knife feels against my skin. No, Lee's blade makes me shiver with fear.

I want to believe he won't hurt me, but I've been told that so many times in my life that I've come to expect the lie. It never ends the way I hope for it to end.

He maneuvers my legs, pulling them apart. I struggle in his grasp, pushing him with my hands. "Stop fighting me. I'm trying to get you dressed." I feel something soft, a fabric of some sort sliding against my flesh.

I settle but only for a moment, and that's when I realize he's not lying. I feel the fabric resting against my hips. It's silky and cold against my flesh. A pair of silk boy shorts, edged in lace, maybe?

"Hmm..." He makes a noise like he's thinking, and I pull my bound wrists up to cover my chest as best I can.

Humiliated isn't even the word I would use to describe this moment. More like assaulted and violated. Tears burn at the back of my eyes, and I don't bother stopping them. He can't see them, anyway, so there's no shame in letting them fall.

I feel the same silky material pull around my hips, not boy shorts, a bodysuit maybe. Its lace tickles my ribs, and he settles a clasp around the back of my neck. I'm covered now at least, and I admonish myself in my head for feeling grateful for that.

A loud cracking sound rings through the woods, and I freeze, my heart in my throat. *What was that? What's going on?* I start to think the worst. Is someone after us? Are they going to kill me? Was that a gunshot I heard?

Lee curses under his breath. "Aw, well, at least you're dressed. Drew wanted me to tell you the rules, but we don't have time for that since I need to get going."

"Get going?" I start to panic. "What do you mean?" My breaths become frantic. "Don't leave me out here alone!"

"Don't worry, the fun is about to start. And just a little heads-up, you should probably run, little one. The fox is a sly predator known for getting what he wants, and if he catches you, he gets to keep you."

"What...? What does that mean?" I'm so confused right now.

I hear something hit the ground by my feet, and then nothing but the sound of the woods around me.

I pause, my heavy breathing making it difficult to hear anything else. "Lee?"

He left me. No. Please. No.

"Lee!?" I scream for him, but I already know he's gone.

I move my hands up and jerk the blindfold down to my neck.

Twilight blinks through the towering trees. Everywhere I look is wilderness. I'm surrounded, swallowed up whole by it. I need to find a way out, but as I look around, there's nothing to signify which direction I should move in.

I take a calming breath and look down the length of my body. *What the hell did he dress me in?* It's some kind of bodysuit. It's the color gray, and dare I say, pretty if I was into strange men dressing me and leaving me stranded in the woods. *Okay, think Elyse.*

The wind howls through the trees, carrying with it a chilly breeze. I shiver, my heartbeat hammering against my ribs.

What if I get lost out here? What if someone finds me and hurts me? What if Yanov gets me? The more I think about the possibilities of what could go wrong, the more I struggle to stay present. My gaze catches on a knife that sticks in the dirt by my feet. *Okay.* At least I have a weapon, something to protect myself with.

It's okay. You can do it. Save yourself this time.

A crack that sounds more like a gunshot and eerily similar to the noise I heard earlier ripples through me, echoing off the trees. Is that what Lee meant? Is that why I'm dressed like a rabbit? Are they going to hunt me down and shoot me?

I slump into the pile of ripped clothing as sharp pain spears through my skull. A memory sweeps through me, threatening to drag me under.

The sharp report of the gun, cold tile under my back. The hot wash of blood beneath me.

Gripping my temples with both hands, I rock back and forth in the leaves, and I remember. *I was alone, cold, and left for dead, but he was there. He found me, and nursed me back to health. He was there the day I woke up in that bedroom, watching me. He's the reason I'm alive today. He saved me, even if he doesn't know it.*

Tears pour down my cheeks, and I lower my hands and

huddle into my knees. It's all I can do until it passes. Then I'll pick myself up and do what Lee said.

I'll run. I'll run away from this place and whoever is hunting me.

I'll return to Sebastian, to the only person I've ever felt safe with.

31
SEBASTIAN

The crowd for the hunt is thinner this year. I don't know if it's a good thing or a bad thing. It doesn't matter since this is my last year hosting the event. If I had known what a shit show this year was going to be I would have moved Lee into my position to take over the big event planning this year. He's done a lot, regardless, while I've been dealing with everything else.

He jogs up the slight hill to join me on a small platform near the front door, set at the edge of the driveway.

"Where were you? I saw Drew run up, too."

He shakes his head and pulls down his jacket. "Nowhere, man, just scouting things out, making sure the lanterns got set and that there weren't any major hazards."

I frown as I watch him. The scent of liquor wafts from him in waves. "Are you participating?"

He smiles wide. "Of course. This is my final chance to get out there and play. Did you bring your little pet?"

I roll my eyes and sigh. "She's not my little anything and definitely not a pet."

He chuckles softly. "Not your employee either?"

I shove his shoulder and stare at the small pack of runners moving and waiting next to the platform, surveying the people who will soon race across the lawn to the woods for the chase.

"Yes, she's my employee, but that's it."

"I have a feeling that's not all you want her to be."

The pregnancy test flashes in my mind. The image of her round with my child. *Fuck.* I can't handle this right now. "I don't want to talk about her with you, or anyone for that matter. Elyse and I are not a thing, never were, and never will be. Whatever you thought you saw, forget it. It's over."

This time he checks me with his shoulder. "I very much doubt that, Seb. You two have something magical going on."

"Oh, you're the expert now because you're engaged?"

His eyes flash cold, and his jaw clenches tight. "No, I'm not an expert at anything, even less love. I'm just telling you what I saw, and that if it's obvious to everyone else, then it should be pretty fucking clear to the two of you."

"Like I said, it doesn't matter," I snap and step up to the podium. My suit jacket is tight around my shoulders, and I shrug to try to shake off Lee's words.

The crowd sees me and goes quiet. I nod at them all and wave to the woods on my right. "Ladies and gentlemen, may I have your attention, please? The Mill House welcomes you to this year's event. *The Hunt* is an annual fundraiser we put on every year. It's a race for the depraved, filthy rich, and elite. You only win when you reach the cabin, and you must be the first runner there. Make it there, and the money is yours. If you're caught... well, the person who catches you gets to do whatever they want to you, outside of causing bodily harm."

There's some excited murmuring from everyone, chasers and hunters alike. I wave my hand to silence them. "As you know, every year we come up with new twists." I whip out my fox mask and pull it over my head.

There's an echoing gasp and some laughter. Then I watch as the rest of the hunters pull masks out of their pockets and bags to place them on their faces. Some are animals, like Lee in his panther mask, Drew, who wears a wolf mask, and Aries, who is a bear. There are other animals in the crowd, each with their own design. There's even one plague mask.

"You won't even be able to see the face of your hunter this year. Maybe...it will inspire our little rabbits to try something new. Perhaps it will give the hunt an added thrill." I keep my voice low and seductive, weaving the spell, adding the magic they expect from one of The Mill events.

I keep an eye on the time and the sun, and signal to Lee, who grabs the flare gun on the stage. At my nod, he raises the gun and squeezes the trigger. It goes off, a sharp crack ringing in my ears that echoes out across the waiting participants.

"Happy hunting..." I say into the microphone as the runners race across the lawn toward the trees.

The hunters stay back a moment, giving the prey a head start. It's usually more fun that way. It allows the runners to hide but also plants the seed of winning in their minds. They believe they can succeed if they get a head start and think they're ahead. It's a psychological mind fuck at best, but it does what it's supposed to.

Lee hops off the platform and tugs his hoodie off over his head.

"You should take the left quadrant if you're going to be on patrol. It seems only right since you seem dead set that you aren't participating this year." He clips each word, letting me know he's annoyed.

I grab the back of his neck hard and give him a little shake, then a shove. It makes him laugh as he catches his balance in motion and turns to flip me off.

"Happy hunting," he mocks and then turns to race off into the trees.

The rest of the pack follows him, and within a couple of minutes, all hunters have disappeared into the forest. With a sigh, I start toward the woods, my steps slow and precise. Fear and sex cling to the air, and I breathe the scents deep in my lungs. Fuck. I should be out there, chasing and claiming someone, but the thought of taking anyone but Elyse makes me sick to my stomach.

A few yards away, I spot Drew, headed toward the far edge of the wooded area. Well, I guess that ensures I stay to the left of the property. No way in hell do I want to run into him and Bel in the woods. It's bad enough that I know for a fact my best friend is fucking my sister, but to witness it? No fucking thank you.

Once I make it to the trees I shove my hands into my pockets and let the allure of calmness wash over me. It's a little chilly tonight—not as bad as last year, but I have a feeling it will get colder as it gets darker. People will take their revelry up to the house as they get tired of freezing their asses off.

A scream splits the slowly darkening woods, and I stop, cocking my head to the side to listen. Screaming, moaning, begging. None of those things are abnormal to hear out here, but that sound... It wasn't a normal scream of pleasure, of play. It was a banshee shout drenched in fear and dipped in pain.

Dammit. *Did someone hurt themselves already?* I race in the direction of where I heard the noise, scanning the trees and brush, hoping to catch sight of someone before I trek the entirety of the fucking property. That would be my fucking luck.

Unfortunately, there's nothing there, and I strain my senses against the gathering dark and sounds of others fucking, moaning, playing in the woods like some great pagan rite. *Weird.* I shake my head and try to let go of the strange impending feeling of doom that I have in my gut. *What the fuck is going on with me?*

I'm tempted to call out to the voice. It sounded feminine, but

I don't want to risk drawing the attention of some of the more zealous hunters. Some participants take things too far, and I'm not in the mood to nurse anyone's wounded pride tonight.

I catch the sound of rustling leaves behind a thicker copse of trees directly ahead of me, and I lean to the side to see if I can catch a glimpse of someone...hell, anything at all. It takes a lot to surprise me, and I'm not even really shocked since this is *The Hunt,* but when a tiny little woman comes rushing through the thicket, her body crashing into my chest, I am. Mainly because something about her, and the placement feels off. Wrong.

Chase participants rarely get this far out.

I catch her by the biceps, and she lashes out, instinctually fighting against my grip like she's fighting for her life. *What the fuck?* She's tiny, and if I wanted to, I could subdue her. Instead, I do a quick sweep of her body, trying to pinpoint anything that might give me a clue as to what the hell is going on. Knotted rope hangs off one wrist, gray rabbit ears adorn her head, and a black sash is tied around her throat.

I can't really make out what she's wearing, but from a quick glance, I'd assume some type of lingerie and black sneakers. *Who is this girl? Where did she come from?* None of the runners I had seen were wearing anything like this. I would've noticed.

She whimpers, trying to twist out of my grasp, which only makes me tighten my hold on her. I won't lie, her cries make my cock hard, but I swallow that desire down. I'm more curious as to who she is, and how she ended up this far out here.

I stare at her face, my gaze roaming over her eyes, nose, and lips in the paltry moonlight shining through the trees.

Delicate. Breakable. Like porcelain.

The ground beneath my feet crumbles, and my entire world shifts into sharp focus. *It can't be.* How? I didn't invite her, and no one else would dare, and somehow here she is, a participant in The Hunt.

"Elyse," I breathe.

Her big blue eyes widen with fear, and there's this faraway look in her eyes. "Please... don't. Just let me go."

Let you go? She's talking gibberish.

"Let you go?" I hiss.

"I don't want to be kidnapped again."

Something spears through me. *Kidnapped?* Who kidnapped her? I scan the trees over her head, half expecting another person to pop out. Yanov, mainly, but could be any unfortunate soul at this point. But, there's no one else there.

"There's no one there," I murmur and then ask, "Who kidnapped you?"

She shoves at my chest again, tears trailing down her cheeks. I don't want to let her go, but it's obvious touching her is making things worse. "Let me go. Please, let me go!"

With a sigh I soften my grasp, and she tugs her arms free like a thread through the eye of a needle. Studying her, I notice more rope, this time hanging off her right ankle. It looks cut. I survey the area for any other clues, and my gaze catches on something shiny. That's when I see the blade of a small knife she's wielding in her hand.

My gaze shifts almost involuntarily to the gray bodysuit she's wearing. Spaghetti straps and silk hug her body. Lace panel cutouts give me glimpses of bare, goosebumped flesh, and I have to swallow hard.

Shit. What the fuck is going on?

I reach for her again, mainly because I need to touch her to ensure she's real, and maybe touching her will give me an answer because I need to know what the fuck is happening. *Is she out here to play? Was she planted here?* I don't get very far because she releases a screech of pure terror and swings the knife toward me like she thinks I'm going to hurt her.

With a long exhale, I snatch her wrist, the one holding the

knife, and tug her back against my chest. At the very least to give her some of my body heat. Her skin is ice cold now that the sun has set. *How long has she been out here?*

"If you cut me before I'm ready to play I'm going to get mad, and then I'll have to punish you," I hiss.

She jerks against me and freezes, her wrist still caught in my grasp.

Is she finally giving up? Then, like her fight or flight has been activated, she moves with precision, twisting her wrist hard, forcing me to lose my grip. The knife knicks my suit jacket, and all I can do is shake my head. Fucking hell, I thought she was done destroying my clothing.

I don't have enough time to grab her again, and like the bunny she's dressed as she scampers off into the woods. Adrenaline races in my veins, awakening needs and desires I'd spent the last couple of days burying.

My instincts beg me to give in, to chase her down and claim her, but if I do that, it's over. She will be mine whether she wants it or not, and that baby inside her will be mine, as well.

Her body, her soul, her life. All fucking mine.

It's not a choice but a need. A bone-deep ache I can't reject. I have no other choice. I can't let her go. The possibility that someone else might find her and claim her makes me murderous.. I strip off my jacket, hanging it on a low tree branch, and tuck the flashlight into my pants pocket.

Then I start to walk, my steps slow but without hesitation. I know this property and have been playing this game since I was a teenager. *She can't escape me. Not at my own game.* I watch curiously as she cuts a path through the trees.

She's fast, faster than I thought she'd be, I'll give her that.

Desire ripples through me, bringing with it heat. I tug the tie I'm wearing loose, letting it hang limply around my neck. I choose not to toss it as it might come in handy later. Depending upon how squirmy she is. I cut around the trees, going left to see if I can cut her off if I move quickly enough. The sheath of my favorite knife rubs against my ankle, reminding me that it's there.

Something hot and molten fills my veins, igniting things I've been suppressing. It's as if my world shifts on its axis like I've been waiting for this very moment, this one perfect second, to come back to myself.

Of course it would be my Ely who brings me home.

"You can't hide from me, Ely. I know these woods like the back of my hand." I taunt.

Leaning into those feelings, I finally race after her, closing the distance between us. She hasn't looked back once, and it only takes a minute to catch her around the waist, lifting her off her feet and taking her down to the cold-packed earth.

There's a soft bed of leaves beneath us, but I know she'll be aching from the hit tomorrow. Being that she's pregnant, I can't risk hurting her out here, or at all, so while I want to unleash myself on her, I remind myself that I must maintain control and be gentle. Something I have no experience being.

"Look what I caught, a little rabbit."

She, on the other hand, doesn't think she has to be gentle, and swipes at me with the knife. I roughly lever my weight off her, pressing my hips into hers and anchoring her arms to the forest floor.

"Mmm, she's got teeth. But so do I." The words come out in a low groan as I lean in and run the rubber mouth of the fox mask down her neck.

She whimpers. Trembles under me, the feeling entering my own body. I stare down at her face, taking note of her pinched features, the way her eyes are squeezed shut, like she's trying to crawl inside herself. *Wait*. The realization of it all slams into me like a brick wall. This isn't a game to her. She's truly fucking terrified.

I slowly raise the mask up to rest on top of my head and lower my face near hers. "Ely, look at me."

She shakes her head hard, and I spot the streak of tears as they slide down the apples of her cheeks. There's a smudge of dirt on her pretty pointed chin.

"Ely," I whisper. "You're safe. Always safe. I'm not going to hurt you. Open your eyes and see. I've taken off the mask."

Her body shudders against me once more, and it's not in pleasure. *Fucking hell.* How did I not see how far down the rabbit hole she'd gone? Trapped in a memory, triggered by the chase.

"Ely, Ely, Ely..." I continue saying her name, hoping to bring her back.

It takes a minute and more patience than I ever thought I'd be capable of possessing, but slowly, the panic recedes, and she cracks one eye open to look up at me. The only way to describe the look in her eyes is relief. Complete relief.

"Seb...Sebastian?" Her voice cracks, ending on a sob.

"Yes." I nod, searching her eyes for sanity. "It's me. You're okay."

She blinks her eyes open, her gaze darting around the quiet forest before coming back to my face. "You...you did this? You had them kidnap me?" I don't miss the way her voice rises, ringing with panic.

"No, I didn't have *them* kidnap you. I didn't know you were out here." All I can do is shake my head. Fucking Christ. I should've known something like this would happen. Why would I ever think she signed up or willingly joined the event? "It was probably fucking Lee."

She nods once, then again. "Yes, he... he dressed me in this... whatever it is...and Drew. He was...he brought me out here." Her lips tremble as she speaks, but at least she is here, her mind present, with me.

I'm a little surprised that Drew was involved, being that Elyse and Bel are friends, but that doesn't matter. I'll deal with them assholes later. Right now, my concern is Elyse.

"Listen, it's going to be okay. They were just trying to fuck with me."

"Wait, why? What's happening? Why did they bring me out into the woods and dump me here?" She questions, her voice small and whisper thin. "And how did you know I would be here? Are you going to hurt me?"

I had hoped this event would come and go without a hitch, but I guess Lee and Drew had other fucking plans. "No, no one is going to hurt you. Lee stuck you in the middle of the annual event for The Mill. *The Hunt.*"

Her eyes go wide. "*The Hunt?* Like the sex game thing."

I feel my neck flash hot at her accusation. "Yes, it's a primal hunt. A lot of people beg for an invitation to this event," I say, almost indignantly. "But you didn't sign up for it. You aren't here because you want to be, so it's okay. I can take you back to the house."

I push up to ease some of my weight off her, but when her tiny hands curl into the fabric of my shirt, I pause. "Wait."

Her blue eyes shine like luminous pools of water. I notice she's breathing deeper now, her features relaxed, and it allows me to calm as well, but in the wake of that calmness, I realize how close our bodies are and how badly I still want her. We never finished our conversation from last night, but discussing that now feels wrong. I know we need to talk about it, but all I want is to be inside her, to claim her, and keep her.

My cock grows thick at the thought, and I realize the moment she feels it pressing against her pussy. A soft breath escapes her lips, similar to that of a gasp but more sexual. Her pretty blue eyes widen with shock that bleeds into curiosity as we stare at each other.

The air between our bodies grows heavy, electrically charged. I find myself panting, a desperate need threatening to tear me apart at the seams. The fate of *us* lies in her hands, and only hers. If she wants me to take her back to the mansion, I will.

But if she gets up and runs from me, there will be no going back. I will chase her, and when I catch her, I will fuck her into submission until the only thing she sees and feels is me.

32
ELYSE

Shock waves ripple across my skin, and I find it hard to admit even to myself how turned on I am right now. As afraid as I was a short time ago, that fear is nothing but a fleeting memory now. Especially with Sebastian's cock pressed against my pussy. If I lift my hips even an inch, I'll have him right where I need him.

No. I can't. This is wrong. I shouldn't be here.

I look away, and the heat, the tension…it snaps.

Shivers wrack my body as adrenaline continues to course through me. My brain picks at the things Sebastian told me. How this is a game—*The Hunt*, he called it. I can't seem to wrap my brain around why Lee and Drew thought putting me in the middle of it was a good idea.

Even worse, now I'm wondering if Sebastian was going to play this game with another woman. That seems to cut through the haze more than anything else. Him taking another woman down to the bare leaves and fucking her like an animal.

Oh. Fuck. No.

I shove at his chest, and his mouth goes slack under the

shadow of the mask. Concern is etched deep into his features. "Move. I want to get up."

He nods and slowly pulls away.

"Why would your friends bring me out here? They said they were trying to help us. That this would help us. I don't understand how any of this is helping us." I feel like I'm losing my mind, and maybe I am.

What was the intention behind all of this?

He scrubs his hand up his face, almost toppling the mask off the top of his head. "Fuck. I'm going to kill both of them."

I scramble to my feet and stare down at him, but as soon as my eyes lock on his, I realize he's not looking at my face. His dark gaze is trained on my body, and the flames of desire blaze a path of territorial need from my thighs up to my tits.

I rip at the blindfold that's still hanging around my neck, and then tug at the fabric, but the knot is too tight. Annoyed, I give up and turn my attention back to him.

"Why are you people like this?"

"Like what?"

"Psychopaths who kidnap people and bring them into the woods to be attacked by other people."

"I'm sure there is a reasonable explanation for why they did this, and I will figure it out as soon as I get you back to the mansion. If that's where you want to go?" His tone has an undercurrent, and it's like he's asking me something without *asking* me.

I'm not sure if I'm reading too deeply into it or not. Is he asking me if I want to play? If I want to be hunted by him? I can feel him watching me, his gaze penetrating deep into the darkest parts of my soul, shedding light on spots that have never seen or felt the warmth of the sun. I trust him. I know this. I trust him more than I've trusted even those that were supposed to protect me and raise me. Sebastian would never hurt me.

He shoves off the leaf-covered ground in one smooth motion, nothing like me scrambling to get my legs beneath me.

"Yes, and that explanation is that you're all in desperate need of psychological help."

Even as I say the words, my heart hammers against my ribs, nervous energy zinging up my spine. But mixed with that nervousness is a deep-seated arousal. Is it fucked up of me to want him like I do? To be taken in such a way that mimics the exact scenarios I found myself in with Yanov?

"Oh, we all need psychological help, Little Prey. Even you, since I know what you're thinking right now, even without asking." His voice is low, dipped in danger.

Shit. I take one hesitant step backward, and he cocks his head to the side. I can almost hear his unasked question in my mind.

Have you made your decision yet?

"Think it through because if you run, I will chase you, and when I catch you—and we both know I will—there will not be a single thing to stop me from claiming you. Do you understand, Ely?"

"What if I want you to stop?" I whisper.

He grins, and it both terrifies me and excites me. "I doubt you'll want me to stop, but if you do then say the word *red.*"

I nod and swallow down the fear and hesitation.

I've made my decision. We both know it.

"Are you sure about this? I need to make certain that you understand the consequences. Are you ready to be chased, captured, and fucked?" His words are still slow and enunciated, like he wants to make sure I understand.

I can't explain it. *Why?* Why is this urge rushing through me? *I want it.* I want him to hunt me down and fuck me in the woods until there is nothing left of Ely, until I'm *his little prey* and nothing else. I want to break free of the hold Yanov has on me. I want to learn to love myself, to trust, and I can't do that if I continue to hide behind the person I used to be.

It's now or never.

"I trust you, Sebastian," I tell him because I need him to know I'm giving up my power and control.

"You really shouldn't say things like that." He takes a predatory step toward me, and I can see the hunter lurking beneath the surface, waiting to come out and play.

"Why?" My voice wobbles.

"Because men like me take your trust, break it, and then shove it back at you. We eat fragile girls like you for breakfast and spit out the bones. Is that what you want me to do to you?"

"I don't think you're the monster you want me to believe you are, and even if you are, I could never see you like that."

"Maybe it's time I let you see the real me, let you feel what it's like to be broken in two."

"That's the problem, Sebastian. I'm already broken, and so are you, but maybe there's still hope for us. Maybe we can break free of the chains trapping us in who we used to be. Maybe we can be whole."

With one last, devastated look, I turn my back on the old me, and I run. Not like I did before, like I was trying to escape, but like I'm running toward something.

Racing away from the death of the woman I used to be. That's what he can give me. The ability to take it all away and make me into someone else. Someone who deserves to be touched and looked at the way he touches and looks at me.

I race through the dark, only tiny lanterns casting light here and there as I go. Adrenaline drives me higher and higher. I hear his footfalls crash behind me a second later. He's fast, even in his suit. It makes me smile before I feel the ghost of his hand near my back. *Shit.*

I burst forward, quickening my pace, trying to stay ahead of him, jumping logs and shoving branches into his line of path.

Air burns in my lungs, the organs aching, but it feels good at the same time. I barely notice the chill on my skin as my body warms from the inside out from the exercise and the memory of his hands on my body.

It started as fear, but now it's different. I quicken my pace but startle when something to my left catches my attention. A man has a woman pinned to the ground while he fucks her from behind, almost like he hates her. She mewls, panting and pushing back against him. It's erotic and puts the porn I've watched to shame.

Distracted by the sex taking place mere feet away, I'm not surprised when his hand closes in around the back of my neck. His grip is hard, and I scramble to get away, but he's got a good hold on me.

Without releasing me, he turns me in his arms to face him, and I'm greeted by the eerie mask of a fox. The usual panic returns, but I stare into his eyes through the holes, reminding myself that this is Sebastian. That I'm safe, and all I have to do is say the word and he'll stop.

"Little Prey," he says, his voice low and dark. "You have no idea what you've just done. Running from me. Making me chase you."

He drags me through a copse of trees but doesn't release me, no matter how much I struggle and swat his hands away. When we are alone again, with only the sounds of the forest for company, he shoves me forward, and I stumble to the ground on my knees. I wince as I fall, but the burn only adds to the rest of it. It's one more sensation to drown out the terror, the fear, the self-loathing.

As he circles me like a predator, I move to get back on my feet, and his hold changes. He digs his fingers into my hair, pulling my head back with my neck outstretched.

"What am I going to do with you, Ely? You deserve a punishment for teasing me, not a reward, but I want you so fucking bad I'm tempted to do just that. To reward you for being a good rabbit and running from the predator."

He tugs me by the hair, and my scalp burns, but it doesn't hurt enough for me to say *red*. It joins the other little stings and cuts to add to the experience. I almost feel like I'm in a haze, standing outside my own body, watching as I give myself to him.

In my mind, we are the only two people in the entire world here right now.

The hunter.

And his prey.

He pulls his knife from his ankle, shaking his leg so his pants fall back over the sheath.

I catch sight of the sharp blade in the little bit of moonlight that cuts through the trees. The blade dances in front of my eyes, and I watch, mesmerized by the flick of it. Then he slides the tip down my right arm. He doesn't cut me with it, just caresses, until it reaches the scrap of rope at my wrist. He jerks the blade hard so it digs into my skin, and the rope snaps beneath the pressure. I'm free. I resist the urge to rub at the small burn marks that reside there now. He does the same to the one on my ankle, then gives me another circle.

"Should I call you Little Rabbit?" He jerks his chin up to the bunny ears I'm still wearing.

I shake my head and tug them off to throw them on the ground.

"Ahhh, there's my Little Prey." His seductive tone reaches inside me and strokes me from the inside out. "I've caught you, and what did I say I'd do if I caught you?"

Crowding me with his body, giving me no escape, he reaches

between my thighs and cups my sex. A shocked gasp slips out of me, and my core tightens in approval as his fingers press against the silk between my thighs.

"Little Prey... you're really trying my patience."

With the knife in his other hand, he uses the tip to trace a path over my collarbones, then down between my breasts and lower to bump over my belly button until the blade replaces his hand, the point of the blade resting toward my opening with the flat of the blade angled up against my clit.

My lungs burn, and while my brain continues to remind me that I'm in danger and that this could end in a terrible way, I lean into that trust.

"You...you said you'd fuck me. Mark me." My voice sounds different, sensual, labored. I want him. I need him.

"Mmm, good girl," he praises.

"Are you going to hurt me?" I ask, my voice hesitant.

Do I want to know? Worst of all, will I let him?

"Do you want me to hurt you?" he counters, cocking his head to the side.

I bite my lip and shake my head. "No, but I want you to fuck me."

A groan emits from his throat, and I won't lie—it's the sexiest sound I've ever heard.

"Oh, Little Prey. I'm going to fuck you. I'm going to fuck you and own you in ways you've never been used before, but before I do that, I'm going to prepare your little cunt. Get your pussy dripping wet, and stretch you so I don't tear you with my cock." He rocks the knife forward and back, giving me a little sensation but nothing like what I need to ease the ache there.

I squeeze my eyes closed, trying to focus on the feeling alone, but he removes the knife, and I blink my eyes open and stare up at him, begging for him to continue.

"Tell me again, do you trust me, Elyse?"

33
ELYSE

I swallow thickly and nod my head. "You know I trust you."

"Trust me not to hurt you?" His voice carries a hint of amusement, and I'm not sure I like where this is going.

"What are you going to do?"

I keep my gaze on him as he watches me so intensely through the features of a snarling fox. I'm left suspended in anticipation.

"Are you sure, Elyse? Do you really trust me?" he questions once more, heightening my fear.

"Yes. Yes. I'm sure."

He takes a step back and grabs the crotch of my bodysuit, pulling it away from my skin. With his other hand, he brings the knife in a downward motion, slicing into the fabric like butter. It parts down the middle, leaving two flaps against my rib cage and my bottom half bare. His gaze lingers over my skin, and I can hear how hard he swallows, mixed with the heavy pants of breath that fill his lungs. He's consumed by me, and I can't say I'm not every bit as consumed by him.

"Get on your knees." It's an order, not a request, and I startle at the darkness in his voice. Doubt flickers in my mind, but I push it away. *You're safe.* Without thinking of the why or the what, I drop down to my knees, trying not to cringe at the cold, damp leaves that stick to my skin.

Sebastian takes a step forward and presses a hand to my chest, pushing me backward. "Lie down and give yourself to me, Prey. Let's see if you trust me as much as you say you do."

I let him guide me to my back and watch curiously as he drops to his knees, the night sky above blanketing us with its stars. I notice the way his hands are clenched tight, braced on his thighs. He looks downright frightening, but somehow I know I've never been safer than I am right now.

There's a slight tremble to my voice, more from the fear of anticipation than actual fear of him. "What are you going to do to me?"

"Whatever I want, Little Prey, and you're going to let me because you're mine. All. Fucking. Mine."

I swallow past the lump forming in my throat and try to wrap my head around the onslaught of emotions that are barreling into me. He grabs me by the ankle and pulls me closer, but instead of putting my leg back on the ground, he rests it on one of his shoulders and maneuvers me, my legs spread wide open to him. The desire to snap my legs closed is overwhelming and not because I don't want him to touch me, but because it makes me feel vulnerable to show the most sacred, untouched parts of my body. Not that he knows they're untouched.

I consider telling him the truth—that I'm a virgin—but snap my mouth closed before any words can come out. I don't want him to reject me for that simple reason alone. I don't want this moment between us to end. By the time he finds out, it will be too late to stop.

I keep my gaze on him, watching intently so I don't miss anything. The air in my lungs stutters out when the knife returns to view.

"Keep your leg against my shoulder, and don't move it. I'd hate to accidentally hurt you." Thought his tone is teasing, I know he's serious from the dead-ass look in his eyes. My body involuntarily shivers at his confession.

What the hell is he going to do with that knife? Even though I question his motives, I don't make a move to get up or stop him.

"Mmm, so fucking perfect," he murmurs, staring down at my pussy. "I can't wait to see how she looks stuffed full of my cock."

Slowly, he lifts the mask up to rest on top of his head. Then it's like slow motion as he brings the hilt of the knife to his lips. Using two fingers, he holds the steel blade and wets the hilt, pressing it deep into his mouth.

It's fucked up, but also strangely erotic to watch. When he pulls the hilt of the knife from his mouth, it's wet with saliva, and I stare up at him, confused. His fingers gently stroke against my inner thigh, and when he drops his hand, the knife disappearing from view, I freeze.

"Wh-what are you doing?"

"Remember, keep very still, Little Prey." His voice is a whisper, and my nipples harden to stiff points as his fingers brush against my wet, sensitive skin.

Holy shit. My body heat rises to a combustible level.

Lifting my head to get a better look, I watch as he flips the blade around the hilt end toward my entrance. *Fuck no.* He isn't going to do what I think he is...is he?

"Sebastian." I'm trembling now, my gaze ping-ponging between where he touches me and his face.

"Yes, Little Prey?"

The hilt brushes over my clit, and every nerve ending comes alive. I can barely breathe, let alone form a coherent thought, but my worry for him overshadows that pleasure. The blade is sharp, and if he's going to put the other end inside me or touch me with it, he'll need to be holding the blade to maintain complete control.

"You can't..." The air escapes my lungs as he slides the end back over my clit, and I whimper from the onslaught of sensations.

"What was that?" He chuckles darkly.

"Stop. You can't. You'll cut yourself." My response comes out in a rush.

He gives my clit one more stroke, and then I feel him slipping through my soaked folds, trailing down to my entrance. I can't move for fear he might accidentally cut me, but I can touch him, which is exactly what I do. Placing a trembling hand on his arm, I use the connection to make certain he both sees and feels me.

"Unless you're choosing to use your safe word, I'm not stopping." His penetrating gaze is back on me, flicking across my face, reading my features. I can't put into words how much it means to me for him to take my feelings into consideration. Especially when I know it's not something he's used to or even does. And a tiny smile tugs at my lips because while he says he won't stop, he doesn't penetrate me with the knife either.

"No, that's not it. I don't want you to cut yourself."

His eyes warm at my admission. "Ely, that's just it. I don't think you understand how fucking far gone I am for you, but let me spell it out." I feel him tug against my clothes, the sound of fabric ripping, but I don't care what he does to this stupid costume. "Pain doesn't scare me; it only intensifies my pleasure, and if I have to endure a little pain to witness that euphoric look in your eyes, to watch your pussy pulse around my knife, to hear that sweet little mouth of yours beg and plead, then I will endure any fucking amount of pain to be a witness to that."

I swallow thickly. There are no words for that response, nor does he wait for me to give him one. Instead, he drags the hilt through my sopping folds one last time before he brings it to my entrance. I shiver from the contact. There's a slight burn as he slides the matte handle inside me, slowly, so fucking slowly. I feel every little ridge in the grip as it enters me. All the way until the colder part touches right at my opening.

I watch until he takes his free hand and places it flat on my belly, forcing me to lie flat on my back. War wages in my mind because I'm torn between watching him and lying back and letting him do whatever he wants to me.

"You look so fucking hot right now, Little Prey. Dripping all over my knife." He speaks slowly as if he's hypnotized by what he's watching.

I sink my fingers into the dirt and use it to ground me as my pussy clasps around the hilt. He moves it in and out of me, fucking me slowly, sending little tremors of pleasure through my core. *Is Sebastian crazy, or am I, for allowing him to do this?*

"Are you going to come for me, Little Prey?"

"Yes," I gasp as he thrusts the knife a little deeper.

"Fuck yes, you are. I need to feel that tight cunt pulse and ripple with pleasure."

"Sebastian," I whimper as he ups the pace, fucking me faster. I tip my head back against the dirt, the pleasure carrying me higher and higher. Oh God. I'm close.

"Give me your fucking eyes, Little Prey. I need to see your pretty eyes when you shatter around my knife."

My gaze snaps back to his, and I swear his eyes are the darkest shade of green I've ever seen. Emerald jewels glittering in the sun. I'm mesmerized by him, and I couldn't look away even if I tried. The muscles in his jaw jump; his features are tight, his nostrils flared. He looks every bit of the unhinged man he hides beneath that emotionless mask he wears. It wouldn't take much to make him snap. To lose complete control.

I want it, want to see him let go.

A low growl emits from his lips, and I feel something warm splash against my skin.

Was that blood?

"Are you bleeding?" I gasp, and lift my head, peering down the length of my body.

It's too dark to see if there's any blood, but I can hear the wet sounds my body makes as he fucks me faster, pumping in and out, setting my nerve endings on fire.

"Don't worry about me, Little Prey. Worry if this tight pussy can take my cock. Fuck, I'm going to stretch you and make you take it, even if you can't."

"I'm close..." I cry out, my toes curling into the dirt.

"Yes! Come for me, Ely. Soak my blade with your juices. I want to see how pretty my blood and your cum look when mixed."

Sebastian's filthy words spur me on, and I explode in a cosmic way, my heart soaring out of my chest, my back bowing. The tension snaps out of me like a rubber band pulled too tight. The ringing in my ears grows louder, drowning out all other noise, and for one moment, I'm weightless, falling deeper and deeper into the darkness.

Will he catch me?

"Beautiful, fucking beautiful," he praises, fucking me through the orgasm with the knife. My pussy clenches on to it tightly, refusing to let it go.

Once I've finally floated back down to earth, he pulls the knife out, and I whimper at the loss, the sudden emptiness I feel without it there. I peer up at him, my chest heaving, and watch as he brings the hilt of the knife to his face, surveying it in the dim moonlight. I catch sight of our mixed fluids, his blood and my juices. Normally, I'd be turned off by such a sight, but something about seeing it makes it all the more real.

Once he's had his fill of staring at the knife, he licks it clean.

His eyelids flutter closed as he moans around it, and when he blinks his eyes back open, I see him for the predator he is.

"It's time to claim what's always been mine." He smirks and places the knife on the ground beside me. Need and excitement twist deep in my gut. I'm not ready for this night to end. When he reaches to undo his belt, I take the heel of my foot and shove him backward.

Caught off-balance, he lands on his ass. I scramble to my feet, dirt and leaves cascading to the forest floor, shaking free from my trembling body with the motion.

"Oh, you still want to play?"

"If you want to fuck me, you'll have to catch me again."

"Hmm. Playing hard to get. That's fine. I like a good challenge. Just know, the next time I catch you I'm fucking you. Hard. Deep. Owning you and your pussy. *My* pussy."

It sounds like he's trying to scare me away, but little does he know I'm not scared. I'm excited, ready for him to do all the things he's promised, but first, he'll have to catch me, and this time, I'm going to make him work for it.

Snagging the knife from the ground, I turn and take off between the trees with a smile on my lips.

"Catch me, if you can."

34
SEBASTIAN

"Catch me, if you can." The words echo through my mind.

Fuck, how is it that I'm even more turned on now than I was five minutes ago, watching as the hilt of my blade slid in and out of her tight cunt?

I shake my head and shove off the ground, smiling while I do it. My hand stings from the cut there, but it was worth it. Worth watching her orgasm and tasting her cum on my knife. Fuck, she's got me so hard my cock aches, leaking pre-cum into my pants.

As I peer through the trees I spot my knife, the one I just fucked her with tight in her grip. Fear constricts my chest. I'm about to yell at her when I notice she shifts the knife so it's point is safely out and away from her body.

If she fell on the blade...*I don't know what I would do.*

I blindly chase her. She's fast. So fucking fast. I can't help it as a swell of pride expands my chest. My girl is so fucking fast.

I keep her in my sights so she doesn't get too far ahead. The anticipation of bare skin under my fingers, as it has been every night since I met her, encourages me to chase her and claim her.

Nothing else matters at this moment but catching her and making her mine for good. That is, after I rip the knife from her grasp and burn her ass for putting herself in danger by running away with it. I charge through a pair of bushes and lose sight of her feet as she closes around a cluster of trees. *Dammit.* I pick up the pace, feeling the cold air seep in and out of my lungs with every gasping breath. It's the end of football season, I'm in the best shape right now, yet she somehow managed to outrun me on land that I've been running for years.

I pause, listening, hoping to pinpoint her by sound, but I don't hear anything but far off laughter and the soft hoot of an owl.

No, she didn't outrun me; she's hiding. I grin into the night. *Clever Little Prey.*

I lift my feet higher to quiet my steps as I cut through the trees toward the area I last saw her. It's still eerily quiet, and I can't see shit in the dark. I have a flashlight, but I don't want to use it. *Not yet.* When I catch her, I want to have earned it, and every second she keeps me on the chase makes my cock harder, makes catching her all the more worth it.

There's a rustle of leaves to my right, and I spot a faint figure dart through the trees.

Caught ya. I give chase, my blood pumping in time with my heart, my breathing becoming deeper, heavier. It feels good to run, to chase, and it will feel even better when I sink inside her as my reward.

She darts left and I catch the glimmer of moonlight off one pale shoulder. It's streaked with dirt and leaves, but I've never seen anything so beautiful. Once we're finished out here, I'll take her out of these woods and soak her in the bath. I'll take my time cleaning every inch of her body until she's warm and languid in my arms.

The thought of caring for her spurs me on more. It's strange;

with other women, I couldn't leave fast enough once the deed was done. Now I'm fantasizing about aftercare and ensuring her comfort. That's after I've had my way with her. Shattered the existence of who she is. I won't stop until she cries and whimpers and begs me to fuck her. Begs me to stop. Begs me for everything.

I adjust my erection as I run, almost holding it now, just needing to ease the ache enough to keep moving.

She's still running, hopping over rocks and around fallen logs. Hell, if she kept going, she might get to the cabin and win this shit. The last time she was out here, she rode on the four-wheelers, but hell, maybe she remembers the way. Not that she'd know 25K sits out there in the woods ready to be claimed since she was just tossed into the event.

There's a noise up ahead, and I drag myself from my thoughts just in time for a scream to pierce the quiet of the night. *Fuck.* I speed forward and enter into a small clearing. A few yards ahead, I spot Ely. My sigh of relief morphs into blind rage. Some random fucker has an arm wrapped around her middle, their hand circling her throat.

At first, I fear the worst, that Yanov has found her, but that fear diminishes greatly as soon as I see the douchebag's face, and recognize him as one of the members of the football team. If he's smart he'll step the fuck back.

"Deakins. If you don't release my prey, I'm going to kick your teeth in."

Ely struggles in his grasp but then seems to remember she's holding my *very* sharp knife. Lifting it, she presses the point up to the side of the man's neck, barely poking him. As if he's been stabbed in the throat, Deakins screams, shoving Ely away. She stumbles forward and winces as she falls to her knees, the knife skidding across the ground in front of her.

Piece of shit.

I launch myself at Deakins, tackling him to the hard forest

floor. We land in a heap, me on top of him, my hand pressed against his throat where a small trickle of blood shows through his fingers. *Pussy.*

"What the fuck, man?"

Tightening his shirt in my fist, I haul him up off the ground and slam him into the nearest tree. Holding him in place, I pull my arm back, clench my fist tight, and punch him in his stupid face. He grapples with me when I go to hit him again, but then I rip the mask off my face, throwing it away so he can get a better look at my face, so who he can see who he fucked with.

Deakins freezes and drops his hands down to his sides. "Arturo, fuck. I didn't realize it was you. I'm sorry, man. If she's yours, she's yours."

"She's mine. More than mine. And you fucked with the wrong person."

I rear back and land one more hit on him, if only to burn off some of the rage threatening to burst out of me like a damn atomic bomb. *Okay, once isn't enough.* I make a move to strike him again but am stopped when a small hand lands against my arm.

I pause only briefly and glance down at Ely, who shakes her head at me. Her expression is soft but earnest. "It's okay. He's going to leave; he didn't know I'm yours."

Deakins chimes in, nodding so hard I feel it up into my arm. "I didn't. I didn't know. I'm sorry. I'll leave you alone."

I keep my gaze fixed on Ely as I release him and then give him a hard shove, just for safe measure. In his haste to escape, he scrambles into a tree, then spins and races out of the clearing. I force a couple of breaths into my lungs in an effort to calm myself. I can't lose control. Not with her.

Now that we're alone again, I spin to face her fully, my eyes roaming over her delicate features. No tears, no fear, nothing but soft, gentle eyes trying to reassure me.

"Better run, Little Prey."

Before she can take off, I snatch her by the neck and drag her backward, my front colliding with her back. Her mouth falls open as she stares up at my face, but I don't give her any time to speak. I kiss her hard, brutally mashing our lips together so they are caught between our teeth. *I want it to hurt.* Want her to feel and remember my kiss. I plunge my tongue between her lips, tasting her.

This small act makes me unravel from the inside out. My breaths slowly begin to even out and some of the anger recedes. I need to finish the hunt without hurting her...at least, not any more than she would enjoy. I caress her tongue and then catch her bottom lip in my teeth as I pull away. When it pops back I peer into her eyes, noticing how soft, and languid she is.

Not yet, Prey.

"Run..." I growl and release her.

She jolts, her eyes open wide. Turning she flees, but this time a little slower. That's fine by me. She's wearing herself out, which means she won't have any fight in her when it comes time for me to sink deep inside her warm heat.

I allow her to get ahead but only a little so that when I start running I dont catch her too quickly. Before I leave, I snatch my knife off the ground and slide it into my sheath. I keep a close eye on her, but she's growing tired, not racing around obstacles, and jumping branches like she did before. Time to catch my Little Prey before she hurts herself.

I scan the woods while I run so if anyone else thinks to sneak up on her they won't get the chance. She's mine. All mine.

It doesn't take me long to rush right up on her ass. She squeals as she feels me and tries to race away, but I grab her around the hips and take us both to the ground, her beneath me, our legs entwining and flailing together.

"Get off me," she shouts, but there's no real heat to her words. Especially not when she's rocking her ass against me.

"Get off you?" I grin. "Are you sure that's what you want when you're pushing your ass back against me? Looks more like you want me to fuck you, Little Prey." I swat at her hips as I tug them up in front of me, then roll her hard onto her back. She winces and shuffles her hips to the side to line our bodies up. "Is that what you want? Me to fuck you?" I want to hear her say the words.

"Yes. Please fuck me." Her cheeks heat with embarrassment at her words, but I love seeing her like this. Vulnerable and unsure. I'm so turned on by her confession that I reach for her, my hand circling her throat.

Her pulse thunders beneath my hand and I peer into her blue eyes, watching for an indication of fear. When I see none, I tighten my hold, squeezing the tender column.

Leaning into her face I whisper against the seam of her lips. "I told myself I'd try to be gentle with you but I don't think I can do it. I want you too much."

"I want you as you are. Don't be gentle, be you." She whispers back, and then presses her lips to mine. Fire ignites in my soul, and I kiss her back hard and fast, punishing us both.

I need her, right now, and I'm thankful she feels the same way. Her hands tug at my clothes, like she can hardly bear to have another item separating us.

As much as I hate it, I break the kiss, and pull away to undress. I glance down the length of my body and notice my shirt is partially undone. *Fuck she wants this. Wants me, after all we've been through.*

I undo the rest of the buttons and toss it to the side. Flicking the button on my pants, I shove them down my thighs. My aching cock springs free, jutting out like a damn sword.

Elyse's gaze roams over my skin, from my chest, down my sculpted abs, and to the tip of my thick cock. I confirm it when I look down at her and watch her staring at me through hooded eyes. Looking down at her I realize she's been laid before me like a sacrificial lamb.

I reach down and drag my knife out of its sheath and bring it up between us. Her eyes immediately latch onto the metal glint.

"What are you going to do with it this time?"

"Don't worry, Little Prey. I won't fuck you with it this time. The next thing going inside that tight cunt is my cock," I growl with a hint of possession.

I caress her calf with the tip of the knife and then slide it up along her hip to insert the point along the seam of the ripped-up silk lingerie. It slides apart like butter, falling away in scraps around her torso.

She's so beautiful, cast white under the soft moonlight filtering through the trees. Like she can't handle the spotlight being on her she lifts her arms to cover herself but I shake my head at her and say, "No, don't hide from me. Let me see your tits, your silky porcelain skin."

Hesitantly she drops her arms back down to her sides, and I drink her in. Her tits are small but perfect, with dusky pink nipples that beckon me to take them into my mouth. Fuck, I want to mark them, mark her. So I do just that. Leaning forward I take one of the hard nipples between my teeth, nipping at her sensitive flesh.

"Oh..." Elyse whimpers, one of her hands coming to rest on my head. I flick my tongue against the hard bud, and alternate between sucking and biting her flesh.

It doesn't take long for her to start lifting her hips, begging me to fuck her without saying a single word. Her pussy brushes against my leaking cock, and I pull away, a harsh breath passing my lips. *Fuck.* I peer down between her spread thighs, and to her perfect pussy.

She wants me, needs me like I need her.

Control yourself. Don't hurt her.

She lifts her hips, seeking out my cock, begging me with her seductive gaze.

War wages inside my head, and I almost allow the physical need to let go of control and have my most basic instincts lead me, but at the last moment I clench my hands into tight fists and regain my footing.

Elyse can sense the change in my demeanor and she whispers softly to me. “I can see you struggling for control. You don’t have to be something you're not for my sake. I’m not made of glass. I won’t break if you touch me.”

“Wrong, Little Prey. You won’t just break for me. You’ll fucking shatter.”

35
SEBASTIAN

The animalistic urge to claim her becomes the only thing I can see or feel. I'm past the point of no return. The predator has been set free, and sweet little Elyse is my willing prey.

I take her by the hips with bruising force, and lift her, holding her at the perfect angle.

She whimpers softly, but I'm too far gone to care. I'm not sure I'd be able to stop, even if she begged me at this point. Fuck I should ease my grip, gently enter her, kiss her, and make love to her, but I can't. I need her too fucking badly to do that. Plus, there will be plenty of time for that later.

"Wait, Sebastian... I..." Elyse murmur.

If she was going to ask me to stop, it's a little too late. I thrust my hips forward. So fragile and perfect. I know I'm going to fucking ruin her, destroy her, but I can't be bothered to give a shit anymore. I no longer care if taking her makes me selfish. I look down the length of our bodies, watching as my cock enters her, my length filling her in one thrust.

"Fuck, Elyse." I curse under my breath as black dots appear in my vision.

It's like a damn out-of-body experience. She's so warm, and tight. *Home.* She's where I fucking belong. I bite back the desire to come right then and there like a teenager. I take a couple of calming breaths and hold myself inside her for a moment, relishing in the sensations. She clamps down on my cock, and I swear I see stars.

When I start to pull out, so I can slam back in, I feel her tiny hand on my forearm, her nails digging into my skin. Pinpricks of pain zing across my flesh.

I tear my gaze away and back up to her face, and what I see makes my insides cold. Her pretty blue eyes are filled with tears that slide freely down her cheeks, and her features are pinched together as if she's in pain.

"What the fuck?" I growl and pull almost all the way out of her.

"No. Please." She whimpers, trying to grab onto me like she thinks I might disappear. I look down between our bodies and notice the red tinge of blood that coats my cock.

"Why are you bleeding, Elyse? Did I hurt you?" I question with concern.

Some of the primal desire fades as I tug her up into my arms, cradling her small body while I swipe at the tears with my thumbs. My cock is still partially inside her, and the movement makes her muscles clamp tight around me. Air hisses through my teeth as I stop myself from thrusting deep, until my balls press against her ass and there isn't a single spot I'm not touching inside her.

"Please don't be mad..." she pleads, and I stare down at her in confusion.

"Tell me what the fuck is going on," I ask, tightening my hold on her.

"You didn't hurt me. I'm a virgin. Well, was." Her legs tremble as she tightens her hold on me. *Virgin?* It never occurred to me that...my mind is reeling. If that's true, what about the pregnancy test? Does that mean...shock gives way to anger, and I sink my fingers into her hair at the back of her neck and tug her head back so I can see her face better.

"Why didn't you tell me? Why did you let me think that test was yours?" I'm practically foaming at the mouth with rage.

"I didn't think you would go through with it if you thought I was a virgin, and I don't want anyone else but you to be my first." She bites her bottom lip, "You bled for me earlier, and now I'm bleeding for you."

You bled for me, and now I'm bleeding for you.

Damn. Maybe she is the antidote to the chaos inside me.

I nearly moan from the knowledge.

She wanted me to be her first?

"Fuck, Ely. And the test?"

"It's not mine, but I don't want to talk about that right now. I want you to finish what you started. I want you to claim me completely." Her eyes burn into the depths of my soul, and I know I'll never be the same after tonight.

"What does it say about me if I'm still rock hard and ready to fuck you into oblivion, even while knowing it's your first time and I should be gentle with you?"

Elyse gives me a small smile. "That you're a man?"

"Yes, *your* fucking man," I whisper against her lips as I thrust deep inside her, before pulling out a little ways so I can do it again.

Her thighs tremble around my hips, and while her eyes still swim with tears, none have fallen yet. Tightening my grip on her, I grapple for control, the need to fuck her hard and fast close to taking over.

I nip at her lip with my teeth. "Is this what you wanted, Little

Prey? For me to claim your pussy with my cock? To own you completely?"

"Yes." Her reply is a throaty whisper.

I love the way her breath hitches in time with my thrusts. She's so tight, her pussy clamps down on me with each stroke while her thighs quake within my grasp as I drive deep inside her, her body acting as if she can't take another inch.

"Goddamn, you take my cock so well. Even if it is a tight fit." I pant, moving her up and down my length, her channel flooding with arousal at my praise.

I watch her facial features closely and notice the slight part in her lips when I bottom out inside her. The tears swimming in her eyes have disappeared, and she peers up at me, her gaze reflecting security and warmth.

"Oh…that feels good," she pants, the head of my cock brushing against her G-spot again.

I've fantasized about this moment for so long it almost doesn't feel real.

"Please, Sebastian. I need…" Her small voice comes out as a whine.

"I know, Little Prey. I know what you need." I piston my hips up, touching that special spot at the end of her channel.

"Don't stop, don't stop," she mewls, her cheeks flush, her blue eyes wild with desire.

Her nails dig into my skin, close to piercing the flesh while she clings to me like I'm the only thing capable of holding her in place.

"I couldn't stop if I tried. You own me, Ely, own me," I grit through my teeth, feeling her tighten all around me. "Yes, come for me, sweet girl. Milk my cock. Fuck, I need to feel that perfect pussy squeeze all around me."

"Sebastian!!" She screams my name and then explodes all around me, her lithe body convulsing with pleasure. I can't breathe. I can barely move, my heartbeat thundering in my ears as she clamps down on me so tightly my vision fades in and out for a moment.

"Good girl. Good fucking girl," I praise against her neck, fucking her through her orgasm, my own release tingling at the base of my spine.

Elyse sags against my chest, her breaths erratic, her eyes shining with contentment. This lazy smile tugs at the corner of her pink lips, and *fuck*... I wrap both arms around her, holding her tightly so she can't escape, and I use her body, fucking her without resistance.

"I can't get over how well you take my cock, how perfect you feel shattering all around me. Fuck, Little Prey, you're ruining me for anyone else."

"Sebastian," she whines against my throat, her voice edged with pain.

"I'm almost there. You can take it, sweet girl, you were made for me. Made to take my cock. Just a little more... oh fuck... yes."

I climb higher and higher, edging closer and closer to my orgasm, even as I try to fight against it because I don't want this to end. Even though I know she's in pain, I don't want to stop. I'll never be able to fuck her for the first time again, so I need to elongate the moment as much as I can.

Her hot mouth places open kisses across my throat, trailing across my skin, stopping once she reaches my shoulder. Her lips part, and I feel her teeth graze my shoulder, the sensation eliciting a moan from my throat. That sound spurs her on, and before I can comprehend what she's doing, she bites me *hard*.

How the fuck does she know exactly what I need?

With the slight edge of pain zipping across every nerve ending, sending jolts of pleasure straight to my balls, I'm unable to hold off the impending orgasm another second. With a feral growl, I let myself go.

"I'm going to come, Little Prey. I'm going to fill you with my seed. Fill you up and get you pregnant so you can't leave, ever. Mine. All. Fucking. Mine." She moans against my shoulder, her tongue lapping over the bite.

My movements become jerky, and with a final groan, I slam deep inside her, holding myself there for the last time. I explode, pumping her full of my cum, my entire body shuddering against hers. I swear my soul leaves my body for a moment. When I return to my senses, my heart hammering in my chest, my chest heaving, I feel our combined juices and my sticky cum dripping down between our bodies.

I need to get her back to the house, clean her up, and make sure she's okay. Make sure I didn't hurt her too badly. I slowly ease out of her body, and she whimpers softly.

"I got you." I stroke her side gently with one hand, while I blindly search for my knife with the other, my fingers closing around the hilt. Lifting the knife I grab her arm, and she turns her head to see what I'm doing, but she doesn't say a word, doesn't object or pull away. She knows I need this, that this is how I show she is more than the others. That there is no one else like her.

My, Little Prey.

Placing the blade against her soft, porcelain skin, I press down. With one smooth jerk, I mark her, right below the other two marks. I grit my teeth against the impulse to keep going. To carve my name over that fucker's name, to cover her in my marks so no one else dares to touch her. I remind myself that I've inflicted enough pain on her for the night, and that there are many days to come where I can do just that.

Catching my breath, I gently place her on the ground so I can get dressed. Her expression is relaxed, and her eyes roam over my body, watching as I pull my pants back up. I snag my shirt off the ground and gently maneuver her so I can wrap her up in the fabric. Once covered, the edge of the shirt hangs loose around her thighs.

Seeing her in my clothing makes me want to rip it off her with my teeth and claim her all over again. God, she's fucking with my head. Destroying my resolve. I know without a doubt, as I look down at her, that I'll do anything to protect her, from her enemies, my enemies, even from myself. From the darkness that seeps out of my pores, threatening to taint her angelic soul.

A scream echoes through the air, followed by laughter. There are still hours until the final runners and hunters stumble out of the woods, finding their way back to the party at the house. I won't be attending that party this year.

I put my knife away and crouch down on my heels, scooping Ely up and taking her into my arms. I hold her against my chest bridal style, my grasp tight like I'm afraid she might disappear if I don't hold on to her. Mine.

After tonight, nothing will ever be the same between us. There is no going back to the way things used to be. There is only the future, and Elyse is it for me.

"Where are we going?" she asks sleepily.

"Home. I'm taking you home."

36
ELYSE

It's strange how one single moment can change your entire life.

One choice. One word. One act.

Even though he hasn't said anything, I know everything has changed. It's all I can think about—that and what will happen next. I try not to let the lack of answers send me into a panic while I listen to the steady, strong beat of his heart. He's careful with me, gentle, and it's a stark difference from the usual way he throws me around like he owns me.

Instinctually, I know I should be scared right now. I should be wondering what else he might do, what other pain he might inflict. What revenge he might be contemplating. I can't be bothered by thoughts like that, though, not when all I feel is...safe cradled in his arms. I'm satiated in a way I've never felt in my life. It feels like I've unlocked this secret door I didn't know existed inside me, a gaping hole that needed to be filled, and he's the single thing I needed to make myself whole.

Sebastian carries me through the woods without complaint. Part of me wonders if I should ask him to put me down since, you know, my legs work just as well as his, but there's something about being carried through the woods by the man who claimed me in more than just a physical sense that makes me all warm inside. It makes me feel cherished.

A few yards ahead, he pauses and grabs his suit jacket off a low-hanging branch, and as much as I'm enjoying him caring for me, it's still more than I'm used to.

"Am I getting heavy? Do you want to put me down? I can walk."

He makes a low noise in his throat, almost like a grunt. "No. If I wanted to put you down, I would have done it already."

He places the suit jacket over my torso, covering me from mid-thigh to chin and I'm grateful, considering he shredded the lingerie I'd been wearing. Ahead, the trees thin out, and soon enough we're exiting the woods. Sebastian passes numerous couples that are mid-fuck, their moans stirring the air around us. He doesn't even blink as he walks past them, almost like he doesn't see them at all.

He carries me all the way to his car and cradles me one-armed against his chest while he opens the passenger door. I let out a squeak when my bare ass kisses the cold leather as he places me inside the car. It takes a minute to get around the other side and turn on the car.

Once in his seat, he fiddles with a few of the controls, and I let out a content sigh when heat blasts out of the vents. I hold my chilled fingers up to soak it in.

"Oh, that's nice. I didn't realize how close to icicles my fingers were."

"Gimme a minute, and you'll be nice and toasty."

I toss him a curious look as he backs out of the driveway, then navigates the car out onto the main road that leads back toward campus.

Heat from the leather seat envelopes my legs and bare butt

after he presses another button on the console. "Mmm, now that is way nicer than a little heat. I think I can finally feel my toes." I flex them in my shoes, the feeling slowly returning.

I sink into the seat and cover myself more fully with the suit jacket.

Sebastian peers over at me, his gaze filled with possession. "I hope you know that tonight changes everything. I tried to stop, tried to fight against the inevitable, but I can't keep fighting against something we both want. You gave yourself to me, and that means you belong to me, and not just in the sense of being my property, Elyse. I mean physically, emotionally, mentally."

I can't even put into words how that makes me feel. It's hard not to have doubt when you've lived a life like I have. I'm happy to know he doesn't just plan to toss me away.

"I don't want to be anyone else's, so I'm happy to hear that."

"Good," he replies gruffly, returning his attention to the road. His hands tighten around the steering wheel, and it looks like he's trying to strangle it.

"Are you okay?" I whisper.

"Yes, just trying to control my emotions. I'm fighting with myself right now because I want to fuck you until I'm under your skin and in your blood, but that's not really what you need right now so..."

Why does that make me shiver, my nipples hardening to the point of pain? A tiny gasp escapes me at the sensation, and he continues speaking.

"You have no idea how hard I've fought against myself in the last couple of months. How much I tried to tell myself that I can't have you, that I can't let my darkness touch you. Now, the dam's broken, and that one little taste has done nothing to subdue the need. It makes me crave you more. I need to unleash myself on you, claim you, mark you, fuck you."

"Is there something wrong with me?" I ask, mainly myself.

He lets out a dark chuckle. "Did you not hear what I just said?" Shaking his head, he continues, "And you ask me if there's something wrong with you?"

I smile. "Yes, only because I want that, too. I want you. I've never wanted anything in my life like I want you, and I'm afraid of that feeling. Afraid that it might end before it can begin."

The car slows, and the gate opens as we turn onto the road.

"It won't. No one is taking you from me, and if anyone is stupid enough to try, I'll kill them." The conviction in his voice should terrify me, along with the ownership he's claiming on me, but it doesn't. In fact, it has the opposite effect, and that's almost just as terrifying.

He drives the car up the driveway, stopping at the entrance of the house.

"You don't want to take the car to the garage?" I sit forward and wrap the jacket around my back so I can slip my arms in the sleeves.

I'm hit with a wave of anxiety then, the thought of any other staff seeing my bare ass, or hell any of them seeing me with Sebastian in this condition at all. I don't need rumors being spread about me.

Soothing some of the worry, he puts the car in park and tells me, "Anyone who sees us and or says a word will suffer the consequences." He's out of the car before I can reply, and he wraps me up in his arms, carrying me into the house. I press my face against his chest, so I don't have to see if anyone notices us. If I don't know, then it won't matter.

We make it to the bedroom in seconds, and using his foot, Sebastian kicks the door closed. The sound of the lock being turned in place echoes through my ears.

And somehow this all suddenly became even more real.

What happens now? I glance at the bed as we pass by it and head into the bathroom.

The overhead lights are bright, and I blink a few times to adjust my eyes. Once my eyes adjust I see the dirt caked under my nails, the scratches, and bruises that dot my skin, hidden under the jacket. He places me on the edge of the counter and then pulls away to turn the shower on.

A shower sounds amazing right now. "I can help. I'm not dying or anything."

"I'm aware, but I want to take care of you. So let me."

Turning away, he starts the bath, the tub filling with water. When his gaze returns to me, I feel the heat in it, the flames of desire flicking against my skin.

What would it be like to let him burn me to ash?

"Stop looking at me like that, or I'll have to bend you over and fuck you again," he snaps, the warning in his tone making my core clench.

"I'm not looking at you like anything," I lie, my cheeks heating, giving me away.

"Yes, you are, Little Prey. You're looking at me like you want me to fuck you until there's no way to tell where you begin and I end. I would love nothing more than to do that right fucking now, but I can't be selfish with you. I have a duty to care for you, to ensure you're clean and content. And fucking you would go against that, especially knowing how sore you're going to be, so please...don't look at me like that right now because I'm barely controlling myself."

I swallow thickly, my mouth suddenly dry. *How do I even respond to that?*

Instead of trying to come up with a response, I shove the suit jacket off my shoulders and unbutton the dress shirt with trembling fingers, shrugging it off as soon as the final button is undone.

A wave of self-consciousness washes over me now that I'm naked in the glaring overhead lights. I'm tempted to wrap my arms around my middle, and use my hands to cover myself, but I don't.

He's already seen all of you, fucked you, I remind myself. He crosses the space, his steps predatory, but I don't dare look away. I don't think I'll ever get over seeing that look in his eyes—the possession, the need to claim. It's such a far cry from the anger and annoyance that I used to get.

"Undo my pants," he orders.

Reaching for him, I slowly loosen the belt on his dirty dress pants until they hang open to frame the bottom of his tan eight pack. I swallow my tongue as I get a closer look at his body, inspecting it like I've never seen it before. Yes, I've seen him shirtless, but I've never openly stared at him, drinking in every little indent and muscle twitch.

He leans in so his face is level with mine, his green eyes burning into mine. "Fuck, Ely, you're so beautiful. I don't think I deserve you... actually, I know I don't deserve you, but I don't give a fuck. It's too late to undo what's done."

Something tightens in my chest at his words, like I can't breathe around the declaration.

He grips my thighs hard and spreads them, his gaze trailing down my chest, over my belly, and then lower. The grip of his fingers changes, becoming almost painful as he takes in the sight of my body. I look down to see the red on my thighs. Not from the cuts or scratches but a lot of red right at the juncture of my thighs.

It looks worse than it really is. I'm sore, yes, but not any more than I expected to be after the first time. I can almost feel his guilt building, stirring deep in his gut. I don't want him to be sorry or feel bad. I don't want him to regret what we shared.

"Sebastian..."

Even as he holds me with all the possession and pride, a tinge of guilt reflects in his eyes when he lifts his gaze back up to mine.

"I should've been gentler. Fuck. I'm sorry, Ely. I didn't mean to hurt you."

"No, you didn't!" His expression is tortured, and I lift a hand to soothe the rigid line of his jaw. "I'm fine, I promise. Better than fine. It's just a little blood...everyone bleeds—"

"Yeah, they might bleed, but it doesn't need to look like a fucking bloodbath. God. What is wrong with me? Your first time should've been different. Instead, I took you in the woods like a fucking animal—"

"Stop, please. I loved it." Grasping his face with both hands, I force him to meet my gaze. "I fucking loved it, and I wouldn't have changed a thing. Please don't guilt yourself into regretting what we did."

He gives me a small smile, and my heart clenches a little in my chest. "I could never regret what we did." Gently, he strokes the inside of my thigh. ""I can't get over the fact that I'm your first, and I know it's fucked up but I'm almost sad to clean you up. It feels like I'm washing away the proof that you're mine, that I'm your first."

Oh crap. The reminder of Tanya's pregnancy test pops into my head, ruining the moment. I already told him it wasn't mine, but I haven't explained anything more.

I wince. "We haven't really talked about it, but..."

Shaking his head, he presses a finger to my lips. "No. Stop. I don't want to know right now. All I want is to sink as deep as I can into this moment with you. Fuck everything else. The problems will still be there tomorrow; let's take tonight for us."

I nod and open my mouth to tell him I'd enjoy nothing more than that, but before I can speak again, he scoops me up in his arms and carries me into the shower. His gaze gravitates back down to my thighs, like he's trying to take a picture with his eyes. Once he has me under the hot spray, he steps out and quickly shoves off his pants and shoes. I stand there staring like a stalker.

How can a man look as beautiful as he does?

He might as well be a Greek statue, every muscle perfectly formed and sculpted like he's cut from stone. The glaring overhead light that makes me feel boxy and short highlights every beautiful curve on his body. He's a masterpiece. A priceless art piece.

Looking at him, I forget to breathe, forget to function. I snap out of it when he grabs his already hard length, a sinister look filling his features as he strokes himself, the blood of my innocence staining his cock.

He steps into the shower stall, turning the big box into a tiny one with his size.

Normally, I'd feel anxious with his frame towering over me, but I feel safe and secure, and the hot water feels so good beating against my sore muscles that I can't be bothered by any other emotions at the moment.

"Mine. All mine," he whispers. I'm not sure if it's to himself or me, but I don't ask. Even if there are a ton of unsaid things hanging in the air between us, I can believe in one thing with complete trust, and that is that I belong to him.

When I grab the loofah and put soap on it, he crowds me and takes over, running the suds over my slick skin until I feel like I vibrate from his touch. After scrubbing me clean, he puts me back under the spray and rinses the suds away.

With a smile, I grab the loofah from him before he starts washing himself.

"Please, let me."

He releases his hold on the sponge, and I run it across his chest, cleaning him just like he cleaned me. There's a calmness that fills me, the pressure, fear, all of it melting away, and it's like I can breathe for the first time in my life.

"You didn't get as many bruises as I did."

"Well, you were the one running." His response is casual.

"I guess you're right." He rinses and turns off the taps, then he reaches for me.

Pausing, he steps out of the shower and helps me to do the same. A puddle pools on the floor, but I can't be bothered with the mess we're making.

Leading me over to the now full bath, he turns the faucets off. A startled gasp slips from my lips when his hands circle my waist and he lifts me, gently placing me in the water. A blanket of warmth covers me from head to shoulder, and I sink into it.

"Oh my God..." I moan by accident.

It feels even better than the shower, and when he reaches forward and presses a button that makes the jets start, I swear I could melt into a puddle. I've only ever dreamed about taking a bath in this thing. He perches on the edge of the tub, his gaze sweeping over me.

"There's enough room in here for three people if you want to get in, too?"

"I would, but then I'd be tempted to fuck you again."

I can feel the heat creeping into my cheeks. He's so blunt about sex. That'll take some getting used to. I shake away the embarrassment and relax into the water, letting it soothe my aching muscles. I tip my head back against the lip of the tub, and his fingers sink into my hair, massaging my scalp gently.

Holy shit. My eyes flutter closed, and I greedily accept his touch.

"I didn't know touch could feel this good. My whole life all I've known is pain."

"I fucked up in the past, and I know I'll fuck up in the future. It's not in my nature to be perfect, even if I try, but I can promise you that no one will hurt you ever again."

"That's a big promise." The words shudder out of me.

"It's more than a promise. It's the truth." The darkness in his voice makes me open my eyes, and I stare up at him. Tragically beautiful. My dark knight.

"I trust you. I just...you might have to be patient with me. This is all so new, and we have so many things to discuss. Who knows, maybe you'll change your mind." It's more or less a joke, but Sebastian doesn't see it that way.

His gentle touch becomes steel in a flash, and he grabs me by the hair. Tipping my head back at an uncomfortable angle, he forces me to look at him and only him.

"I know you're afraid of what happens next, but you have no reason to be. I don't regret what we did, and I don't think you do either. Nothing we will discuss will change that you're mine, completely, in every single way. Remember that whenever you have doubts. I've wanted you for so long, Ely. I'm done playing. I'm done pretending."

I push up, needing his lips on mine.

He understands and leans forward, kissing me, and my entire world shifts. He devours me like he's starving and possessed. His tongue probes my lips, and I open for him, letting him massage my own tongue, tasting me in long, hot strokes.

He's breaking me free of my shell, helping me to see that I'm more than the old version of myself. I'm more than the maid, more than my father's bargaining chip. I'm a woman who can be loved and cherished.

By the time we pull away from each other, my body is wrung tight, desire and need clinging to my bones.

"Beautiful, Ely. You're so damn beautiful," Sebastian murmurs as he strokes my cheek. "Are you ready to get out now?"

I nod, my body relaxed, my muscles liquid. *How did we get here?* I'm almost afraid that I'll wake up at any second and realize this is a dream.

He helps me into a sitting position and then lifts me out of the water, placing me on my feet. It takes a moment for me to get my legs to work, and I catch myself against his chest.

"Sorry. I think I forgot how to use my legs." I laugh.

He uses one hand to steady me and grabs a towel off the counter with the other. He wraps me up in the fluffy towel, securing me like a burrito, and then we're moving.

"Hey, I can walk. I got my legs to work," I announce.

All he does is grunt as he carries me into the bedroom and lays me out on the huge bed.

He disappears from view, and that's when the thoughts pop into my head. The debt I owe him, Tanya, our future together. Is there even a future for us? He reappears holding two bottles of water, and I find I'm even more consumed by the thoughts.

"What about the debt? I don't think I can work as a maid for you anymore." I think a moment longer on it. "I could always get a job and pay you that way."

"Stop, Elyse. You're thinking too much into it. Fuck the debt. I don't care about the money."

Climbing up onto the bed, and he twists the cap off one of the bottles. Bringing it to my lips, he orders me with his eyes to drink.

"You act like I'm incapable of caring for myself."

"No. I act like I let you care for yourself long enough. Now it's my turn to care for you, so please let me and take a drink."

I do as he says, keeping my eyes trained on his face. I believe him, believe his words, but there's still that trickle of doubt. It all seems too good to be true, so all I can do is lie here, waiting, watching, and counting the seconds until he changes his mind and throws me out the door. After I've drunk enough water to satisfy Sebastian, I unwrap myself from the towel and use it to dry my long hair.

He settles against the pillows, and I follow suit, letting any awkwardness I might have fade. Resting my head against the pillow, I bury my nose into it, inhaling his scent.

Sea-salt and spice.

It calms me, and when I lift my head to resituate it I realize just how tired I am. My head feels like it weighs a hundred pounds.

Sebastian tugs me into his chest, and I snuggle against him, letting the warmth of his body encompass me in a cocoon. In his arms nothing can hurt me. Not my father. Yavon. Tanya. No one can touch me.

I'm overwhelmed with emotion, even as sleep lingers at the fringes of my mind.

"This feels like a dream..." I whisper.

His gentle laugh vibrates through me, "No, Little Prey. This is very much not a dream."

"Hmmm, it might be." I smile, while struggling to keep my eyes open.

"It's not. It's real. You're real. What happened is real."

"In that case..." I blink my eyes open, but they fall closed just as fast, the exhaustion finally overpowering me.

"What was that?" Sebastian hums, his fingers stroking my skin.

"I think...I...I love you." I give up my fight to stay awake and let my eyes fall closed at the confession. There is no response, and fog fills the spaces in my mind, dragging me down into the dark depths of sleep.

Right before I succumb I swear I hear Sebastian whisper, "You're more than I deserve, Elyse. I just hope when the truth is revealed you still feel that way."

37
ELYSE

It's dark. There's an overhead light shining down on me, but not fully as a person towers over me, blocking out part of the light. No, this is different. This nightmare is different. I don't see the tattooed hands, or hear Yanov cursing. My entire body aches, pain radiating throughout my limbs. I strain to hear something, anything, but it's quiet except for the soft whisper of a fire crackling nearby. Even if I can't feel the heat of it, I hear it.

I try to squint, to make my eyes work so I can at least make out the features of the person towering over my body, but there's no point. The light is too bright, and I'm barely holding on as it is. I wouldn't be surprised if that very light was me passing into an alternate dimension. Death clings to me. All I can do is brace for the fists that will inevitably come.

But after a few seconds, there are no fists.

Forcing myself to focus my gaze on one thing, I finally make out the barrel of a gun pointed at me. It's weird how a tiny part of me relaxes. All I can think is, yes, *finally, someone is going to do the right thing and put me out of my misery.*

I don't hear the gun, but I feel the bullet. Feel it as it rips through my skin, pulling the flesh from my bones. A cry of pain catches on my lips.

I wake with a gasp, and find myself sitting up in bed. My shoulder throbs, like it's trying to send me some unwritten message. I flex my arm and try to massage the pain away while I ignore the sweat beading my brow, and the hammering of my heart against my rib cage.

Shit. It's okay, it was just a dream. Well, more like a nightmare.

It takes me a couple of minutes to calm down, but once I do the events of the night before return. *Sebastian, myself. The Hunt.* Never in a million years did I think yesterday would end the way it did. I turn to look at Sebastian and find the bed empty.

I try not to feel disappointed. I'm sure he got up to make breakfast or get coffee.

I scoot closer to the edge of the bed so I can hop down off it. My ankles shake, along with my thighs when I land on my feet. Every muscle in my body aches, and I hurt all over.

I spot Sebastian's football shirt folded neatly at the end of the bed, and I grab it, smiling as I pull it on. I don't need a mirror to know my hair is sticking up all over the place. Not that it matters. I don't know anyone who wakes up looking like they're ready to compete in a beauty pageant. My belly rumbles loudly, and I head off to find Sebastian and breakfast.

I poke my head out into the hallway. It's empty, thankfully so. The last thing I need is Tanya making an appearance and catching me sneaking out of Sebastian's room.

I look down the length of my body, watching the light catch on the scratches and bruises that mar my legs. Somehow they feel like a badge of honor. Along with the fresh cut on my arm, which matches the previous one. It might be stupid, maybe even silly, but it makes me feel special and desired. Knowing that even if he's been with others, there is no one like me.

The trip downstairs is short, and when I reach the bottom

step I turn to go toward the kitchen but pause when I notice a light is on in the front room, the study to be precise.

A feminine voice echoes out into the foyer. *Tanya.*

"We both know you can't treat me this way, Sebby. I'm going to be the mother of your child, for heaven's sake."

What? My heart freezes in my chest, threatening to fall out and shatter.

I tiptoe closer to the door and plaster my back against the wall.

The sound of a fire in the fireplace undercuts Tanya's voice. "Let's do this the right way. We can raise the baby together." There's a desperate edge to her voice, and it makes me sick to my stomach. "It's what we always wanted, Sebby. This isn't a death sentence. It means we can finally be together."

Seb answers, his voice low and ice-fucking-cold. "From the moment you took my virginity, Tanya, I've made it clear that I don't want you. That I've never wanted you. Throwing yourself at me in a fit of desperation doesn't change that."

"Stop; you don't have to lie to me."

"No, you fucking stop. This is disgusting." The air shudders out of my lungs. "Even if you were pregnant, and it was mine, which I don't fucking believe for a second, what in the fucking world would make you think I'd want to raise a child with you?"

Something that sounds like glass, or maybe marble, shatters. *Shit.* I automatically flinch away from the noise, as if what used to follow at my father's house will come barreling out of the office at me.

"Sebastian," Tanya tries to subdue him, her voice twisting into something seductive.

My insides knot and coil into one big ball of anxiety. This can't be true. It can't be. Even while I'm afraid to know the truth, to hear another word spoken, I can't bring myself to walk away either. I tiptoe closer so I can peer through the crack created by the hinges.

What I see makes me want to throw up in my mouth. Tanya is splayed across Sebastian's lap, her pencil skirt shoved up around her hips as she straddles him.

She's his fucking mother, or aunt, or I don't fucking know. What I do know is that no matter who she is, this is wrong, so wrong, and it makes me burn with rage. I can barely restrain myself as she leans down, her dark hair curtaining her face along with his, so I can't see him through it all. But I can hear her just fine, unfortunately.

"I've always thought what we shared was special. I need you, and we both know that you belong to me. The sooner you realize that, the better it will be for you and that little maid you're sleeping with."

I press a hand to my lips to stop myself from speaking. Sebastian wraps his hands around her hips and lifts her off his lap, sending her to the floor. She scrambles to her feet and lashes out, her nails cutting red lines into the side of his cheek. Tears sting my eyes.

The assault and mistreatment. It's suffocating.

He stares up at her, murderous rage flickering in his green eyes. That look is so powerful and searing that it makes me afraid. She might be towering over him, but it won't be long until he unleashes fury on her.

With a smile, she runs her hand over her flat stomach. "Certainly even you remember that night. Don't you? It happened right here on the couch."

That murderous glare fades from his eyes, and I watch him crumble right before my eyes. He looks sick, pale. One look at his face, and that's all the confirmation I need. Even he knows there's a chance.

"Deny the baby if you want, but it doesn't change the truth.

We both know you're the father, Sebastian."

I resettle my shoulders and keep my hands plastered over my mouth. I want to scream, to tell her to get away from him. But it wouldn't change what's already happened. The whole thing is disgusting, even if they aren't related by blood.

Her voice grates on my nerves as she stalks closer to him, like she might try to straddle him again, but he stands and stalks toward the fireplace.

"Enough of the games, Sebastian. Let's talk about this like adults."

"There's nothing to talk about."

"There is plenty to talk about. I'm going to give you the heir you need to hold the Arturo business. This couldn't have happened at a better time. We can run it together, as a family. If you want, I'll even let you keep your little pet as long as she understands her place and doesn't get in my way."

It takes me a second to realize she's talking about me.

She's telling him he can keep me...while being with her. Not that I think Sebastian would ever consider it, but even if he did, I would never allow it.

Sebastian stares straight ahead into the flames for a long moment, then he grabs a bottle off the mantel. His sweats hang low on his hips, and I have to look away from the bare expanse of his back as he flexes his fist against the stonework in front of him.

"Tanya. You need to leave before I do something I won't be able to undo."

His words *ping* inside me, and I'm not sure why they make my stomach turn even more.

Tanya doesn't seem to care about his warning and approaches him anyway. As if that's not enough, she skims her hands up and over his shoulders and then back down his back. He doesn't move, doesn't even appear to react.

How can he stand there and let her touch him?

"Sebby. We were so good together. I taught you everything you know...we can have that back."

Sebastian shrugs her hands off of him. "Tanya..." he warns.

Oh no. It occurs to me then that if she comes out here, there will be nowhere for me to hide, and I don't want to be on the receiving end of her wrath. If she's horrible enough to hurt her own...the man she raised this way...she will have no issue with hurting me.

I need to get back upstairs. The idea of eating after what I just witnessed makes me sick. I need a moment to wrap my head around things, and maybe build up the courage to talk to Sebastian about what I heard.

I tiptoe toward the stairs, but freeze when I spot one of the security guards standing there. Robin, I believe is his name. *Weird.* They usually don't come into the house, that is unless Sebastian calls them. Hm, maybe he did. Maybe he's going to have Tanya removed?

Robin leans down and waves at me to come closer. There's a concerned look etched into his features. Over the weeks, I've come to trust Robin, as he's always watching out for the animals and making sure I'm okay while I walk between the house and cottage.

With one final peek over my shoulder, I creep up the stairs, stopping once I reach the landing.

"What's wrong?" I whisper.

"Sorry, I know I shouldn't be inside, but something is wrong with the dog in the cottage. He's been crying and barking for hours. I feel bad for him, and the thought of leaving him there to suffer. Plus, shift change is coming soon. The other guards might shoot him instead of questioning if he's someone's pet if they hear him."

The words "shoot him" send me back down the stairs and into the kitchen. I can't do anything about the situation with Sebastian, at least not yet, but I can take care of that dog.

Robin follows close and disables the alarm at the door, sliding it open for me. I rush out into the cold, dark night, goose bumps skating across my skin as I jog across the brick patio, my bare feet sinking into the dew-dotted grass.

"When did you first hear him crying?" I ask, carefully picking my way across the grass.

"Couple of hours ago. I was looking for you, but I didn't know how to find you without Mr. Arturo seeing me."

Shit. A couple of hours. What could've happened? I guess anything. He could've eaten something? Or something might have fallen on him. The possible scenarios are endless. God, I hope he's okay.

My heart lurches in my chest, fear ruling my instincts. Once I reach the cottage, I grab onto the door handle, but that's as far as I get before someone's hand closes over my mouth, clamping down and sealing whatever scream was going to escape back inside.

Struggling, I crash into Robin's chest.

"Sorry, Elyse. It's just business, nothing personal."

My eyes go wide as I stare up at him, mumbling against the hard grasp of his hand. "What?"

He wraps an arm around my waist and turns me, dragging me into the cabin, back first. *What is he doing?*

The cottage is dark and quiet. *Too quiet.* A different kind of fear unwinds in my gut, urging me to fight harder. So I do. I thrash in Robin's grasp, but his hold is tight, and he's so much stronger than me that I don't even manage to land any hits on him. Opening my mouth the salty taste of his skin fills my mouth. I know how to get him to get me go.

Without thought to the consequences, I sink my teeth into the palm of his hand.

"You fucking bitch!" he growls and pulls his hand away, giving me a hard shove now that we're inside. I stumble, nearly falling to the dusty floor.

"Oh, Robin. You made a fatal error in judgment."

That voice.

That terrible, thick voice trickles out of the dark like it has so many times before, the sound circling around my throat and tightening. Every moment in my life seems to be threaded with that voice, taunting me, beating me, yelling at me.

"She fucking bit me," Robin growls and leers toward me.

I take a wobbly step back. "You don't know what you've done."

"There are consequences for every action, and I told you what would happen if you did anything other than what I instructed you to do."

Robin stops mid-step, his gaze falling on the man who's behind me. "I didn't do anything to her."

A sharp crack ripples through the room, followed by a flash. It all happens so fast; one minute, Robin's standing, and the next, he's falling flat on his back, a bullet hole in his head. Paralyzing fear tightens its grasp on my throat. I have to get out of here. I have to find a way to escape because I'll be the next person with a bullet in their head.

Dazed, I turn to face the man I've hated since I was a child and figured out what it was that he truly wanted from me.

He sits in a chair on the far side of the cottage near the small kitchen. I stare at him for a long moment before my eyes drop to the small lifeless body...*no...I can't.*

A sob rips from my throat, and tears flood my eyes. *No. No. No.* I press a hand to my mouth to stop the agony from spilling out.

"Ah, my beautiful Ely. I knew we'd get here. It took a little work, more than I expected, but we're back to where we were before."

"No! No!" I scream and step away from the monster in front of me.

I forget Robin's lifeless body is behind me, and in my haste to escape, I trip over his legs. I land hard on the cracked and pitted floor, my head bouncing like a basketball against it.

Get up. Move, I scream at myself.

Black spots appear in my vision, and try as I may to blink them back, to hang onto the present, the throbbing sensation in my head makes that impossible.

"Yes, Ely. Mine. All fucking mine." Yanov's voice haunts me, even as the world around me goes dark.

Thank you for reading *The Prey*.
Please be sure to preorder *The Predator* which will be the conclusion to Sebastian and Elyse's story. If you're new to the series and have yet to meet Drew and Bel, you can check out their book which is called: The Wallflower

About the Author

J.L. Beck writes steamy romance that's unapologetic.
Her heroes are alphas who take what they want, and are willing to do anything for the woman they love.
She loves writing about darkness, passion, suspense, and of course steam.
Leaving her readers gasping, and asking what the hell just happened is only one of her many tricks.
Her books range from grey, too dark but always end with a happily ever after.
Inside the pages of her books you'll always find one of your favorite tropes.
She started her writing career in the summer of 2014 and hasn't stopped since.
She lives in Wisconsin and is a mom to two, a wife, and likes to act as a literary agent part time.
Visit her website for more info: www.beckromancebooks.com
Stay up to date on sales, new releases, and freebies by signing up for her newsletter here: https://forms.wix.com/r/7054249734898188429

ALSO BY J.L. BECK

Oakmount Elite

The Wallflower

The Wildflower

The Prey (Releasing August 2024)

The Predator (Releasing September 2024)

The Misfit (TBD)

Moretti Crime Family

Savage Vow

Violent Delights

Stolen Innocence

The Obsession Duet

Cruel Obsession

Deadly Obsession

Devil Duet

Devil You Hate

Devil You Know

King Crime Duet

Indebted

Inevitable

Also By JL Beck

Doubeck Crime Family

Vow to Protect

Promise to Keep

Bound to Darkness

Bound to Cruelty

Bound to Deception

Bound to Punish

Dark Lies

Perfect Villain

Beautiful Monster

Cruel Beast

Savage Vow

Torrio Trilogy Series

Empire of Lust

Empire of Lies

Empire of Pain

Dark Knight

Project Series

Killer

Rogue

Also By JL Beck

Blackthorn Elite

Devious Hate

Ruthless Rivals

Sinister Obsession

Vicious Regret

Northwoods University

The Bet

The Dare

The Secret

The Vow

The Promise

The Jock

Breaking the Rules

Flirting With Love

Flirting With Fate

Flirting With Love

Ties Series

Dangerous Ties

Severed Ties

Mended Ties

Also By JL Beck

Bittersweet Series

Bittersweet Revenge

Bittersweet Love

Bittersweet Hate

Bittersweet Trust

Bittersweet Symphony

Mr. Book

Mr. Alpha

Mr. Heartbreaker

Sold to the Billionaire

Seducing the Virgin

Seduced By the Billionaire

Taken by the Billionaire

Standalones

Lumberjack Love

The Billionaire's Nanny

Quiver for Me

Stranded With My Brother's Best Friend

Worse than Enemies

Her Mafia Bodyguard

Also By JL Beck

Sin For Me

Their Spoiled Virgin

Be Mine Smut Collection

Bad Boy's in Blue

His Obsession

Hung

Their Best Friend's Little Sister

Their Spoiled Princess

Her Ex's Dad

Giving Her A Baby

Their Spoiled Stepsister

Teasing Daddy's Best Friend

Their Spoiled Brat

The Billionaire's Assistant

Babysitting Love

Daddy's BestFriend

Off Limits

Taking What's His

Also By JL Beck

Made in the USA
Monee, IL
19 May 2025